London Skies

A novel

Paul Tomkins

Praise for Paul Tomkins's debut novel *The Girl on the Pier*

Awarded the Kirkus Star, for books out outstanding merit.

"Beautiful and chilling—a brilliant debut.
Tomkins' prose is evocative and devastating." *Kirkus Reviews*

"A Classy psychological thriller." *The Bookseller*

"A beautifully written, thought-provoking psychological thriller."
Araminta Hall, author of the best-selling *Everything and Nothing*

"Reflective, atmospheric, and written in gorgeous prose."
Laura Wilkinson, author of *Crossing The Line*

For Lillian Tomkins

**With special thanks to Siân Pursey,
Palomi Kotecha, Emma Fox and Paul Leahy.**

*Dedicated to the memory of my father,
and to his career in the aviation industry,
and to all those lost in the air.*

© 2024 Paul Tomkins

All rights reserved. No part of this publication may be reproduced, distributed, or transmitted in any form or by any means, including photocopying, recording, or other electronic or mechanical methods, without the prior written permission of the publisher, except in the case of brief quotations embodied in critical reviews and certain other noncommercial uses permitted by copyright law.

www.paultomkins.com

Prologue

1956

Within the matrix of movement and chaos, Charlotte Bradbury finds stillness. Jet-age adjacent — transcontinental glamour by osmosis — she soaks in the bustle and scurry of London Airport's sparkling new terminal. She sits, serene and composed, a study in tranquility in her prim camelhair coat buttoned to the collar, her hair clasped neatly into a chignon bun with an elegant sweep just above the nape; her internal world covered, concealed.

The terminal, with its walls of floor-to-ceiling glass, bristles with irregular motion — paths crisscrossing, haphazard trolley-wheels wobbling and squeaking, sharp-heeled shoes clacking on the highly-polished brecciated marble — but she sits to one side, detached, glancing out through the walls of windows. Despite the advent of the jet, all aircraft are propeller-driven: the world's first jetliner — the de Havilland Comet — recently taken out of service, following a series of tragic crashes.

She turns her gaze inside, at the people arriving and departing; at the clusters of family members taking turns to exchange desperate or welcoming hugs; at the pilots and their crews in immaculate uniforms striding confidently in lockstep formations to work.

She has no ticket — at least, not one that's still valid. *This* is her destination. Aside from one occasion, she has never gone airside, to the realms of passport control and customs officers, although she likes to watch those who step into such privileged corridors, to soar, within the hour, into the sky at a twelve-degree angle. For well over a year, ever since the terminal complex first opened, she has made the journey — almost daily — to a seat on the concourse, to study this new world. As has been a habit since her teen years, she jots something in her journal: perhaps a quick sketch with brief annotations, or a few lines of descriptive prose full of sharp detail, in which, she feels, the truth, and the beauty, resides; descriptions that help her to re-see a scene with crystal clarity — time travel, via the mind's eye, as it zaps into view with a visceral sting. Sixteen years earlier the rudest interruption of war destroyed her dreams of a life of words; destroyed so much more, with damage that refuses to abate. Still, she continues to document her world, unread by others, as if a beloved correspondent read by millions.

Emotional pain, she concludes in a new note, flattens over time. Its razor-sharp peaks become shallower, duller. But in flattening, pain also compacts, taut and compressed; calcifying, ossifying, petrifying. It thins, but in doing so, hardens to dense granite. And with each passing year, layer upon new layer falls: further losses, failures, sorrows, injustices and ignominies — stilted dreams, dashed desires, butchered hopes — like soft soil scattering over deep strata tamped by decades. In time, it too hardens and thins, and turns to stone. She realises all this, yet with a stoic spirit, and a necessary hint of self-delusion, carries on all the same.

Occasionally she takes a photograph with her battered Argus C3 — maybe one or two shots, on a good day, to eke out the cheap film. On this afternoon, however, she breezily shoots over half a dozen. They will reside as forgotten photographs, left as undeveloped negatives in their canisters, until rediscovered and unspooled, to shed black-and-white light.

Fifty yards away, a commotion breaks out: a posse of people gathered around a fully obscured figure who walks across the concourse. Men with notebooks chase in a circling herd, and three photographers fight to capture the scene. Charlotte swiftly lifts her camera, frames the moving throng; her focus purely in the surrounding droves, and their behaviour, with no interest in the encircled figure. She has seen enough movie stars in her time, in the different terminals: rat-pack contenders in fedoras and dark glasses, disembarking from Pan Am and TWA airliners; British icons, strolling confidently on their way to try and crack America; and Mediterranean actresses with black shades and headscarves flown in on Alitalia, Swissair, Air France, walking hurriedly to limousines with running engines. She feels no thrill, just a curiosity about how silly those surrounding them become — and never more so than in the summer, at the arrival of Marilyn Monroe, and a day of chaos that Charlotte would prefer to forget. She thinks of the ticket, now months out of date, scuffed and dog-eared at the bottom of her bag; a trip to nowhere, now.

This is a great-light day. The bright midwinter sun — swiftly lowering in the afternoon sky — floods in through the panoramic windows, conjuring sharp highlights and deep, long shadows; so much more dramatic than the overcast days which paint the scenes in wearisome, low-contrast greys that flatten and deaden the dimensions. The way today's sunbeams catch swirls of cigarette and pipe smoke adds a sense of otherworldliness, as if unseen travellers — transmuted into clouds of vapour — are sneaking along for the ride.

And yet that very same smoke also brings to mind those aircraft she has seen consumed with fire, and the men set aflame; men whose seared, foul-smelling skin sloughed off like loose-fitting silks before he eyes. So many men who died, and whose disfigured faces — if she squints — appear in those random arrangements of exhaled tobacco, for just the briefest of moments, before the shapes unfold and diverge and dissipate. Men, alive again in her dreams; to die again in her nightmares. And that *specific* man she saved, and who, in return, gave her own life a new sense of meaning.

The vicarious pain and pleasure endures, as people rush for flights, while others say long, tearful goodbyes. Children run about in play, hopscotching across the variations in tone and hue of the marbled floor, while some of those old enough to know what's actually happening in the grownup world around them wail and stomp, or step aside and turn their backs to sulk; a teddy bear or a doll also turned to face away, to join them in pouting. Families in tears, lovers torn apart by final calls to board, and then, in amongst them all, the aloof, detached trilby-clad businessmen, who move from one part of the airport to another with minimum fuss and an optimal stride, their worlds contained within slender attachés and briefcases, their emotions as indiscernible as the classified paperwork hidden behind locks and catches. Some stop at telephone kiosks, others queue for duty-free spirits. They read newspapers in cafés, or sit bolt upright in the seats that line the concourse, too well-mannered to slouch; although occasionally those with exhaustion recline across seats in the corners, jackets covering their faces like shrouded corpses at the scene of a disaster.

Eventually they will all disappear behind partitions — into the funnelling system that pre-sorts passengers into distinct channels — emerging in the fresh open air a hundred yards away, to be led, by foot, across the tarmac towards their allotted aircraft, where movable staircases await; their next footfall on terra firma in Paris, Berlin, Hong Kong, New York.

And some, with a poignant, personal yearning felt by Charlotte, to Keflavík: hub for a country to which, despite her desires, she has still failed to travel.

Charlotte once felt, at her very core, the kind of nerve-raw emotions on display in the gleaming new Europa Terminal, but now, stretching beyond her mid-thirties, she cannot bear to open herself up to it again. In this way, the compression of pain feels slightly different; more like an overpacked suitcase, her past locked down, every ounce of her own bodyweight having forced the catches closed — with no way for it to come unhinged without explosive decompression; but also, no longer any room for even the slightest addition. It feels that full, that overbearing. And although she doesn't wish that kind of heartbreak and sadness on anyone else, it comforts her to see that it goes on all the time, if she just looks in the right places. The pain she constantly subdues, she realises, is not exclusive to her.

Christmas lights add to the sense of occasion, reflecting — doubling, tripling, quadrupling in multicoloured patterns — on the abundant chrome, the marble floors, and the endless panes of glass; all part of the palpable frisson of festive travel, with a clear increase in traffic. That it's also a Friday afternoon, with the weekend edging in, adds to the buzz of excitement in the air. It further fuels her fascination with the daily churn of untold stories, from which she tries to decipher snippets of information: the quality and cut of the clothes; the length of time it takes to say goodbye, and whether or not both parties seem equally torn; the colourful stickers, adhered to careworn suitcases, on which all manner of destinations are depicted; the conversations she overhears, and the many languages and dialects, and how at times she thinks she knows what they are saying without the need for translation.

Despite this, she doesn't feel any desire to pass time at a train station or ferry terminal, where similar stories can be found.

The aircraft beyond the walls of windows provide the familiar propeller-driven thrum. She remembers hearing the distinctive spiky wail and whistle of a Comet — watching from the old airport buildings a couple of years ago, as it soared into the air. It signalled the future; a future now mothballed. Progress is more successfully epitomised by the new terminal building in which she sits: in operation for eighteen months, but only officially opened by Queen Elizabeth a year ago. Charlotte attended that auspicious day, too, but the crowds left barely any space to move, even in such a large area. Crowds — when a dense sea of jam-packed bodies — bring back anxieties of 1940s London, and the fear of being carried and tossed by a sweaty tide of humanity; the panicked memory: unable to make her feet find the evasive floor during the teeming V.E. Day celebrations as, amid the pandemonium, she searched for the man she'd lost. Although willing to watch people going about their business, she does not care for anyone getting too close, and crowds pushing in.

Along with the terminal, Her Highness opened the adjoining eponymous Queen's Building. Charlotte held some vague interest in catching a glimpse of the fresh-faced monarch — how weird, she thought, to be older than the head of state — but she felt in no way starstruck. As a fresh-faced nurse she'd seen too many dead bodies — torn bodies, dismembered bodies, bodies turned inside out — to think that people were not basically the same, when reduced to states of dislocation and disarticulation. Not even royalty could withstand the kinds of physical forces that, via too many aftermaths, she had witnessed; celebrities likewise fallible. Who were they to think themselves better?

War at close quarters, she once noted in her diary during a coffee break in the mess hall, reduced everyone to clothed corpses, where, outside of the deepest, most reinforced bunkers reserved for those in power, no privilege existed if the bomb landed at *your* feet. The poshest pilots, she soon learnt, could be flayed alive in a crash, the same as working-class lads who fought their way up through the ranks of the RAF; and those who survived were just as likely to suffer the same torments on the road to recovery, if they remained lucky enough to get through those hellish initial stages, and held onto hope. Perhaps the upper-class had more to return to, but no one got out unscathed, unaltered, undamaged. She hadn't become a nurse at the outset of war to become so acquainted with death, but she came to know it intimately all the same. If anything, the commotion during the Queen's grand opening only disrupted her own airport routine. She felt much happier the next day, when things returned to normal.

The vast Europa terminal — surveyed through Charlotte's camera viewfinder as it sweeps across the panorama through a narrow field of vision — comprises a sparse and simple design, with straight lines and endless sheets of glass on two sides, joined together at either flank by wood-panelled walls with entrances and exits to different parts of the airport, and elevators to the upper floor and mezzanine. A patchwork world of squares and rectangles, almost everything perpendicular; curves and circles barely visible in the architecture, beyond a few features: a modern, unfussy, fine-handed clock; the deep light-wells of the mezzanine ceiling; the downward ever-rolling arch of the escalator handrail, endlessly looping. Otherwise, nothing but clean, unbroken lines. 'This is *Modernism*', she thinks, trying to see it afresh. Minimum fuss. And even though it bears no resemblance to the old English cottage in which she grew up, she approves — her old-fashioned tastes gradually won over by the simplicity, the understated elegance, the sense of scale in the high ceilings and the gloriously flooding light. Aside from the occasion when Her Majesty cut the ribbon, it somehow retains a sense of space, even on the busiest days.

She turns, shifting to the view outside. In the distance, way beyond the runway, the skies are darkening — a brewing storm; snow, they'd said, on the forecast. It looks the right *colour* for snow clouds, she thinks, without ever having wondered what differentiates snow clouds from others. Perhaps it's the Prussian blue mixed in with the dark grey? She jots the thought down in her notebook, then walks across to Forte's café.

Ahead of Charlotte in the café queue stand Frank Carter and his red-headed son, James; the pair killing time before their flight to Glasgow is called. She hears the father ask his son for a second time what he wants to drink, and the boy impatiently repeats his order. "Yes, of course," says the father, staring out, into the distance, at the great expanse of *aviation*. "Silly me."

Once served, Charlotte takes a seat with her coffee, and studies the pair, now sat at the adjacent table. Discreetly — a skill she has honed over many years of low-key, covert observation — she starts to take notes, and sketches their appearance. Despite no formal training in art, through practice she has developed a reasonable skill for quick-drawn likenesses.

Frank: a round-faced, middle-aged man with horn-rimmed spectacles and a balding pate, covered by a sweep of hair from the side pressed down by a dark grey trilby, which he occasionally removes to scratch or wipe sweat from his scalp. *Blubbery lips*, she notes — seeing them as awkwardly full and round — that emit a clipping sound as they smack together as the words form; small specks of saliva and food projects as he speaks. James, in his early teens, is slender and faintly moustachioed — the finest downy orange-red hairs on his upper lip; his face dotted with a mix of calm and angry acne. Lanky — already taller than his father — his nose and ears spike outward, resulting in a slightly disjointed face that hasn't quite yet grown together. Perhaps his features will appear less jagged once he fills out, Charlotte ponders, although she once heard that the nose and ears continue to grow throughout life; and with this thought she pities the poor mite's luck. The gingerness of his hair — fashionably quiffed — darkens to a deeper red with the oily Brylcreem, whose aroma, from ancient intimacies, she can still evoke at will. The confident hairstyle disguises his innate pubertal awkwardness; the short sides leaving those ungainly ears awkward and exposed.

"So, are you excited, Son?" Frank asks, as the pair sit facing each other over a tray of tea and scones.

"You keep asking me that," the boy huffs.

"Sorry. You just don't seem too excited," Frank says, heaving stacked spoonfuls of sugar into his tea; three white mountains of gradually avalanching granules that partially spill into his saucer and beyond.

"I'm excited, *okay?*" James says, his irritation clear.

"Okay. It's just that you've wanted this since you were seven."

"Well I ain't seven anymore, am I?"

"No. I guess you're not," Frank says, scooping the stray sugar from the table into his palm; momentarily tempted to tip it into his cup, before discarding it the ashtray.

"There's no guessing about it."

"No."

"I'm looking forward to it. Just leave off asking." The boy sighs, and returns to his yellow-jacketed *Wisden,* as thick as a bible, which he inspects almost forensically, imbibing numbered codes of leather on willow. His father opens his untouched copy of the *Daily Mirror,* and stares blankly at an inside spread.

The last half-inch of Charlotte's coffee stands cold. The father and son — Frank and James — are on their way to the boarding gate and its filtration system, but still she sits, as if time passes differently for her. The serving staff are used to her eking out a single drink, and only ever ask her to move on if there's a queue for her table. Often she'll leave a small amount of coffee in the bottom of her cup, to argue that she's not quite finished. "Look", she'll say, with a wry smile. "I'm not done yet."

There's a little more roundness here in the architecture, she notes, as if seeing it all for the first time: long conical lampshades; the feminine curves of the cash tills; the familiar circular shapes of cups, saucers and plates. It's warmer, more human.

People queue to order cream teas, buy sandwiches wrapped in cling film, or take cakes from under glass domes — yet more curves — on the counter. Despite some other predilections in the past, her undying addiction remains coffee: white, two sugars. Initially, after years of abstinence due to rationing, two sugars tasted far too sweet — awful, even — but it seemed silly to pass up on the newfound abundance, especially when, in a café, it cost no extra. Two years on, its sweetness has become the norm. On certain low-energy days she adds a third spoonful to her drink. It takes her back to the late summer of 1940, and the nurses' mess hall, and her desire, amid the frightful chaos, to switch from tea to the punchier coffee.

A familiar, handsome young man — late teens or early twenties, sharp-suited but not overly groomed and his hands free from the gaudy gold signet and sovereign rings that seem so popular with his peers — joins the queue. When it's his turn to order he gets stuck on the 'p' of the opening word — *Please* — and after several aborted attempts — *P-p—pl-p* — changes it to "Cup of tea, ta". He takes a seat at the table vacated by the father and son, wiping the stray sugar granules onto the floor. She has seen him several times before, to the point where they occasionally smile in faint recognition, but nothing more. What's his story? Does he work here? He is always smartly dressed, but never in uniform. She knows him by sight, and nothing more.

In time she will learn that he is Stanley Smith — a local man, with good reason to make frequent trips to the airport.

Flight has long been a part of Charlotte's life. Or rather, for many years she has experienced an adjacency to it. Despite this, she has never actually flown.

She has never flown, and yet she has witnessed aircraft crash.

The first — and the one at closest quarters — changed her life. The man on fire. The burning plane, losing altitude; trading sky for ground like a pheasant pierced by twelve-bore birdshot.

A time of passion and terror; the best and the worst of times. But that was over a decade ago, in the war, before London Airport even properly existed; before the vast fields and small villages — including a little hamlet called Heath Row — were flattened and concreted and built upon. Back then, London Airport was just a grassy testing strip for the Fairey Aviation Company, headquartered in the nearby industrial town of Hayes.

Even now the construction work continues, as the airport expands like a concrete organism — a sprawling overland concretion — spreading ever outwards, consuming the adjoining acreage, paving over pasture and woodland and boscage.

From her seat in the café Charlotte can see both the terminal concourse and the apron beyond, albeit a far smaller portion than when sat at her favourite bench, and much less of the sky. The darker clouds continue to roll in, the snowstorm moving closer. In the mid-distance a Vickers Viscount taxis past: Iceland Airlines, which always causes a stirring, a flutter. One day, she tells herself — when she can muster the gumption, and hold her nerve — she will fly with them, to the airport near Reykjavík, and then, via a smaller airplane, on to Akureyri in the north. One day, when finally able to board a plane, and *trust* it. The Icelandic Airways' Viscount provokes just one of many reminders of the war, and that special pilot.

Was he a myth? Her 'Iceman', as she called him — *still* calls him, to herself — contradictorily brought into her life by raging hellfire, on the brink of death. It had been so long. Could she trust her memories? What parts were real?

Unable to eke any more from the cup, Charlotte wanders across from the terminal to the adjacent Queen's Building, then, from cool to cold, out onto its long, multi-levelled concrete viewing terraces — harsh brickwork softened by boxed greenery, circular planters and streamlined wooden benches — overlooking the vast tarmac. It's the best view of airside, from the apron out all the way back to the monolithic BEA and BOAC hangars and cargo sheds in the distance like docked ocean liners on the horizon; the intersecting lines of lengthy runways and taxying strips resembling a foreshortened Star of David.

Out here the rawness of the sounds bursts right into eardrums, with no glass barriers for protection. But she sees less observable human life, as dusk descends, and thickening, portentous clouds loom ever closer. Still, a couple of dozen people brave the bitter temperatures — the schools shut for Christmas, many parents clocked off work until the New Year. Yet they are all spectators, engaged in watching, which mostly negates her interest in watching them. There's not a great deal of *doing*.

Still, there are discernible small stories all the same; little dramas that gently play out, if she takes the time to observe them.

She stands close to a man she will come to know: Geoffrey Freeman, prematurely grey-haired and silver-suited, with his bespectacled five-year-old son, Montague. The pair lean against the cold balustrade; Charlotte snaps a quick photo, of which they're unaware. The boy, in paroxysms of joy, literally shakes with excitement, as if a whole toy shop had come alive before widening eyes magnified by thick lenses. Ahead, an aircraft comes in to land; to one side, another thrusts along the runway and up into the sky. It's all too much for him.

"Father, Father!" he screams, jumping up and down. "Look! Look!"

Down below, a glistening, silver British European Airways DC-3 starts up right in front of them; close enough to see fine engineering details. The emphysemic rattle and roar of her engines, as they attempt to fire, temporarily drown out the boy's shrieks. Airscrews slowly spin, stutter, sputter, splutter and spin again — and this time the three blades on each power-plant become a blur of motion with a great *whoosh*. Grey smoke chokes from the exhaust pipes on the cowlings, as the aircraft pivots on its tiny back wheel. Its passengers press their faces against the half-dozen windows that line the fuselage, some looking up at the big terminal building — perhaps trying to spot family, who in turn are somewhere, trying to spot them. At the rear window she sees the father and son from the café: Frank and James Carter, father leaning over son to get a glimpse of the airport as they finally begin to taxi; their faces momentarily lost to Charlotte behind the slope of the wing, until the angle of the plane alters and they are visible once more, albeit now diminished by distance. A few seconds later, as they taxi away, the window shrinks too small to discern the pair.

"You see that?" Geoffrey says to his son, pointing across to a grounded de Havilland Comet in the distance, outside one of the hangars, where it has sat parked for over a year. "That's a Comet. A jet plane."

"What's a jep plane?" Montague says, looking up at his father with his magnified eyes.

"*Jet. Jet* plane. It's a new kind of aeroplane. Much faster than the old ones."

"Did you work on that one?" Montague asks.

"No, Son," Geoffrey says with a smile. "I only work on them after they crash. I did work on another Comet."

The boy points to the distant plane, which he can barely see. "That one didn't crash?"

"No — unfortunately, the ones that crash don't usually fly again."

His son looks puzzled. "Why don't they fly again?"

"Well, usually they end up broken, in pieces."

Montague looks aghast. "Don't you put them back together again?" he asks, pushing his glasses back onto the bridge of his nose.

"No, there's usually no way to put them back together again. A bit like Humpty Dumpty, I suppose. My job is to find out why they crashed, by looking at the pieces."

"Do lots of planes crash? Will we see one crash? Will we, Father?"

"No, Monty. And it means lots of people get badly hurt. Of course, these days I'm told it's safer than driving a motor car."

Charlotte observes the pause, as Montague tries to process the information. "Do lots of *cars* crash?"

"I suppose they do. Although they don't travel as fast as planes, and they can't fall from the sky either."

"Do you look at why cars crash as well?"

"No, that's someone else's job," Geoffrey says, patiently; accustomed to his son's incessant lines of questioning, yet also slightly distant in reply. "But we will be seeing more aeroplanes. Your mother and I will be moving here in the New Year."

"Here? To the airport?"

"Well, nearby, Monty. So we'll be able to pop in as often as you want. See some planes. My job will be in one of those buildings over there," Geoffrey says, pointing across to a cluster of office blocks beyond the tips of plane tail-fins.

And with that the first specks of snow start to drift down, and people begin to hurry inside.

The cold having infiltrated her bones, Charlotte returns to Forté's, for another coffee, more for its warmth than its reviving properties. She doesn't like to have caffeine after four, nor too many cups each day — with it comes a fidgety anxiety — but its kick has long-since been a crutch. Now, however, she just wants something warm, before taking the bus home.

Once seated at the table, she watches a mother park a pram at the table beside hers and go to the deserted counter. Smartly dressed and fairly well-spoken, the woman is a pilot's wife, seen a few times before, and spotted and photographed a little earlier in the afternoon. "A cup of tea, please. And if it's no trouble, can you warm this milk for the baby? Thanks ever so much."

The baby is Michael Marston. Oblivious to the world beyond the proscenium of his pram hood — his eyesight not yet developed enough to focus any further than the colourful toy that dangles inches from his face — he lies on his back awaiting his bottle; far too young to realise what a monumentally fateful day this will prove to be.

He will grow up to see things, and tell all kinds of stories.

Part One

1955

The pair met under a spinning star: a big wheel of light that cut circles through the seeping hues of dusk — orange to cyan to violet, and on to deepest indigo, as the sun slipped from the horizon.

July 1955, the evening air warm and fragrant. Stanley Smith stood languidly at the front of the queue as Alice Mortimer stepped off — her delicate poise and balance apparent as she descended, resplendent with red-carpet grace amid the boorish clanks of industrial machinery; as light as a feather, he noted, barely causing a ruffle in her elegant green chiffon dress as she moved. Their eyes met: a palpable pause, as everything slowed to a stop. They didn't speak — at least, not yet — but a connection sparked between two strangers. In that moment he felt, on some inexplicable level, that he *knew* her.

Alice lingered in the shadow of the Ferris wheel, talking to her friend Nancy, as Stanley took his open-air seat on the ride. He watched Alice shrink as his seat pulled him backwards and up into the air — his stomach lurching, his legs suddenly lolling. He didn't shift his eyes from Alice — not once, while she remained in view. She looked away, but then glanced up — flashes of coloured lights bristling across her elegant features. At the ride's highest point he could no longer tell if she remained looking directly at him. Were their eyes still meeting?

As the ride passed the apogee she slipped from view, motionless beneath his seat as he moved away. He dare not crane his neck over the side of his seat, to try and keep her in his sights, as — even replete with naiveté — he recognised such a gauche tipping of his hand, in addition to the rudeness of staring. And yet in those few seconds she could have wandered away, lost in the crowd like a small pebble cast onto a vast shingle beach. As the first revolution neared completion, their eyes locked again, as if she were awaiting his re-arrival. He almost revolved *around* her, orbiting a celestial body; yet totally out of control of his own movement, at the whim of physics and machinery. His heart pounded — partially due the unnatural suspension in mid-air, all sense of terra firma absent. He felt his palms sweating against the metal guard rail; holding tight, while his grip somehow loosened. Gradually his dangling feet moved back towards the ground, as the wheel completed each circuit, and then dragged him back up into the sky. He lost count of the number of revolutions — too many, it seemed — until finally, *mercifully*, the mechanism ground to a halt. She remained there, in the same spot.

Alighting, he sensed a slight trembling in his thighs and calves. After a momentary hesitation Stanley moved towards Alice, his body and mind giddy with adrenaline. Not once in all his nineteen years had he ever approached a total stranger — let alone a *girl*, or a *woman* — outside of the interactions with store clerks and usherettes and librarians, and other enforced and often awkward social exchanges; and certainly never an unfamiliar young woman *in public*. And yet he couldn't let the chance pass. Instinct: moving toward her with a blank mind, pulled like a migratory bird or fish drawn by an invisible magnetic field. It just seemed to happen; as did saying *Hello!* before even reaching her — hurrying it out before he lost his nerve. The ability to intervene in his own actions felt elusive, with no plan as to what to say next. Alice smiled, demurely, and returned his 'Hello' with one of her own, along with a gentle nod of her head.

What she did not yet know: *hello* one of the easier things for Stanley to say; words starting with certain other letters would jam in his throat, stuck before stammering out in stages, if at all.

"I'm Alice," she said, offering a soft hand: soft grip, soft skin, which Stanley, after wiping his sweating palm on his trouser leg, took gently in his own; careful to not squeeze it in contrast to the overly firm manner his father had drummed into him at a young age — this was, after all, not a bank manager, headmaster or prospective employer — and yet not wanting to offer a limp clutch. Why hadn't his father taught him how to shake hands with the fairer sex? he thought, as he tried to figure out the correct pressure. The contact of her skin felt thrilling, yet he knew that, as the seconds passed, he had to buy more time. For some strange reason it hadn't occurred to him, as he made his approach moments earlier, that he would have to say his own name. The force that pulled him towards her had rendered thought superfluous, yet his whole life had been about planning ahead, detouring around the words and sounds that ambushed and tripped him up; including his own name. Unlike other names, with shortenings and variations starting with different letters, there could be no escaping the sibilant hell of *Stanley*, with its unhelpful reduction to *Stan*. To double the indignity, his surname — Smith — evoked further dread, although at least the need to share it rarely arose in such an informal setting.

"I'm S-s-s…" he said; or half-said. Feeling like he would choke on unsayable sounds, he turned his eyes away; in so doing, catching sight of Nancy nudging Alice with over-widened eyes, as if to suggest that this meant trouble. He glanced back at Alice, gripped with anxiety, and anticipating further humiliation — half ready to cut his losses and walk away — but she held his gaze, and smiled, sweetly, without a hint of fear, and free from any kind of patronising gesture. She simply looked at him in a friendly, patient manner, as her friend again gently dug her in the ribs.

He tried once more, to no avail. Words were allergens, his tongue in anaphylaxis. He took a deep breath. Then another.

"…*S-Stanley*," he finally said, after a long pause, followed by an extended exhalation.

His name finally unhooked from his throat, he felt grateful for Alice's patience. To some small degree it eased his nerves. Adrenaline rushed, in a positive flux from anxiety, as his self-loathing eased into relief and then up into joy. Here stood someone who would not mock him. Not that she *looked* the sort to do such a thing — she projected a warmth, a most welcoming air with her open expression, but painful experience had taught him never to take it for granted. People could be so cruel, and it wasn't always from those most suspected.

Words flowed a little easier, albeit altered by a strange new affectation: a quasi middle-class accent unexpectedly tumbling out as he spoke. *Charmed to meet you,* projected in an attempt to disguise his estuary vowels, as well as avoid those debilitating trigger syllables of esses and pees, that sat separate and slippery, like oil on water. Usually, *pleased* became *nice*, and yet here it somehow became *charmed*.

The tactic of avoiding words that provoked stutters was nothing new, but this enunciation arrived out of nowhere. Despite humbly-educated parents and a working-class background that, although relatively poor was nowhere close to penurious, Stanley possessed a good sense of the Queen's English — having read classic novels via an inspiring teacher; been to the cinema to watch acclaimed British dramas portraying upper-class life; and seen highbrow plays on his parents' basic-model television bought two years earlier for the coronation — but no one on the railway estate would ever dare talk like this, nor accept him doing so. And yet, having started, he knew he couldn't stop.

Occasionally a word would come out all wrong — some half-dropped aitches, an errant *ain't* before he corrected himself — but she didn't seem to notice; or if she did, she had the good grace to let it pass. In contrast, he had her pegged as distinctly middle-class. The daughter of a schoolmaster — a fact he would later discover — elocution had been important; clearly apparent in her accent, her vocabulary, her grammar. And yet to Stanley she did not seem *excessively* well-heeled, and in no way haughty or aloof. She appeared exotic, but not *too* exotic; a slight sense of mischief about her, that brought her closer to his level.

"Hadn't you better go and find your sister?" she said to her friend. This time Alice nudged Nancy, who, after an extended stare, finally took the hint to leave the two alone. Stanley smiled — inwardly — at the way Alice clearly didn't feel the need for a chaperone. As she retreated, Nancy gave Alice one last open-eyed look, tilting her head in disbelief, but Alice simply patted her on the arm and then, ever so gently, ushered her away.

"Are you here alone?" she asked Stanley, once Nancy skulked off with an exaggerated shake of the head, before disappearing into the throng.

"Yes. I mean no. I'm here with a p-pa … with a friend, Eddie, but he hooked up with an old flame."

"How very rude," she said, but then smiled, undercutting the harshness of her judgement with a hint of pleasure.

"Where are you from?" Stanley asked, unsure of what to do with his hands, which suddenly felt utterly — *ludicrously* — outsized, as if suddenly wearing the cumbersome wicketkeeping gloves he once donned during a brief foray into cricket. Eager to look relaxed, he did not want to risk the disrespectful act of slipping them into his pockets, or crossing his arms, which could hint at boredom or defensiveness; yet, untamed, they wanted to flit in all directions, like unwillingly grasped doves. In the end he clasped them behind his back, safely out of view.

"Ruislip," she said. "You?"

"Here, in Hayes."

"Where are you stationed?" she asked, starting to walk slowly in the direction of the carousel, with an understanding that he would follow.

"S-sssss-stationed?"

"Your national service? Or have you already completed it?"

"Oh, I won't be doing any."

Alice paused, slightly taken aback. Given the viciousness of his speech impediment, Stanley felt uneasy at *any* silence, even before one lasted long enough to become awkward by normal standards; made worse by the fear that the responsibility would fall on him to fill it.

"Oh, you're not a conchie, are you?" she eventually said. Her tone *seemed* playful, but he wasn't entirely sure; too aware of occasions in the recent past when aspersions were cast on his failure to be drafted.

"What if I were?" he said, trying to sound insouciant — even mysterious — in reply, before quickly adding, in case it came across as antagonistic, "But no, I'm not. I'm exempt from conscription. I have asthma. Quite bad, really. Well, it can be. S-s-sometimes."

"Oh my," she said, with the first hint of pity: a pause, as if she were saying to herself: a stutter *and* asthma? And then she gave him a strange look, as if pondering if his handsome face, and his imposing height, and his kind demeanour, proved some kind of natural balancing of the deficiencies with which God — in whom she only half believed — had stricken him. Yet to Stanley, the look signalled *doubt*.

"I wanted to join up," he said hurriedly, slightly wounded, inferring some kind of disapproval. "Really, I most definitely did. But they wouldn't take me. Nothing I could do."

"Thinking about it," she said, "I'd probably be a conchie — if us girls had to enlist, that is. Don't get me wrong, I'd help Queen and country in the threat of invasion — well you would, wouldn't you? — but I could never be a soldier, if there ever comes a time when we'd be forced into such a ghastly duty. I'd simply have to object. To be honest, I don't even like to harm a fly. But I guess you boys are much more gung-ho about fighting."

"I'm not. Well, I wouldn't mind it terribly — if the war was justified, and they would take me, well then I wouldn't run away. I'm not a coward. But I'm not one of those who wants to charge around with guns blazing and all that. I'm not keen on fighting, especially just for the s-s-sake of it. Nor am I a conscientious objector. I just … have asthma."

"I have to say," she said — as fiery reds and oranges fizzed and flickered over her shoulder as they strolled — "I'm glad it's not because you're too young — you not being in the forces, I mean. I'd feel rather foolish talking to you, having made an assumption — if you weren't even seventeen yet. You just look the right age to be called up, that's all. And so tall."

"I'm nineteen. Nearly twenty, actually."

"Well that's good, then," she said. "I'm nineteen too, although only recently so."

The pair navigated between a steady flow of revellers, and around the amusements, without paying too much heed to the environment; slipping seamlessly into paths on the flattened grass despite facing each other for what seemed too long as they walked and talked; some other sense, almost like sonar — rebounding about the night air — guiding them through unscathed. Never had Stanley imagined that small-talk — hitherto so hated —

could feel so invigorating. He didn't care too much about the *meaning* of the words they shared; delighted mostly by their exchange. A deep and intellectual conversation — the type he always imagined requiring to impress a girl — did not feel necessary to elicit a thrill. He marvelled at the sounds of the words — the ability to trade them, the ebb and flow, once successfully extracted from his relaxing larynx; the meaning arriving in the fact that communication proved possible, a connection made.

They came to a stop at a nexus of glaring, clanging attractions. Only now were they unsure of which of the many paths to take; a circus-like junction in an over-illuminated maze.

"So, where do you work?" Alice asked.

"At Fairey Aviation. Just over there," he said, pointing in the direction of the factory beyond the vast white rectangular EMI buildings, which were themselves obscured by the banks of flashing attractions. "I'm a draughtsman. Well, nearly finished my apprenticeship. What about you?"

"Just a secretary, I'm afraid. For now, at least. But I like aviation, too. Not designing or building the aeroplanes, though — I'd like to be an air hostess, one day. Unfortunately I'm not quite old enough yet. Father thought I should have gone to university, but I wanted to do something simple to bide my time, until I could apply to work for an airline."

"University? My, you must be very s-s-sm— … very clever."

"Oh, I don't know about that. Perhaps if I worked my hardest I could have scraped an acceptance somewhere, but I'm not sure I'm suited to academia. I would prefer to travel. I want to see the world. Father thinks I'm too good to do such a job, but who on earth is too good to travel?"

"Maybe you'll travel in a Fairey p-plane? Although we don't really make airliners — it's only really been military aircraft for decades now. But that's changing. There's a wonderful project I've been working on — the Rotodyne. You might have read about it?"

She looked nonplussed. "Can't say that I have, I'm afraid."

"It's an airplane, of sorts," he said, eagerly, "but with rotors, so it takes off vertically, like a helicopter or gyroplane. It will s-s— surely revolutionise travel — albeit more city to city, rather than country to country, due to limited range. But it could still go from London to P-Paris or to other northern European cities, and that would be quite exotic I should think."

"Sounds most unusual," she said, perhaps with a greater sense of wonder than the average young female in terms of expressing an interest in engineering. He had talked to the sisters of friends about his work and their eyes just glazed over. "And rather splendid," Alice added, enthusiastically.

"Oh, that it is. Early days, of course, but a few years' time they will be everywhere, filling the skies like London buses. Mark my words. Buses of the sky."

"Then maybe I shall be riding in one," she said, with a smile. "From London Airport to Paris," she added, lifting her hand into the sky like a soaring aircraft. "Although if mine were to go wrong, I would now know who to blame," she added, with a sense of mischief that garnered a smile from her companion.

"The Comet is a worry, though," he said, suddenly sombre. "I'm glad I'm not at de Havilland having to deal with that. P-pushing the boundaries can be a painful p—process. So far ahead of its time. Revolutionising air travel. A few crashes, and now look what's happened."

"I would most definitely like to fly in one of those — once they are deemed safe again," she said, as if its return were inevitable. "All that jet power. I should imagine it feels like travelling at the speed of light."

"Yes, I would most like to experience that, too. Once it's all sorted."

As they talked Stanley kept Alice's face steadily fixed, as would a cameraman — framed, centrally focused — but everything behind her, in his peripheral vision, flared as a flurry of blurred light and movement. It only accentuated her stillness; fragility amid the chaos. Diesel fumes blew about them from chugging generators, mixing with aromas of cooked meat and onions from the nearby hotdog vendor, and all kind of clanks, clangs and steam-based hisses — rising above circling piped organ music, the shrieks from the ghost train, the shrill teenage laughter — failed to distract him. Time almost stood still. Everything, aside from her face, faded to fuzz.

"Ssh-sh-shall we try a ride?" he asked, suddenly aware that the conversation had ground to a halt. He looked around, turning full circle to survey their options. They stood central within the fairground, surrounded by all manner of amusements. Each ride, he felt, would say something about him, about his personality, were he to suggest it. The simplicity and relative slowness of the dodgems, and next to them, the waltzers — not quite as gentle as the name suggested, especially if the attendant proved mischievous in the way he span the carriage, which he recalled from painful experience. Back at the far edge loomed the Ferris wheel, which they'd both already ridden. He didn't even know what type of ride she liked. Did he want to look cowardly or boring, by suggesting one of those fairly sedate attractions? Suddenly this simple decision seemed primed to encapsulate his essence; especially when added to the knowledge — out in the open so soon — that he could never be a member of the armed forces, with such sadly deficient lungs. He tried to see himself through her eyes, without — from his limited perspective, as an only child whose friends were all boys — any great real-world insight into the workings of a young woman's mind, and how she would process such information. He looked around, buying more time. She looked around too, following his lead; silently assessing the possibilities — each and every option labelled with a brightly-painted sign demanding their attention.

For a time, it all felt too much. To Stanley, the Moon-Rocket, directly opposite, looked fairly adventurous: cars on an angled loop, shaking from side to side, lights flashing overhead. Quite fast, with the seat titling inwards; a type of rollercoaster that rumbled in circles, albeit with yet more spinning stars overhead. The Hurricane-Jets appeared more dicey: a dozen-or-so oval-shaped cockpits attached to struts fanning out from a central hub. The ride swirled around and around — *every* damn thing here seemed to swirl around and around — with the cockpits taking it in turns to rise incrementally until the highest ones appeared fully airborne. *Maybe that's what flying feels like?* he thought, never having taken to the air, despite his vocation. Maybe she'd like that?

"Which one?" Alice asked, with a slowness to the words that betrayed ongoing cognition.

"Which one," Stanley replied, almost mirroring her pace and tone, but with it sounding less like a question.

Adjacent to the Hurricane-Jets stood the Dive-Bomber, where capsules at either end of a vertically rotating arm swung around, twisting on their own axes as they span through the air at great speed. The ride resembled a giant clock face with the hour and minute hands in opposing rotations; the riders strapped to the tip of the timepiece's hands, and presumably praying for dear life as the world flew past in a circular motion. It looked *absolutely terrifying*; if the Hurricane-Jets seemed reminiscent of flying, this looked like it evoked the panic-stricken moments before crashing.

Perhaps sparked by a childhood mishap on a fast-spinning roundabout from which he couldn't alight — some older children tormenting him about his speech impediment, forcing him to stay onboard as he tried to get them to cease projecting it round and round, faster and faster, only to find it harder and harder to vocalise his objections — he imagined himself being physically sick, if forced to try it. Alice seemed to genuinely like him, but vomiting next to her — or indeed, *all over her* — felt like a good guarantee of changing that. Equally, he didn't want take her onto a ride that might also make her ill in any way, and with this in mind he finally shrugged and suggested the dodgems, with their insulated, fully-buffered recklessness.

"Actually," she said, after a short pause, "I'd like a go on the big wheel again. That is, if you don't mind?"

"No, not at all," he said, relieved to avoid one of the faster, stomach-churning rides; leading her back to the attraction, with a renewed sense of control.

"Some of the other ones do look frightfully rough," she said. "I like the speed, but not all the swirling around."

"The views are wonderful, though, aren't they?" he said, looking up at the carriages hanging highest on the wheel, above the rest of the funfair. "Much better than being spun so fast you can't see a single blasted thing."

Suspended side-by-side in a gently rocking chair, a metal lap-bar holding them in place, the pair gradually rose high above the shimmering lights of the funfair, which contrasted vividly with the now fully darkened sky. Stanley carefully kept his hands to his side, even if he desperately wanted to try and hold hers. Dare he? No, not yet.

He had never even kissed a girl before — at least, not since the chasing games of primary school, and that almost certainly didn't count. Indeed, if the recipient screamed and puckered up her face, eager to run away, that surely did not count as a *proper* kiss.

On the ascent he glanced across at Alice, and every now and then she glanced back; a glance he met and held for a fraction of a second before something forced him to look away, often just as she herself averted her gaze. Such striking beauty, particularly the almost unreal, translucent blueness of her eyes — even with so many other colours skimming their surface. What made *her* so much more beautiful than any other woman he could ever recall seeing? No one, from memory, came even close. In glances, he took in the uncanny symmetry, and the faultless complexion, with no blemishes or beauty spots. Her lips, though fairly full, weren't overblown, even with the accentuation of a tasteful red lipstick; her nose neither petite nor oversized, nor did it have a particularly pronounced ski-jump upturn that he tended to find alluring: in no way misshapen — simply slender and straight and normal. Eyebrows neatly plucked, and skilfully — he concluded — left neither bushy nor pencil-thin.

He motioned to say something, and Alice turned to meet his gaze. But now, even those initial syllables couldn't be conjured; not due his stammer, but because they no longer seemed important, when it came time to try and eke them out. And she seemed to appreciate that; quietly smiling, or pleasantly sighing, before they returned to wordlessly sharing the view, in between fleeting glances of one another.

Even her *teeth*, so perfectly shaped and aligned, bestowed a sense of kindness and intelligence, although he couldn't figure out how mere enamel, and its alignment, could impart such information; perhaps their straightness, and whiteness, and the lack of unbecoming gaps, implied good health and fine breeding. She wore her dark blonde hair at medium-length, just above the shoulder, with loose curls that fell as little more than gentle waves. As such it appeared more feminine than the proliferating, shorter Italian styles — an awkward bastardisation of which he had earlier observed on her friend Nancy, with what he saw as some unfortunate butchness; and the popular pixie cuts, shorter still, that some girls were able to pull off with elfin élan, but which were still not to his taste. Something about longer hair made him want to touch it, caress it; sample its fineness, hold it in his palm to test what kind of mass it possessed, like feeling for the weight of a butterfly's wings.

As time slowed — an inversion of his heart-rate — the ride stretched into eternity; his mind a muddle of thoughts and impressions, that he sought to untangle. To the ceaseless analytical churn of his brain she had suddenly become a puzzle that needed solving. Why *her?* Why *now?* What made Alice seem so perfect?

Stanley glanced down. The couple in the car below waved and said hello, and Alice waved in reply.

"Do you know them?" he asked.

"Not in the slightest," Alice replied, with a smile.

As she looked up at the cars above, Stanley returned to studying the young woman — so suddenly, so surreally beside him, in the grand scheme of things; a complete stranger less than an hour ago. At such a length, her hair — on which he found himself fixated — looked in no way unfashionable; indeed, he concluded that she somehow appeared *beyond* fashion. This close, with a warm summer breeze above the fairground, it smelled of the most heavenly floral bouquets — some magical perfume, left to settle upon the strands, he pictured, like a fine mist. He then pictured her as he had first seen her: her figure, clear to discern from the green chiffon halter-neck dress — pulled in at the waist by a broad white belt with gold clasps — slim and svelte, but not lacking the pleasing, proportionate curves of hips and bust.

To some, this overall lack of any irregularity might be considered bland, but to Stanley it represented elegance of an almost regal nature: beauty in order and symmetry, with nothing too ostentatious or showy. Since hitting his teens he had occasionally found himself superficially attracted to what his dad dismissively called 'tartier'-looking women, with their bolder, brasher form of sensuality — heaving bosoms with the clear display of cleavage, lascivious lips painted with what seemed the reddest of all possible hues, shorter skirts that left less to the imagination — but he felt unable at his very core to *love* such a girl. He would rather marry a mousy librarian with kindness and intelligence than a brassy blonde who put too much on show.

At the apex of the ride, with Stanley lost in this reverie, Alice tenderly took his hand in hers: lifting it with her right in order to slip her left into the grip of his fingers, which she then closed tight, her right hand resting over the top, holding the union in place. He could hear his heart pounding within his ears, sense the sweat in his warm palm.

Whilst nervous — beautiful girls *always* made him nervous — he felt the wash of a strangely reassuring sense of disbelief, as if now detached from the confines of reality: a feeling that 'it' — everything that this encapsulated — could not last. Whilst clearly still elated, it seemed unreal — too far beyond any normal expectations — and that somehow suddenly made it harder to worry about. The most sumptuous dream gives way to opened eyes, just as assuredly as the worst nightmare. There seemed no point in even pinching himself, to feel the sharp dig of the present moment; a sting in time and space. Its realness, he concluded, must be some kind of living mirage — palpable … until not. Then, a swift return to his body; a sense of weightiness upon the airborne seat.

There sat Alice, still beside him, to root his ruminations back in the real world. His speech defects, and the physically-limiting effects of his asthma, undermined the kind of confidence that his good looks might have otherwise provided; occasionally a self-possessed girl would approach him — perhaps outside school as he approached graduation age, or near the shops — but he'd lower his head, and blush, and find a way to extricate himself from the situation, if his attempts at speech had not already killed all potential interest. As such, Alice felt out of his league to such a ludicrous degree. It reduced the pressure; the night itself, he concluded, could now be seen as a mere ride — carefree fun, with thrills felt in the belly and through a quickening of the heart — but which, he admitted to himself, could only prove fleeting. He had to alight soon — *awaken* soon — and that prospect, as he mulled it over, seemed strangely fine. As long as he didn't start getting any grand ideas, and projecting some kind of future — creating the illusion of an 'us' — he sensed he would be okay.

He glanced across, and she glanced back. Every time their eyes met he turned away; at once eager to kiss her, in order to unknot the timber-hitch of tension rippling in his gut, but afraid of ruining the moment; afraid of making it *real*. So he held her hand, and let the world spin.

* * *

Walking with cold ribbed bottles of Coca-Cola — to them, a sweet new treat, thick with the sugar denied throughout childhood — Stanley and Alice nibbled at pink bouffants of candyfloss whose syrupy webbing clung to their cheeks. Their hands full, they could not partake in any of the amusements, so they just ambled through the crowds, side by side, taking it all in.

In amongst the suburban mix of revellers swaggered a louche gaggle of Teddy Boys, roughly Stanley's age: greasily quiffed hair, leopard-skin brothel-creepers, suits of drainpipe trousers and varicoloured drape jackets, Slim Jim ties, and an intimidating air of *owning* the place. He envied their bravado — that ability to *strut* — but never liked being part of a group, on account of feeling consigned to the bottom of any pack; the more people, the greater the chance of someone mocking his speech, which became trickier still with everyone talking over one another. No one ever waited for him to get his words out. He and Alice gave the gang a wide berth, even though, aside from their loudness and their language, and some occasional inter-gang pushing and shoving, they caused no obvious trouble.

Once free of their candyflosses, Stanley and Alice strolled past the shooting gallery, rolled coins down shoots in the penny arcade, circled the carousel; steering clear of the sideshows and tented attractions set back towards the rows of caravans, and the seedier elements on display, all advertised for a shilling: dwarves, stripteases, knife throwers, magic acts.

"I don't know about you, but I'd p-ppay to see a ssss-stripteasing, knife-throwing dwarf," Stanley said, getting past the difficult syllables quickly enough to not strangle the joke, and Alice laughed.

"Only if he then cuts a woman in half," she said, smiling.

Empty Coke bottles dispatched into a bin and their cheeks warm with smiles and fine specks of sugar, they stopped at the coconut shy. A swarthy carnival attendant — oily-haired, hand-rolled cigarette quietly smouldering from the corner of his mouth — growled "Watcha darlin'," without even acknowledging Stanley's existence.

"Two, please," Alice said abruptly, in reply.

"Ladies first," Stanley insisted to Alice, as the attendant — still ignoring him — handed her the wooden balls.

As Alice lined up a shot — methodically, as if more than a mere teddybear hung on its outcome — the attendant tapped Stanley on the shoulder. The man — only a few years his elder — pointed at Alice and then violently grabbed his own crotch through thick denim, vigorously shaking the clutch of grimy blue fabric that balled up in his greasy hand, lewdly sneering with a foul-breathed, gap-toothed leer. "*Phwoar,*" he whispered, with a lascivious wink. Caught completely off-guard at what felt like a clear violation of Alice — even though she remained unaware — Stanley's only response in a pique of anger to shout *Stop that!*, but the ess stuck hard in his gullet, like a stylus locked and jumping in a vinyl groove. "S-s-s," he said, trying to force the words out, his eyes widening in discomfort; "S-s-ssss", as Alice, wooden ball in hand, turned sharply between throws to see why a strange noise suddenly hissed from her companion.

"Ha! — he's a fuckin' *spastic!*" the attendant bellowed in delight, looking at Alice. "Right proper nancy boy, ain't he!"

With a heat of anger the like of which he could not recall — the familiar resentment over the shaming of his stammer exacerbated by both the desire to protect Alice and the wish to not be humiliated in her presence — Stanley drew back his arm, ready to punch the man, but she grabbed it, held it still. "Come on, Stanley, let's go," she said, dragging him away, as the man — shorter, but full of bristling, itinerant machismo — laughed; the tall stuttering stranger seen as no threat. For a moment Alice considered throwing the remaining ball at the man, but instead hurled it in anger at the array of coconuts, narrowly missing.

"You're a right smashing bird, you are, luv," the attendant called to her between long, self-satisfied drags on his cigarette, delight clear in his coarse voice, and, to *his* mind it seemed, conveying an air of flirtation; as if simply working his charms, and that it would win her round. "Lovely bit of skirt. Too good for the likes of a poofter like 'im," he added, in a more serious tone, as if this observation would somehow make her see the error of her ways and turn swiftly on her heels. He then added something, possibly in palare, designed for his own understanding, and sputtered out an unwashed laugh.

"Are you okay," Alice asked Stanley, sweetly, once out of sight, as he slumped down against the outer wall of the carousel in a semicircular spot away from the crowds, the champing grins of gold horses galloping overhead to the distorted wail of piped organ music. The energy of words stuck in his throat seemed to rebound inwards; syllable after syllable stored up, like a blocked steam outlet, waiting to either unblock the pipe in a cataclysmic release — *whoosh!* — with what could sometimes lead to aggressive-sounding volume; or explode internally, tearing through his innards, dislodging his organs, slicing through his heart and kidneys, like shrapnel from a pipe-bomb. Despite Alice's calmness he wanted to *scream* — humiliated by the lout, and by his own verbal inadequacies. He'd claimed earlier that night to not like fighting, yet he rued not landing a blow. Anxious, he felt his chest tightening, and heard its first telltale wheezes: the familiar bronchoconstriction underway. He took sharp gulps of air that only partially reached his lungs; like breathing through a thin straw, suddenly squeezed halfway. A few attempted breaths later and the wheezes were audible.

"Oh my, Stanley. What do you take for your asthma?" Alice asked eagerly, placing her hand on his forearm; matronly and, in the eery spinning light, almost angelic.

"Eph—edrine. An elixir. It's … at home. I'll be okay. Just need to … s-s—s-stay calm. Ain't nothing to … get het up about."

"Okay. We shall stay calm," Alice said, without stifling her look of concern, and yet, reassuringly, clearly not panicking. "I think I saw a St John's ambulance-man earlier. Maybe I could go look for him? Or what about your pal? Eddie, was it?"

"No. I just need … to get home," he said, lowering his head between his highly-arched knees, before fumbling with his hands on the grass, trying to push himself upright.

"Are you sure?" she asked. "I'll walk with you."

"No. Honestly. I'll be … okay."

"No, Stanley, I insist," Alice said, her posture full of composure but her eyes still drawn tight in concern. "Really, you must let me. Please — for me?"

"Okay … For … you."

Dizzy upon standing, and assaulted by the spinning lights, the speeding horses and the full-force of the eerily breezy music, the decrease in oxygen in his brain made it hard to think clearly. But he felt certain about one thing: he didn't want her to see where he lived, or to meet his parents. While not an all-encompassing shame — he would, if pressed, accept it rather than die alone in the neighbouring streets as he gasped his last breaths — it felt like another negative on a night that had already shone plenty of light on his shortcomings. His dad, he just knew, would say something ultimately harmless, but daft and unhelpful: a lame joke, at his son's expense, to underplay the seriousness of the medical situation; or some kind of awkward backhanded compliment about Alice, and what the hell was she doing with *him*. His mum would be friendly, but her accent could make her seem uncouth, her coarseness exacerbated during times of stress. Both parents would undo the illusion — if still in place — of his newly acquired elocution, revealing in one fell swoop his working-class roots, from which Alice would feel misled. His home — a terraced house on a railway estate — in no way qualified as a slum; mostly everyone kept the road tidy, and trouble rarely arose. And yet — still plain and unremarkable, and distinctly *salt of the earth*. Good people — apart from a suspected burglar three doors down, and a cantankerous drunkard at the far end of the road, as well as a smattering of roguish kids with excessive energy — but it failed to represent who he now saw himself to be. A street he yearned to leave behind, feeling himself swiftly outgrowing it. And so to take her there — even in distress — would have somehow served to root himself to the past.

"You know, the hospital isn't too far," Alice said. "If you really need treatment — and it seems you do — then I shall walk with you. To see that you're all right. It suspect it would be quicker than getting home and needing to call out the doctor."

Hillingdon Hospital, in the opposite direction, stood closer than the walk home. "Okay," Stanley said, after calculating the distances, and glad of the alternative plan. "S-s-s—" — deep breath — "Sss—sorry," he added, in a voice reduced to little more than a whisper.

"For what?" she asked, leaning in to hear.

"For p-putting … you out."

"It's no trouble", she said, hooking her arm through the crook of his. "Really. Don't be so silly."

"What about … you … getting home?"

"I shall telephone Father when we get to the hospital. He shall come and get me. We can telephone your parents, too."

"Okay," he said, not wanting to admit that they did not have a telephone at home — relying on a communal callbox on the corner. "But really, they … won't be worried. They won't be up. They often go … to bed early."

"That's good, then," she said, as they took their first slow steps. "We need not worry them."

"What about … Nancy?" he asked, half-heartedly looking over his shoulder, in a token gesture of searching, without craning his neck far enough to see anything; the name suddenly jarring with what the carnival lout had said.

"Oh, she'll be fine. She lives nearby, just over the way there. She has her sister, too."

"Oh, okay."

"You're sure you can walk it?" Alice asked, bearing some of his weight.

"It'll be fine. Just take … it s-slow, like this. It may even … just clear up. Often it does. If I don't p-p—panic."

Together they slowly left the fairground, crossing the road lined with parked cars; all the noise and commotion suddenly behind them, as they wandered west, into the increasingly peaceful night. His balance felt fine, the minimal gulps of air enough to keep him upright, and he certainly didn't want to give the impression of being lame. But he let her take a little of his weight, so that she nestled closer into his stride, and gripped him tight.

"I'm … really grateful," Stanley said, in a rasp of wheeziness, as they shuffled along the narrow pavement.

"Please, no need to talk," she said, gently rubbing his forearm. "Save your breath. Talking can wait."

And this, for Stanley, made for a kind of paradoxical heaven: his body failing him — all rasping lungs and jittery larynx — but walking in the moonlight, arm in arm with the most beautiful and caring young woman he had ever met, and to not have to worry about *words*, and their angular awkwardness, their sharp traps, their spikes and catches; like walking in the protective, non-judgemental care of a nurse, who had seen him for who he really was — perhaps in wartime, cut apart by shrapnel — and did not flinch. Even the difficulty of simply putting one foot in front of the other, and of *breathing* — usually second nature — seemed worth every last ounce of his energy, with Alice close at his side.

2010

Beneath a curve-peaked baseball cap, eyes obscured behind sunglasses on a bright early-spring lunchtime, Michael Marston — half hidden behind a tree — stood outside the local primary school, looking through the wire perimeter fence during playtime. He felt his pulse race, his clammy hands clutched tight in his pockets. Amid the chaos of kids he saw the young boy, and experienced those familiar yearning sensations: heart skipping a beat, breath momentarily taken; overwhelmed by rushes of desire, mixed with the fear that he could get arrested. Never mind that Ethan was his own son; this remained prohibited.

He desperately wanted the boy to notice him, and with the broadest smile acknowledge his presence, but if Ethan were to tell his mother, or the school — as he surely would, exclaiming "I saw Daddy!" — then all hell would break loose. But then, a darker thought: after all these months, would the boy even recognise him? How long does a memory hold, in one so young? Does even a *father* start to fade?

Michael sensed he only had a few moments to stand around, before his behaviour would start to seem suspicious — an adult man doesn't get long to loiter outside a school these days, he concluded.

Just a fraction longer, he thought, backing away slowly; his eyes still fixed on the boy.

Ethan looked so small, so fragile, and yet, in a strange way, so independent — playing with other children, part of a community. Four years old — a mere infant — and already in the big world of school. In truth, none of the kids looked old enough. They all appeared so tiny. He saw his son's little legs, his stubby fingers. Not a scrap of excess weight around his trim torso, but still the baby-fat on the limbs between the joints; no leanness, no muscle definition, just smooth plump flesh that curved out from the wrists and curved in at the elbows, doing the same between elbow and shoulder, beneath his short-sleeved shirt in the spring sunshine. His blue eyes, even from this distance, glowed big within his face. His uncoordinated running a study in awkward motion. *Careful, son!*, Michael wanted to shout. *That's concrete!* If Ethan were to trip and hurt himself he'd hurdle the fence, and get himself arrested. Even the *thought* of his son falling over made his bones quiver — a strange darting of nerves within his shins, up through hips and along his spine, into his neck — as he internalised a very real pain for something that hadn't even happened. Just the mere *thought* of it bruised, along with his helplessness.

He watched his boy run, and play, and try to catch a ball. Ethan's voice, which Michael could discern above the choir of shrill exuberance, made his legs go weak. He wanted to cuddle him tight — too tight, probably — and smell his hair. How he missed that smell. He felt a lump in his throat, the itchiness of moistening eyes.

He would recognise Ethan anywhere, and yet his son had changed so much in such a short space of time. Every *minute* he grew, changed; and yet months had now passed. How could he stand to miss any more of it? But what the hell could he do about it? Carry on like this, however, and the authorities would not be impressed if they discovered; and nothing, he knew, could be allowed to jeopardise the custody battle, and the court appeal, set for the summer. 'Drug and alcohol abuse', she had claimed, as a way of blocking access, bolstered by bolshy solicitors and a swiftly acquired new boyfriend who, Michael sensed, as a team, eagerly agitated against him.

Michael thought back to the dingy rented flat that still didn't feel like home, and, in the corner of the front room, the cheap plastic Christmas tree, which he had struggled to find the enthusiasm to erect back in December as hostilities with Pippa escalated — the decision to deny him visitation decreed mid-month; then never found the energy to dismantle. To take it down, he felt, would somehow signal failure: the conclusive end to a Christmas that never got to happen. Beneath the tree sat a stack of lovingly wrapped presents, all bearing Ethan's name; a film of dust like frosting on the shiny metallic wrapping paper.

Time had come to get away.

* * *

Light early-April snow drifted idly on the late-evening Icelandic breeze, until a sudden harsher gust sent flakes spinning in circles across the dimly lit airport carpark, keeping them airborne, inches from the ground, in a delicate, playful vortex. Higher up, on the horseshoe-curve of hillsides and mountains, the snow had settled, layer upon layer, white upon white. Above it all, with the sun having set, the sky shimmered with an ethereal, translucent shade of blue — the same colour and density seen by pilots and astronauts at the very edge of space — in the minutes before it all turned black; the whole landscape painted in icy hues, as oranges and yellows from the terminal building burned hot in contrast, to the sounds of engines — ramping up and powering down — drifting from the adjacent tarmac.

It had not been a smooth flight, and Michael felt an increased anxiety when cramped in planes ever since hitting middle-age. Maybe a sense of his own mortality arose after becoming a father; or perhaps all the magazine and newspaper articles he had written over the years about myriad plane crashes, and the scenes he had visited for some of those stories. Now, the chance to work on an Icelandic wartime mystery, as a chapter in his first non-fiction book; multiple aircraft and multiple men, including a famous artist along for the ride, vanishing into *thick* air. Bravado and indestructibility, taken for granted in his youth, had waned — the sense that this could never happen to him — and now he pictured his mangled body amongst the wreckage that someone else photographed and documented, his dignity lost on the tarmac or mountainside.

He hopped into a cab to Reykjavík, slumping silently in the back and sighing as rural Iceland sped past; miles of road cutting through volcanic valleys and grassy fields, bereft of anything but the hardiest of life. He hadn't even bothered to prebook a hotel, with the fallback of friends and acquaintances to call upon if he couldn't find a room. It felt imperative to travel light; unfettered by the weights of heavy baggage and concrete plans.

He texted Siggi Leósson, a friend from previous visits, where they had met on an amateur archaeological aviation dig.

Where are you? Just landed! On my way into Reykjavík.

Twenty minutes later Michael dragged his tired frame out of the taxi and walked to Prikið on Laugavegur: the oldest café restaurant in Iceland, dating back to 1951 — a few years after the American wartime colonisation, that usurped the British — according to its gaudy sandwich board, whose legs stood proudly astride; the same bright red and green livery also framing the entrance, bringing Christmas, and the impotent tree, back to mind. Surrounding these primary-colour assaults to the senses stood a sober, wine-coloured façade, striped horizontally with a thick white beam, from which two-dozen evenly-spaced orbs spread an eery light into the night. He knew of the venue from a previous visit, although only from what Siggi had told him: by morning a café; by lunchtime an American-style diner; by evening a pub; and by the early hours of the weekend — of all things — a hip-hop themed nightclub, whose flickering disco lights were scattered by a lone mirrorball. The mirrorball would then sit sadly unreflective when the party ended and faint daylight streamed in through the venetian blinds, as hangover-cure breakfasts and black coffees were brought by waitresses to tables, the circle complete.

Groups of revellers loitered in the street as Michael, unsure if he actually wanted to go inside, lingered near the threshold. He'd have thrived, a decade earlier; in his milieu: a crowded bar, alcohol flowing, jukebox pounding. He'd have walked in and *owned* the place; or at the very least, felt right at home. The music in such venues now always seemed too loud, and too modern. Beyond that, he felt off-balance, destabilised around strangers, increasingly uneasy in confined spaces. He texted Siggi, asking him to come outside. Michael now planned to just say hello, and then make his excuses, find a hotel room. He had come to Iceland for its remoteness, to find space, to wander under open skies — not to be hemmed in. He fiddled with the strap of his canvas shoulder bag — packed to bursting in the absence of a suitcase — but which still amounted to an insignificant supply of luggage for a stay that could, in theory, last months; anything to avoid the dank flat, which still did not feel like home, and to damp down the overpowering absence of Ethan.

A wave of warmth blasted like a shockwave as the doors clattered open, hot air spooling out with bursts of chatter and music and the smell of fried food and beer, and that unique mingling of sweat and alcohol and a multitude of man-made fragrances that combines as *nightlife*.

"Hey man!", Siggi said in his American-influenced Icelandic drawl: part Nordic, part midwestern, before bestowing a bruising bear-hug from his slim but powerful frame. *"Fokk!"* He said, in Icelandic, but in no need of translation.

"Good to see you," Michael replied, once able to breathe again.

"What are you doing here?" Siggi asked, his breath warm and beery. "It is way too early to dig, man!"

"Yeah, I know. But I can do some rekkying."

"Rekkying in Reykjavík!" Siggi said, smiling at the wordplay; the *vík* stretched into *veek*, rekk*yay*ing inheriting the capital's middle syllable. "Of course, not that you'd find anything to excavate in the city."

"Of course," Michael said, taking a step back, as if Siggi might wrestle him inside. "Not so much about the digging this time — I leave that up to you guys, and the summer. It's more about research — for a book I'm writing. Or hoping to. Wartime stuff, amongst other stories. And, well, things at home … I just had to get away, clear my head. You know how it is."

"I hear you, man," Siggi said, an arm on Michael's shoulder. "I hear you."

Siggi's slightly dopey expression — one eye ever so slightly lazy — and lengthy, tousled hair belied a sharp, rapidly-shifting mind. He looked permanently stoned: the toll of late nights and booze, rather than dope, that aged him beyond his early thirties — particularly around the eyes, with their near-concentric bagging circles — but he possessed an enthusiasm bordering on the manic, an energy overload from within a sleepy-looking soul; something almost childlike, infused with unfeigned innocence.

"Come on, come inside," he insisted. "Get warm. I know how you pussies are always moaning about the cold."

Michael pulled away, catching his host by surprise. "Look, maybe another time, Sig. On second thoughts, I'll probably be better off just checking into a hotel. I'm shattered."

"Nonsense. You can stay at mine. Come, come and have a drink. All the best doctors swear by it."

Michael yearned to say *no* — a weariness in his bones that craved a horizontal bearing, after hours of upright seating and traipsing from point A to point B, herded and stowed like cattle, bounced and rattled by turbulence — but now, even when he tried assertiveness it lacked conviction. In a way he wondered if he overcompensated with Pippa towards the end: trying harder to assert himself, and being bullheaded about it; not wanting to bully her when putting his foot down, but rather, to locate a strong sense of self, a strong sense of his own standing, whilst on unstable ground. His shoulders slumped slightly, and he allowed himself to be ushered inside; although the smile he displayed for his host shone as genuine. "Just one drink, though," he added, three miniature whiskeys from the plane already wearing off.

"Go and meet the others," Siggi said, pointing to their table. "I must take a piss. I am *always* needing a piss. Too much beer!"

Michael nodded, but then just stood alone, observing the overpacked bar. He briefly considered walking out — the door *right there* — but felt it rude. He didn't want to test a friendship, especially as a guest in Siggi's country, and as one of just a handful of Icelandic contacts in his phone; another, on the far side of the island, three-hundred miles across glaciers and mountain peaks. For now, he'd had enough of alienating people.

In addition he had the offer of a bed for the night, which required no searching, no checking in, no fake smiles and hollowed-out customer service.

Instead he just waited, leaning wearily against the wall, surveying the scene: heel-marked floorboards, dusty and chipped; the rough wooden walls lined with dark-framed black-and-white photos set within stylishly spacious white borders; the distressed-steel menu board with its chalked-on specials; creaking stairs leading up to a second floor, to which Siggi had headed. Michael looked over at Siggi's friends: a man and a woman, their backs to him, slouched on maroon leather bench-seats in a booth designed for four people, two either side of a careworn table etched with knife scratches and coffee-scorched circles. He just couldn't bring himself to make an introduction — so at odds to the younger man who could walk into a room and befriend anyone, even when stone-cold sober.

Nowadays, being half-cut felt absolutely vital, and even that didn't always work. A couple of whiskies sometimes livened him up in social situations, but as on the plane, it ran the risk of the flip: tipping him over into morose, and in danger of dragging others down with him. Beyond a blur of heads he saw himself in a mirror, still and alone, adjacent to *life*, like a scientist standing at a safe distance from his experiment, observing; uneasy at what he detected. Upon the publication of his first novel, before eventually falling into aviation journalism, he had felt like a rock star; now he felt like an ageing rocker, of whom the 'kids' had never heard, and whose old hits were no longer even played.

What the fuck am I doing here? he thought, feeling utterly alone within the crowd. He stared at his reflection, trying to make sense of how he got to look *like this*. Though his hairline remained full, beyond a slight widow's peak, far more grey than black crept into his semi-swept quiff and wispish sideburns, and age, like a vandal, spattered white sparks in his stubble. His eyebrows hung thin and low; his eyes hooded and bagged. He tried to smile, to see what it looked like, but it provoked a nervous twitch at the corner of his mouth, flickering without conviction. The flight had been too short for jet-lag — there were no crossed timezones — but on such a long day, his body felt like it had just been stuffed into a suitcase and dragged from London to Tokyo and back.

In the mêlée of chatting couples and incipient flirtations, he felt as single as at any point since his separation. How would he ever find a new lover, like *this?* Several months on, he knew he had to excise Pippa. It was over; she had moved on. All the anger and hostility towards her still clung tight, yet some strange kind of guilt held him back; a guilt, residual and obsolete, that had needed overriding. He needed to erase whatever remained.

He tried to set it out in his mind, in a way that he would later write down, when alone with his notebook.

He needed to clear the memory of her scent, inhale an unfamiliar perfume; feel a different texture of skin, taste a different mouth, bite another lip; hold a different heft of bosom, caress an alternate nape of neck, clutch a contrasting thigh. Thinner hair, lighter, longer, shorter, fuller: *whatever.* Just not the same. To interlock fingers in a different way — a way that would not remind him of her; a way that drew him into the present moment and out of the past.

But how? It had always seemed so easy, in his overactive imagination, prior to the split — the ease with which he could casually move on, as, bit by bit, his marriage broke down, in the time before any sense of finality. The possibilities seemed endless, when still able to dream; thinking back to the approaches young female fans would make at those early book signings, as if he were still that man, and those fans were still prepared to queue. Then the reality hit hard, like a haranguing, head-punching hangover. He wasn't just middle-aged, but he reeked of *defeat*.

He sidled over to catch a bartender's attention, and ordered himself a Jack Daniels. "Make that a double," he added, over the hubbub. Then he glanced around, eager to see if a solution — a woman to wipe out Pippa's lingering sense-memories, a full-disk erase, a write-over — stood nearby; but none caught his eye. What would he say, anyway? His chat-up lines were always pretty natural, in the days when he could address any stranger. And often they approached him. He didn't need anything smart or snappy; they'd ask what he did, and he'd say 'novelist', and their intrigue often instantaneous. Now he wouldn't even know how to start.

Siggi returned just as Michael's drink arrived. "I thought I'd better order myself something first," he said, following his host to their table. Once there, Siggi introduced Michael to Magnus Sigurjónsson and Jóhanna Leósdóttir.

The beguiling smile of the latter — so warm, so beautiful — suddenly had him thinking about *fate;* forgetting that he didn't believe in such superstition.

1940

Even to a novice such as Charlotte Bradbury, there could be no doubting that the Spitfire would crash. It wasn't simply that the war had so recently introduced her to the inevitabilities of doomed flight: the maimed and mutilated survivors of so many crashes stretchered into her wards, burnt and shrivelled, broken-jawed, blinded and deafened, absented limbs or with the jagged bone of compound-fractures spearing out through their own flesh; some for patching up, and others, after the very best that could be done, toe-tagged and wheeled on squeaking gurneys to the morgue.

No, the movements of the fighter across the clear blue sky were far too irregular — clear even to the non-mechanically minded — as if something crucial to its performance had reached the irreversible point of shutdown. The aircraft roared and screamed like a wounded beast, coughing and spluttering, trailing swirling vortexes of black smoke as, in one last effort, the pilot sought to defy the laws of physics and make it safely to the adjacent RAF airbase. In her heart Charlotte knew, beyond all doubt, that a victory for gravity awaited, and defeat for anyone brave and foolish enough to try and cheat it. You can only push things so far. The broken elements of the machine — so obvious in the gnashing, gnarling sounds, in the acrid, smelting smoke from an engine burning itself up — would inevitably overwhelm those parts still functioning; it took, she realised — even without the slightest expertise in engineering — just one or two components askew or detached to destabilise a thousand highly-tuned and immaculately manufactured pieces of steel and aluminium, leaving it with no option but to tear itself apart. A lacerated engine, a punctured fuel tank, a severed control cable: none could heal themselves; there were no proteins to bind together, to coagulate, to stem the fatal flow. Fire, once lit, will not ignore the highly combustible source that gushes towards it, greedy for its consumption. The plane would crash — if it didn't first explode.

Gazing in silent awe, Charlotte came to an abrupt halt on the hospital's lush green quadrangle as the Spitfire approached, flames now flickering in a cockpit filling with smoke. One by one, half a dozen other nurses and a lone male orderly on their lunch breaks stood beside her, thunderstruck, watching on helplessly; their bodies as still as statues — neither fight nor flight, but instead that immobile middle-ground of freeze — as their heads followed the aircraft. What could they do anyway? — run towards it, when no one knew where it would come to rest? And who would want to stand in its path? One nurse raised a hand to her mouth to stifle a gasp. No one said a word.

And yet a voice in Charlotte's head — which she tried to suppress — momentarily detached her mind from the scene: prime fodder for her wartime journal, written — albeit patchily, the busier work got — under the auspices of the Mass Observation project. She felt a strange tingle of excitement, some kind of elicit thrill; a distinct counterpoint to her caregiving urges. The nursing instincts — the instincts for the protection of life — soon spiked back into the foreground under the auspices of guilt, and begged — for many of the best stories include a happy ending — that the pilot safely eject.

For a few seconds she viewed the scene as if from behind herself, perhaps from the top-floor windows of the buildings to her rear, looking down, over her own shoulder, like those craning their necks for a view. It hadn't even finished playing out, and yet she already wanted to record the events; words and sentences forming, but chaotically so, like the action itself.

Did this, she wondered, mirror life as a correspondent on the front line? Surely such reporters had to crave action, and all its subsequent atrocities, or why even be there? To write about the weather? In another life, journalism might have been the path taken, had she been given the time to go away and study; but the war — which had, in its way, come to her — and her dual senses of duty and compassion, led her to enrol in the Princess Mary Royal Air Force Nursing Service. For months she wondered if she'd made the right decision, with no shots fired — the Phoney War, all talk and no action — although that also meant nothing much to write about as a journalist on the home front, for those who took that path. But now the Germans were trying to destroy the Royal Air Force, on their way to invading Britain.

She snapped back, to within her own viewpoint; the horror suddenly very real again, the poor pilot still entrapped, still fighting the greater forces of nature. Somehow he managed to at least level the plane out and keep it reasonably straight as it sped away from the airbase towards the hospital roof, with a trajectory perhaps not too far removed from a normal landing, only five times too fast.

Only then did the pilot, his gloves clearly on fire, wrestle back the cockpit canopy. The standard bail-out procedure — told to her by those convalescing, often ruefully, as if supposedly as easy as walking on water — entailed flipping the aircraft belly-up, in order to let gravity induce a safe fall; but such a procedure required a far greater altitude, and some kind of control of the machine. This pilot, with no such option, stood on his seat, ready to fling himself clear. Charlotte held her breath as she watched him jump. He seemed to hang in the air for milliseconds — an unseated jockey, the colt blindly galloping on. Time slowed in her mind, as it must have in his to a far greater degree; every detail within her narrowing field of vision as sharp as a kestrel's focus when looking at that one spot of land where its prey quivered and twitched; tensed to pounce, at the exact right moment. Hands on fire, the pilot appeared to grasp for the release cord of his parachute, but with insufficient time for it to deploy.

Perhaps by luck, or possibly by judgement, he didn't have too far to fall; crashing onto the asphalt of the hospital roof with the brittle break of bone as crisp as a fine frozen twig snapped in two. Within a heartbeat the Spitfire skidded along the far end of the roof in a hail of sparks and screeching metal; flipping over, at the expense of both wings, before the fuselage exploded into the coppice flanking the building. A fireball — of undeniably beautiful golden hues and stunning power — burst over the roof of an unoccupied auxiliary Nissen hut.

In the chaos, her primed muscles full of elastic energy, Charlotte led the way in the frantic rush up the iron fire escape staircase, her heart pounding within her ears. She raced over to where the pilot lay supine, his tunic smouldering, his gloves burned clean through, his hands bright red and drawn-in like clamped-tight rooster feet. He lay unconscious, but — *Thank God!* a nurse arriving beside her cried in a thick Irish brogue as the woman frantically crossed herself — still alive.

With a strength of purpose and clarity of mind that only later seemed strange as she looked back on her actions, Charlotte took charge: ordering a nurse to go fetch a stretcher and gather up some capable bearers, as she knelt over the crumpled, unconscious man. His boots and jacket gave off a mist of smoke, but the remnants of his gloves were still actively burning. She removed her tippet with a swish from her shoulders, placing the outwardly grey cape — with its vivid red underside — over both the man's hands, to starve the oxygen. That was the easy part. Her training at Cranwell — information gleaned through a series of stomach-turning large-scale photographs whose vivid horrors sent retches echoing about the lecture hall — dictated her next actions, as, those lessons suddenly fresh in her mind, she sought to stabilise the airman. His jaw unnaturally askew, she placed two fingers into his mouth to root out any loose teeth; fishing out two bloody molars from where his jawbone caught his full falling weight, although fortunately she could detect no apparent fragments of splintered bone. From her pocket she took a sewing needle, that she somehow threaded with a surgeon's hyper-stillness. Grabbing onto the pilot's lolling tongue — such an odd sensation, holding that private wet limp muscle, as it moistly squirmed, squid-like, between her fingers — she skewered the sharp tip of the needle straight through with an ooze of blood, pulling the thread tight towards the top button of his uniform. Again, her hands remained unnaturally steady — the steadiest she had known — as she wrapped the cotton round and around the button, to ensure the tongue stayed clear of his throat. As she snapped away the excess thread her sense of hearing — which must have been overridden in the mêlée — returned, and she heard the group at her side, with a stretcher now laid out beside them, and the sounds of the fire crew racing toward the Nissen hut.

Moving aside as the new arrivals took charge, she stood and watched the team awkwardly descend the emergency staircase with the prone airman. The staff formed a strange eight-legged creature, bending at the knees, hands reaching out to the iron banister as others held the stretcher handles or pressed down on the pilot to keep him secure. Charlotte looked down at her bloodied hands, her fingers now fluttering wildly like wheat-stalks in the wind, her forearms quivering, the tremors racing fast up her arms and forcing their way into her pounding chest. Her knees wanted to buckle, but she sat herself down, just before falling over.

* * *

Days later the pilot reawakened to the world, a gargled groan that grew into a guttural growl projecting from a body threshing and writhing on the mattress. His jaw wired shut, he could not get the words out; and so they echoed in his throat and escaped, in distorted bursts, through flaring nostrils.

A dose of morphine soon quietened him down, shooting fast and sure and smooth into his bloodstream. He let out a deep breath through artificially gritted teeth, and his body slumped back against the sheets, as if in post-coital repose. His grimace softened to a twitching, awkward smile, within the harsh metal armature, as, gingerly, he looked up at Charlotte, his bruised eyes narrowing in an attempt to focus. With her halo of curls under a white cap there could be no mistaking the angel replacing pain with a lightheaded glee; his *saviour*, he concluded without even realising the true extent of her interventions, back on the hospital roof. He managed to convey such gratitude when thanking her, the words — indistinguishable, beyond a probable "Thank you" — squeezed out through wired teeth and lips initially quivering with the last remnants of receding pain.

The name tag at the foot of his bed read 'Viktor Hallfreðsson'. A pilot — or, at least he *was*, days earlier; now — for the time being, at least — a total invalid, consigned to a bed and drip-fed a lifeline. A fairly strapping young Icelander, he possessed the upper-body build of a swimmer, his dark blonde eyebrows singed away, his scalp partially burned; none of it as severe as other areas of his body — his hands in particular — with clear third-degree damage. And, of course, all those broken bones, including a tibia shattered like smashed porcelain.

Coming to his aid on the rooftop, Charlotte expected him to be British — a natural assumption, she felt, when concerning the Royal Air Force and its fighter pilots. At the very least she expected him to hail from within the Commonwealth — Canadian, perhaps, or an Australian or Kiwi, with a carefree countenance born of rugged landscapes; less fussy than the Brits. But Viktor Hallfreðsson definitely didn't hail from these shores. She wondered why her general preconception lingered, given that a pair of Eastern Europeans — a Czech and a Pole — had been two of the first through the doors that summer, having rushed to England to enrol with the RAF after their own countries collapsed. Still, most of the other men did hail from the Empire.

The way he looked at her, with such gratitude, left Charlotte breathless. The words were irrelevant, lost in the clamping mesh. And then, his deep, soulful blue eyes blanking as he looked past her, as if cast upon distant landscapes; before squinting to focus much closer, but still beside her, perhaps at an imagined figure at the foot of his bed.

* * *

Back in her billet for the night, and freed of constricting shoes that blistered her heels and shaped an angry-looking bunion on a big toe, Charlotte took her leather-bound journal from beneath a petticoat in the dresser drawer, and opened it to the page marked by a slither of satin ribbon. With a fountain pen dipped in blue ink from a fat glass bottle she jotted down a brief entry before the lights were due out at ten p.m..

One does one's best for these wretched souls, and then hopes — although many of my Sisters pray to their Gods — that it is good enough. Yet never can it be, not all the time. Sometimes one's best is utterly useless.

Never in her many months with the RAF's nursing service — which already marked her out as a veteran — had she felt such a sharp sense of responsibility to a single patient. Witnessing the man sustaining the injuries caused it to resonate far more deeply. For once she had the full, uncensored — unavoidable — narrative, complete with a second-by-second sense of his mental torment; a man burning alive, no less, in front of her very eyes. She watched a living soul dying, knowing — for certain — that he *would* die; and with the poor man himself also knowing, surely, that he would die. Then, no … still alive, somehow. She too had prayed, in her unreligious manner, that he would survive, and survive he did.

And days later, with her help, *still* alive. This was not some distant injury, shipped into their Sussex hospital from afar; nor one of those from just beyond the hospital perimeter, on the occasions the staff treated those injured in training exercises on the adjoining airbase — pretty much all they had to deal with before the Luftwaffe unleashed lightning war. This occurred closer still.

I feel for those men too, believe me, she wrote, conscious of a slight tremor in her hand, the scourge of strong black coffee towards the end of her evening stint; the mixture of those exotic dark beans having recently taken over from tea as the hot drink of choice in the need to power through seemingly endless shifts replete with chaos and tragedy.

2009

Bloodhounded eyes, and a mouthful of teeth that made no sense. Someone once told Montague Freeman that he had too many teeth. There existed an oddness to how his thin, lower incisors — including a tiny baby tooth, fused to the jawbone in childhood, that added to the odd sense of spacing — were buttressed by prominent canines at unusual angles, whilst from his overcrowded upper row projected a central snaggletooth, like a guilty child forced forward from the lineup by its peers to shoulder the blame. Since slumping and sighing into his fifties, the wear and tear, along with distinct nicotine and black-coffee discolouring, had further damaged a smile even his mother had struggled to love. It certainly didn't help that no one took him to a dentist beyond the age of seven, or that, once old enough, he never tried to correct this oversight.

Unfortunate — the kindest way to describe his looks; the way his mother often used. He broke his nose at the age of six, falling down the stairs; flattened, and never properly straightened, meaning that in adulthood he barely retained a bridge on which to perch the pads of his wiry, unfashionable spectacles. His nostrils wheezed with every breath, in and out; a thick greying moustache, and thicket of nasal hair, like a ragged doormat, dampening the sound.

He smoked hand-rolled cigarettes, to ease nerves that first started to shred in secondary school, where his mere name — *Montague* — proved enough to elicit bullying, and where his appearance only added to his troubles. Everything about him seemed suited to attack, in a fairly rough secondary modern. His tormentors could see that he offered no resistance, and although never badly beaten — he never angered anyone sufficiently for that — the teasing remained merciless, to the point where he regularly welled up behind milk-bottle lenses, which only served to magnify the tears and highlight his weakness. Such crying only served as a triumph for onlookers, and those joining in with jeers and laughter. Rather than needing to see blood, his tears were enough to signal their victory and his humiliation. Even some of the girls joined in. His peers at primary school had mostly been kind — even helpful to one other classmate, with a wooden leg — but it all went wrong once Montague moved up to the bigger, wilder world of the secondary modern; a world to which he ended up consigned after flunking the eleven-plus, even though he had the intelligence to breeze it. Rather than a satchel or holdall for a schoolbag, his mother supplied him with a tan leather briefcase — one of his father's, found discarded in the back of a wardrobe — which invited further ridicule. And yet he couldn't bring himself to get rid of it, out of a loyalty to the parent who handed it to him, rather than the one who purchased it. At one point he felt tempted to pretend he'd lost it, after it got thrown on top of the bike sheds, but he dutifully retrieved it — needing its contents for class — and respectfully persevered. There were also cruel rumours about his mother, which the bullies threw at him, and only then did he fight back, but only in words — words of denial, rather than spite — and all to no avail.

But his general anxiety could be traced further back, to much earlier in his childhood. At the age of six he experienced his world turn upside down.

* * *

By the end of 1956, Montague's father Geoffrey had, somewhat reluctantly, set about finalising his time as an air accident investigator at Farnborough's Royal Aircraft Establishment, to take up a job at London Airport. Aircraft had been his passion since his late teenage years — from piloting fighters in WWII to different kinds of investigative work thereafter — and as such he made aircraft the life of his son too. Geoffrey had bought Monty the very first Airfix model kit — a 1:72 scale Spitfire upon its release in 1955 — and, starting in Christmas 1956, took the boy to the viewing gallery at the Queen's Building at London Airport. A few months into 1957 — later than originally planned — Geoffrey relocated their lives to a house flanking the airport, and then, less than a year later, abandoned them there.

Montague's mother, Dorothy, suffered shellshock at the rejection; her nerves — already wrought with an ever-tired edginess that could be traced back to postpartum depression — irreparably damaged. Within a few years she took to sleeping in her armchair, and aside from just two occasions — the second in a hearse — never left the house again. Anything she needed now had to come to her, or she despatched Montague to fetch it.

The mortgage remained paid, and money regularly transferred into Dorothy's bank account — Montague took it as a small mercy that his father wasn't *that* terrible to them — so mother and child never went without anything. They never finalised a divorce, as far as he knew. Each day after school the boy ran home, to help take care of a woman whose ill-health he could not be expected to properly understand. Yet he knew, all the same, who merited the blame. From the age of seven he did all the shopping at the local store, the checkout ladies familiar with his situation and always eager to help locate items — at first he'd just hand over the lists his mother had written in the shakiest, spidery script — and pack the tartan trolley bag he wheeled to and fro; something else ripe for bullying, whenever spotted. The doctor occasionally used to visit his mother, but no one intervened over the pair's situation; she wasn't *technically* handicapped, and no social workers or carers ever came by. Prescriptions of nerve medication — benzodiazepines, which she called by their nickname of 'mother's little helper' — were fulfilled monthly, but rather than bring her back to life the drugs just left her groggy and morose. The two were left to get on with it, and although they never discussed it, in a strange manner they both increasingly liked it that way. At first, the only thing Montague wanted, aside from his mother's love and some happiness in her life, was for his father to return, even if that would diminish his own sense of purpose; without doubt, a conflicting desire. Every new day that his father spent away, Montague felt a growing resentment towards him. However — initially, at least — he felt he could temper the rancour if he returned, and if it somehow managed to put things right. But his father never did return, and things never were put right. So the resentment only grew. Geoffrey had always called him Monty, but to Dorothy he was always Montague. Once abandoned, he he never let anyone call him Monty again.

Despite sufficient intelligence, Montague never made it to university, mostly due to his mother's sickness. He worked hard on his schoolwork, but he had so much else to take care of. She anchored him to the home, fully weighted down. The worsening of her nerves left her unable to face the world; and then, possibly through lack of exercise and any form of fresh air beyond the occasional open window, allied to an unhealthy diet rich in fish and chips from the nearby takeaway, other health issues arose. Weight piled on; blood pressure rose; joints grew inflamed. Before long a commode arrived for the front room, to complete what became a comfortable, if self-imposed, prison cell. At first some of the neighbours would occasionally stop by, but these interactions grew increasingly awkward, until they avoided the house entirely, and only sought updates from Montague when he passed them on the street. When they enquired as to how she was doing he would tell them to pop in, that she would very much like it if they did, but they always deferred or demurred, with vague promises of 'another time'.

* * *

Years after his mother's death, Montague steadfastly remained in the family home, directly beneath the Heathrow flightpath. It kept her close by, to stay in the space they shared. The place where he had spent all that time, year on year, fruitlessly awaiting his father's return; the nexus of their lives. Even as an adult, Montague sometimes thought *Maybe, just maybe* — although by that point, merely to give the old man a piece of his mind. In truth, if he were to sell up, where would he go? Moving house seemed such a colossal effort, especially with the tonnage of furniture and possessions.

As in his childhood, giant jets skimmed the rooftops, shaking the windows, rattling the foundations; by 2009, the modern planes were larger still, their engines more aggressive, their passage much more frequent.

As a child he had recurring nightmares of one of the bigger airliners crashing through the walls, obliterating everything. He'd wake at night screaming, his head held under the pillow, his eyes tightly shut, his body trembling as if the whole house shook, the bedsheets wet and yellowed.

Decades on, the thought still terrified him, and yet he also wondered what it would feel like: that moment of utter inevitability, and in that split second, as death approached at 500 miles per hour, the paradoxical euphoria of letting go of all his fears. Once such a conclusion became clear *there could be nothing left to worry about,* nothing worth hanging on to, and no point even trying, as the world dissolved to dust; his bones and his blood and his brain and his heart all instantly atomised, his hopes and dreams and fears lost in vapour, his time at an end so fast that he wouldn't even get the chance to feel it.

Terrified of pain, he didn't *want* to die. He obviously held no real desire to see his house razed by one-hundred tons of fast-moving aluminium and burning jet fuel; but the fantasy — if that's the word that captured its essence — remained vivid all the same. Would it be perversely thrilling? An analogy sprang to mind: the only sport he cared for was cricket — although his only attempts to play proved hopeless — and every now and then a test batsmen would get bowled by a delivery so violent in its pace and its movement through the air that nothing could be done except admire the way it sent the off-stump spinning, the bails exploding upwards. "Nothing you can do about those," the radio commentators would usually say. And therefore, no point fearing it; a lifetime of proliferating neuroses rendered obsolete.

Montague even pictured looking out his bedroom window to see a fuselage impossibly large as it darkened the world, bearing down at a speed and a scale beyond comprehension: like the moon unmoored, careering into its mother planet at a million miles per hour. Too big, too unreal. Sometimes, in both daydreams and recurring nightmares, he saw it clearly: the dark brown curtains reaching into the room like spooked horses rearing up on hind legs; the ungodly screams of full-fury engines as they sucked in masses of oxygen to feed ever-hungry turbines; the eerie change in barometric pressure, as all the air got pulled from the room. Running becomes futile — left or right making no difference to something that big, at that speed, at that proximity. There existed nothing, beyond the initial horror, except The End.

Montague wanted to know what all of this would feel like, whilst harbouring a terrific fear of pain, and of a prolonged, agonising death. He had never once flown, for those very reasons: an aviation aficionado afraid of the sky. Of course, he knew the sky to be the safest place — the landings, and the takeoffs, proved far more perilous. He never boarded planes, and he never bought lottery tickets. It all felt like tempting fate. If a bus ever mounted a pavement to wipe him out, then, well, that's just life.

He knew only too well, without ever having sought psychiatric advice, that he owed the phobia to his father, whose work brought him and his mother to this house, adjacent to one of the world's great aviation hubs, before so callously walking out on them. Albeit not in harrowing detail — beyond the images Montague illicitly uncovered in the manilla envelope — his father sometimes discussed the various crashes he'd worked on, telling the young boy about metal fatigue or birdstrike, rather than the mess of human life. Even so, but for his father's work, none of this need be an issue. But for his father's abandonment, his life could have been normal.

1956

Flying blind in a blizzard; England a whiteout, the night sky obscured by dense, endless banks of cloud shedding thick sheets of snow. Frank Carter and his son James sat side by side on the back row of a British European Airways DC-3, taking tea from an air hostess as the storm buffeted the aircraft; their world an inverted, heavily shaken snow-globe, bounced and swept by malevolent winds whipping in from from the east.

Their destination: Glasgow, to stay with Frank's in-laws. His wife, Gloria, had taken the train a couple of days earlier with their other child, nine-year-old Lucy, to help prepare for the festivities, while Frank stayed on at work to finish an important project before the Christmas deadline. It gave him the excuse — overtime supplying the money — to fly for the first ever time, and to help fulfil his son's long-held wish to do likewise. Indeed, years earlier Frank had promised James a trip in a plane before his fourteenth birthday — a day now only a few months away. As a young boy — all freckles and red hair, and often a toothless grin — James had been obsessed with aviation, his earliest recallable memory consisting of a squadron of Spitfires flying low over the neighbourhood. Frank, a skilled and experienced capstan lathe operator, worked at the thriving Fairey Aviation Company on the outskirts of west London, to help manufacture military aircraft.

He too had always wanted to fly, having failed the medical for an airborne role at the RAF. Fairey, one of the war-effort's key manufacturers — supplier of Swordfish and Battles, Barracudas and Seafoxes — had experienced setbacks since 1944, when the Air Ministry sequestered, without compensation, its testing aerodrome at Heath Row. The Swordfish alone — a basic biplane known affectionately as 'stringbag' on account of what appeared to hold it together — credited, via the single bomb that each fragile frame could carry, with the destruction of a greater tonnage of enemy shipping than any other Allied aircraft. By the mid 1950s, Fairey had bounced back, doubling their annual pre-tax profits to over two million pounds, for a company that, just forty years earlier, spent £807 to build its first five sheds at Hayes, quickly followed by its first brick office building, costing just a fraction more. Though production had slowed since the war years, Fairey moved from churning out simple but effective aircraft that performed steady wartime roles to developing state-of-the-art machines. Earlier in 1956, the Fairey Delta 2 became the first aircraft to exceed 1,000-mph — indeed, surpassing that target by an additional hundred-and-thirty miles per hour, just for good measure — and thus set a new flight airspeed record. James had been so impressed by the feat back in March, when Frank had shown him all the newspaper clippings, as if it were some kind of personal achievement. Yet seven months on the boy seemed more guarded, almost indifferent.

The air hostess attending to rear of the plane — an attractive brunette, neat black cap pitched at just the right angle, and a beautiful lipsticked smile not in the least dampened by a slight gap in her upper front teeth — offered Frank a newspaper, but he declined, pointing to his copy of the *Mirror*. Her smile seemed personal — the front-teeth gap in her grin making her seem a little more homely — even if he understood professional courtesy, a reflex of the lips repeated time and again throughout her working day. The good ones can fake it, he thought, without passing judgement — before correcting himself: it did not mean that *every* smile lacked authenticity. Even for the genuine staff, the task must grow tiresome. He need not smile once all day long at the lathe. He tried to remember the last time he saw a woman this attractive up close; he'd encountered bubbly barmaids and pretty sales assistants, and a glamorous nurse or two, but this young lady — Gladys, according to her name tag — looked just like her colleague at the front of the plane in terms of clear complexion, bright eyes and immaculate presentation. Neither would win Miss Great Britain, he concluded, when trying to place them, visually, into such a pageant, but they would surely do well in the regional heats. Where did the airline find them?

Buoyed, he turned to James. "You enjoying the flight, Son?"

"Give it a rest, Dad, will yer?" James said with a sigh, his eyes unmoved. "I'm reading my book."

The passenger compartment of the Douglas DC-3 comprised eight rows — the port side double-seated, with starboard organised into a single line, the aisle offset to the passengers' right as a result. The only unoccupied seat out of the 24 — incongruously numbered 25, due to the skipping of 13 by either the manufacturers or the airline on the grounds of superstition — sat adjacent to Frank and James.

"Your order, sir," Gladys said to Frank, holding out a tray containing a glass with ice and, beside it, a miniature whiskey bottle. In that moment the plane hit a patch of turbulence, but she held the contents steady, like some roller-skating waitress in an American diner or drive-in, as seen in the movies.

"Thank you, my dear," he said, smiling broadly. "This is the life," he told his son, laying his newspaper flat on his lap before lighting his pipe and, in a deliberately ostentatious manner, swigging at his drink; missing only a footstool, and his tatty slippers, to have made himself right at home. "Feels like I've won the pools," he added, as saliva with a hint of single malt sprayed from his thick lips.

"Uh-huh," James said, with no inflection at all.

"Course, some lucky sod at work *did* win the pools a year or two ago. Young lad too, in the draughting office. Nothing to retire with, but a few hundred quid. Lucky so-and-so. Got himself a car. Most I've ever won is a few shillings."

James looked up from his copy of *Wisden*, but as he began to turn his head to meet his father's eye he noticed a heavily-freckled dark-haired girl approximately his own age, looking over her shoulder at him from the row in front. She smiled, with unashamed brashness and unerring intensity; slightly goofily, but in a way he also found sweet and attractive, as well as jarring. For a moment he just stared back, wide-eyed and confused, before hurriedly looking back down at his book. Only then did he allow his facial muscles to offer any kind of reciprocation, with the mild aftershock of twitching, upturned corners of his mouth; feeling his face flush as red as his hair, as he stared down at what became a jumble of words and numbers in his annual, floating around the page. When, seconds later, he dared to look back up again — brave enough to perhaps smile directly back — she now faced away, looking forwards, listening to her mother talk nineteen-to-the-dozen about their festive plans.

Did she see his belated grin, when he looked down? She reminded him of Valerie, the girl who smiled at him through the wire fencing that separated the boys' and girls' schools, and sometimes at the bus stop, where he pretended not to notice. Earlier that day, as the two schools emptied out, she gave him the warmest of smiles as they passed. "Have a merry Christmas, Jim," she said, and he wondered how she knew his name — everyone at school called him Jim — even though he definitely knew hers. He returned an awkward smile; a smile of glee only possible once at a safe distance, no interaction required, as the warmth and sweetness of her tone sunk in. Indeed, he had replayed it all the way to the airport in the taxicab. While some of his pals spoke about their desire to engage in sexual congress — one of the group even claimed to have already done so — it seemed to him that nothing could trump seeing Valerie's smile. And so, with the holidays underway, he suddenly didn't want to go to Scotland on some stupid aeroplane. He had often noticed where Valerie got off the school bus. Had he not been on the silly plane he could have gone there, to hang around on her street, on the off-chance of bumping into her. He felt his adrenaline pump at the mere thought. And yet what would he say? Aside from his younger sister, whose interests were still quite callow and naïve, he had no idea how to talk to girls. Lucy still loved her dolls, hopscotch, skipping rope — as well as a few boyish interests — and when they did talk it often descended into squabbles in the pettiest manner. He felt fairly certain that such an approach would not work with a girl of fourteen, who for all the world seemed like a *woman*. Now he had a new enigmatic smiling girl to contend with.

James shifted nervously in his seat, hormones sparking wildly, energy coursing through his body in the confined space. Had his father noticed this clumsy foray into the befuddling world of adolescent girls, and the way they smiled at him? If he had, Frank would tease him, without doubt. He always liked to tease. Not mean-spiritedly so — not with any nastiness — but discomforting all the same. He looked across: his father's head bowed, eyes firmly fixed on the fine newsprint.

The front of Frank's tabloid told of two elderly women whose bodies were set for exhumation earlier that day, the opening paragraphs noting the "sheets of canvas, portable floodlights and cameras" carried to a cemetery in Eastbourne late the previous night, in preparation. Next to the main article, the story of a man who proposed to a young woman within a month of meeting — on the surface a tale that seeming utterly un-newsworthy, but the catch, explained beneath a photo of the pair smiling as if in some American-influenced advertising — selling toothpaste, he thought, given their grins — was that she had spent most of the past five years in hospital, encased in plaster up to her armpits, after seriously damaging her spine.

Frank turned to the inside. On page three: the tragic story of a heavily-bearded schoolteacher with financial troubles, whose students nicknamed him 'fungus face'. Up to that point the story again seemed somewhat trivial. But the teacher had exited the caravan in which his family lived carrying a shotgun, and proceeded to shoot himself dead. Neighbours later found the bodies of his wife and three children — aged seven, five and three — inside the mobile home. *"By the children lay their toys,"* the article stated, *"a blue plastic duck, a little wooden canoe, and two buckets and spades."*

"Can you believe that?" Frank said to James, shaking his head. "Killing his own family. The nippers, too. Beggars belief. Hanging would be too good for him," he harrumphed, before realising, "Of course, he's already taken care of that himself, the bloody coward."

James nodded, without adjusting his gaze. "Uh-huh." He then glanced up at the girl in front. Disappointingly, she sat nose-deep in her own book, never once looking up or back. Not as alluring as Valerie, whose smile captured his heart — but she'd piqued his interest.

Viewpoint, on page two of Frank's newspaper — letters from readers — had the headline *"Ere — wot abaht this lot, mate?",* in which Mrs H. A. Chester questioned the proliferation of Cockney accents in films and radio broadcasts. What's wrong with working-class accents, Frank wondered — even if a little of the harshness of his own speech had been smoothed away during years spent dealing with engineers and draughtsmen; albeit not as dramatically as his son's improved locution since attending grammar school, even if James tended to let it slip slightly when away from his friends and teachers. Frank still sometimes chided his son whenever he dropped an aitch or said *ain't,* but in truth — and he knew it only too well — the boy had become the better spoken of the pair, and he'd become the more likely to drop an aitch or say *ain't.* The difference grew particularly noticeable in times of stress, when Frank reverted to his own boyhood tendencies, without the time to think — or worry — about getting things right. His son — the occasional bout of laziness aside — had few such problems. But Frank had always wanted what's best for James; desiring a better education for him than the pathetic excuse of one he received, and to provide things — such as air travel — that would have remained well beyond anyone with his own humble upbringing. And yet he also worried that it had taken his son from their shared roots, to the point where — when James offered his own criticisms, or corrected his father's grammar — Frank sometimes felt like the child, scolded by a superior who knew better. He never once pondered — ahead of time — the gap, the divide, that could arise due to the elevation of his own offspring. James, he thought — with his head for numbers — had the potential to become an engineer; maybe he could get him a job, when it came time, at Fairey.

Frank turned the page, then straightened the paper. Page five told of the arrest and arraignment of Dr John Bodkin Adams, accused of killing the two elderly women from page one. "Can you prove it was murder?" Adams had stated in the dock, which Frank took as an odd declaration: surely if you are innocent you only focus on your innocence, and nothing else? If truly innocent, then of course they could not *prove* he committed the crime. You can't prove something happened when it didn't. And with that Frank concluded that he must be guilty, and thus in need of hanging.

Frank flipped to the back page of the paper, whose top half covered two stories connected to the Suez crisis, with the Prime Minister questioned in the Commons about secret talks between Britain, France and Israel, which may have led to the whole farce. Below those, the result of an inquest into the crash of the new delta-wing Vulcan jet — the first such fighter in service, ahead of his own firm's still-experimental, record-breaking, Fairy Delta 2. The Vulcan had crashed in bad weather at London Airport, no less, just a couple of months ago. According to the Air Minister — quoted at length — the pilot descended improperly, and the controller in the tower, 'talking him down', gave inadequate guidance, failing to warn that the aircraft had slipped below the glide path. Three crew members and a passenger died, with two others — those with the luxury of ejector seats — only surviving thanks to their swift deployment. It did not make for comforting reading, as Frank shifted uneasily in his own seat, which he knew had no such emergency escape mechanism. He thought about mentioning it to James — joking that he wished they sat in similar ejector seats, and if deployed, the thrill of surging into the air with a parachute to catch their fall — but, having smiled in anticipation, he decided to keep it to himself, lest the comment fall flat.

Several minutes later, Frank looked up from his paper to intercept Gladys, and requested another whiskey. She smiled, that same smile. *Perfect*; or perfectly rehearsed. Not a handsome or important man — far from it, he understood all too well — it felt like a pleasant perk, in those moments, to pretend that he really mattered.

The aircraft continued to occasionally bounce and drop, although never anything too disconcerting; at least, until it hit a particularly violent patch of turbulence, with both air hostesses almost toppling into the laps of passengers. The woman directly in front of Frank and James, between frantic drags on her cigarette — drawing it as if to extract every ounce of nicotine in one go — told her daughter to buckle up, but the girl took no notice. Moments later a man seated halfway down the cabin vomited amid some truly awful retching sounds; his paper bag swiftly taken by Gladys without fuss, skilfully holding the seat-back to steady herself, and replaced with a fresh bag. The acrid smell, however, proved harder to dispel. Frank put his glass of whiskey to his nose, to stave away the odour, and fumbled for his pipe.

Elsewhere in his newspaper were adverts for Christmas shopping, including Bisodol — the antacid tablets that, it claimed, all grown-ups would like to receive in their stockings. "Now there's a lie!" Frank said to himself, chuckling. Next to that, a jolly Santa overlooking a selection of Bata shoes. Frank also found amusement in a small story on the centre spread, which declared the occasional spanking of children a perfectly fine punishment, according to experts — before warning not to try it after adolescence, whatever the provocation, as "*There is always the risk of coming off worse*".

"This here says I'm not to spank you, when you're naughty."

"Very fun–" James said, the words suddenly high and squeaky. "Very funny," he repeated, after a cough.

On another page of the newspaper, a small article about a new musical sensation. Frank sighed, shaking his head. "I don't understand your modern music," he said to his son, who, lost in rows and columns of cricket statistics, wondered where this latest topic has come from. "All that heavy drumming. Why do they have to play it so damned loud?"

"Sounds better, doesn't it? It's meant to be like that — the beat. It gets inside you. Sounds great down the youth club."

"But you can't hear the *tune*. It's all thump, thump, thump. It's not a patch on the good old songs."

"*God*, Dad — you're not gonna go on about bloody Vera Lynn again, are you?"

"Watch your language, my boy. You're not with your pals now," Frank said, his tone softer than the harsh words. "You don't want me spanking you," he added, and laughed. "But those were *proper* songs."

James turned to look at his father, lifting his head from his book as if unhooking himself from some strong magnetic force.

"Look, you're not gonna start signing are you? This ain't no charabanc. You can't just start singing away on here."

The girl in the row in front laughed.

"Don't be so cheeky," Frank said, although he quite liked his son's resistance. "That's how music's *supposed* to sound. 'Nightingale Sang in Berkeley Square' doesn't need no banging drums. Sweet music, Son. Melodic."

"They'll love you down at the Darby and Joan club. With all the old fogeys."

"And 'Shine On, Harvest Moon'," Frank said, undeterred. "That's the best one of all."

Finally James softened. "You were always singing that when I was little."

"I know," Frank said, smiling at the thought.

"Used to drive me loopy."

"You sang along, you cheeky little bleeder!"

James laughed. "Yeah, I know. But it's not exactly my cup of tea nowadays."

"No, I know. You like all that rocking-roll nonsense."

An easing — but not a complete eradication — of the turbulence meant the meals could be served. The trainee air hostess attended to the three rows nearest the flight cabin, while Gladys — the senior hostess — dealt with the five at the rear. Each carried two trays at a time — on which sat an array of fine food on china plates flanked by gleaming cutlery — but the difference in their competence remained clear. Frank marvelled at how effortless Gladys made it look, as if accustomed to delivering silver service whilst bouncing on a trampoline; so light on her feet, almost balletic. By contrast, the trainee at the front looked more like a first-timer skating on ice, but still managed to deliver the food without spillage. With his own balance, he thought, there'd be food everywhere: on the ceiling, against the windows, in people's faces.

"Have a good nosh up, Son," Franks said, with the meals placed on the tray-tables across their laps. "It'll help if you're feeling a bit peaky."

"I'm fine, Dad. It's just a bit of bumping. No different to a ride at the fair is the way I see it."

Frank leant his head back against the prim white headrest cover and reclined the chair. Blasts of faintly-lit snow swirled an inch or two outside the windows, beyond which all sense of distance disappeared into the blackness. For a moment he seemed set to relax, before looking around the cabin, checking for signs of something.

"This is taking an age," he eventually said, checking his watch.

"Yeah," James said, still finding new details in his copy of *Wisden*.

"Shouldn't we be coming in by now? It's time to land."

James shrugged, all sense of time lost in cricket data and stories.

"So … is it all you hoped it would be?" Frank asked, nudging his son.

"What?"

"Flying."

James sighed, then looked up from his book. "Suppose so."

"Suppose so? Is that it?"

"The takeoff was fun. The rest is — I dunno — just like being on a train in a tunnel. It's not as though we can look out and see anything. It's just darkness and snow."

"You know, I never really got into cricket," Frank said, looking down at his son's annual. "I enjoyed playing it at school. But never followed it or anything. Football's more my speed."

"I know, Dad."

"So why cricket?"

"All my friends like it. The people at school prefer cricket. We don't play football."

"All those rows of numbers, though. You need to be a mathematician or something to understand it."

"I like the numbers. Batting averages, bowling averages, wickets taken, that kind of thing. You can see over time who are the best players — their numbers—"

The crackle of the intercom interrupted James, after a disconcerting squeal of feedback. "Good evening ladies and gentlemen…", the Captain said, his accent smart and clipped, exuding the comforting tones of authority, control, education.

Gladys — attending to the mother of the dark-haired girl — paused mid-pour of her silver teapot.

The pilot continued, his voice occasionally breaking up in hisses of static. "As you may have — we're experiencing some delays. As you can see through the windows — much heavier than forecast. We have — get above the weather but the cloud is thick even at our ceiling of ten-thousand feet — no choice, it seems, but to stay within it. If it — worst case scenario is that we divert to an alternate destination. For now, however, please just sit back and relax, and — refreshments from the crew as they pass down the cabin. I will update you as and — necessary. Please fasten your seatbelts, and enjoy the rest of the flight."

With crumbs of biscuit caught on his wet lips, Franks asked his son, "Do you think he sounded nervous?"

"Nope," James said, not listening properly, his eyes still fixed on the page.

Ken Mackay topped the batting averages with 1,103 runs, at an average of 52.52.

1955

Engine idling with a steady, half-throated thrum, Stanley's car lingered on a broad, tree-lined street of reasonable-sized semis and detached houses fronted by immaculate lawns, spotted with varicoloured flowerbeds and overhung by lovingly-manicured bushes and pampas grasses. He gave two quick parps of the horn. After a few seconds — had he got the right house? — he saw Alice's face appear in the living room window, as she pulled aside the delicate net curtains; a big smile forming once their eyes met. His heart, pounding furiously, seemed to be inflating; already feeling outsized within its cavity, squeezing into other organs as it expanded with joy and fear. The evening felt unfeasibly warm and humid — even with the sun starting to lower itself in the sky. He got out, moved around to the pavement. While waiting he reached behind his back, pulling the sticky, sweat-soaked cotton of his white shirt away from his clammy skin, then, with fingers damp and visibly shaking, tried straightening his hair.

Should he have rung the doorbell and announced himself? Given his nerves, waiting by the car seemed easier than speaking to Alice's parents. But did it seem rude? Some people ignored social niceties, he told himself; those who *seem* rude simply paralysed by the prospect of not quite striking the right tone — and he frequently fell into that category. He didn't want to make a bad impression, and yet the prospect of stuttering and stammering like a fool — her father, he imagined, impatiently imploring 'spit it out, man', like so many of his teachers had done, or, just as horrifically, staring back silent and aghast, as if he were mute, or mentally handicapped — might not exactly make for a good one. What if she hadn't warned them? He felt his throat constricting, as if the words to greet her — as yet unformed — were getting ready to shatter into sharp syllables to slice and shred his trembling vocal chords. For a horrible moment it all felt like some dreadful mistake, some grand folly — like attempting to swim the Channel the very moment the armbands came off.

Why hadn't he thought this through?

Too late to back out, fear still pushed hard for the upper hand in his ambivalence. At the funfair, beyond moments of silence on the Ferris wheel, he'd had little time to think, to worry about all the things that could go wrong — all the dangers inherent in putting himself out there with his malforming mouth, his malfunctioning larynx. Although he hated the helplessness, the asthma attack had freed him from the pressure of having to maintain his composure — and to conjure words — and Alice had been so compassionate when seeing him at his worst; staying with him at the hospital until he seemed okay. Yet he now had to find words afresh, and possibly for a new audience. Why hadn't he even thought about the presence of her parents?

Thankfully, Alice emerged from the front door alone. The curtains in the front window twitched again — two shadowy, adult figures, and a smaller sibling silhouetted. His attention moved swiftly to his date for the evening, as she closed the door behind her, shutting her family inside. She seemed to glide down the path in a pink dress with flowing skirt, over which she'd wrapped a petite white Orlon cardigan; the same simplicity and easy style of the fairground. Why Alice, he thought, again; how is *she* so perfect, and — almost surreally, all of a sudden — in his life? All of this was real — he knew that, without needing to pinch himself — but it still felt a little dreamlike and dissociative, like a sunstroke fever, fuzzy at the edges; more visceral than a dream, with their skewed narratives and jump-cuts, but more unreal than normality. He felt alive to the reality, but also slightly detached in moments, as if, split in two, he also watched from afar; with twice the emotion, as both subject and observer. Could it simply be that — even though true — it remained *too good* to be true?

"It's no Rolls-Royce, I'm afraid," he said, holding out a slightly quivering hand, as Alice moved through the open gate. She stood and stared at the olive-green Morris Minor, with its clunky wooden panelling and scuffed whitewall tyres, the car further tarnished by a couple of slight dents and scratches along the bodywork. Then she moved to its rear, giving the vehicle an exaggerated once-over, as if a trade inspector. She laughed. "Well, you're definitely right about that — it certainly *is* no Rolls-Royce. But it has what I think they call *charm*."

"One not ss–so-careful p-p—previous owner," he said, kicking a tyre gently, for no other reason than mirroring what his father did upon seeing it for the first time. "But it runs okay, and it does for me."

"Any car is a good car if it takes you places," she said, moving towards the passenger door.

"It certainly does that."

"And, of course," she added, "if it brings you back again."

"It does that too," he said, smiling. "And we could always p—pretend it's a Rolls-Royce, couldn't we?"

"We certainly could. Luckily for you I have quite a vivid imagination."

"S-s-so …" he said, adopting a formal, upright posture, "would milady like to ride in the back?" — but then instantly worried that she might say *Yes*, to play along with this impromptu joke, and the situation might become odd. He already felt beneath her — an uneasy sense of unworthiness in her presence — without the complications of becoming her chauffeur, even in jest. She chuckled, but he quickly opened the door and she eased into the front passenger seat, to ensure that the charade went no further. Even the way she slipped into the vehicle suggested a natural elegance, as if nothing about her could be awkward and ungainly. Had she attended deportment classes?

"It might be best to hold on to that strap on the door," he said, sliding into his seat.

"Why so? Are you not the safest of drivers?"

"P-p-precious cargo," he said, smiling.

"How very flattering … I think!" she said with a hint of excitement and the broadest of smiles, straightening her dress at the hemline across her knees. "Although I've never been called 'cargo' before. So where are we going?"

"It's a s-sss–s—urprise," he said, unable to think of a synonym. Indeed, one of his prized possessions since childhood remained the now dog-eared copy of *Roget's Thesaurus*, which helped him to navigate around the trickiest of words, to expand his vocabulary out of necessity. But on 'surprise' he drew a blank.

"Hmm, I really don't like surprises," she said, a little abruptly. "Oh," — she quickly added, placing a hand on his forearm — "I don't mean to sound ungrateful. I'm ever so sorry if that seemed rude. I just like to always know what's happening. It's a terrible quirk of mine."

"No p—p-problem. I thought we could head up town," he said, releasing the handbrake. "You haven't eaten, have you?"

"No, I followed your instructions on that. Even if the rest of what you said was rather mysterious."

"I've booked us a nice restaurant, really s-sp–sp– … really lovely."

"Oh, how delightful!" she said with a noticeable bounce, as Stanley checked his mirror — more out of habit than need, given the quietness of the road — and pulled out. "Although you didn't need to go to too much trouble," she added.

"It's not too much trouble," he said, slightly unconvincingly. "Not for you, at least."

Days earlier Stanley bought a magazine that listed London's attractions and eateries, then made his way to the nearest telephone box to reserve a table at the one that caught his eye: the Café Royal. The name stood out — he'd seen Alice as an almost

almost regal figure at the fair, and his naïve ideas of courtship were that you simply treated a young woman like a princess, even if unclear to all that it entailed; and even if not the paradigm modelled by his parents, whose relationship seemed respectful and collegiate, with neither party treated as even remotely regal by the other. Still, he would not be aiming so low. Next he purchased a road map, and did his best to memorise the route, so as to not keep stopping and referencing it — although he felt pleased that, on the page, once safely on the Great West Road — picked up close to London Airport — it stretched as one continuous — if not exactly straight — road into the West End, through Brompton Road and Knightsbridge, into Piccadilly. Though imprinted on his mind by rote, he chose to stash the map under the driver's seat, just in case. After reserving a table he then telephoned Alice's house, and felt mightily relieved when she answered; fearful of how awkward it could be when a stammer struck before he'd even introduced himself, and the person on the other end took it as some kind of rude call. Even non-trigger sounds could cause a problem with the added strangeness of talking to someone miles away, unable to see their face, unsure of their true reaction, as nerves set in. Often they'd hang up before he even got a chance to gather his words and explain; had her mother or father answered, he may have done the same.

"Have you been there before? — to the restaurant?" she asked, one hand on the canvas strap that hung from the door as a handle, the other placed neatly on her lap.

"No, never. To be honest, I never really go up town. What about you? You go up much?"

"Occasionally — with Mother, to shop. So you've never been into the city?"

"We went up as a family when I was a lad. Did all the s-s– … all the s-sights. The Tower, Big Ben, all that. Went up on the Metropolitan line, from Uxbridge — a lovely day out. But I always wanted to drive up to the West End, once I got my own car. I only got my licence a few months ago and, well, I never found the excuse until now."

As he talked, Stanley found himself fighting a continual urge to look across at Alice — to maintain some kind of eye contact; and yet also because it felt difficult *not* to look at her. In the movies they always held such easy conversations in cars, with the driver rarely looking at the road — although Stanley often noticed the background slipping from alignment with the vehicle. It proved far more difficult to drive and talk than he ever imagined, with his brain working hard to find things to say, and to avoid his trigger words, whilst trying to comprehend the moving traffic and unfamiliar road layouts — quirks and surprises that no two-dimensional map could prepare him for, no matter how much he had studied it; and all as a relative novice behind the wheel. Conversations with his driving instructor — a strict, older gentleman with alarmingly thick glasses, a hearing aid and little patience — were much easier, given that they didn't contain anything contrary to his task in hand: just what to look out for, what gear to be in, the need to check his mirrors, make hand signals, and so on, all while driving around familiar, fairly quiet local streets at a slow rate of speed. Chit-chat wasn't an option with Mr Whittaker. And yet he received no lesson on how to deal with a beautiful woman in the passenger seat, and how to talk to her without accidentally mounting the pavement.

The traffic, initially, proved not as heavy as expected — he always imagined London as constantly heaving — but it still felt a little overwhelming, and far busier than the familiar suburban roads of Hayes and the surrounding areas. He caught glimpses of colourful cars parked on kerbs, but encountered mostly taxis and buses hogging the lanes as his Morris drew closer to the city. There seemed so much to contend with as he tried to keep alert and focused on the view through the windscreen, with no fellow drivers aware of his inexperience. It felt like a kind of assault course: gaudy billboard posters — which proliferated closer to the heart of the capital — designed to deliberately catch his eye; pelican crossings, flashing lights; wayward and wonky cyclists; bold red postboxes, black and yellow road signs — and then, out of nowhere, a sudden careless pedestrian who went to cross the road without first looking, before suddenly — thankfully — stepping back. All flickered in and out of his narrowing peripheral vision. GPO, Lyons' Tea and Zeeta and Co. vans, with bold logotypes, blocked the view ahead; the sounds of engines and horns, occasionally drowning out Alice's voice, so that he lost half a sentence and had to ask her to repeat herself, or instead, guess the missing words. The traffic flowed with the Morris in its slipstream, past brightly-striped shop awnings, and the bold, sometimes illuminated lettering on the signs of banks and pubs; and then, ever closer to the centre, regiments of overhanging trees — oak, birch, laburnum and the flaky-barked London plane — outside imposing Georgian and Regency townhouses, conveying an increasing sense of wealth and power — all hinting that he really didn't belong here, an interloper passing through. Everything felt so new — even the façades of old London — and that made it all the harder to let it blend into the background.

"Beg your p-pardon?" Stanley asked Alice as the sound of an over-revved bus engine died down; relieved to not slip and say *Beg your pudding?*, or *Beg your pud?*, in the way that his mother would.

"Oh, nothing," Alice said, breezily. "I was just pointing out something down a side street, but it's gone now."

Finally Stanley spied a parking spot at the entrance to Old Bond Street, outside Scott's the hatters, and fearing that it could be the last for a while, decided to pull in.

"This may be the best we can do. It's not far from here," he said, opening his door, eager to rush around to her side of the car. "Are you okay walking?"

"I may regret wearing these new shoes," she said, levering her legs, knees pressed together, out into the road, shielded by her open door. "Alas, I have no wings, so walking will have to suffice."

"There's no rush," he said, contradicting himself as he scurried to help her out of the vehicle; disappointed that she'd already opened the door herself and edged halfway out. "We're early anyway," he added, escorting her onto the pavement as a lorry gave them a wide berth. "Didn't take as long as expected."

They began to walk north, but soon found themselves sidetracked by the shop window displays, with dozens of retailers crammed into barely two hundred yards of street, their flagpoles proudly leaning out over the pavements, their wares groping for attention.

"I don't think I've ever been along this road before," Alice said, scanning left and right. "I've shopped all along Oxford Street, but never here. How have I missed it?"

They quickly passed Frost & Reed, whose sign spoke of 'Fine Paintings' — which might have interested Stanley on another day, simply to browse — he dared not even think of the prices — but Alice signalled to cross the road, to Charig Ltd, who proudly boasted the status of 'Court Jewellers'. Initially Stanley read it as Court *Jesters*. Even in the shade — the last bursts of sunlight hitting the other side of the road — its displays coruscated, precious metals and stones aligned and shining upon plump velvet cushions as dusk reflected from the windows opposite: emerald brooches, gold bangles, platinum rings; Cartier diamond bracelets, Van Cleef and Arpels silver necklaces; sapphires and rubies, garnets and opals by various makers, inset into 18 and 22 carat gold earrings and hairpins and clasps and chokers — including types of jewellery Stanley never even knew existed. More and more diamonds, all at prices that would buy cars; *houses*, even.

"I hope you s—shan't go getting any ideas," he said, both excited and appalled at what he saw; thrilled by their beauty and their precious nature — you simply didn't see such opulence around his way — but crestfallen at the cost, and the years it would take to save for virtually anything on display. The sign may as well read: *You really don't belong here, Sonny.*

"Heavens no," she said. "But they're all so beautiful, don't you think? Well, the less ostentatious items — the gems themselves, I mean. And the way diamonds are formed, the time it takes — a billion years, they say! Not only are they so beautiful, but it's the unimaginable length of time wrapped up in their creation. So it's beauty, and time. You can't skip the time part, can you? The jewellers are artists too, clearly — but the precious stones are something that cannot ever be man-made, just found."

"Well, yes. I'm with you on that."

"But really, I could never justify the expense of such ... well, they're luxuries, aren't they?" she said, shaking her head. "It's exorbitant, don't you think, when you look at the prices? Such beauty but really, so unnecessary. If I had that money — or if I were married to a man who had the money — then such sums should be spent on travel, seeing the world, not inanimate objects that may then just sit in a closed box, only occasionally to be shown off."

"Quite right," he said, seeing his own head nodding in his glass reflection.

"Or spend the money to help the poor and needy, of course," she added, as if correcting herself. "Yes, that would surely be far more satisfying. You could feed and clothe entire villages on what these things cost. But still, those gems — so lovely to look at, and to admire their journey, from there to here."

"I guess that's why they call it window shopping."

"It's the cheapest form, I find," she said, spinning and walking towards Yardley, its stylish shopfront curving around onto Stafford Street, above which a further four floors of the company's office space. The store's front door lay within an immense square window, in whose corners swished furls of curtain, as if a proscenium arch opening to a performance. "Oh, I absolutely adore their perfume," she said. "If only they were still open. Now these things I can afford."

"What's it called? — the perfume."

She laughed. "*Bond Street*. Which suddenly makes a lot more sense, now that we're here."

"Is that what you're wearing now?" he asked, leaning in slightly, to inhale top notes — not that he could name them, or even separate them from the overall heavenly fragrance — of bergamot and orange, and hints of vetiver and sandalwood. A very pleasant aroma, it may still have meant little to him on anyone else; but on Alice, as first experienced at the funfair, it sparked and tripped across his neural wiring — not just within the olfactory cortex, but in all other lobes — so that he could almost *see* it, *taste* it. It now lived within his memory, hardwired, as an entity with dimensions, trapped as if inside a glass jar — ever since the ride on the big wheel, when he really caught its power. Two nights ago he had lain in bed having awoken from a dream, and felt it with him. He knew then, for certain, that were he to ever lose his sense of smell he would still be able to recall it, clear and piquant.

"Indeed it is", she said, pointing at the bottles on display. "It's the only perfume I wear." She angled her head against the window to see further into the store. "Only, I'm running quite low."

"It's rather lovely," he said, closing his eyes, to focus purely on its bouquet as a fraction of the scent wisped on the breeze; a fragrance that mixed with the indefinable smell of hot London pavements and sweltering tarmacadam — a smell that, in the moment, he couldn't separate from the perfume, and which in itself proved neither pleasant nor unpleasant, but somehow tied up with adventure. Even the less appealing aromas of car exhaust, cigarette smoke and stale beer from pub cellars, that at times wafted and hung in the evening air, were signals of excitement. They too flooded into the deep recesses of his brain, to anchor themselves to amygdala and hippocampus, connected to *this* moment.

"How are we doing for time?" Alice asked.

"Oh, we're fine," Stanley said, checking his watch.

They wandered a couple of doors down. "How would you like to be fitted out here?" Alice asked, outside Gieves the tailors. "My," she added, "such stylish clothes. And all at a pretty penny."

"Beyond my means, I'm afraid," he sighed.

"But that's a nice suit you have on," she said, looking him up and down, smiling. "You carry it well."

"Thank you," he said, and wanted to offer a compliment in return, but too many arose, to flood his mind; and some would seem far too excessive, at this early stage. So he simply said "Thank you" once more.

Having dallied for long enough, Stanley and Alice eventually turned onto Burlington Gardens, then Vigo Street, and out onto the parallel curves of Regent Street; London unfurling in ever-more opulent vistas as they strolled east. And there it stood, up ahead: the Café Royal. They paused across the street from the restaurant, their eyes unavoidably drawn to what lay a hundred yards further up the road: a cross-section of chaos, Piccadilly Circus framed between grand buildings. Round-roofed red buses and hunchbacked black cabs lurched around its famous statued fountain, as if on an endless loop; the brief interjection of a brown Austin or a blue Rover, or of a different eye-catching advert running along the length of a bus, confirming a constant flow of new traffic, and not simply some bizarre eternal merry-go-round.

"Come on," Stanley said, taking Alice by the arm — linking elbows — and escorting her across the road, then through the arched doorway and into the foyer of the restaurant. The maître d' swiftly greeted them, asking in an accent that sounded more Italian than French if they had a table reserved.

"Yes," Stanley said. "S-S-Sm…"

The maître d' — long-faced, pencil-moustachioed, with fright-white hair — raised an eyebrow and leant in ever so slightly, as if to say *Go on then, sir, tell me*. Stanley looked to his side, wondering if Alice would take over, in the way that his parents had forever jumped in to finish his sentences, obliterating any pauses, bulldozing any half-formed words. But she simply squeezed his hand. "S-sm..Sm.. S—Smith," he finally said, after a deep breath.

The pair followed to a table for two, set within a large room divided by ornate partitions: the walls awash with mirrors and clusters of gold-plated lanterns, each reflective of the other, in a garish feedback loop, distance and perspective thrown into disarray, repeating ad infinitum, lurid and jarring. Stanley pulled out the heavy, red-velvet chair for Alice; imitating chivalrous conduct — mirroring David Niven in the movies rather than anything witnessed in his own domestic life. Despite following the protocols of etiquette as inferred from films, he found himself *wanting* to do such things to help Alice. Far from helpless, it felt like a duty to assist her.

After a brief delay, a young, impeccably-suited waiter presented them with large gatefold menus, the full colour cover image a lush pastiche of Botticelli's *Birth of Venus*; the back of the menu explaining it to be of a painted ceiling within the restaurant, although after looking around the pair could not spot it.

"Oh, it's in French," Stanley said, sounding despondent, looking up and down a list of dishes that mostly made no sense.

"You don't speak any French?" Alice asked.

"Well, we didn't do it at school. Or if we did, it wasn't for long and I didn't p-p-pay any attention."

The prices next to each dish were steep, but not quite as excessive as he feared. Unnerved by the Gallic titles, he felt a little more settled that he could afford to pay for anything ordered; at least, this once. The downside: that he couldn't tell what those dishes actually were.

"So, what food do you like?" Alice asked. "I can tell you if it's on the menu. Or if you'd prefer I could go through and read all of the dishes out in English?"

"I get mostly the s—same old stuff at home — steak and kidney pie, liver and dumplings, fish and chips on a Friday, ham salad or a roast on a Sunday, kipper or egg for breakfast. But that's just Mum's cooking, not fancy restaurant food. I'd actually like to try s-something a bit different. You know, in the s-s—spirit of adventure."

"That's a good idea," she said, nodding her assent. "I think I shall do the same."

"I take it that *poissons* isn't a misspelling of poisons," he said, smiling — with the unexpected pleasure of getting the words out in one go — as Alice laughed. "I can buy arsenic for half that price," he added, letting out a small laugh of his own; not at his cleverness, but consciously, audibly, to share in the moment with Alice — wanting his laughter to mingle in concert with hers, like the deeper timbre of cello rising in harmony with the lighter tone of viola.

"And you're far too much of a gentleman to offer arsenic to a lady," Alice replied, and he laughed again, through a broad smile.

After a long *hmmm*, Stanley asked, "What's *Homard Mornay Thermidor*?", a little embarrassed to not even be able to make an educated guess — none of the three words made any sense to him on their own, let alone as a trio — but safe in the knowledge that Alice wouldn't look down on him for it. "It sounds like some country esquire," he said. "Please let me introduce you to S—Sir Homard Mornay Thermidor...."

Alice laughed, then said brightly, "Homard is lobster. It's in a Mornay Thermidor sauce, although to be honest I couldn't tell you what that consists of. Something *very* French and *very* fancy, I'm sure."

Stanley snapped the thin menu shut. "Then that's what I will have."

"Heavens!" Alice said, a fraction too loud. "It's expensive," she added, lowering her voice, at the same time as she lowered her head. "Ten and six."

"This is a s-sp-special night."

"In what way?" she asked, almost absentmindedly, while intently studying the list of dishes.

"Isn't it obvious?" Stanley said, his face showing slight signs of dejection.

"Well, yes — of course," she said, looking up from the menu, her eyes over the brim. "I just wondered if there was something else. A promotion at work, or something like that."

"No, nothing else. Just … you. Here with me. S-so, what will you be having?"

"I think I'd like to try the Haddock Colbert, if you don't mind."

"Not int he s-slightest," he said, smiling. "S-sir Haddock Colbert it is."

After ordering their meals, a waiter asked Stanley to taste the wine — a chablis he'd picked from the list without even knowing its colour, or even how to pronounce it. He never actually cared for wine of any variety; only choosing it now to be sociable, to be grown-up, and with Alice leaving the decision with him. It simply felt like a wine occasion; and surely much more civilised than pawing at a pint of beer all evening and needing to excuse himself every thirty minutes to empty his bladder. He nodded his approval to the waiter, although the drink had the same stark sourness that always struck him any time he tried a glass. Had he been asked to test a tub of turpentine by the sommelier he'd still never dare reject it. "Very good," he added, nodding with what he hoped came across as authority.

With still a few morsels left on his plate, Stanley laid down his knife and fork, and looked set to say something. Alice wondered if he had found himself caught on a word; preparing a verbal detour around problematic syllables, to which she had so quickly become accustomed. But then — "You're *s-ss—so* beautiful," — said almost solemnly, in a reverential whisper, undiluted by the stammer.

"Don't be silly," she said after a moment to take it in, waving a theatrical hand, complete with haddocked fork, at him; looking away, before swiftly looking back, to meet his gaze, to assess his seriousness.

"Well, you are. I was brought up to tell the truth."

She paused, placing down her cutlery. "You really think so?"

"You don't believe me?"

"I do," she said, then added, after a short pause, "I suppose."

"How do you mean, you *ssss—suppose*?"

"Well, you seem like an honest man, Stanley. And people do sometimes tell me that I'm pretty," she said, holding his gaze. "They have since I was little. But, deep down, I don't particularly feel it. Well, most of the time. Sometimes I'm happy with the way I look, but … a lot of the time I think it's all smoke and mirrors — good make-up, a talented hairdresser. I'm really nothing that special behind all these layers. It's a mask, you see?"

"Now it's you being s-s—si…silly," he said, a hint of frustration clear at the stammer's interruption of his sincerity. "You're hardly wearing any makeup. I can tell. Not like a lot of girls."

"You have to understand that it's hard for me to take such comments to heart," she said, looking down. "Don't ask me why, but something stops me from quite believing them. I learnt at a young age that not all compliments on one's looks feel wholesome. It's not easy to explain, as not all the attention felt right. Although, trust me, it's ever so nice to hear it from you. Even if I can't quite accept it myself, it's lovely to know that you think it so. That you mean it. That I trust that you mean it."

"Maybe you'll learn to think so, too," he said. "But it's not just how you look. You're kind, too. I can tell. Ss-ss-o very kind."

She laughed. "You just haven't got on my wrong side yet."

"I'll bear that in mind," he said, taking her hand, which she accepted with a quick squeeze.

"But what about someone like *her?*" Alice said, gently motioning at the woman on the next table with the slightest tilt of her wine glass. "Surely she's genuinely beautiful?"

Stanley went to fully turn his head, before Alice whispered, "Be subtle!"

The woman looked glamorous, for certain. A doubled-up pearl necklace draped around an elegant long neck so flawless that not even veins were visible, with larger pearls set into earrings — all of which seemed muted in contrast to the extravagant diamanté spectacles whose frames caught and reflected light at every conceivable angle. She wore her hair short — styled into elaborate curls set fast with the modern wonder of hairspray — and tinted pink, to match the silky magenta stole draped over her shoulders. She looked utterly fashionable, inescapably eye-catching, and in every sense immaculate.

"You're much prettier," Stanley said, with a series of swift, sharp nods of his head, as if this exercise had merely confirmed his suspicions.

"Oh, come now," Alice demurred, with a modesty Stanley took as genuine.

"No, you are," he added, leaning in to whisper; the occasional glance across at the woman used to prove the comparison and confirm his point. "It's all so showy. Don't confuse beauty with things that s-s—sparkle. Look, she needs diamond frames to make her eyes light up — yours need nothing."

Alice let out a sigh, and squeezed his hand more tightly. For a second it looked as if she would protest some more, still feeling uncomfortable at such praise, but then she smiled — *beamed* — and let it go.

2010

Jóhanna Leósdóttir: cascading curls of strawberry blonde hair, highlighted with a fiery streak of bright pink dye. In no way a modern vision of mainstream western beauty, she possessed an almost Pre-Raphaelite aesthetic. Hers was a look predating Hollywood glamour — a hint of Frank Cadogan Cowper's *Vanity*, although the title of that painting in no way applied. Or, to travel much further back, Johannes Vermeer's *A Girl Reading a Letter by an Open Window;* a similar profile: high hairline, slightly hooked nose, full and naturally rouged cheeks. Also perhaps, something in the way she held herself.

Michael — alone with Jóhanna in the Reykjavík bar after Siggi and Magnus left to meet some other friends — found himself captivated by the ease of her appearance, with no great reliance on make-up, aside from a dark and striking eyeliner. No caking, no gaudy lipstick, no unnecessary lipliner for exaggeration. Round of face, and slightly fuller of figure, and yet not exactly plump or shapeless, or in any way frumpy.

"So, are you from Reykjavík originally?" Michael asked, testing out her keenness for eye contact: her gaze returned in a friendly manner, but not without natural interruptions and glances away.

"No, Akureyri," she said, in a moment when she met his stare. "A more sleepy place."

"That's weird. I always assumed Siggi came from Reykjavík," Michael said, swilling his drink around its glass, tracking its soothing motion; then tapping it absentmindedly on the table, as ripples spread.

"I think people assume everyone in Iceland is from Reykjavík. It is where everyone ends up, of course. Well, the younger people, most certainly. And, well, we moved to Reykjavík when we were young. Maybe he prefers to seem more cosmopolitan."

Her speech rolled and listed with a lilting, mellifluous quality; harder to understand than Siggi's, with less of an obvious American influence. Icelandic words — such as those for place names — slid seamlessly into sentences, lost in seas of syllables, with the English words — themselves hard to discern at times due to her accent — caught in their wake. Skólavörðustígur, the downtown district of Reykjavík where she lived, sounded to him like it should end at *ðust*, with the *ígur* appearing at the point where his mind already listened for adverbs, verbs, prepositions. Upon complimenting her jumper, she seemed confused, and then said "Oh, my sweater?" but it came out as swet*trrr*, with emphasis on the final syllable and the 'r' extended for a beat too long, until it purred.

Hours earlier they had never even met, and he barely even knew of her existence; the sister of a friend, mentioned in passing, with no memorable anecdotes –– just the acknowledgement that she existed. He started the day alone in England, and finished it in Iceland, in a stranger's company. Life so rarely felt like this anymore. When younger, he'd meet new people and wake bleary-eyed, blinking up at unfamiliar ceilings, having been carried by the flow of the previous evening. More recently such flows were viewed as if from the riverbank, detached and unaffected; spontaneity, fun, floating by fast on the tide. That was, until this night. Just meeting Jóhanna in the bar proved a jolt to the system, especially in such an unfamiliar environment. He could simply have walked to a pub near to where he lived in Brighton — to escape the miserable flat and its unquenchable dankness — and only encountered unwelcoming strangers, unwilling to share their stories; and which, were those people to instead feel that their stories were worth sharing, he would probably find mundane anyway, with their familiarly dull, local lives. Interesting folk in there somewhere, perhaps, amongst the crowd, but if talking, telling only the kind of tales he had heard before. Instead he found himself a thousand miles away, sat across from Jóhanna Leósdóttir; her routine, her very existence, inherently exotic through the lens of his own experience.

Siggi and Magnus had departed an hour earlier to meet some other friends at a neighbouring bar; Siggi happy to leave his sister — who didn't care for the group her brother intended to meet — in the company of, to her at least, a stranger, to whom she then offered her sofa for the night. And so Michael found himself alone with this intelligent and alluring young woman, the pair nursing the last dregs of their drinks as midnight approached, and as a long and surreal day, for him, drew towards its end.

*　*　*

Jóhanna's sleek apartment: a layer sliced within a narrow, modern Reykjavík high-rise; but still essentially a *low*-rise, to anyone familiar with an even vaguely densely-packed city. Her home — a whole storey — not so much sparse as barren; its off-white walls free of any adornments, spared of all signs of habitation.

They stumbled into the apartment in the early hours, fairly drunk, and as promised, Michael took the couch. At first he just slumped onto its plump supports, vaguely upright, while Jóhanna brewed some coffee; but, after reclining — to project an air of insouciance — he closed his heavy eyelids to the sound of the kettle's whistle and he was gone, sleep drawing him into the cushions in an instant.

He awoke with a jolt in the dark two hours later, his head pounding, his panicked mind eagerly racing within a few heartbeats — *shit*, he was falling from a great height! — until he felt the reassuring lack of downward motion, and the firmness of some type of upholstery holding him securely horizontal. Shame pricked at his conscious, as he recalled remnants of a dream: Jóhanna, naked on a reclining seat of a plane, from which, after making an unwelcome sexual approach, he then somehow fell — or had he been thrown? — from 30,000 feet. Then, hit by the sense that sleep had been and gone after finding himself wide-eyed and dry-mouthed and bolt upright, he noticed his body had been covered by a woollen blanket, as one might place over a sleeping child. His earlier intentions — emboldened by several double shots of whiskey — to make advances at Jóhanna once back at her apartment had been thwarted by sleep, and thus he hadn't made a fool of himself. The conclusion that she *hadn't* pushed him out of a plane, even in a dream, came quickly, but the truth of the night before hung a little foggier as he fumbled on the sofa, trying to feel for his surroundings. Definitely alone; definitely on the sofa. The tender placement of covers to keep him warm provoked a new stab of guilt in the darkness, at his inebriated idea — his host a kind-hearted person offering help, not a quick drunken fumble. He reached inside his canvas bag for his sleeping pills, to kill his mind and dampen his newly-sparked adrenaline — his nervous system still alerted to falling through the clouds — to get through to sunrise. Their power, he knew, guaranteed sleep until the thumping headache passed, but the addition of the pills at such a late hour would leave a fuzziness in his mind, as well as a metallic taste in his mouth, well past lunchtime.

Michael awoke to the same sound that originally sent him to sleep: the crescendo and diminuendo of the kettle's fluty boil as it rattled on the hob. Through sore eyes he saw light stretch across the ceiling and walls, the rectangular shapes flooding through the windows starkly bright against the shadows on plain off-white walls; abstraction adding interest on the canvas of the minimal.

"Mor-*ning*," Jóhanna said, the *ning* almost dinging; disconcertingly bright and perky as she handed him a black coffee. "Sugar," she said, as she set a bowl and teaspoon down on the coffee table. "Help yourself. There is milk in the refrigerator, although you strike me as a black coffee kind of guy."

Michael nodded, his eyes still smarting from the penetrating brightness. "Eurgh — so, you're a morning person, then?" he said gruffly, his throat hoarse, his mouth full of the tang of chewed iron filings and sawdust; but then he coughed out a laugh, to soften the exchange. "It's too early for me."

"It is *eleven a.m.*," she said, sitting cross-legged on a beanbag, in a saggy grey t-shirt and baggy sleep-shorts.

"Then it's *definitely* too early for me."

Coffee mugs stowed in the sink, Jóhanna took Michael on a quick, dispassionate tour of the apartment, pointing out the rooms with an air of indifference. "It is just a space," she said, a hand casually held out, after Michael expressed his approval. "It is not like I built it, or worked the land, or my family did before me. It is not my heritage, my culture — not some turf house, from centuries past. It is just a flat-pack home, for now. That is all it is. I pay money, they give me this."

"It's like a palace compared to the shithole I've moved into."

Aside from the light-play, the off-white living room walls — into which the front door directly opened — stood almost callously bare, as if somehow malnourished. The wooden floor lay bereft of anything aside from a beanbag, the sofa on which Michael slept, and a small, simple coffee table, with some type of driftwood sculpture — entwined limbs of whitened, desiccated birch — hunkered in the corner like an emaciated Victorian child serving a punishment. Jóhanna's bedroom also stood sparse, aside from the bed itself, and one freestanding lamp, with several books placed in a pile on the floor. By contrast, the hallway that joined the two areas seemed hectic: lined with rows of cleverly inbuilt bookshelves, densely packed with spines of different colours and heights and thicknesses, with those books most often read showing vertical scars and stretch-marks; striations of love, of frequent holding and unfolding and bending, causing the printed letters of their titles and authors' names to partially flake away.

He could pick out her passion for Margaret Atwood, Sylvia Plath, George Orwell, Toni Morrison, Iris Murdoch and T. S. Eliot, with at least two books by each; and huddled amongst those, Icelandic authors whose names and book titles appeared indecipherable; although he did recognise Halldór Laxness, whose work Siggi had once recommended, but which he'd never taken any further.

The bed-less spare bedroom housed the rest of her possessions, many still packed in boxes; as well as clothes, divided between a wardrobe and a chest of drawers, on which rested an aluminium MacBook. But even this room felt airy, and the few pieces of furniture and her library aside, everything in the apartment would fit into the back of a medium-sized estate car. He could see no knick-knacks, no photographs, no personal paraphernalia, and certainly no clutter.

"Where are your family?" he asked, looking around the room.

"Miles away," she said, flatly. "Siggi aside. They moved back to Akureyri."

"Do you get along with them?"

"Of course," she said, bemused. "Why would you say this?"

"But where are they in your apartment, I mean? You have no photos."

She pointed to her head — "They are in here," — and then to her heart, her tone matter-of-fact — "and in here, too. Can you not picture loved ones in your head?"

"But don't you want proper reminders?" he said, thinking of the laminated print of his son in his wallet, and the various framed *occasions* hanging on hooks at home like captured trophies: hunted fractions of time, hung for posterity.

"I have memories too, of course," he protested. "But, well … a printed image helps to unlock them."

"Photos are just still moments in time," she said, squinting, as if to sharpen her focus on him. "I have reels and reels of real life memories stored up here. Of course, I also have some actual videos, and a few photographs, on my computer. But that is it."

"And on your mobile phone as well, presumably?"

"Mobile phone? I do not have a phone. At least, not a cellphone," she said as they stood in the corridor, surrounded by books.

"Really?"

"I have a telephone, with a tape machine. And a letterbox. And a pigeon hole at the university. And email. This is quite enough, do you not think?"

"Well, obviously not — I've got a mobile," he said, fumbling in his pocket. "To tell the truth, I'd be lost without it. Although as you can see, it's not one of those fancy new ones. I was tempted to get an iPhone a couple of years ago when they first came out, but I still have this crappy old thing."

"But do you not hate being contactable all the time?" she said, absentmindedly tipping books from the shelf at forty-five degree angles before letting them fall back into their upright stances with a satisfying *thump*. "In the shops, in your car, in the toilet. In the countryside, on the beach?"

"I can switch it to silent."

"But it is always there. I bet you check it when it is on silent, just in case."

"Maybe. I used to check more — when Ethan was still allowed to phone me. His mother would dial, and then he'd be on the other end, sometimes chatty, sometimes silent for a while. I would be in the middle of a sentence and he'd just say *Bubbye* and put the phone down on the table and wander off, back to his toys, or the film he was watching. But he doesn't call anymore."

"That is such a shame," she said, and appeared about to say more — perhaps delve into details — but instead stayed quiet. Finally she added: "He will call again. One day."

She had one more room to show: a tiny but large-windowed bedroom, which, aside from a single bed, housed nothing but limbs of driftwood and other detritus from the shorelines — shale, shells, fragments of lava, rusty debris — stacked in piles based on size, colour and texture.

"You make the sculptures yourself?" he said, thinking of the example from the front room.

"I do."

"I didn't realise you were an artist as well."

"I am not — not really. It is just something I do. I drive my car also, but I am not a *driver*." She paused, hearing her defensive tone. "Sorry. I just like to be able to do what I like to do, and not be tied down to doing this or doing that. I am not keen on being put into boxes. Well, aside from this one," — she laughed — "but we all need somewhere to live. Until we move to the next box. Or they put us in one, one last time, six feet under."

They returned to the living room and its adjoining open-plan kitchen. "Have a seat. I will go get dressed," Jóhanna said, pulling at the neck-curve of her grey t-shirt, like some muscle memory of undressing that she interrupted just in time. "Then I will show you the shops, if you can bear such excitement."

From the fifth of six storeys Michael looked out over other elegant, dark-grey rectilinear modernist boxes of similar stature, but also at multiply-pointed roofs of red and blue houses, where the smaller triangular juts of dormer windows echoed the main gables; everywhere the clash of the new and the old, with little in-between. Scores of corrugated façades, their innards outside. But also yellow houses, green buildings, pink walls, orange roofs. Day or night, Reykjavík, with all its colours, appeared permanently backlit, as snow reflected from the surrounding mountains.

"Such a beautiful view," he said, looking across to the island of Viðey in the distance, as Jóhanna returned, dressed for the cold. "Those white mountains," he added. "Amazing."

"I love to look at the mountains," she said, with a deep, warm sigh. "It grounds me. At least it does for now — but so much of Iceland is melt-*ting*," — the final syllable ringing out like a wine glass tapped with a fork.

"Really?"

"Sadly, yes. You should come with me to the glacier–" she named Sólheimajökull, but the syllables made no sense to Michael "–sometime. On the map it looks like this crooked finger, pointing down from the fist of–" again a blur of sounds "–Mýrdalsjökull. Although in a few years it may just be a stump. Or maybe," she said, holding out her hand with it clenched into a fist, "no finger at all."

They left the apartment and walked towards Hallgrímskirkja, the strange church at the end of the street, that, despite construction commencing during the Second World War, took decades to complete. Michael's association to flight meant he couldn't help but see its similarity to a Concorde, stood on its tail; its spire the iconic nose, the wingspan spreading ever outwards, in brutal blocked concrete, towards the ground. Or perhaps, more accurately, a Fairey Delta, whose wings provided the template for the Concorde, and whose development in the 1950s he had researched, along with the company's other aircraft, for an as-yet uncompleted book; or better still, the Avro Vulcan, whose wings — unlike those of the Concorde — curved right to the very rear of the plane, subsuming the tail cone, to complete a triangle. He considered sharing this observation with Jóhanna, but would she even know of the Vulcan? And even *Concorde* — that stopped flying years earlier, after the Paris crash in 2001, about which he'd been asked onto radio shows to discuss. Surely everyone knew Concorde? The age gap, and the societal differences, undermined the surety of his usual cultural references — how old would she have been? — and this struck him with a sudden debilitating sadness, sucking hard at his stomach, and he felt hit by the sense of being a thousand miles from home: Pippa would have understood even the most obscure of his observations, given their shared experience. He could say anything and she'd know what he meant. They met with common interests, and then, over the years, interwove their knowledge and experience, coauthoring and editing each other's lives. And yet, of course, she eventually became bored senseless by those same references, having heard them a hundred times. She grew to hate his predictability, his fascination with arcane details. *Not more bloody planes.*

The choice of his life, in that moment on Njarðargata, seemed to be between the familiar but bored — not that he could go back to that life, and to Pippa, anyway — and this new life, unmoored from his past, and wandering free in some foreign land, where he could be interesting and unfamiliar and exotic, but also lost and misunderstood.

Carefully, out of the corner of his eye, Michael studied Jóhanna as she walked across the warm café-cum-bookshop on Laugavegur with their coffees. Sat at a breakfast bar by the window, he first looked out through skinny trees to boutiques and strolling shoppers, until he felt the urge to fully look her way; the sense of her movement dragging him in. He turned, and there she stood, her cheeks still glowing from the cold air outside.

Her physical appearance, he felt, spoke fully of her personality: warm and welcoming, smart and mischievous. "Takk", he said, doing his best to fit in, as she handed him his drink and took a seat beside him.

Again out of the corner of his eye, cast over the rim of the mug, he studied her some more, up close, in the midday light, as the conversation fell into a comfortable lull; trying to fathom what made her so appealing: dimples dipping inwards either side of a delicate but heartbreaking smile; yet more dimples higher up, curving around the tops of her rosy cheeks; bright blue eyes that popped against the whiteness of her lightly freckled skin. And that mouth. My god, he thought, that *mouth*. The full, naturally-red lips screamed of sensuality, but he knew this to be a projection. He experienced a strange, almost unnerving sense of familiarity, that lasted until he stopped to consider the cultural differences, the chasm in age, the lack of shared experience. Still, something reminded him of someone he had met before, although he couldn't place who, nor where, nor when. In return, she seemed to like him — but how could he interpret that warmth, he wondered, the age gap? He already felt like a cliché, thrilled by the attention — or at least, the company — of a much younger woman, and yet should he give a damn about that? She seemed to defy convention, and the only opinion that mattered on such matters, surely, belonged to Jóhanna.

Indeed, she seemed older than twenty-four. Not physically: her skin, still fresh and taut, nor her hair, lush and full. She didn't seem prematurely middle-aged, nor sensible to the point of dullness. He just sensed *something* — her expressions, her mannerisms: like she had lived before, somehow; returned from the nineteenth century with her Pre-Raphaelite aspect and demeanour. Earlier that morning he had surreptitiously watched her walk around the apartment with hands clasped together under her chin, almost like a prioress, and yet, while spiritual, she followed no religion.

He liked the contrasts, too. Undermining her demure, delicately oil-painted air, the streak of pink hair, the eyebrow piercing — a bolt bookended by shiny metal spheres — and an upper-arm tattoo of the Buddha, in monochromatic deep blue ink; visible beneath the short sleeve of the grey t-shirt she wore around the house, which, Michael had keenly observed, displayed no visible bra straps underneath. A contradictory mix of sweetness and impurity, he thought, before correcting himself: concluding that body art and piercings were not in and of themselves indicative of any kind of deviant behaviour — just a willingness to tarnish the skin, and to not care that some people disapproved.

However, their time together — for now — stood at an end. She had to visit the university library, with research to undertake, and he needed to head out, to a remote location for research of his own; and with it, a desire to shrink, under sweeping skies, and feel humbled by overpowering vistas.

1956

Frank tapped his watch, held it up to his ear to listen for the sound of ticking, then checked it again. "This is getting beyond a joke," he said a little too loudly, breaking the uneasy silence; the air cut as sharply as if screaming obscenities during silent prayer in church. Heads turned, ears pricked, eyes widened. For almost two hours the cabin had been eerily hushed. In the first hour following the Captain's announcement the compartment buzzed with the rumbling hum — audible above the thrum of the engines — of moaning and tutting and griping, which rose to a crescendo of sighs and grumbles and calls to the hostesses to explain the situation, and how this all seemed very unacceptable, and that plans were now in absolute tatters, and that letters would most certainly be written.

Silence then spread minutes after Gladys, as the senior hostess, went in to see the crew, and reappeared ashen-faced, only to smile and say, when asked, that everything was fine. "We're just waiting for the airport to reopen," she told one passenger, while Frank thought he heard her mention something about Inverness to the other hostess at the front. Were they diverting? Then the two women stopped serving drinks, and sat solemnly at their stations at either end of the plane, buckled into the jump-seats. No further announcements from the cockpit had been forthcoming — its door, wide open earlier in the flight, now firmly closed, as if the crew were sealing themselves into a secret meeting. The grumbling of passengers had given way to what seemed an everlasting pregnant pause, as everyone listened out for cues to their fate. Soon after, the onboard lighting flickered and died, sending the cabin into darkness; a collective gasp, and worried glances in the ambient light, but nothing more, as the hush returned. No one dared to speak a word. To speak meant confirming the truth.

Frank turned to his son. "We must still be circling the airport," he said, although in the blizzard it became hard to get a sense of forward movement. Everything felt normal — almost stationary — until the brusque jostle of pockets of turbulence, whose brief violence, through successive lurches, reminded of the ongoing experience of flight.

Hours had passed since the air hostess emerged from the cockpit, and still, with no new news, they flew — with no sign of landing. It felt like they simply hung at high altitude; aimlessly bobbing like a wind-blown weather balloon. Then, out of nowhere, the thump of a thunder-snow storm, lightning strobing in the darkness, highlighting the flaky precipitation. The first crack and boom elicited screams and *Dear God*s in the cabin. The gas from a lighter sparked into furious orange life as the woman in front, with shaking hands, lit another cigarette.

"These are damned good airplanes, Son," Frank said, gripping his seat's armrests with taut fingertips, a tremor in his voice.

"Really, Dad?"

"Really, Son. So don't you worry now."

Frank knew the aircraft well, from his time with the ground crew of the RAF. Although no expert on the commercial variant — the DC-3 — and its full flight parameters, he did know of its long-range capabilities through its wartime incarnation as the

C-47 Skytrain, or Dakota; famed for its almost unique capability of lasting in the air for a dozen hours — a quality that helped make it a star aircraft of the Allied efforts. Of course, it required full tanks at takeoff. Indeed, he had even refuelled a fair few in his time. But even those wartime workhorses had their limits. Without enough fuel, he knew only too well, they'd soon be nothing more than a metallic meteorite, falling fast across the snowy night sky.

"I was just thinking—," Frank was midway through saying, in between a nervous puff of his pipe, when the worst — so silently feared, with a couple of dozen people poised for its arrival, but ambivalent with denial — finally happened. The dark-white world outside in no way prepared them for the collision in the unseeable pall — the flight violently interrupted within a fragment of time too short to naturally measure, the G-forces pulling their lap-belts with unimaginable pressure sharp into their midriffs. They heard no warning to brace for impact.

Everything seemed normal — at least in terms of unhindered forward motion — and then, with no chance to comprehend the change — no opportunity to even *think* — everything irreparably ripped apart.

2009

Precious little light permeated Montague's stygian Victorian house, its unkempt front and back gardens populated with tall, wide-branching trees that blocked the sun. Beset into the front door nestled a tiny stained-glass window, just above a rusting letterbox cage, letting in the faintest coloured light. The walls of the dim corridor — darker still when the interior doors were closed — were lined with brown wallpaper, and cramped with fussily framed photos and artworks, including several faded Constable reproductions; Turner far too radical, too abstract, too avant-garde. *The Hay Wain* and *Salisbury Cathedral from the Bishop's Grounds* represented a perfect England, a simpler time; indeed, a time Montague sometimes felt to which he belonged, like the sense of being the wrong baby taken home from hospital, only in his case some far greater mixup, involving the incongruities of space and time. There existed a family rumour that an ancestor once owned an actual Constable, but if so, it never remained in the family long enough to alter Montague's fortunes.

Greying net curtains, saturated with dust, hung limply against every window, further curbing the light. The furniture, which cluttered the hallway from the front door to the foot of the stairs, and spilled over into — and out of — every room, comprised a sombre mix of mahoganies, walnuts and teaks, over-busy with filigrees and burdened with ornaments and knickknacks. Chintz reigned, from rugs covering the wooden floorboards to the flocked wallpaper reaching up to the high, corbelled and corniced ceilings. A grandfather clock stood sentry outside the front room, inside which the mantelpiece bent slightly with the weight of another clock, whose chimes were out of time, and in a different key, to that of its taller relative. Yet another clock, in the back room, started its peals just as the others finished theirs, and one more, on the upstairs landing, rang wobbly and mournful Westminster Chimes every quarter.

They all hailed from the time when Dorothy's family had money, before most of it vanished during the Second World War. The Taylor-Smythes lost their mansion, along with their fortune, but Montague's mother later inherited much of the furniture — some of it retaining reasonable antique value — and somehow managed to find room for it all, despite the suburban squeeze. A sense of superiority clung to her side of the family even after the slippage of their social standing. The Taylor-Smythes insisted that Geoffrey Freeman –– a man of great intelligence and accomplishments, but from a lower middle-class background — still failed to meet the standards for their daughter, but Dorothy wouldn't listen, and married him in spite of their bitter protests. That permanently sundered the familial relationship, and as such, she never told them, years later, that they may have been right all along, after he walked out on her and their son.

Dorothy's belongings remained largely untouched since her death a decade-or-so earlier. Aside from her absent self, there existed little evidence of her demise. Visitors — not that Montague often entertained any — would never have known that she had long-since passed away. The blankets were no longer on the sitting room armchair, and the commode, which in later years Montague had to empty and swill out with his nose held — or rather, the one still-functioning nostril pressed in by a thumb — sat idle in the garage; cleaned that final time, but never fully disinfected. Her bedroom remained untouched, even though she slept downstairs, choosing not to venture up at all in later life. Her wardrobes remained cluttered with moth-bitten dresses, her dresser stuffed with garments that reeked of old drawer-wood and must, while the room itself retained a faint hint of stale lavender perfume. Occasionally he dusted the room, but never more than a cursory brush with a cloth. Keeping her door closed most of the time meant that, whenever opened, the essence of his mother hit him like a warm breeze. Occasionally, often at Christmas or on her birthday, he would lay on her bed, sometimes sobbing uncontrollably; every fibre of his being, in those moments, reduced to that of a little boy.

He continued to sleep in a single bed in the much smaller back bedroom, which he had occupied since the age of five. It was the only room that didn't retain its old decor, with the Spitfire and Hurricane wallpaper his father had adhered replaced with simple blue and white stripes; the toys boxed-up and stored in the garage with the commode, on top of the turquoise two-door Morris Minor saloon that his mother never drove after 1957. She had promised the car to her son when he turned eighteen, but he never got around to taking lessons. With all the detritus, it would take a day or more to extricate it from its tomb — packed like an ancient pharaoh's final resting place, only rather than scarabs, amulets and canopic jars, the space instead crammed with tat, junk and dust; the layers of his and his mother's lives piled upon one another, squeezed tight in the dark.

* * *

Stephanie Ogilvy: unveiled to Montague through furtive glances, tentatively stolen from his mother's bedroom window; peering down at his new neighbour through lustreless net curtains, as, without assistance, she unpacked a plain white transit van, unaware of her audience. Even if she were to look up at his window, aiming her gaze to where a fuzzy grey figure might be delineated beyond the semi-opaque curtains and beside the drapes, the fine flecks of snow moving on the breeze made such an observation virtually impossible. Perhaps it never occurred to her that someone might be watching. By contrast, from his vantage point he gained a much clearer view: the precipitation, like the net curtain, easier to see through when the target on the other side stood fully lighted, with the low winter sun arcing under the snow clouds to provide an orange-hued spotlight.

The house next door had been empty ever since the old lady — with whom his mother used to argue over the garden fence, in the distant days before Dorothy stopped venturing out the back — died six months earlier. The neighbour's house sold quickly, to a developer, who worked on the property on weekends, until it soon sold again; and so, Montague presumed this woman — as she carried boxes from the van into the hallway — to be the new owner.

He considered it perfectly normal to head outside and introduce himself, and offer to help, especially in inclement weather; but instead he stood and stared, as if observing a rare creature at the zoo through protective glass. He felt a jabbing sense of guilt at his voyeurism — but then again, how could it be a sin to simply observe a new neighbour moving into her house? Wasn't curiosity perfectly natural? It's not like she seemed vulnerable, or in a state of undress; and she stood outside, not locked away in private. What if she didn't want his help, and felt patronised were he to offer? — wasn't that a problem these days, ever since women's lib? Would she snap at him, make a sarcastic comment about her own feebleness? He pondered how he might make such an offer clear and inoffensive — nothing but a kind-hearted gesture — and, as he ruminated, some safe-sounding opening gambits sprang to mind. Yes, he could say *that*, he concluded. Yet he just stood there, watching, careful not to tweak the voile of the curtain as he pressed close against it.

The van contained nothing too large: potted plants — calathea, ponytail palm, and a rugged-stemmed yucca; boxes no bigger than her arms' reach, hugged as she carried them down the path; a reasonably tall and sturdily-framed abstract art print, glimpses of whose manic expressionism made him uncomfortable; two suitcases: one old-fashioned and faux-leather, one sleek and modern Samsonite; and bags of all shapes, sizes and materials, carried and lugged indoors, through the fine sleet and snow.

Over the coming days and weeks, either side of Christmas, additional vans, branded with furniture or appliance company livery, parked up outside, and items freshly boxed or wrapped were wheeled to her front door. And again he watched from the bedroom window, at times holding his breath as long as possible, as if such tiny movements would give away his presence.

In those early months he knew everything about how Stephenie looked, but little about who she *was*. The items she took into the house that first day, and those subsequently delivered, gave insights into her taste, but mostly it amounted to practical stuff that any other human being would own or purchase; and a lot of it lay obscured in boxes or bags. He never saw a man enter the house, beyond those delivering goods.

One day in early February he thought his luck might be changing. She came to his front door, and he stood frozen in the hallway, able to glimpse her face through the grubby stained-glass window. He flinched — thinking at first she would see him, but she appeared oblivious, as if it were a two-way mirror; and then, again, tensing up as he anticipated the doorbell's chimes. He took deep breaths, straightened his back. He'd rehearsed how he would introduce himself, should their paths cross — by the front gates, or on their actual front paths — but he still wasn't ready. His mind emptied, like a fast draining sink, as if the words sank into the useless pit of his stomach; leaving the sense of a swirling mental vortex, in which nothing firm could form.

However, there were no doorbell chimes; instead, an envelope slipped through the letterbox to fall into the metal cage, as, still utterly inert, he heard her footsteps recede. Had she written him a letter? Could this be an invitation to some event? Or even an early Valentine's card? His heart raced, until he reached in and picked up a mis-delivered phone bill bearing his name.

His childhood fear of new people and new situations never really went away. Leaving his comfort zone, he concluded, had rarely gone well.

* * *

Dusk snuck in early. Up there with the warmest of summer days — but a few weeks past the equinox, and thus far from the longest. It grew dark with surprising speed, and soon it would be time for father and son to start heading home; Geoffrey's instruction to be back with the boy by dark. First, however, a treat. In the moment that Geoffrey turned toward the vendor when buying Monty a candyfloss — as he handed over the coins with one hand and took hold of the stick with the other — the boy had gone, hypnotically following a gaggle of older children like the last in a line of ducklings, turn after turn, until out of sight from his father. When the kids suddenly ran off, too fast to keep up with, Monty found himself disoriented and alone. The panic felt like a sinister adult hand around his throat, gripping tight.

Spurred into movement, Monty ran past the various rides that span and gyrated with grotesque light. He tried to run faster, as if increasing his speed — simply imparting more effort — could somehow turn back time, and put him back at his father's side. But no, he just grew more confused, and disoriented, as everything flashed by at an even greater pace. Then, the sense that the rides would crash: that the Ferris wheel would topple, that the capsules, like cockpits in the aircraft that he later came to fear, would fly from the rotating arms. He ran, often in circles: around and around the carousel — catching glimpses of the gurning golden horses, wild-eyed and champing crazily at the bit — until exiting along a different aisle. He saw a friendly-looking young couple walking with candyfloss and bottles of Coke, but ran past them, as his mother said never to talk to strangers. He recognised the individual stalls and rides and kiosks, but could not join them together; like knowing all the planets but not the order in which they regressed from the sun, when needing to hop from one to the next.

Suddenly, out of breath, he sensed that the rides and lights were behind him, as he stood in an enclave of caravans behind a row of sideshow tents. Clearly he'd strayed too far. He heard voices, and as his eyes adjusted behind his thick lenses peppered with sweat that fell from his forehead, figures — some with faces shrouded in the smoke of cigarettes and pipes — emerged from the dark: a man as tall as a telephone box; a woman with a web-like maze of tattoos crawling up her neck and across her lower face; a man with no arms, dressed in a dinner jacket and bow-tie; a young lady with a beard; and someone else, back in the shadows. Some moved towards Monty, and he froze in panic. "Are you lost, sonny?" asked one of the voices; deep and male, yet somehow female. "It's okay, little man," said an even deeper voice, which he realised came from the giant.

Was he dreaming? A nightmarish dark fairytale? No, he was awake; it felt all too terrifyingly real. Without feeling the release, he sensed the liquid warmth in his underpants, and the wetness of his trouser crotch, as his bladder abruptly emptied. As the quartet drew closer, and he clenched, he saw that the faces were kind; even the one with all the dark inky lines, like literal crow's feet curved around her mouth. "Where's yer mum, laddie?" asked the tattooed lady, maternalistically, as she knelt down and put a heavily-painted hand onto his forearm.

Before he had a chance to reply, having paused to weigh up whether or not he could trust the people, a passing policeman — the bobby in the familiar helmet, emblazoned with the initials HR — moved their way upon the call of the giant. Handed over by the strange collective — everyone relieved at the swift resolution — the officer and the boy walked hand in hand, around the central complex of rides, until father and son found each other outside the coconut shy.

On the drive home, Geoffrey told Monty that he *must not* tell Dorothy; framed with compassion, to avoid causing her worry. Monty did as planned, bottling up the story and holding it tight in his stomach — for that's where the emotions felt crammed. Arriving home well after dark, he went straight to bed, without having to explain. The next day, however, he felt suffocatingly inhibited; strangely silent, scared to speak in case he said the wrong thing. He couldn't eat, his belly full of lies. Dorothy could tell something wasn't right. Eventually it all burst forth, in one big explosion of tears and words and emotions. Even though safe and well — home, wrapped in her embrace — his mother did not take the news phlegmatically. She scolded Geoffrey in front of the child; giving her husband a dressing down for his irresponsibility. Did he not realise what could have happened? A little lad had been abducted from a fairground just a couple of years earlier, and found dead in a canal a week later — had he forgotten? What the hell was he thinking?

1955

Stanley and Alice emerged from the restaurant into the warm twilight, blinking into a night whose explosion of heat and colour caught them off guard; the old city lost behind a vast array of dazzling, flashing lights as bright as that fateful funfair's as they turned towards Piccadilly Circus. It could be considered a travesty, with such beautiful, historic architecture obscured by gaudy advertising: classic doric columns, arched and pilastered windows, elaborate architraves and cornices, and the proud portico of the London Pavilion — all blocked out by vulgar commercial touting; and yet it instead felt to Stanley like landing on another planet, buzzing with energy, as, with every conceivable colour, innumerable lightbulbs and neon strips twinkled and flashed and pulsed. Everyday items — batteries, chewing gum, fizzy drinks, stout ale, tonic water, beef stock — rendered as deities on four-storey walls of light.

The pair crossed the road to the steps of the statue at the heart of the circus, and in awed silence looked around, from Regent Street to their left, to Shaftesbury Avenue up ahead, and to the right, along Coventry Street, drinking in the dazzling displays that burst from their façades. They had met under spinning stars,

Stanley thought, but this seemed on a whole other scale. The multitudes of lights reflected on the circling buses and car rooftops, and bounced back from shop windows, amplifying the giddying effect.

"It's not Eros, you know?" he suddenly said, matter-of-factly.

"What's not?" Alice asked, momentarily puzzled. "The statue?" she added, looking over her shoulder at what clearly *was* Eros. Everyone knew that.

"People *think* it's Eros, but it's not."

"Really?" she said, still appearing puzzled.

"Yes, really."

"How strange! Who is it then?"

"It's Anteros, his brother. The god of requited love. He's the lucky one. Himeros, another of the brothers, was the god of unrequited love. He wasn't s-so lucky. Eros was more about p-passionate love, physical desire."

"How do you know all this?"

"I read it s-s-somewhere," Stanley said, recalling the library, with the colours of its stained glass windows falling across the tiled floor, the fug of the warm room rich with the smell of a thousand old books. "Although I guess it's not much help if you arrange with someone to meet them at *Anteros'* statue. Probably better to p-p—purposefully get it wrong, so they at least know what you mean. Shall we stay here for a while?"

They sat themselves on the wide, shallow steps — Stanley carefully brushing away the dirt before Alice lowered herself — and watched the wall-bound fireworks coruscate: the Catherine wheel of the *Coca-Cola* sign, with its giant red circle — a circumference the size of two double-decker buses, and in much the same shade of red — swirling in a circular motion, hypnotically swooshing round and round, before the words REFRESHING and DELICIOUS flashed up in yellow uppercase lettering; no place for the apologetic lowercase form, the subtle gesture. Across Shaftesbury Avenue an animated stick of Wrigley's Spearmint Gum flew into the foreground, trailing a rocket's tail; forming an arrow that pointed at its slogans: HEALTHFUL, REFRESHING, DELICIOUS. Beneath a clock imprinted with GUINNESS TIME stood a neon zookeeper midway between two seals, the animals flicking a pint of stout back and forth, over the beleaguered man's head. Beside this, SCHWEPPES TONIC WATER sparkled, the blue and white lines of the display dissolving into bubbles before reforming. And further down Coventry Street to their right, another entire four-floored façade completely lost behind the lights of the Osram Lamps, Cinzano vermouth, Nescafé coffee and the airline BOAC.

To Stanley, they sat at the heart of the universe, where all life converged; seeing it, in that moment, like an actual heart, with the energy pumped out through arterial streets. There were shows all around them — theatres and cinemas, big and small — but it would feel odd — absurd, even — to take seats in the dark and witness a work of fiction, when they experienced vibrant reality. And there could be no greater beauty on any screen or stage to fantasise about than his companion — of that he felt most certain.

He took Alice's hand, and — spurred on by the energy all about them in the humid air — leaned in to kiss her lips. For a moment she hesitated, aware of the strangers sat on adjacent steps, and the gurning blur of faces peering out of bus and taxi windows, and the tourists passing by on the pavements. But then she let all that go, and sunk into his warm lips in the hot night air.

With their eyes closed they heard laughter and singing, and boisterous shouts; drunk people crossing the road, a screech of tyres, a horn honking, a revved engine. *You silly bugger!* More laughter. *Sod you!* All heard, yet dreamily so, like a distant wireless not quite tuned in to a station.

"I don't ever want it to stop," Stanley said, when they finally broke from the clinch.

"What?"

"This. *Everything*. I want to stay here forever," his stutter largely diminishing, but neither of them noting its general absence. "With you. Although, of course, it will get later, and quieter. And we'll get cold … and then it will get light, and it won't be the same — of course it won't be the s—same. I know that. I'm being daft. But I just wish it *could* be. You know? I want this moment to last."

"It *can't* last, Stanley," Alice said, resting her head on his shoulder with a sideways tilt. "That's life. But we can make other moments. That's how it works. And we can remember this. I mean, how could we ever forget?"

1956

Crushing, crumpling metal churned in the snowstorm; the crunch and clatter of still-spinning engines twisting up on rock and ice morphing into the wails of disembowelled banshees, the nerve-shredding screeches of a thousand — a *million* — fingernails dragged down chalkboards, as the DC-3 smashed and split apart, its body sundering in stages, its wings ripped clean off — as if a mere balsa wood model in the hands of a reckless child — the tail fin torn in two, all within a few blinks of an eye.

All bags and belongings in the overhead racks fell loose and flew away; Frank's glasses swiftly fleeing his face, his pipe breaking free of his clutches, although James instinctively clung to his copy of *Wisden* as if now an actual bible. Frank grabbed for his son's forearm in the dark, as the fingers of his other hand dug into the armrest. The entire front of the fuselage dropped from view — *gone* — and the mid-section, shorn of its wings, just seemed to simply fall like the heaviest imaginable stone, for whom aerodynamics — lift and glide — were never applicable. All seven rows in front of Frank and James vanished straight down, as they, at the rear, slid onto the crest of a slope and, after a sideways bump, slipped backwards down the incline at unimaginable speed. So fast, yet comprehended so slowly; the marvel of how much could be seen and discerned, even in a blizzard, when adrenaline pumped and the mind's focus sharpened to its very keenest. In the moment of disintegration the girl with the black hair, sitting loose and unbelted, had drifted up, out of her seat, and continued on up, soaring — arms flailing, head lolling like a rag doll — with a kind of momentary weightlessness, as, strapped in at the back of the plane, the Carters started to slide away. Through the fog of precipitation, behind which she rapidly paled with distance, they witnessed the girl lose her upward momentum and start to fall, chasing the midsection — where seconds earlier she had been seated — in a losing battle with gravity; her screams lost in the tumult and clangour. Shortsightedness further blurred Frank's view, but he saw *enough*, in the way shapes moved, and the noises they made, to comprehend the horror.

He and his son bellowed out what felt like never-ending screams and yells — an escape valve for the terrors flooding their minds and the forces jolting their bodies. And yet, with all the other noise, they couldn't even hear their own cries and shrieks.

Facing in the wrong direction, theirs became the front seats — the *only* seats — belted into some kind of horrific backwards ride, the tail-tip to their rear now a nose-cone; a roller-coaster gone awry, the icy elements rushing at the back of their heads and nipping at their ears, swirling around to their faces, still managing to sting their eyes, as the rear portion of the plane careened down snowy mountain terrain; tobogganing in the unabating snow, until another jolting collision sent them up in the air — they flew again, briefly, with spin and turn — as the rear of the cabin flipped over to land on its roof, without somehow caving in. The vessel thundered on, upside-down, before something colossal and unbending in the landscape brought it to a forceful and conclusive, stop. And with that the pair were knocked out cold. There came an unheard whoosh at a dislodged pile of snow, as the spattering of flakes fell around them. Then silence.

* * *

Still belted into their seats, Frank and James slowly regained consciousness. Their heads hung heavy with blood as they dangled upside-down in the night whiteout, their pulses beating in their sinuses and foreheads, their faces cold and numb. Nothing made sense. Fading fires burned on the horizon of their inverted world, paled through sheets of snow that rose from the ground to settle in the sky. Arteries of electrical wires rose from the broken fuselage, severed at different lengths from its aluminium skin. At first Frank could not recollect the impact, his eyes opening to inexplicable devastation — for a moment unable to even recall that he'd even been on a plane, while his relative shortsightedness did not help clarify the situation, a blur within a blur, that contained ice and hellfire. It almost felt like a dream, but the sensations were too real.

James, who had regained consciousness moments earlier, tugged at his father's arm as the pair hung from the ceiling. "Dad... Dad... *Dad!*"

Then, for Frank, it all clicked. "Are you okay, Son?" he asked, eagerly, in the immediate moments after reality — if not total comprehension — dawned; images of the air hostess — Gladys? — serving him a drink, then the eerily silent flight; and finally, the poor girl flying through the air.

"Yeah, I think so," James said, ice-wind whistling wild and sharp in their faces.

"Are you hurt?"

"A bit," James said, gently rotating his head. "My neck hurts," he added, rubbing it, and then flinching as the pain shifted down to his shoulder, and further, down to his shoulder-blade.

"Mine too," Frank said, as he started to rub the back of his own neck; pain and discomfort setting in after the initial shock wore off. He then instinctively shook his head, as if to wake up, or to see clearly, before twingeing at a pain shooting into his temples — liquid nitrogen injected with a sharp needle through the fine side-walls of his skull.

The cold coiled around them, the chill punching their organs. Hair follicles turned to threads of ice, moisture on eyelids to icicles. The air stung their nostrils, and cut sharply at their throats; every in-breath a bag of broken glass.

The relief of surviving quickly gave way to the terror of their predicament; the unspoken realisation that dying in an instant — unaware in the moment of death, unaware forever more, when put to permanent sleep — could prove preferable to some long, lingering demise, cut off from civilisation. As part of some primordial paternal drive, Frank kept such worries to himself, in his role as protector — even though he possessed no similar primordial knowledge pertaining to survival in the wild. Instincts, and not instructions, had endured via evolution; alas, he did not have the skills of the Eskimos he'd once read about, and their generational wisdom. A few boy-scout summer campouts in Cranford Park were hardly adequate preparation.

Even his wartime travails were sedate and unthreatening, apart from the one time the airbase got bombed — but even that occurred at a safe distance from his bunk, with no casualties aside from some fighter planes, a runway and a hangar.

And yet, he concluded, all was not lost. Without serious injury they at least had a chance, even if the terrain, and the weather, and the apparent remoteness, posed an obvious threat. Still inverted in their seats, they could see little but snow, stained dark by the night sky; the only thing discernible, aside from snow on the ground, and snow in their faces, and snow at every distance from near to far, were scraps of plane debris, a couple of nearby suitcases, and the smattering of small, faltering fires. The cold felt beyond bitter. They had packed for winter, but the plane had been moderately warm, and their coats, stored in the overhead racks, were lost in the impact; their suitcases stored in the luggage compartment, whose whereabouts they could not discern. Had that part of the plane remained? They could only hope, fuelled by the two suitcases that lay below them. On their top halves they wore nothing but thin pullovers, with slender cotton shirts underneath. Frank also wore a vest that, at such temperatures, counted for little, but felt better than nothing.

There had been no explosion, he recalled, trying to piece together what took place; if there *had* been, neither would have survived. It confirmed his hunch that the plane had flown its last minutes on fumes, given its extended duration. Why hadn't they diverted to another airport or aerodrome? Or even found a safe place to ditch? Why did they spend hours circling Glasgow, caught in a white squall? Or had they diverted to Inverness, as he thought he heard the hostesses discussing?

Beyond a few fragments of metal, and the pockets of snow-doused fire — fuelled by mere dregs of avgas, the precipitation batting down the flames — they were alone in a wilderness, set apart from the rest of the catastrophe; wedged upside-down on a narrow ledge, their section of fuselage jammed between two small peaks in the topography, at some unknown altitude, in the middle of nowhere.

An eery silence: no screams, no cries for help, not even any distant sirens growing closer — just the spiteful wail of the wind;

the remainder of the aircraft, and its passengers, lost somewhere out in the crystalline whiteness.

"We need to get down," Frank eventually said, fumbling with hands blue and shaking. "I'll go first," he added, unbuckling his belt with quivering fingers that for several moments could not release the clasp. Finally flipped with a metallic chink, he fell from floor to ceiling, onto which snow had already drifted; sliding a few feet as the wetness gave way on the torn fabric lining and the partially-exposed aluminium beneath, the skid further hastened by the slight decline in the tilt of the tail section. With giddiness — that shooting pain again in his temples — he forced himself to a stand, finding his limbs all still worked, even if riddled with soreness; the orientation of the world now righted. He kicked and pushed a mound of snow to below where James hung suspended, and told his son to pull the release clasp. The boy did as told, collapsing down onto the softening pillow of snow.

"Where are we?" he asked his father, as he struggled to his feet and looked out at a landscape obscured, in layers, by snowfall and darkness.

"God knows, Son. Ben Nevis? Somewhere in the Grampians, I imagine. We hit a mountain, although thankfully not head-on. There was something about Inverness, wasn't there? Did you hear them say that? Certainly not Glasgow. This sure as hell ain't a cosy street with warm boozers. I can't even see one city light."

"Bloody hell," James said, and then flinched for his father's reaction at his language. None was forthcoming. "Will anyone find us?"

Frank shook his head. "I've no idea, Son." He went to add 'Your guess is as good as mine', but stopped himself, aware that he needed to remain optimistic. Give up *here*, he sensed, and death waited mere hours away; quicker, even. Stop fighting, and it would take you, swiftly and without mercy. "Now that I think about it," Frank said, his tone artificially upbeat, "someone *must* be on their way to find us soon. This is Scotland, for Chrissakes. Not a city, clearly — but we must be *close* to Glasgow, or on the route to Inverness. We're not in Siberia, even if it bloody-well feels like it."

The aluminium tail cone — the remnants of the very thing that transported them to what felt like a peak in remote Scottish highlands — became their refuge: a type of igloo shielding against a severity of weather neither had ever before experienced; something far beyond what London ever presented, even in its direst winters — although the January of 1947 had its moments. Frank laughed, lightly and laden with irony, then sighed. Back then James loved the snow — a little boy enraptured by its potential, by the way it could be scooped into balls or rolled into the shape of a corpulent belly, onto which could be placed the hand-dented sphere of a head; but the boy could always run back inside to warm up by the stove, or be handed a warm cup of cocoa.

They could discern nowhere safe to venture out to, in the darkness, with the blizzard raging — no clear path to take, no sense of anything beyond a hundred or so feet, if that. To leave represented a suicide mission, as ill-advised as Oates leaving Captain Scott's tent at the South Pole. And at least that ill-fated gang knew their approximate location, and possessed the tools and accoutrements — even if outdated by current standards — for an expedition. Here, neither could leave the other.

"I'm freezing, Dad," James said, wearily perched on an inverted luggage rack, jutting from where the upended fuselage roof curved, his breath a fog that enveloped the falling snow in front of him. "I'm not sure I can stand it much longer," he added, the coldness snapping harder as adrenaline ebbed away.

"Look, let's see what we can find to open these with," Frank said, stepping out gingerly to gather the two suitcases lying loose on their narrow escarpment. His feet instantly sunk twelve inches — maybe more — into the snow, and he quickly reached back to James for some stability. After some teetering, Frank finally grabbed the suitcases and between them, one after the other, they dragged the dead weights up into the plane, like hauling soaked bodies onto a lifeboat.

"Locked," Frank said, stepping away from the lifeless luggage when its ice-cold latch refused to release. "Damn. We need to find something to open these up with."

The galley behind their seats lay in total disarray: trays, teapots, broken china and various utensils in a heap on the floor, amid scraps of unserved sandwiches, the bread suspended like archipelagos in fast-freezing puddles of tea and coffee. They rooted through the scatter, picking up several pieces of cutlery whose icy stainless steel felt painful to the touch. With shirt sleeves pulled over their hands each tried to jemmy the locks of a suitcase. Frank's brute force got nowhere, but James, angling a dull-bladed butter knife, managed to dislodge the damaged latch on his. The lock flipped open with a satisfyingly springy *thunk*, and the pair peeled back the lid with the eagerness of archaeologists anticipating a hoard of Viking treasure in an ancient wooden chest; the pair knowing that, in their predicament, a pair of gloves, or a scarf — or perhaps some stowed food — would have a value far greater than any conceivable weight of gold or silver, with its cold and pointless beauty.

Inside they found tightly-packed articles of women's clothing, still neatly folded despite the various collisions and the extreme G-forces. A reassuring scent of perfume wafted, wisp-like, from the fabric: a human touch, some feminine softness and delicacy — hints of sunshine, summer meadows, floral bouquets; hints of *life* — so welcome, and unexpected, against the stark coldness and endless dark. A red velvet clutch coat with a capelet collar sat on top, below which a blousy blue knitted jumper, with a neat row of buttons. "Put these on, Son", Frank said, handing them quickly to his son to the point where he almost shoved them into his hands. Neither thought twice about any possible oddness, nor saw the funny side in cross-dressing, which usually gained an easy laugh in the music halls and school plays.

"Drat. None of this will fit me," Franks said, despondently tossing aside a formal deep-blue rayon dress, several silk petticoats and slips, and a few pairs of balled-up stockings, before returning to the stubborn suitcase at his side. "It's all too small. Far too small."

"Don't be getting it all wet," James said, stretching his arms into the sleeves of the coat, then wrapping the body of the garment around himself, holding it tight against his scrawny chest as he shivered. "They may be of some use," he said, sharp and staccato, through chattering teeth. "As scarfs, or something. Pillows, maybe. I dunno."

"Good point, Son," Frank acknowledged, unballing the stockings. He could sense his thinking faltering. He felt dulled, slowed. Still, he carried on, trying to will his brain to sharpen up. "These might make decent gloves. At least until we find something better." The pair tore the crotches out of the garments, and unfurled a leg of material up each arm.

Frank, losing patience, lifted the obstinate suitcase, to throw it against the rear interior wall of the aircraft — a bulkhead housing the toilet door, and what remained of the galley — but decided against it, with no knowledge of just how secure the aircraft lay within the landscape, and with no way, in the blizzard, to leave it and check. He knew he couldn't afford to lose his temper, but the urge to yell and kick the luggage felt overwhelming; exacerbated by the irrational sense of guilt at landing them in this mess, and the responsibility of being the one who should have all the answers. But if staying on the escarpment and hoping for the best didn't fill him with optimism, it still beat skidding down the mountainside in a giant tin can, or perhaps worse still, causing an avalanche to bury them both alive.

The wind howling ever stronger, and with snow slanting into their makeshift shelter, Frank picked up a jagged strip of metal from the broken shelving of overhead racks, and jabbed relentlessly at the dark brown leather exterior of the case, trying to force a hole; attempting to spear and skin, once again, the defiant animal who gave its hide. With no success, he went at the lock again, with this bigger implement. Finally it gave way, snapping apart rather than unlocking. The lid flipped back to the welcome sight of men's clothing, through which he eagerly rummaged: a neatly folded Harris Tweed three-piece suit, with a brown and red herringbone weave; a plain burgundy polo shirt; a hand-knitted Aran jumper; a coarse-knit bright blue tank top; and various undergarments: underpants, socks and vests. "Bingo," Frank said.

He held up the jumper, then sighed, his head slumping forward, like a defeated child. "Can you believe it? Looks a bit on the small side."

"It'll stretch," James said, shuffling on the spot and flapping his arms to keep warm. "That's what Mum always told me when I started to grow out of stuff. Give it a good stretch."

"Look Son, you need to get some of this on too," Frank said, handing a clutch of garments to the boy. "It'll fit you, no bother. The vests, shirts, and the tank top — get 'em on. I'll see what I can do with the rest."

James unbuckled the coat, slipped it off. He lifted the woman's jumper back over his head, then his own thin pullover, below which just thin white shirt. His mother always told him to wear a vest — and he always ignored her. If only she were here now, he thought, suddenly in dire need of her touch; and then, *No*, he wanted her safe, away from this calamity, along with Lucy — still far too young, too brittle. Down to just one layer, the cold felt like a tight new skin: frozen grafts of ice all over his body. He hurriedly put the vests on over his shirt, one after another, although the shakes, and the numbness in his fingers and thumbs, made it hard to perform such an otherwise perfunctory task. He held buttons in his grasp, but the tremors rattled them to and fro in front of the hole, until eventually, one by one, he fumbled each into place. Next, the polo shirt, and then all the other layers laid out before him, ending with the red coat — now tight and constricting, but whose discomfort, in the circumstances, felt somehow reassuring, like an overly-tight and smothering hug from his mother; perhaps with the sense, when a toddler, of a hot towel wrapped after a lukewarm bath.

Frank squeezed into the tweed waistcoat, whose flanks refused to meet — the divide several inches, buttons well beyond reach of the holes. Then, having stretched it out, he struggled into the Aran jumper like a large animal trying to squeeze into a narrow tree-hole. Gloria had been on at him to lose a little weight these past couple of years, as his midriff expanded from a small potbelly to something decidedly more portly. Silently, and belatedly, he conceded the point. And then he thought again: perhaps she *wasn't* right — he had some natural insulation, after all, unlike their poor boy, who would need all the help he could get.

"Can we build some kind of door?" Frank wondered, surveying the scene as the snow blew into the chunk of fuselage. "Block out the worst of it. What d'ya say?"

"Wouldn't hurt to try, I s'pose," James said, looking around at their raw materials.

They collected the strewn drapes that once hung at the rear of the cabin, but could find no way to affix them to a floor which became the ceiling. They tried tying the cloth — rendered near-rigid with a starching skin of ice — to some protruding electrical wires, but it proved too fiddly. Nothing held.

"What about the lavvy?" James asked.

"You need to go?"

"No. I mean, it's a *room*, isn't it? At least, it's got a door."

"I hadn't even thought of that," Frank said, turning to face it. "It ain't very big, though. I could barely fit in it when I had to spend a penny. But anything's worth a try."

James led the way, but let his father overtake and assume control. "How did I not think of this?" Frank added, unnerved at how his mind — initially ramped up with adrenaline — slowed with the cold, and grew confused by panic. Facing the door, he instinctively pressed the handle down, before remembering it's inverted nature, and so lifted it up. Initially it wouldn't budge — ice sealing the door shut with a clear adhesive sheen — but eventually, after James helped in pushing as hard as they could, it opened to a tiny compartment, into which two adult-sized males could just about squeeze. The inverted attitude of the tail-cone provided a bonus: adequate clearance on what became the floor; the toilet and handbasin, so cramped into the tight space, now conveniently hanging overhead, out of the way. "This'll do 'til morning," Frank said, nodding to himself.

"What about keeping an eye out?" James asked. "What if someone comes looking for us? Won't we have to attract their attention?"

"No one will be out looking in *this*," Frank said, weariness clear in his voice, the wind howling through the open door. "At least, not right now," he hurriedly added, trying to sound brighter. "It's too difficult for them to come find us now. They won't see a bleedin' thing, will they? But in the morning, when the storm has passed, they'll be out looking — mark my words. We just have to take care of ourselves. The storm will pass, soon. If we don't get warmer pronto, we'll be done-in by hypothermia. We don't want to freeze to death before they arrive, do we? Come on, let's find something to use as bedding."

They clambered back outside the WC, to gather all the soft material they could find: the unused items of clothing from the two suitcases, and the unhung curtains. Frank, by far the stronger of the two, reached up to tear some cushions from the three remaining seats; James, with his extra height, lending a hand for leverage, as his father's greater weight dragged the upholstery apart. They laid the drapes on the cold, wet toilet ceiling, the cushions set aside for pillows. Several loose items of clothing — cold, but blissfully dry — were jumbled together, to spread over the area, to plump the nest; the remainder retained as makeshift blankets. "If we curl up just right, we should both be able to lie down," Frank said, looking at the bedding. "Here, you lie down, and hold all this until I'm sorted," he told his son, passing the heap of clothes to the boy once down on his side. Frank then closed the door, which in an instant cut dead the maniacal howl, as well as extinguishing what little ambient light remained. The tiny cabin turned pitch black, but, to their great relief, felt as safe as a womb.

1957

To the sound of distant whining engines, Charlotte looked up from her coffee, and away from the intriguing Rorschach test of a stain its froth left around the inside of the mug. Seated in a comfortable low chair at a small, equally low round table on the carpeted mezzanine — adjacent to the terminal café, but still part of its seating — she could see straight through rows of glass panes fixed between highly-polished steel balustrades and bannisters; and beyond the shallow-decline staircase, those same architectural combinations, out onto the distant airport apron, and its taxying airplanes. Inside the terminal, passengers ascended and descended the stairs, and queued at the ticket desks below.

She fumbled in her bulky shoulder-bag, unloading items onto the table like a hot-air balloonist frantically shedding ballast: her copies of T. S. Eliot's *East Coker* and *Burnt Norton*, both particularly dog-eared; less-battered copies of George Orwell's *Nineteen Eighty-Four* and *Under the Net* by Iris Murdoch; a spiral-bound notebook, with pencil in its wire spine; a bumper box of Aspro; a silver fob-watch, wrapped in a protective silk handkerchief; her trusty Argus C3 camera; an undeveloped 35mm film in its little tin canister, and two identical canisters of fresh film; a small box of feminine napkins; and her target — a packet of Craven A and its necessary matchbook — all tossed out onto the polished glass surface. She set the cigarettes and matches to one side, along with her notebook, and, holding the bag open below the level of the table, scooped the contents back inside.

She lit a cigarette, then flicked open her notebook; writing with her right hand while smoking with the left. It had struck her, whilst drinking her frothy coffee, that, removed from the sky, these planes weren't at all *birdlike* — the descriptor so often used by the pilots she knew during the war. Viktor had called his Spitfire "my falcon", she recalled, but he had not understood the word 'peregrine' when she added it in enquiry, trying to affix it to the more generic species. "It's the fastest," she noted.

These were, at least in terms of their *bodies*, entirely different kinds of animals — sea mammals, manatees, elongated saddlebacks, sloping silverbacks — all aligned on the tarmac, or taxiing to runways. Flightless fat-bodied creatures, essentially — their wings all skinny and hopeless, as if an afterthought. How did they even take to the air? The Spitfire had grace. *That* was birdlike.

'It's all about the engines', she concluded. All that additional power, tacked under those slim wings. Taking the pencil from the ringed spine of her notebook, she carefully jotted down these reflections. She had sat here, and at other vantage points, often enough to know the names of all the manufacturers, and the titles and model numbers of each style of aeroplane, as well as the origins of airlines with unusual appellations like Lufthansa, Qantas and Sabena — but seeing this zoomorphic connection to the aircraft felt fresh. All the time spent here, and suddenly she saw something new. "No peregrines here", she inadvertently said out loud, as if Viktor could hear.

The long-fronted Constellation: mammalian, small-headed; the bulging curve of the fuselage filtering to a strangely narrow nose. Distinctively triple-tailed, it seemed ungainly, its wings situated too far to the rear, its neck an awkward, almost phallic protrusion. Then, the fat, snub-nosed Stratocruiser: orca-faced, its double-barrelled belly drooping down, concealing the lower-deck lounge, from which its low-slung wings angled sleekly back. It looked too corpulent to gain any lift. And the dolphin-nosed DC-3 — her favourite — with its comforting curves disrupted only by an angular caudal fin, which jarred in place of a more organic tail. Smaller and older, its wing design at least appeared closer to avian physiognomy, and thus suggestive of natural flight. As one such aircraft emblazoned with British European Airways' livery taxied past she had to shield her eyes as the low, harsh sun reflected on its polished aluminium; the airport mirrored, with distortion, along the aircraft's shiny body.

A DC-3, indeed, had gone missing a week or two earlier, on what had initially been a similarly sunny winter's day, before the dark clouds drifted in. It took off into a snowstorm and, heading to Scotland, never arrived at its destination. She followed the news in the paper. She had seen the plane taxi to takeoff, with a father and son whom she'd made notes on onboard, but only later realised it to be the one that vanished. She'd taken quite a few photographs that day, but the film, along with many others, lay undeveloped; mixed together in a near-full shoebox, indistinguishable from the rest.

She put down her notepad and, lifting herself out of the low seat with a sigh, wandered over to order a fresh coffee.

* * *

Alone at a sunlit mess-canteen table during her break, enjoying some rare tranquility away from the war-wrung wards, Charlotte dropped a single rationed sugar-cube into a mug of barely-milked coffee and stared into the swirls created by the swish of the spoon, careful not to let any of the drink spill into the saucer; stirring it at just the right speed, over and over, to see the contents rise to the lip of the china and no further, in an absentminded test of dexterity. The ripples soothed, the patterns rising and falling with such complexity — the interactions between liquid and rim causing reverberations, echoes of earlier forces, rebounding inward to interact with those heading outward. All so controllable, so predictable, so contained; stopping, at her behest, just short of chaos. So much drama — a little squall — all within a small china cup.

Her thoughts kept looping back to Pilot Officer Hallfreðsson — sleeping in the adjacent ward — and the deep impression made on her psyche by his cataclysmic arrival, as if gouging a path directly to whatever resided at its core. He had already permeated her dreams. The crash that played out in her mind's eye, when fast asleep, stayed just the right side of a nightmare. In the dream, from which she had startled awake that morning — mere moments before her alarm sounded, so that, unable to go back to sleep, the imagery remained fresh and piquant — no other nurses arrived, and he lay relatively uninjured. No one else even knew of the crash, or his stricken body — just the two of them in an unpopulated world. Despite his injuries, he seemed fully cognisant, and free from pain. In his gratitude he leant in, and they shared a passionate kiss that felt strangely familiar; a kiss so full and wet as to tingle the nerve endings of her lips. In a way similar to her dissociation in the quadrant when viewing his stricken Spitfire speed across the sky, she witnessed this passionate clinch at a remove — over her own shoulder, with a cinematographer's elegant framing, and a hazy focus at its edges. They became movie stars, up on the silver screen. Yet she also felt very much at the heart of the shot, eyes closed, almost melting into the contact. She awoke to the evaporating sensation of his lips on hers, and almost immediately the twin bells of the alarm clock beside her pillow brutally clanged and rattled as it jigged and kicked out on the bedside table; as distressing and stomach-churning as an air-raid siren, or the sound of falling munitions. It felt like a *violation*, to disturb the exit of such a tender and spellbinding moment. Once silenced and stilled — she wanted to throw the bloody thing out the window — she sat up and ran a finger over her lips, in slow, full circles, as if, miraculously, his warmth still lingered.

* * *

The indolent preamble — the 'phoney war', all talk and, surreally, no action — had long-since concluded; the harsh realities of conflict now inescapable. In those earlier days — that phoney phase — Charlotte could take a coffee break without danger of interruption. The staff were troubled by the occasional training accident on the neighbouring airbase, but at that point the wards were always at least half empty, with overnight stays for minor illnesses, and only the sporadic case of something more serious.

Though still in its way incredibly distant — before the battles raged overhead, and men like Pilot Officer Hallfreðsson were shot down over East Sussex — the Dunkirk evacuations of late May and early June changed all that. The drama, occurring across the Channel, transmitted itself into the air of the wards. In what she initially deemed a callous decision, the injured and lame were left, vulnerable and in agony, until last on that hellish French shore. Fit soldiers were given priority, their presence needed to protect England from invasion, should it swiftly occur; famously, to even fight them on British beaches, if necessary. It came to make a certain kind of sense, in a world of imperfect policies and cruel compromises.

Within minutes of the first arrivals — shipped in by the busload — the most dreadful, retch-inducing stench began to permeate the entire building: wounded men who had been walking north across France and Belgium for a week in the summer heat, without food and water. Many, as part of the massed ranks of hundreds of thousands, were trapped on the beach for days on end: targets for bombs, strafing and rifle fire, as they lined up like sitting ducks. The challenges they faced were evident in the putrid odours that accompanied them home, the situation woven into their clothes, tattooed on their skin, entwined within their hair. Blood, urine, damp wool, trousers soiled with diarrhoea, septic wounds, and layers of foetid sweat heaped upon sweat and grease and oil and ash, all mixed together in the wards and corridors. *Ghastly,* Charlotte noted in her dairy.

Bograts vomiting in hallways and at bedsides made it all the worse — these girls, one fears, shall not last long here. Not even as long, perhaps, as the dying men. A wretched state of affairs.

In truth, she too struggled. But the sights, sounds and smells were not enough to disrupt her outward demeanour. And, amid the chaos, she found her mind too busy to overthink her own ill-preparedness in the face of rampant trauma. She felt like the entire nursing crew were tossed overboard in their pristine white uniforms, and given the chance to sink or swim — and she found herself doggy-paddling like crazy; treading water, keeping her head from going under, surviving moment by moment on instinct and adrenaline.

There had been no option for the medics in and around those beaches — targets themselves in the unimaginable panic and confusion — to do anything other than patch the men up and only later, when possible, ship them out. Even though the healthy went first, they lacked the time — and the equipment — to treat the injured and the mutilated. Many wounds were treated with the closed-plaster method: a quick fix with plaster-of-Paris that bought the patient more time, leaving the task of proper care to those back in England. The method entailed crudely cutting away the dead or damaged tissue around the affected area, and plugging the wound with a sterile Vaseline pack; then encasing the entire limb in a plaster cast, to ensure full immobilisation, so that any possible breakages did not grind, and if performed properly, the injury could be left unattended for a couple of weeks.

Charlotte later noted that unwrapping such capsules — prepared and wrapped in the smoke-filled air of combat — had been *A test of one's constitution*. The shores and all their inherent terrors were trapped within: the sea spray, the black ash and debris, sharp glistening grains of golden sand, spilt avgas and globules of oil; and boiled and burned blood, spattered from combusted comrades, to mix with the flow and coagulation of their own. Above it all, the rancid reek of *death* — enclosed in plaster, irrespective of how much effort the frantic medics made to seal a perfectly hygienic package.

Later, in her notebook, she wrote, *Most queerly, it was as though we were somehow exhuming corpses from WITHIN these men, with dead flesh from the limbs decomposed for days in the heat while only superficially attached to the body.*

Trainee nurses — barely out of school — continued to faint and vomit; one bolting from beside Charlotte to the toilet block, but spewing into her apologetically open palms before she made it. Thankfully, Charlotte thought to herself, the girl had not returned by the time they cut the next man free from his leg plaster: his wound teeming with an infestation of ravenous, bloated maggots, feasting on his decaying tissue. That tableau even took Charlotte by surprise, and at first she had to turn away, before steeling herself.

Curiously, it has to be noted, his wound looked the cleanest.

It all transported her, in no small way, to the front-line, as she imagined the scenes. Yet she still found it more than terrifying here, one hundred miles away as the crow hurriedly flies.

Prior to Dunkirk, the patients seemed to see the largely empty hospital as an excuse for games and pranks. Brash young airmen, hyped up on testosterone and unresolved pre-conflict tension, showed up on the pretext of some kind of ailment that required the removal of their shirts — perhaps even their trousers — and in need of a nurse's gentle touch to help diagnose the issue. The young nurses soon wised up; the call — made as loud as possible, so that the whole ward could hear — sent out for any doctor currently available to perform a full rectal examination. "Please bring your largest pair of forceps," Charlotte once added, laughing to herself at what kind of image that may arouse in the hastily retreating man's mind.

But then Dunkirk, and an end to the fun and games. No sooner had the wards started to thin again when the Luftwaffe began attacking Britain day and night.

Silly little boys, she thought, looking back — and then sighed, at the realisation that, just mere months later, several of those pranksters were already dead. Another had lost his legs and half his face after a takeoff went horribly awry, and had found himself back in the hospital — this time his ailments very much real; youthful braggadocio replaced with the most vehement melancholia and self-repugnance. She thought back to their games — irritating at the time, but rendered harmless fun, in hindsight, by everything that had followed; innocent, good-natured, and essentially innocuous — the nurses always having the last laugh as the young men quickly belted and buttoned up and scampered back to their barracks. She found it flattering, too, in its own way; recalling her thrilling sense of power when sending them packing.

However, another airman — more senior — proved more sinister. As she took his blood pressure, he put his hand between her legs; asking, as his fingers squirmed about while she tried to clamp her thighs together, if she liked it. Other airmen had tried to touch her — and she could successfully ignore it and reposition herself so as to curtail — but never in such a vulgar and forceful manner. She dropped the rubber air bulb and left the room, and refused to return; Matron threatening her with a severe reprimand for gross unprofessional conduct — 'So what if an officer touched you?' — until hearing the pilot's name, at which point Matron's countenance changed. She dropped the matter, never raising it again. Charlotte received a new task, and Matron herself went in to complete the checkup.

He'd recently died in combat, although Charlotte struggled to muster any sympathy upon hearing of his violent demise. A highly capable pilot — dubbed one of the bravest, who flew, alone, into formations of yellow-nosed Messerschmitts — she had come to realise that not *all* of those were fine, upstanding officers full of honour, concerned only with derring-do and saving the country. Some were proper bastards.

Even so, the allies needed all the talented airmen they could muster — even if some were safest to society at ten-thousand feet.

* * *

A scrum of men in suits and ties, some covered by thin long macs, jostled and shoved and elbowed for room by the terminal's *Arrivals* threshold, holding aloft their clunky press cameras, from which armatures extended out flash bowls the size of dinner plates to amplify each bulb's light. Confused by the chaos, Charlotte took out her own camera — a fraction of the size of theirs; fascinated by this roiling mass of well-turned-out men, frantic-faced and expectant almost to the point of drooling. Some kneeled to the side, others stood on seating at the rear to get an angle above their competitors. As Charlotte checked to make sure she had sufficient exposures remaining on the reel of film, there came a cry and a surge; shouts of "Marilyn!", "Miss Monroe!" and "Mrs Miller!" — not that any of the men cared to focus on the pinup's new husband — merging into a cacophony, as what seemed like a thousand crackles of light popped into the electric air. In the process of lifting the camera up to her face, in the milliseconds before she realised how the situation started to unfold, Charlotte found herself knocked backwards, onto the floor, as desperate men hurdled her in the chase towards their quarry. Only the plump soft bulk of Charlotte's oxblood bag saved her from serious injury, breaking her fall against the harsh marble floor.

A frazzled policeman called for order, as Charlotte, dazed and bruised, crawled to some seating; the photographers and press-men oblivious as they ran beneath a series of bright flashes, two policemen in tow, as if chasing a gang of fleet-footed burglars. A couple of fellow travellers — Japanese, she assumed — helped Charlotte up onto the seat with words she didn't understand, and then they bowed when she thanked them.

Aching, but with nothing broken or dislocated — beyond her sense of calm — she grabbed a coffee and sucked hard on a cigarette in the Forte's café. In truth, she hadn't felt especially calm to start with; the nerves ahead of the monumental step awaiting later in the day. Still, walking around the airport after an early arrival eased some of the tension — until straying into the path of stampeding, besuited wildebeest.

She grabbed her bag — full of all the usual paraphernalia, but additionally stuffed with several changes of clothes — and made her way to the boarding queue for the flight to Iceland. Her legs hurt as she walked across the tarmac to the portable boarding stairs. All the years, building to this point; finally ready to fly.

Faced with the first step, she remained inert.

"I can't," she said, to a smiling stewardess whose name-tag read 'Ingrid'.

"Let me help," Ingrid said, easing an arm under Charlotte's shoulder, to help her ascend.

"No, you don't understand. It's not that. *I just can't.*"

"What do you mean?"

"I'm so sorry."

Ingrid pulled Charlotte to one side, to let the other passengers board.

"It's okay, I've seen it before," the stewardess said. "Some people panic."

"It's more than that," Charlotte said, earnestly, tears welling in her eyes. "I've … just had yet another warning. The most terrible omen, believe me. I fear I'm just not destined to fly."

1955

They curved a smooth path through the countryside's pitch blackness, Stanley's car headlights the only illumination for miles around. The human world packed away, somewhere else, with just the view of gravel and greenery ahead, stained yellow by the cut of the high beams. Within this spray of light a rabbit's eyes glared from the long grass of the autumnal undergrowth, reflecting their approach back at them as the Morris followed the bend of the road. Both Stanley and Alice met the creature's unnaturally-lit gaze, and watched as it twitched, as if ready to throw itself into their path — a pointless midnight sacrifice — before it turned and ducked back into the hedgerow.

"Stop the car," Alice said, moments later. "Pull in here," she added, motioning towards a long farmland track.

"Why?" Stanley asked, his eyes fixed on the turning ahead, his foot hovering over the brake.

"I don't want you to drop me home yet."

"Really? Won't your parents be expecting you?"

"There's no rush. They'll have gone to bed. They trust you, now that they know you a little. We can turn off the engine and look at the stars."

Parked up, headlights off, they awkwardly angled their heads forward to look up through the slanted windscreen and its flanking quarter-lights, unable to see much at all. Stanley leaned back into his seat and wound down his window. The aroma of burnt wheat, its stubble freshly incinerated in the adjacent field, hung over the dark farmland, along with the occasional wisp of lingering smoke that lifted itself from the scorched earth.

"Let's lay down in the back," Alice said, aware of the gap between the two seats, and the awkward jut of the steering wheel.

"I can fold the back s—seat down?" Stanley said. "Although it's not comfortable to lie on. More like a wooden bench, to be honest."

"No," she said. "No need for that."

They awkwardly squeezed their bodies between the two front seats and into the rear, and lay themselves across the width of the car; Alice's spine pushed flat against the backrests as Stanley shifted alongside her, his knees bent at ninety degrees, the soles of his shoes pressed against the back of the driver's seat. Again they turned their heads up, to look through the long side window. Telegraph poles thinned upward from the pair's low perspective, to narrow tips from which wires drooped. Beyond that, stars — whose presence only became apparent in stages, like multitudes of nervous twitching rabbits emerging, one after the other, from an unlit undergrowth.

Alice broke the silence with a kiss — deeper, more intent than anything they'd shared up until now. She looked him deep in the eyes. "I want you," she said, forcefully.

Stanley paused, unsure of quite what she meant.

"But, well…" she continued, after a heavy sigh, "were we to … my mother and father would blow a gasket, if they found out. Or if, worst of all, it became *obvious*."

"I hadn't even …" he said, although he clearly *had*, before their lips locked again.

"I wish we could. Here. Now," she said, through bursts of kisses. She began to move her lips behind his ear, which tingled with warm, wet touches. "It feels right," she continued, her breathing heavy. "Don't you think so?" She then moved her head back a little, still staring deep into his eyes. "I so very much want to risk it. And yet …"

Stanley stared, mute and confused, his hormones surging, his mind racing; words harder than ever to form and emit.

"I just don't think I could wait much longer," Alice said, her voice tremulous between short sharp breaths. "Could you?"

"Wait? Not easily," he whispered.

"Oh, damn and blast it," she said, pulling away. "You know I'm not that kind of girl."

"No, I know you're not," Stanley said.

"I don't mean to tease you," she said, a hand placed tenderly on his forearm.

"You're not. Don't be s-silly. Maybe we just need to be married."

"Married? ... Is that a proposal?" she asked, half-joking.

"P-p ... Maybe," he replied, half-joking.

A silence fell between the two; the kind of pause described as *pregnant;* a pause for the thing they knew to avoid at all costs.

"I can't really ask you, can I? Not like this. Even if you wanted me to."

"What if I did want you to?"

"Do you?"

"Do *you?*"

"Of course," Stanley said. "Ever since we met, I've thought only of how lucky I am. I never assumed you'd s-say yes."

"But I would. I *would* say yes. So ... are you asking?"

"I haven't got a ring."

"I'm not after a ring. I'm interested in *you*, Stanley, not jewellery. Although" — she laughed — "at some point, of course. You won't get off that lightly."

"Of course."

"Well, then?"

"Okay ... My dear Alice, will you marry me?" he said, rolling out a majestically smooth sentence with no snagging syllables.

"I will, my sweet, sweet Stanley," she said with a crescendo of enthusiasm. The two embraced, then kissed with renewed vigour.

Moments later he felt Alice unbutton his shirt, pulling it wide of his chest, out onto his shoulders. "We can do other things," she whispered, now unbuttoning her blouse. Suddenly: warm soft skin up against warm soft skin, the smoothness and warmth a hitherto unimaginable delight.

She laid back, and pulled him onto her, and into the crook of her skirted open legs. "Keep your trousers on," she said, as she moved her hand under the grip of their belt, feeling him through his underpants. "Like this," she said, removing her hand to place both hands on his hips, encouraging movement as their pelvises met through layers of cotton and wool and silk. "Imagine our honeymoon, Stanley. Like this, but nothing in the way. Our skin touching skin, down there. You … inside me."

She held tighter to him, as if all points of their bodies had to meld together. He felt an instinctive desire to move, his lower body momentarily detached from thought. She squeezed harder still, as a sign of encouragement, pressing her fingers into his back. And then she pushed her open lips harder against his, and almost sucked away his breath with a kiss. Through the cotton friction of his underpants he thrust, awkwardly, straight-backed — his entire body like one unbending plank of hardboard, with no sway in the hips, no smoothness or steadiness of rhythm; his knees digging into the side panel, his chest a little wheezy.

They now existed in another world, silent and dark and detached. A partial hint of moonlight; the creaking of the wheels as the car rocked on its suspension, and the sound of their kisses, and whispered groans, and the imperceptible hiss of fabrics shedding tiny sparks. Beyond that, nothing but the buzz of insects, and the occasional call of an owl.

The peace shattered with the jarring sound of a car in the distance. Moments later its lights grew visible. At its closest the headlights drifted across the ceiling of the Minor, angling along the sidewalls and the wooden window frames. Stanley froze, his body flat upon hers, as inert as a toppled statue, as they held their breath; neither wanting to rush to move to a more innocent posture, lest they lose the moment, and yet both anxious about being discovered in a state of partial undress. But the lights drifted further along the country lane, straight past their turning, and in that moment she felt Stanley's shoulders loosen, before his clunky movements resumed. She didn't have to wait long — she could feel his muscles tense, and his rhythm change, and grow frantic, and suddenly he froze; then, with a judder, his entire body spasmed, before he collapsed, exhausted, into her arms.

2010

With a sigh and a sharp exhalation — hit by a cutting wind that buffeted the car door, pushing hard in resistance — Michael stepped from his hired SUV out into the inhospitable, open Kaldaðarnes landscape: big sky, vast panoramic tundra, rolling riverscape. He scanned the spread of ice-tipped cliff-faces in the mid-distance, and beyond them, the towering white *jökull* — the word he had learnt from Jóhanna — that stood as backdrops for the whole island. The land seemed to suck in the wind and rain, funnelling like the aeronautical testing tunnels in which he once stood, then swirled and shifted it in circles. The ground lay barren, but for moss and lichen, and the tufts and quiffs of wild grass, intermittently blown flat and crooked like bedhead. No trees, he noted, and then turned full circle, to try and spot one, to no avail.

After the coffee with Jóhanna in the café bookshop he'd hired the bulky silver SUV and driven south to Kaldaðarnes: the location, on the banks of the Ölfusá, of a British airbase during the Second World War, and an infamous series of disappearing aircraft. Jóhanna promised to be in touch soon, to take him to Sólheimajökull, the glacier they had discussed — *sunhomeglacier*, if translated as one word. Siggi also texted earlier in the day, to check in, but Michael left it unanswered.

He walked slowly to the adjacent river, aware that his body and mind were already on a different speed to when he left England just over twenty-four hours earlier, with the stark absence of hurrying people, rapid vehicles, constant communication; an absence of almost anything manmade, and, most pleasant of all — for the time being, at least — of all other human beings. He'd taken himself to a clock-less world, rid of the tyrannical metronome of the ticking second hand, and of other people's demands. Bar a few scraps of evidence — of occupation that came and went many decades ago — this tiny outpost on the map of Iceland, in its current state, could even predate the industrial revolution. Even Reykjavík felt like Tokyo compared to Kaldaðarnes.

Out of nowhere, Michael wondered what Ethan was doing at that very moment, and tensed up — a reflex, like a spasming muscle — at the sadness, sharp and deep, that he could not even take his son to the local park, let alone to an otherworldly place like rural Iceland. All the *experience*, large and small, which he could not share with the one other human who mattered most. Maybe one day he would get to tell him about it, show him pictures, if ever permitted some type of custody. Maybe he'd even get to bring him to Iceland; share a Coke and some fries in Reykjavík, maybe even at the bar-cum-café he'd visited the night before.

And yet, thinking back to earlier that morning, he found he'd missed his son even more when in the company of Jóhanna, back amid the gentle crowds on Laugavegur, with all the little hands reaching up to hold bigger hands as families window-shopped, and all those boys of Ethan's age — they appeared everywhere — smiling under colourful knitted hats with furry bobbles, or playing on the safe sidewalks in town. In Kaldaðarnes, it felt — in moments, at least — as if no life need exist anywhere else; and so, when making an effort to put daydreams to one side, nothing could be missed.

For a while, at least. He checked his phone, and as expected, it had no signal: a blessing, a curse.

He wandered over to watch the fast-flowing Ölfusá push again and again against its banks, lapping like coastal tides, but its briskness, its chaos, felt somehow calming. Floes of bluish ice slipped along in the current, but winter had almost passed, and across the island glaciers the size of cities, inching imperceptibly along, shed fractions of their colossal mass. The big thaw; not that it felt anything less than the coldest place on Earth with the windchill.

Michael turned back and walked to within the ghost-lines of the airbase abandoned after the war; left to recede, unneeded, into the landscape, while other allied airbases — such as Akureyri — developed over time, into national or international hubs. He sought ghost planes, at a ghost airbase.

He had excavated all over Britain, but Iceland felt like home, for no logical reason he could evoke; the only guess he could muster were childhood holidays spent in the Scottish highlands — the remoteness, the rugged terrain, the big sky — even if, by comparison, those outings seemed cosy and warm. With the earth — even if clear of snow — far less pliant, digging in Iceland made little sense at any time other than summer. Ground-penetrating radar provided archaeologists the ability to see below the surface, but putting spades in the ground, to access any anomalies, remained a challenge. With tens of thousands of uninhabited square miles at the heart of the island, and so few people even at its outer reaches — a country with the population of a large English town, dispersed over great distances — plenty of aviation history simply lay on the surface, untouched by scavengers and explorers. Perhaps to everyday folk it resembled junk, harmlessly discarded on unused pastures, hillsides and abandoned farmland; not quite enough metal to reclaim — the big stuff had already been salvaged — and not in anyone's way. Tourists — to a country that had yet to spark global curiosity — rarely ventured here, away from the well-worn trails. Much of the archaeology didn't even require a metal detector: scraps of aircraft and crumbling architecture — strips of fuselage and corrugated walls — clearly visible amid the stubbly vegetation.

Then, the *buried* aircraft all over the island: the many planes that, like those Spitfires and Hurricanes Michael helped to excavate back in England, ploughing into the ground at high speeds; burrowing metres below the earth, and covered over by time, if not with an immediate avalanche of ice, snow or soil. How many were lost under layers of snow and ice, up on unreachable plateaus? — mountainside crashes through fog and cloud. But at Kaldaðarnes, parts resided plentifully in pieces on the topsoil, along with the remains of the airbase, untouched by everything bar the elements: rivet-pocked strips of twisted metal; a tangled mesh of wires; oxidised springs, snarled in dull-green tufts and black rock; bent hydraulic pipes, caved-in cowlings; and rampant rust, almost bright-orange in hue, glittering in the grass, spread across sprockets and struts and cogwheels like a virulent pox. In the fine reeds of the riverbank sat a petrified ring of rubber, its jet-black form now a sombre grey: a worn tire, inexplicably — after half a century — still inflated. Michael kicked it gently, as someone might when checking over a car. It wasn't the first he'd seen survive with a lung-full of air.

The airbase, as he walked from one side to the other, remained roughly delineated, marked out by the stubs of walls and the indentations of long-fallen Nissen huts, and the US version, the Quonset. Detached to one side, an archway and a gate rendered almost a work of surrealist art: leading into, and out of … nowhere. Sporadic concrete limbs projected from the ground, inner spikes of rebar exposed, protruding like untreated compound fractures whose blood had turned russet. Curls and swirls of barbed wire lay pointless — keeping no one and nothing at in or out; nails jutting crooked from wooden splints; an obelisk of concrete, further carved by the weather, proud amid piles of collapsed and mouldered masonry. The runway — the very key to the entire airbase — lay under moss, its flatness still visible against the low, uneven land either side.

Disaster had struck here, as it had most places during the war. But there were mysteries, too.

Built in 1940 by the British Army, the Royal Air Force used the base from March 1941 onwards, until later US control. At least six planes were written off within its perimeter during the war, according to the records a colleague uncovered: three Lockheed Hudsons, a sizeable Armstrong Whitworth Whitley bomber, and two Fairey Battle light-bombers. No fatalities were recorded in those crashes, although in August 1941 one of the Hudsons — whose pilot, upon takeoff, attempted to avoid, of all things, an errant sheep — almost caused a major loss of life; in swerving sharply, the left-hand undercarriage buckled, and the unsupported wing collided with the runway, which in turn caused the plane to collapse and catch fire. The crew escaped and made it to safety, just as its cargo of depth-charges — destined for U-boats in the North Atlantic — exploded, obliterating the aircraft. A nearby engineer proved less fortunate, his arm cleanly severed by a detached propeller blade that twirled through the air like a gigantic throwing star despatched by a maniacal mechanical ninja. Two months later the Whitley, coming in to land, found itself pushed by a tailwind too far down the runway, speeding towards the icy Ölfusá. The pilot span it off the landing strip to avoid ditching in the river; averting a catastrophe, but in so doing damaging the aircraft beyond repair.

These were the documented crashes, but there had to be others: the ones that occurred in the dark or the fog, with no evidence ever recovered: those that vanished into apparent thin — or not so thin — air. This included the specific series of interlinked mysteries that had drawn him here, to research; a chapter, in a book about vanishing aircraft.

It all centred around the English printmaker, illustrator and noted war artist Eric Ravilious, who arrived at Kaldaðarnes on September 1st 1942, on the very day a Hudson with four crew members failed to return to the airbase from its patrol. The next morning, as an observer, Ravilious asked to join another crew of four in a Hudson that, as part of a fleet of three, sought to find the missing plane; only for the artist's aircraft to also disappear. Four days later, the nine men on the two Hudsons were declared lost in action; Ravilious' body never recovered, the planes never located.

Bracing against the cold, Michael found the past nipping at him as unavoidably as the bitter winds: a similarly blustery, if somewhat warmer day in the south of England, six months earlier, when his marriage — already suffering under a variety of pressures — finally collapsed. It wasn't a day he liked to recall, but it always crept back, until he found himself pondering what alternate courses of action may have produced. And yet to undo the foolish final deeds would not reverse the years of decline and subtle separation.

The only vanished person he cared about right now was Ethan. But until that could be resolved, writing about — even if unlikely to solve the mystery — Ravilious and the missing Hudsons would at least offer something to occupy his self-torturing mind.

2001

The comfort of routine: the morning cup of tea, milk and two sugars; left to stand, to cool a fraction, and to brew. Then, the teabag scooped out and squeezed over the sink — its dark mass lightened to a tighter, less-dense ball — and tossed into the bin. Putting the milk back into the fridge, Montague's attention drifted to the half-full jar of olives, its brine a yellowish hue that, unlike the little green fruits, sat full to the brim. Most of the remaining olives lay sunken in a clump at the foot of the glass jar, but a trio floated, one to the top, the other two hanging suspended in the liquid. All were strangely magnified, with an eery distortion, like a dozen lizard's eyeballs pickled in formaldehyde at a natural science museum.

The wireless — a term never updated in the Freeman household to *radio* or *stereo* — broadcast BBC Radio Four: a discussion about the tragic crash of the hitherto indestructible Concorde, in a Paris suburb. As the presenter talked with a retired pilot and two aviation journalists — an older writer of whom he had never heard, and a younger man called Michael Marston, whose work he occasionally read in a magazine to which he subscribed — visions of the stricken plane, seen the day before on the television, came sharply to Montague's mind, almost with a synaesthetic splendour: the kind of vivid-coloured imagery, with full clarity, that flashes up, but cannot be held onto; the kind that quickly fades, the greater the attempts to override, in the moment, the *actual* refractions of light cast onto the retina. Soon, he saw the kettle, the teacup and the kitchen worktop again, with just a ghostly image of the ailing plane lain across that reality, paling in his field of vision. Then, briefly, the images came to life again: that eery ultra-orange fire, bellowing from the engine, trailing a bilious pall of black smoke. Though only an amateur expert — in contrast to his father — he knew, or least told himself, that he would have foretold the outcome, if it had unfolded right in front of him; if he'd been a passenger in that Parisian car as someone else filmed the footage through the window. He then examined those very thoughts, and tried to balance his own judgement — he obviously already knew the outcome, and therefore possessed hindsight bias; but all the same, he would have said to the others in the vehicle "this will crash". It looked doomed. And yet the colours, replayed in his mind's eye, were so beautiful, and the sight of the plane out of control — simply unable to gain altitude — a shocking marvel; a terrible wonder.

No one suffered — not in his version. No one died, in this internal deception. Just an aircraft, on fire and losing altitude, that exploded, out of sight, on impact with a building: mere aluminium, mere bricks and mortar. He knew that to be a despicable lie, of course, and in truth, over one hundred people perished, including several in the hotel that halted its momentum; but the cognitive dissonance allowed for an appreciation of the *spectacle*.

And he knew that no one could be more traumatised by the up-close aftermath of such an event than he; he had neither the stomach nor the bravery to sift through the avgas-choked debris, black and oily and rancid, and collect the disarticulated limbs of children and the stray heads of adults; that is, if their entire beings — their bones and blood and organs — were not liquified in the cataclysm. That one ghastly photograph he saw as a child in his father's study, at the front of the manilla envelope, had proved one too many. How emotionally stunted, he wondered, were the men and women — although mostly men — who could do *that* for a job? Is that what affected his father? What did seeing such things do to a man like him?

Though the memories had grown weak and distant, Montague retained a sense that his father never spoke about anything other than the material aspects of his work — the kinds of planes that crashed, the locations, and the vague reasons why. After all, how could a young boy hope to understand such things? How indescribably horrific were the sights his father had to comprehend? In ascribing a callousness to the man who walked out on them, he hadn't really thought about how he might have got that way.

The tea started getting colder, although his mother's hands were not so steady these days — far safer to serve it a little more cooled. He himself preferred coffee, especially the type served in the café around the corner — a refuge from the house, the drink a form of rebellion from a childhood home that never stocked the stuff — but his mother remained a stickler for tea.

As a child in the fallout of their abandonment by his father, the routine involved taking a cup up to his mother in bed, before the acquisition of a Goblin Teasmade in 1969 had the service automated within arm's reach, and with a mere flick of a switch she could have the machine deliver the drink as soon as she awoke. But ever since she started sleeping downstairs, all those years ago, the old routine returned; he became tea-boy again, the Teasmade gathering dust upstairs on the bedside table.

As ever, his mother lay asleep, reclining in the armchair that became her bed. The sheet she used to cover herself had fallen over the side. She looked cold; her face bluish and sallow in the pale morning light that crept through the gap in closed curtains. She also felt cold to the touch, as Montague gently prodded her with one hand whilst holding the saucer in the other. The warmth of the tea, felt in the fingers and the palm of his right hand, contrasted sharply with the gelid flesh of her forearm, as discerned by the fingertips of his left. He had told her — as if *he* were the parent — to make sure she kept covered up. Although warm at night, it could turn chilly in the early hours. She would tell him to stop fussing, even though she only ever fussed him. She always took a while to rouse, so he prodded again, and said "Mother, time to wake up". The prod turned to a gentle shake of her shoulder, before putting the tea on the side table. He shook her, and shook her some more. Still no response. His eyes adjusting to the semi-darkness, the back of her thick neck displayed a purplish hue, gravity having pulled the blood so that it pooled in one place. Had she banged her head, he wondered? How did she get so bruised? Then he noticed the same pitted pattern along the bottom of her arm. He watched her chest, and could see no movement. She looked at peace, eyes closed, deep in slumber.

"Mother," he said, now with the voice of a child. "*Mother!* Wake up!" He had the strangest sensation — that he needed *her* help; her opinion. What did *she* think he should do? He wanted to ask her, but the only person he ever went to for advice now lay cold, still and unbreathing in front of him.

After making the necessary phone call — 999, to explain that "something was wrong" with his mother — Montague sat with her, holding her cold, unfeeling hand, until blue lights reflected on the walls and there came a knock at the front door. He hurriedly led a pair of paramedics — a man and a woman, each carrying cases of equipment — down the hall. As soon as they entered the room they stopped, and shared a look of recognition that Montague did not detect.

Having confirmed their suspicions with a quick inspection — postmortem lividity does not, as the name suggests, build up in the living, nor even the very-recently deceased — Montague argued after they said, "I'm afraid she's gone".

"No, she *can't* be!" he implored. "She was fine just last night."

With childlike abandon — hollowed out in an instant — he sobbed and wailed, strange and squeakily, as it became clear, upon their manhandling of her body, that all life had indeed ceased. As quickly as it began his wailing stopped, as denial crept back in.

The paramedics lifted her, lifeless, limbs lolling, onto a gurney — it took the man and the woman, as well as the male driver, to manoeuvre her sprawling mass — and having moved a grandfather clock out of the way, wheeled her out the front door; her broad shoulders, despite the straps, hanging over the trolley's sides, squeezed through its Victorian jamb.

Monty, now reduced to some younger version of himself, went to find his shoes. "Give me a moment," he shouted, as, covered in a sheet, the team wheeled his mother up the garden path, towards an ambulance that doubled as a hearse. "I just need to lock the back door and then I'll be with you."

"Sir, you can't really come with us to the morgue," the female paramedic said as he arrived at the vehicle, with just the right mixture of authority and compassion. "Is there anyone you can contact to come and stay with you?"

* * *

Simultaneously the end of his world and an overdue, blessed relief, Dorothy's death left Montague at a total loss, and yet finally free to live his life. The problem: he didn't know how to actually go about it. His cloistered, cloying existence came to an end early in his fifties, and, long overdue, he could perhaps start to find a partner. But how could he develop the right social skills, and perhaps more onerously, an attractiveness to the opposite sex, when whatever charms he once had — youthfulness, potential, fine sinewy physique, and white, if wonky, teeth — had faded and waned and sagged and yellowed?

In the end, as her health issues mounted and her weight ballooned, he had wanted his mother dead — to put an end to her suffering, but also his own. Yet when it came it hit like a ball-peen hammer to the heart. Escaping her overbearing, passive-aggressive tyranny felt like floating; the fear that arose from such an otherwise wonderful feeling of freedom that he might simply float uncontrollably away, as if filled with helium. Did he need those tethers? Could he survive unfettered? — like a horse, champing at the bit and pulling at the reins, bucking and braying, only to stand still and confused when finally released and able to run free?

She had denied him the chance to live *his* life. Other mothers would have said "Go! — go be a man, go make your way in the world, go start a family, go make your own mistakes. Live *your* life." Yet not once did she even hint that he should spread his wings; indeed, she constantly clipped them with tales of how she would die a horrible and lonely death without him. "I *hate* you," he'd think, in those moments, but he knew he'd hate himself even more if she did indeed die a horrible and lonely death without him. She wasn't evil, he always concluded; she just manipulated him to stave away her own crippling fear of further abandonment, in a life of crushing disappointments and betrayals. Her oversized worries about the outside world meant that, in her own way, she tried to protect him — with what she saw as maternal care — but with the caveat that, kept at home, he might then protect her in return. *Look at what love does to you*, she could have said about his father, although she never put it so succinctly. Should Montague ever grumble, the response, with her weak voice trembling, reminded him that she never asked to be left in the lurch by such a rotten bastard — probably now shacking up with some floozy — and rendered ill and housebound as a result.

Although not fully aware of it, Montague, in his own way, had become institutionalised; like a lifer finally paroled in his dotage he simply didn't know how to *live,* and felt too afraid to find out. Even months after her death he still felt scared to leave the narrow orbit of his previous existence — mindful about travelling too far, lest he be unable to get back to help her. His own freedom remained to visit the café around the corner, and occasionally, the Queen's Building at Heathrow, to watch the planes — that he could see more panoramically than from his house — amongst fellow enthusiasts.

For a while he even continued to run errands, stocking up on her favourite tinned soups until the cupboards were overflowing. He'd brew her tea in the old china teapot. Quickly he'd realise the error, but continue with the act all the same; the pot never emptied until the tea had gone cold; the soups still paid for, even if he realised his mistake before reaching the checkout.

Almost a decade on, he still felt her presence. When in the house he still heard her voice — not in some ghostly, disembodied sense, but within his own head, disapproving of his decisions, passing judgement, offering criticism, promising to make everything right again. But still he felt lost without her; the sound of her voice — a spectral echo within the recesses of his mind — never enough to fully reassure.

At first he thought of his father. Could Geoffrey still be out there — a remaining length of tether, so that he might hitch himself to *something?* He'd harboured such contempt for the man for decades, but suddenly it seemed, in the aftermath of his mother's death, that this elusive figure could be all he had left.

And yet even so, as he dealt with the uneven, shifting stages of fresh grief, the question quickly passed; resentment outweighing any possible desire to track him down. It would feel like a heinous betrayal of his mother to go looking for his father, the moment she turned her back. A *floozy* — that's the word his mother kept using. He's off with some floozy.

But all these years later … things felt different. After all this time he felt able to allow himself to also betray his mother; her once powerful voice diminuendoing year by year. In time he learnt, through trial and error, that he didn't have to slavishly adhere to her wishes, even if those wishes were evoked by nothing more than his own mind, echoing her ideas. He had learnt to argue back, and overrule the demands he imagined her making.

And yet, at the grand old age of 88, would Geoffrey even still be alive? What were the odds of a man living to almost 90? One in five? Even less? And what could Montague hope to achieve if he found him? To give him a piece of his mind for the cruel desertion? Or to find some kind of healing; to tie himself back, with reassuring tightness, to a familial anchor?

Could he rediscover that gentle man — that ever-more shadowy figure, with all photographs destroyed by his mother — who held his hand on the observation deck as the planes took off, and let him look through his binoculars, even though he could never keep up with, and focus on, whatever he was supposed to be watching? The man who bought him his first model kit, and patiently helped unstick the incorrect pieces of plastic his son had hurriedly stuck together, and who peeled the dried curving skins of glue from his tiny fingertips. The man who called him Monty — *my little Monty* — and whose goodbye one day, which he'd taken as just another goodbye, instead proved a final farewell, cloaked in normality.

1956

Huddled together on the floor: father and son, bloated with layers, silent in the blackness; the occasional drip of near-frozen water falling from icicles forming on the rims of the toilet and sink above. The cold had far less bite with the wind blocked out — its vindictive sting, its darting venom, kept at bay — but lying down hindered the circulation. Physically and emotionally exhausted, it still felt impossible to fall asleep after what Frank and James had been through. Their bodies simply would not allow it. Even so, it felt to Frank that they must stay awake at all costs.

"Don't fall asleep, Son, whatever you do."
"I won't."
"Promise?"
"Promise … But Dad, I'm scared," James said.
"So am I, my boy," Frank whispered. "So am I."
"Really?"
"Yes. Really. Listen to me — ain't no shame in being scared. You hear me? You can be scared and still have hope. Here, snuggle in a bit more. We gotta keep each other warm. Only thing for it."

Sharing such intimacy with his father, whose affections were usually displayed through handshakes, backslaps, shoulder-grips, sharp-elbowed nudges and the occasional hair-ruffle, seemed alien to James. He felt reduced to a young child again. Even though his father never kissed and cuddled him as an infant — perhaps he had done so when he was a baby, but his memory wouldn't stretch that far back — Frank would still pick him up as a small child, carry him about, give piggyback rides and wrestle on the ground; *manly* things, displaying his strength and size relative to that of a small boy. James — whom his father then called Jimbo — recalled raspberries blown on his cheeks, being lifted upside down by his ankles, pretend tippings into the coal-chute. The horseplay had obviously ceased many years earlier, although James couldn't recall an exact moment; replaced by this strange — and yet simultaneously natural — distance, that seemed to him to occur between all fathers and sons. The fathers of his friends didn't go around fussing and hugging their boys, and most certainly didn't talk about feeling scared; some of them were always away on business or with the forces, and didn't even see their children. Fathers didn't kiss, and they didn't cry: the natural order of things. And yet in an emergency, for all its oddness, such physical closeness made sense. Not just to keep warm, as a kind of protective paternal shell, inside which he could cower.

"I'm hungry," James said, stomach cramps snapping and pulling at his gut as he lay still, bereft of anything else to focus on.

"Me too. We'll look for some food in the morning, when it's light. There may be more suitcases out there — who knows? Hopefully someone packed something good! Imagine that, eh? Custard creams, chocolate bourbons, a tin of Quality Street — maybe all wrapped up as Christmas presents."

"Wouldn't that be stealing?"

"I think the owners would understand," Frank said with a rueful laugh. "Same as with the clothes," he added, before pausing. "If they're alive, that is. And the presents ain't gonna be delivered now, are they?"

"No, s'pose not."

"We can buy them all the biscuits in the world when we get home. Worst case scenario, there's always all those scraps of food on the floor just outside the door."

"That's disgusting."

"If you're as hungry as you say then, well, you'll be happy to eat it. As will I. It'll keep us going. Anyway, it's not like it's going to turn bad due to being left out in the sun, is it? It's *food*, and if necessary, you'd do damn well to eat it."

"Wonder what Mum's doing now?" James said, wriggling in the dark to get comfortable; feeling his father's hot breath in gentle waves. "You think she'll know something's wrong?"

Frank exhaled, its unexpected force — evoked by an image of his wife and daughter — causing him to cough. "I expect so. We should have landed hours ago. Hours before the airplane — well, you know. We should have been at your Nan's this evening."

The pair fell silent, and time drifted by in the unique way that it can when there's nothing to mark it: no clocks to track the passing of each minute, no shifting light or adjustments in the firmament — of sun, of moon, of stars — to explain the progress of day or night, and the transition from one to the other, with dawn's gradation from deep dark blue to plum, then orange-blue, then lighter, whiter blues; and then, with dusk, the same shades and hues in reverse. They had only the gentle ticking of Frank's wristwatch, occasionally audible above the muted wind and the eerie creaks of the fuselage. The ticking meticulously denoted each and every second, but — as mere sounds — did not add them up into anything meaningful and measurable. Just *noise*;

albeit noise that told them that life carried on, tick by tick, second by second.

They lay in the dark, floating in half-sleep — fighting its pull; the scent of perfume from an unknown woman's clothing mixing with the cigar smoke of an unknown man, to provide a sense of distant worlds of warmth and life, of cosy firesides and smouldering King Edwards in a pub, of the touch of a mother, a wife, a sister, a daughter. Beneath such smells, the unpleasant tang of the toilet, thankfully frozen.

Talking grew increasingly difficult: their jaws in spasm with the rat-a-tat-tat of chattering teeth. Their entire upper bodies ached from the persistent, percussive shaking — muscles tired and rigid, but still, without pause, their bones rattled away. One by one the soft-tissue injuries from the crash began to nip at them: the throb in the neck, the twinge in the back, the tenderness around the belly where the belt dug in. Out of the boreal storm, and covered in layers, they lay inert in a giant tin can in the subzero abyss; no sense of any warmth beyond a hint from each other's cool-skinned bodies, as the blood fled from the extremities and pooled in vital organs. Perhaps even the dead, in most climates, were not this cold to the touch; but, trapped in a metal mausoleum, they were, internally at least, warmer than corpses in a morgue, with their still-beating hearts, heating their cores as best they could.

And yet, despite the difficulty, to not talk, and to just face the silence, seemed even more painful. The fear, unspoken since earlier, of falling asleep and never waking up.

Such thoughts filling his mind, Frank fidgeted in his pocket, fishing out a near-empty box of *Bryant & May*s and lifted it above the makeshift covers. It took three strikes for his trembling fingers to light a match, as its bright-white phosphorescence startled their eyes — like staring hard into the midday sun — before it cooled and shrunk to a yellow halo that stayed on their retinas even with eyes closed, until it too, like the flame, diminished. Frank held the match above their heads as they lay on their sides, the flame now just a tiny orb shimmering around the tip. They felt the faintest whisper of warmth, blown gently like hot breath, but too fleeting to make any significant difference. Still, while it lasted it lifted the darkness. Frank saw his son's face: almost blue, he sensed, even though bathed in weak orange light; his pallor now puce, his eyes sallow and bruised with shadow, as the faint flame flickered. Never before had he studied him as intently as this — just been still and stared; at least, not since when, as a newborn baby, this as-yet unnamed boy arrived in his arms outside the maternity ward, and, flustered, he tried to make sense of a set of features — beneath a fine mop of red hair — that were in some ways instantly recognisable, and in other ways utterly unfamiliar. Almost fourteen years on, and even without his glasses he could see that the boy looked so grown up in so many ways, and yet at the same time resembled the frightened young child he knew a decade earlier, such as when awaking from a nightmare, confused and despondent. Frank had already left school at James' age — straight into a gruelling, hand-blistering apprenticeship — but in his son he saw someone wholly unprepared for such a life; and yet, of course, the boy didn't *need* to be ready yet, with the school-leaving age subsequently raised, with at least one more year after this. He wouldn't need to fall into blue-collar work, if he kept at his studies. He had that mind for numbers.

All the minor disappointments, accumulated from years of fatherhood — all the interests he hoped he would pass on but which just did not arouse his son's passions, all the failed corrections and adjustments to his own inherited flaws that he hoped to obviate with guidance and yet still somehow bequeathed — seemed shallow and irrelevant, as the match, with a whisper of smoke, gently extinguished itself, and as the imprint of flaring phosphorus and chlorate continued to fade from their eyes.

"I don't have too many left," Frank said, resting the matchbox between them in the dark. "I'll save the rest for tomorrow. We may need to light a fire — to send out a distress signal, or even just to cook something if we can find anything, and to keep warm." He sighed at the thought. "The air-sea rescue helicopters will be out in force tomorrow. Those wonderful Westlands."

"You think so?"

"I *know* so. Although, funnily enough — ain't no use to us now, of course — but the Rotodyne would be ideal for this kind of thing. Gonna change the way we fly, once it's ready. It can take off like a helicopter, then fly like a plane." He laughed. "I don't know how they dream it all up, but by golly it's gonna be the best thing in the air, Son — mark my words."

"Yeah, you told me about it before," James said, in a slight drawl. "I wish they'd hurry up and finish building them."

"Well, it's just a prototype right now. But those Westland things — they'll do us just fine. Sturdy as hell. Mountain rescue — the Scots, they know all about this kind of thing. They'll be out in force. The RAF, too, I reckon."

"You were in the RAF, Dad, weren't you?" James said, as if surprised at his own recollection. "So why did you never become a pilot?"

Frank laughed, taken aback by the question. "A pilot? My eyesight, for starters. Failed the medical. Was never smart enough, neither. I joined up and ended doing maintenance. But that was good — good enough for me. The pilots weren't able to fix the planes — they could fly 'em but they couldn't bloody-well fix 'em — and of course they didn't have the time to keep things checked. And yet without us there'd have been all these glorious pilots — talented blokes, I give you that, although some of them fancied themselves something rotten — sat in the mess hall, doing sweet Fanny Adams. So we did our part, kept it all ticking over. But I'd have loved to have gone up in one. At least," — he laughed, this time sadly — "until today. Now, all of a sudden — well, turns out I'm not so keen on flying."

"Me either."

"Let's focus on happier times, eh?" Frank said, fiddling with the matchbox in this pocket, to the sound of a handful of tiny wooden sticks cascading within as he flipped it round and round. "Do you remember when we went to Butlins in Saltdean, down Brighton way?"

"Of course," James said. "It was only three, three-and-a-half years ago."

"Feels longer. You were so young."

"I was nine, almost ten. Three-and-a-half years younger than I am now."

"Well, yes. Now that *was* warm. What glorious weather that was! You learnt to swim in the lido."

"I learnt to float a bit, then sink," James said, a little chuckle warming his voice, which turned to a cough in his red-raw throat.

"Then you cut your head open and that was the end of that."

"You told me not to run around the pool. But … I ran around the pool."

"You never listened to your old man," Frank said, good-naturedly nudging his son in what, in the dark, he took as his chest. "But crikey, the *blood*. Never seen nothing like it! Even during the war. You were sopping wet anyway, and then the blood just gushed out, and it streaked all down you. Looked as if you'd been attacked by a shark or something. A shark in a lido! How many stitches was it in the end?"

"Four."

"Just four?"

"Maybe four big ones. The cut was maybe only an inch long."

"Your mother turned pale as a sheet. Good job she was sat on the lounger or she'd have collapsed, bless her. She's good in emergencies, is your mum — the best. But not with blood. Anything but blood. I wrapped her best towel round your head, and for once she didn't complain at me for ruining her clean linen. Good job the infirmary wasn't too far, eh?"

"I still have the scar. Under my hair," James said, feeling for it in his mind, his hands too cold to lift out of the covers, and the sense of touch impossible through so many layers of material wrapped around numb fingers. "It doesn't grow quite right on that bit."

"They were still happy times though, weren't they?" Frank said, exhaling a sharp, gentle snort of pleasure. "You were right as rain the next day."

"I couldn't go back in the pool, though."

"Nope. And your mother was having kittens when you were running around on the concrete again. She'd have wrapped you in cotton wool."

"I was wrapped in cotton wool, kind of. At least, my head was. Bandages, anyway."

"She'd have wrapped the rest of you in it, too," Frank said with a sigh that captured the bittersweet contrast of fond memories of a happy family life, felt in warm sunshine, now evoked in a situation where they faced nothing but fear and frigid temperatures; no Casualty department just around the corner to patch their wounds, no mother and wife to hug and hold, no daughter and sister to complete their neat nuclear unit. Perhaps this too would make for a humorous story — the time they lived through a plane crash and, after a day, maybe even *days* of shelter, were eventually rescued; then, finally, the lighthearted fact that they had to wear women's clothing would, with the passage of time, become amusing after all.

"Funny, isn't it?" James said, in between a burst of vigorous teeth chattering, "all that blood from a tiny cut by the swimming pool, and yet no blood on us now — not really — after our aeroplane crashed."

Frank shook his head, his thinning hair rustling in the dark against the fabrics beneath. "Sometimes life just don't make no sense."

After a pause, James said, "What you said earlier — do you think anyone else is alive? In another part of the airplane? Will there be other people who survived?"

"I honestly don't know, Son. I mean, we're here in one piece, ain't we? So … maybe? But the rest of the plane — well, you saw. Even without my specs I could see enough. She broke up bad, didn't she? We we got lucky."

"*Lucky?*" James croaked, sounding incredulous.

"We're alive, ain't we? Luckier than the others is all I mean."

"The girl?" James said, a tremor in his voice. "Did you see the girl?"

"I did, Son, I did. It's … well, what's to say? You saw for yourself. Poor lamb. Should have listened to her mother."

Frank fell silent. James heard his father's breathing grow faster. "What are you thinking about, Dad?" he asked.

"Buttered bread with beef dripping. Warming my feet by the fire, sat next to Mum, Lucy playing something on the recorder," — he broke off to laugh – "although it used to grate on me, the noise she made with the bloody thing, *Three Blind Mice*, but I'd give anything to hear it now … Smoking my pipe. Mug of hot Bovril. You reading your cricket books on the settee."

"I'm so cold I'm not sure I can even remember what being warm feels like," James said, then shivered harder, as if the contrast — trying to bring actual heat to mind — proved too much for his body to take.

"It's far warmer in this here lavvy than out there, that's for sure," Frank said, rubbing his son's back through layers of fabric to generate tiny sparks of heat. "Who'd have thought we'd be grateful to be stuck inside some piddling little loo? Small mercies and all that, Son. Small mercies."

"You just mentioned Mum," James said, lining up a question that he would never dream of asking in other circumstances, "but … is everything okay with you two?"

"Why do you ask?" Frank said, surprise clear in his voice.

"I dunno. Just seems like you don't have much fun anymore. And you squabble a lot. And you don't — y'know — kiss and cuddle like you used to."

"Well … I guess these things are difficult. I don't really know how to explain it, to be honest. Life is … never as straightforward as you expect. And you and your sister are getting older now, ain't yer? We don't mess about in front of you kids."

James felt tiny specks of saliva spritz from his father's lips; the barest heat in the molecules cooling in an instant. It helped him picture his father's face as he talked, the awkward mass of lips that he himself had not inherited, but Lucy had. Usually embarrassed by his father's slight impediment, it soothed him here; a good man, who said good things with that slightly malformed mouth. "So, you're not unhappy?" James asked.

"No, Son. Not unhappy. Not at all. Just … *weary*. You have a lot of energy and a lot of plans when you're younger, and slowly it all just — I dunno — *vanishes*, I s'pose. Except you don't notice it happening. You get into these routines, these ruts, and you take stuff for granted. And then something daft like this happens and you wonder why you didn't take more care. You wish you said and did a lot of stuff different, because it matters so much — only it didn't seem to matter at the time."

"How did you two meet?" James asked, his teeth suddenly chattering more violently, so that each word escaped in a sharp staccato burst. "I don't think you ever told us."

"At a dance, in an old village hall. I was on leave from the RAF for the weekend. I cut in, and I think I made an impression, although mostly for my two left feet. She was a lovely mover back then, was your mother."

"Was it love at first sight?" James asked.

Frank laughed, an air of wistfulness evident in its tone and duration. "For me, probably. For her — well, let's say she took some convincing. But she came round." He then let out a shallower laugh, which blended with a sigh, and then a slight cough. "So, do you have a sweetheart, Son?"

"*Dad*," James said, defensively. He felt his cheeks warm, albeit almost imperceptibly so in the bitter cold; as if his body could find just a few spare millilitres of blood to divert to his face. "Give over."

"What's the matter?" Frank said, softly.

"I'm too young for all that," the boy said, his voice cracking high then low within the space of three words, all riding the rattle of the chatter.

"You're right, you *are* too young — to be going steady. But even so. You can still have your heart set on someone special. If she's a good type an' all that. You don't wanna be falling for no troublesome sort, always messing you about, blowing hot and cold, that type of thing. Not at any age. And you don't want to be doing the same to them, cause that ain't fair neither. So … someone you'd like to be your sweetheart?"

James stayed silent, before a quick "Um…".

"So, what's her name?" Frank asked, pleased with himself for decoding the pause.

"Valerie."

"But you're not courting?"

"God *no*, Dad. I've not even spoken to her. Not properly. But she smiles at me. And says hello. She knows my name. She's always saying hello."

"If she likes you then you're halfway there. Would you like to go steady with her, in the future?"

"I dunno. S'pose so. I'm not really sure how to go about courting and all that. Wouldn't know what to do," he said, suddenly aware of letting his father into a world he'd wanted to keep private; a world he hadn't even dared share with his mates, who would just tease him about it, even though they harboured their own — often more lascivious — desires for girls in the neighbouring schools. He had never wanted to lower his feelings for Valerie — and by proxy, to lower her too — to such schoolyard taunts.

"Just be yerself. That's all I can say. I was hardly a Romeo, but I've seen how it all works. Talk to her like she's one of yer pals — although maybe –" he laughed "– not about *cricket*. Take her to the pictures, then afterwards if you're stuck for things to say you can talk about the movie, can't you? But not the back row — you don't want to be starting any of that nonsense yet."

"No, Dad," James said, squirming slightly in the dark.

"So, I'm asking you to think of … Valerie, did you say?"

"Yes."

"Think of Valerie, and how it would feel to hold her warm hand come the summer. Hold that thought if you ever start to feel too tired and want to give in. I'll think of Mum, a hug from little Lucy, and being back in front of the fire. Home again. Safe."

Out of nowhere, his voice tremulous at the bubbling up of memories, James asked, "Sing it for me, Dad? Like you used to, for me and Lucy."

"Sing?"

"Yeah."

"Sing what?" Frank asked.

The boy cleared his throat. "*The … The night was mighty dark … so you could hardly see,*" he blurted, half spoken, half sung; the coldness, and the emotion, adding a marked tremolo to his partially-broken and tuneless voice, the melody barely discernible. "*For–*" a cough, sharp in his gullet "*–the moon refused to shine.*"

James heard movement beside him, felt his father's readjustment. "*Oh, Shine on, shine on, harvest moon up in the sky,*" Frank sang, skipping straight to the chorus, his voice warm and soothing, the words now wrapped around a melody.

James had requested it for reassurance, and it did indeed reassure. And yet it also conjured the overwhelming urge to cry. He tried to fight it, squeezing his eyes tightly shut, holding his breath in the hope that, like an errant sneeze, it would pass; but it just got bigger, brewing behind his shut eyelids like a tornado gathering up other tornadoes into its swirl. He somehow managed to keep it at bay, without extinguishing its presence.

"I love you, Dad," James said, for the first time in years; the words, though spoken through half-stifled sniffles, suddenly easy and natural to locate. Hitherto jammed tight behind some kind of unidentifiable, unfathomable blockage, it all washed free with tears.

"I love you too, Jimbo. Now, try and get some rest, but try not to fall asleep. I'll be here. We'll be okay. Trust me. Ain't ever nothing we can't get out of, you and me."

Moments later the sound of half-held sobbing once again speared the dark.

"Dad … are you crying?"

1940

Without doubt, Charlotte's most prized possession: the Imperial Good Companion typewriter, bought as a present just a few years earlier by her father, before his sudden death, and before her dream of a life of words metamorphosed into the life of wounds, of wards, of war. A machine of elegant beauty and efficiency, little wider than the sheets of paper she turned into its roller, and manufactured to fit snuggly into a neat wooden carry-box. The aesthetics of its exposed semicircular wheel of slender metal typebars totally satisfied, like the strings and hammers of a grand open piano, just awaiting fingers to turn them into music. The Good Companion, by stark contrast to a grand Steinway, produced just a single staccato note, whatever the key struck — but, to her ears, a dulcet tone all the same. Music lived in those clacking, percussive rhythms, as her fingers rode up and down, until — as happened every ten or twenty seconds — two typebars jammed together and required prising apart, like quarrelling children, pulled carefully back in line. Above the type-basket sat the simple carriage, and the feeding and receiving ribbon spools; the whole contraption a masterpiece of ergonomics finished in a matte black lacquer and stamped with the Royal seal. Just to touch it brought pleasure. The faint smell of coffee rose from beneath keys heated by her rapid typing — a ghostly reminder of a drink spilled a year earlier, that proved impossible to fully clean.

After months of procrastination she finally sought to type up her handwritten diary entries, to submit to the Mass Observation project. Dating back less than half a year, her earliest entries felt like they had been written in another time, by another person entirely; every single month since the evacuation of Dunkirk bearing a full lifetime of death and tragedy. How her concerns had changed.

She stopped typing, and, with a sip of cold Horlicks, stared at the rest of the handwritten paragraph in her diary. Her fingers rested on the keys, feeling — but not depressing — them, as if reading braille. Could she trust the anonymity of the Mass Observation project? She had judiciously reduced Pilot Officer Hallfreðsson to the more coded *V*, but she had discussed his nationality. How many Icelandic men raced to England for the war effort? If there *were* others, how many were downed RAF pilots, or had a name beginning with V? And of course, no other Icelanders, as things stood, could be traced to her hospital.

Then, the more general conundrum of how much of her private, innermost world could she dare share with the faceless editors of the Mass Observation project, and potentially, end up in some public anthology? The words seemed too personal, when starkly expressed on the page. It was one thing to write a diary exposing the soul, and even to do so addressing an imagined reader, despite then — as so many diarists preferred — concealing the document from prying eyes; quite another to send it off to others to read, and maybe — as happened with the two-hundred who wrote of their experiences of the coronation of the King and Queen — to appear in a book, such as *May the Twelfth: Mass-Observation Day-Surveys 1937*.

Her compromise: to continue to judiciously jot down as much as she could in her journal — recorded for posterity — and then select carefully edited highlights to type up for submission to the officials. She could censor herself, water it down. Detailing the life of a humble, anonymous nurse was one thing; it was another entirely to discuss fast-developing feelings for one specific and highly identifiable patient.

* * *

Viktor Hallfreðsson, his faced shrouded in metalwork, stared at Charlotte with contempt; what she took as pure hatred burning in his half-glazed eyes.

Without question, the worst part of her job involved a small number of cruel-to-be-kind treatments. Witnessing horrors proved hard enough; *causing* them — even unintentionally — proved harder still. The changing of dressings, in particular, brought fast and fierce to the patient such vivid echoes of earlier tortures — a repeating, over and over, of their very worst living moments, when they screamed in agony and fear and, whether church-goers or atheists, screamed for God to intervene: either to save, or to put a swift and final end to their misery. Except now, in a bed rather than a burning cockpit, most could not hope for the blessed relief of death. There could be no way around such essential procedures — Matron had sternly told her as much, early on, after she'd broken down in tears, churned up by the two-way torment. Cruel to be kind, she had been told. Get it over with, no messing about. Chop-chop.

It made little difference. Charlotte abhorred seeing their faces, screwed up tight, puckered in a grimace. It wasn't like an Elastoplast, that could be ripped off swiftly, for a short, sharp shock; to do that with skin already more fragile than thin sheets of sopping-wet tissue paper would prove an even greater torture, like pulling out fingernails with pliers. However, no matter how the dressing came away from a wound the result always, to her, felt as if every last layer of skin clung to its fabric, flaying the poor man alive.

However much one tells oneself that it is for their own good, at the moment their bodies course with pain then YOU are responsible for those horrid sensations, not some blasted Jerry.

The patient's pain transferred itself like an electric current into her nerve endings, and her heart plummeted. Each time she had to staunch her tears, to stop them welling before it showed. She *coped*; but never comfortably.

It had finally came Charlotte's turn to remove Viktor's bandages. She never wanted to hurt any of her patients, but he was the last person in the world she wanted to put through this kind of pain. Yet, for his own good, his dressings needed changing. She made the mistake of looking into his eyes —

through the matrix of steel holding his face together — at the crucial moment, as her slightly trembling hands unwrapped the gauze from around his wrist and hand; seeing what she interpreted as loathing burning back as the pinkness and the pus seeped from his flesh, with scraps of his skin, and the gooey fluids of its defences, adhered to the back of the bandage. That he could not speak — mute, dumb, behind grids of wire — left the strange sense of attending to a wounded animal: a dog, unable to understand the reasons for the agony so cruelly inflicted; as confused and uncomprehending as if she were callously kicking the creature. Logically, she knew, with his ability to comprehend English clear on previous occasions, that he understood her words, and that he surely appreciated the task's necessity. And yet, as if treating that dog, communication from the animal arose via a series of growls and howls and yelps through a constricting muzzle, and in the sorrow conveyed by darkened, frightened eyes.

In spite of the agony, once over, he twisted the corners of his mouth — as much as the armature allowed — up into the faintest of smiles. She felt her lip quiver; a sense that she did not deserve such beneficence.

Later that evening, tucked up in bed with the lights out, she would let it all go: the tears, flowing hot and fast as her heart tried to hold the conflicting concepts of his pain, felt as her own, and the mercy of that gentle smile, and the exceptional effort it must have taken to produce it for her.

She then lay in the dark, and without the distraction of sight — with just the blank canvas of nothingness — sought to bring his appearance vividly to mind. And when it slipped away, growing vague and elusive in a swirl of confusion or blur of other patients' faces, she found that she could focus her attention and bring him back, clear and true, for a few seconds more. Even through the bruises and cuts, and the armature erected like scaffolding around his face, she could sense his brooding handsomeness. Over a decade later, when she first saw a young Marlon Brando on screen, it instantly brought to mind Viktor's face. Back in 1940 there existed no such reference point. Wishful thinking, perhaps; the passionate young man of *A Streetcar Named Desire* a mere surrogate for her fading memories, and the lack of photographic evidence, beyond the tiniest sepia face, as one of a group of many men outside the dispersal hut, on a picture little bigger than a thruppence postage stamp.

Her diaries described Viktor's deep broad chin, with its delicate cleft. Eyebrows, where not burnt away, thick and straight, the same hue as his golden-brown hair. A strong nose — albeit, she observed, not strong enough to avoid breaking in the crash, but also, thankfully, not flattened to the point where he resembled a punch-drunk boxer.

A little crookedness will be its only flaw, and that 'flaw', I think, shall only add character. The most piercing blue eyes, that at times I think look straight into my soul. My body shivers at the mere thought.

Did he really look like Brando? Viktor's face seemed thinner, she would later recall, and his hair more blonde, but otherwise the comparison still made sense. But by the 1950s she could no longer lay in the dark and ask her mind to evoke his true likeness from the mist; she would get *something*, of course, but never as fully vivid, never as solidly Viktor. Why on earth did she not invest in a camera during the conflict, to capture his likeness? It seemed so obvious an oversight, all those years later. And yet the war, in that first year, mixed chaos, tragedy and endearment. Looking back, with time condensed — concertinaed into just the drama — life presented few intervals to stop and take pictures. It constantly moved forward at breakneck speed. Back then, words were her only recourse.

* * *

Elbows resting against the cold enamel of two separate wash basins, Viktor Hallfreðsson tried to maintain his balance on his one good leg — the other thick with splinted plaster — but Charlotte sensed the pain sending him giddy. The intimacy rendered her strangely nervous, and acutely aware of her surroundings. Dripping taps held their rhythm, each sounding out a different note: blip, blop, *blap*; blip, blop, *blap*. Every now and then the tap on the empty bath at the rear of the room sounded a deeper tone. Accidental music: accompanying her as she gingerly removed his pyjama top, which had in some places adhered to weeping grazes whose ooze seeped through bandage fibres and dried like phenolic resin. It revealed broad shoulders and lightly burned skin, and a smattering of fine blonde hair on his chest.

For the most frightful moment I feared he caught my gaze lingering, as, with a queer and unabating fascination, I took in his splendidly well-defined torso. Yet when I looked into his eyes he seemed so utterly unaware, as dope fogged his mind.

Due to staff shortages — a bout of gastric flu halving the number of available nurses and orderlies, and two new recruits having already quit in horror — she worked unaided, no one else present in the cold porcelain washroom, with its chilly ceramic echoes, its eery dripping taps. With cotton wool clasped in the forceps' pincer she gently swabbed his forearms with sweet-smelling ether — he squirmed — and then moved slowly down, past a tattoo of a dagger encoiled by a serpent, onto the raw scaly mess of his most damaged hand; his sore, tender subdermis, red like a brightly boiled lobster. The liquid anaesthetic gave off a faint mist as it quickly evaporated. He winced, squealing out what she took — perhaps imagined — to be "Worse ... than ... crash," through fixedly gritted teeth, the sounds generated by guttural echoes. Even stranger sounds slipped from his pursed lips — too odd for Icelandic, she assumed; as if pain had its own language to a man whose mouth could no longer form fully functioning words.

In the absence of smalltalk — a distracting and disarming tactic in such awkward situations — Charlotte became acutely aware of all other sounds, from the continued dripping of the taps, to the distorted distant squeaks of a trolley wheeled along an uneven corridor, and the hearty whistle rising from the path below the open window; the slightly mournful, bluesy tune of *If I Didn't Care* filling the room, echoing against the ceramic walls in an otherworldly manner. It felt like a reverie, a subtraction from time; possessed of a dreamlike quality, with everything at the edges fuzzy and muted. Discretely, she pinched her upper arm, and felt reality sting.

"You need to be one hundred per cent clean and disinfected for the operation," she said, gathering her composure, preparing a razor and a warm towel. "Hold steady," she added, although despite telling him stay still, she herself felt an uncertainty about the sureness of her touch; acutely aware of every movement she made, which in turn further inhibited her steadiness. She took a deep breath, chiding herself — *Focus, you silly fool* — and set to work. He looked on glassily as she ran the blade back from the edge of the burns at his wrist, at the point where the follicles had not been singed away. His eyes, almost hypnotised, followed the razor to the bowl; staring at the wispish hairs floating in the milky water as they slid from its blade.

One has to feel for the flinch — that dreaded moment before the blade takes skin, not hair.

"Right, that part's done," she said with a disguised sigh of relief, placing the razor and the towel on the metal tray. "Onto the next task. I need to take these down."

Charlotte could feel herself blush as she asked permission to remove his pyjama bottoms. Never usually anxious about eye contact, it suddenly felt impossible. She became the shy schoolgirl again, at the front of the class, asked to explain her personal poem by an impatient teacher. The surgeon had already explained the procedure to the patient — Charlotte had been present at Viktor's bedside, where she duly noted every detail — but in the fog of pain and fading opiates it seemed he'd failed to fully comprehend. He appeared somewhat confused as she prepared him for the first of many grafts. He held out his hands, as if to highlight the problem. Didn't he remember what the surgeon had said? The skin from the inside of his thigh, she explained once more, would replace the lost dermis of his hands, once it too had been sanitised. He seemed to listen, but said nothing. Had he understood?

Out the corner of her eye she saw him nod his head, and heard what she took as a mumble of consent. And yet, consent or not, she needed to disinfect his inner thigh, and with the operation imminent, there could be no argument. With that, she gently lowered the garment. Not at all unused to seeing male patients in a state of undress, this felt different. Even though her partner in this confined closeness — trying to hold himself upright — appeared far from lucid, the intimacy, to her at least, felt more than strictly professional. She felt a connection — ever since the day of the crash, once she'd had time to take stock of the drama.

Soaping his inner thigh, she tried her hardest to avert her gaze from what loomed in the corner of her eye — feeling as nervous and bashful as on her first week of training, when, in her diary, she had described herself as *Frightfully green*, and that she *could do no right*. She found herself holding her breath as she washed upwards, up to where the skin of his leg met the hang of his genitals. The more she tried to avert her gaze the greater the compulsion to look. She had never been particularly interested in the appearance of male sexual organs, which had always struck her as odd — almost alien — but now she wanted to know what *his* looked like, as if of vital importance; an additional intimacy, illicit and revealing; something others would not see. *Get a grip of yourself,* she said — to herself, but it half slipped out under her breath.

"Ehh?" she thought he said, glancing down, but his eyes unable to fix on hers as she looked up.

"Nothing," she added, turning quickly, guiltily, to cast the sponge into the bowl, before retrieving the razor and towel. Upon turning back she positioned herself so that she could only see his thigh, her head turned with an exaggeration. She held the flesh taut as she moved the razor back and forth, breaking away to foam more lather against his leg, and then to slosh the blade in the bowl, and finally, a wipe of the towel to clear any remaining gloop from the sharp steel edge.

Why was this happening to her? What was this man, without even realising, *doing* to her?

Everything felt strangely inverted. She had already been *inside* him: her fingers, deep within his warm, bloody mouth. She had felt the organ of his wet tongue, within her tautened grip — even if, at the time, it slumped as a limp muscle, dead and impersonal in his unconscious state as he lay at her feet. She had penetrated him, with a needle, through that very tongue. And now, alone together, she had taken off his clothes, and looked at — felt — his body. Washing it, preening him. How, she wondered, would his weight feel pressing down against hers? If unencumbered, would his hips start to move? Clearly so strong, and yet so vulnerable. So masculine, and yet so childlike, in his doped-up state. So innocent, yet he had, from what a fellow patient had told her — brimming with respect — killed several other men in the air. So fast and free, at speeds of up to four-hundred miles per hour, and now so trapped, so slow, so immobile; and doped to near-dumbness. His body, shorn of clothes, shook with the cold, his leg trembling under the strain. He was hers — fully hers — in these moments, utterly unable to escape her or fend for himself; and yet she felt terrified that, for all his remaining solid muscle and sinew, she may somehow further break him.

"Enuff?" Viktor finally asked, the gargled words strangely clear — could he be learning a new way to speak, or she a new way to listen? — as she set down the razor and tenderly dabbed his leg dry.

"Almost. One more coat of this stuff," she said, gently applying the ether to his inner thigh. "From me, at least. Then, off to surgery I'm afraid. But you won't feel a thing — I promise."

2009

The openness of the vast wheat-field on its eastern edge allowed the wind to whip in and pummel the western flank, where the small woodland — an island in a sea of grains — gathered in a tight huddle; gusts adding spite — and loose flecks of chaff — to the fine specks of rain. Michael Marston sipped at his Thermos lid of coffee, its steam stinging his eyes, but its warmth welcome all the same; a comfort within the autumnal drizzle.

Not a day conducive to outside work, the Sussex War Aviation Team had a permit, and an allotted time — a weekend, with day-jobs and partners to return to, lives to resume — and they hardly faced a typhoon or tornado. The work centred within a clutch of trees that partially protected them from the elements, but rain still dripped from the leaves and branches. Part of the spinney remained missing, torn through more than half a century earlier by the destructive dive of a MKII Spitfire. Even so, the area presented an awkward proposition for mechanical equipment, with two half-fallen boughs and a stump blocking the path.

Late September, the leaves on several trees were turning, glowing golden amidst the green, growing red and orange at the outer edges. One particular tree held up high an outspread of bare branches, atop a skirt of russet foliage, while others defiantly retained their full summer verdure. Spreading from one broad trunk were the raised veins and knuckles of roots breaking the earth, half-covered by moss and a blanket of flat yellow-green leaves, upon which lay a spattering of brown leaves, furled like the outer sheaths of a cigar.

Michael stood within the lattice of trees and looked out at the ploughed field, with its loose speckles of harvested hay, the shallow dome of a rangy grain silo, the church in the distance. To the south, close to where he'd parked, the remains of a dead fox, half in the road, half in the lay-by, its bloodless red and white fur browning with dirt and decay as flies darted about its corpse. Beyond the hedgerow, a tractor with a squall of squawking gulls at its rear, the birds rising and falling as if riding ocean thermals behind a trawler. In another adjacent field circled a dozen-or-so haughty crows, its trees — on the side that faced the road — shaped by passing lorries and buses, which whittled away the branches. In a break between rain showers, Michael watched the shadow of a single cloud shift swiftly over the wheat-field, soft-edged and eerily dark as, momentarily, the sun picked it out, before the light dimmed, and it merged into the blanket of grey.

He thought of Ethan, the one bright spark in his life, and then of Pippa, and how strained things had grown. 'Don't you dare go on this dig', she had said the previous night; and so, pigheadedly, he felt even more compelled to participate. Since the birth of their only child four years earlier he felt his wife forever ordered him about, although maybe, like a small cut on a finger that only stung once later observed, he simply noticed it more. He'd arisen early that morning, to drive to the site, eager to leave before she woke. He kissed his son on the side of his head as he slept — his warm, sweaty hair smelling of the previous night's shampoo, and damp, freshly-laundered pillow fabric — and drove in the dawn light, still indignant about being told what he could and could not do. Who did she think she was?

But hours later, remorse spread and hardened, which in turn softened his ire. He removed his gloves and flipped open his mobile phone, sending a short but sincere text of apology, with the promise to explain in full once he got home.

After what felt like endless deliberation — or perhaps just total indifference, and possibly non-consideration — permission finally arrived from the Ministry of Defence to excavate the Spitfire of Pilot Officer Edwin McPherson, who baled out of his burning plane — little more than a torpedo with wings, at that point — and parachuted to the relative safety of the woodland. The trees' canopy further slowed his descent, before a less-benign branch, snapped and sharpened like a skewer as his descending boot broke it in two, speared his thigh and lodged firm against bone. In great agony, he was rescued, and restored; unlike his Spitfire, whose heavy engine, with its propeller spinning at two-thousand revolutions per minute and projecting the fighter — with the additional help of gravity — at four-hundred miles per hour, bored itself deep into the ground. After the impact, according to witnesses, its fire raged on, but with insufficient fuel for an explosion. Once it had burnt itself out, the lighter parts of the aircraft, detached in the collision, were lifted from the smoking crater, as well as from all across the field and the spinney, where wing tips and horizontal stabilisers — and one of the rubber tyres — had skipped and bounced and cartwheeled; all carted off in their crumpled, concertinaed form. A few additional pieces were taken by souvenir hunters and curious children who were first on the scene. For this particular crash, that proved the extent of the contemporaneous recovery effort; no easy access for any heavy-lifting machinery, which, in the chaos of war, often amounted to little more than a simple lorry-mounted crane, or more frequently, a rudimentary wooden sheerlegs with pulley. And so the engine, and everything still firmly attached to it in compression, received a permanent burial, having dug its own deep grave.

In stark contrast to the overstretched nature of wartime recoveries, modern retrieval efforts — even though largely peopled by amateurs — had the benefits of superior equipment, and the relative lack of time restraints. During the war, they needed to retrieve the injured and if possible, recover the dead; and yet, sixty-four years after the war had ended, the dead still posed a problem — permits to excavate refused if the aircrew were believed buried with their aircraft, with unexploded ordnance another reason to deny access to a site. The late 1960s and early 1970s saw a fervour sparked by the Michael Caine movie *The Battle of Britain* — a wild approach at a renewed interest in the conflict, from which followed a backlash. The general public, stoked by outraged columnists in newspapers, grew irate at stories of how the bodies of war heroes were retrieved by amateur and often *amateurish* archaeologists rooting for finds with little apparent respect for the dead. It seemed that anyone with a shovel could go and dig up an aircraft and its entombed aircrew, with no special assignation as war graves.

During the war it required the location of a mere three kilograms of body matter — often from within a deep cavity — to constitute a 'recovery': able-bodied men just hours earlier reduced to the equivalent of three bags of flour. Mere fragments were often all that a coffin contained on its march from church to grave, along with a few rocks or weighted sacks to give the impression to pallbearers of a whole human being encased within the wooden box they stoically shouldered.

Over six decades on, men like Michael — as long as the corpses of the aircrew were officially recovered at the time — dug up planes in which men died, and in so doing, tried to tell their stories.

Michael felt the familiar vibration in his pocket, and quickly rummaged for his phone, flipping open its lid in eager expectation. Had Pippa accepted his apology? But rather than his wife, an old friend messaged to see if he fancied a beer later in the week.

* * *

Michael's very first dig, decades earlier, would also stay with him forever: a giddy time in his life, the weekend would also be marked by the shock of finding human remains; the moment he realised, in horror, that he held a scrap of a pilot's skull, as the inescapable evidence of death.

The summer of 1987, that dig also concerned a fast-moving Spitfire impact, discovered between the mediaeval village of Winchelsea, situated on the East Sussex coast out towards the

Kent border, and its nearby beach; the wider region known during the war as Hell's Corner, due to the ferocity of the action. Shortly before the dig he eagerly awaited the galley proofs of his first novel when he read something in a local paper about a group of aviation archaeologists who covered the combined eastern and western Sussex counties. That very moment, without even needing to think about, he phoned the number listed at the end of the article, and asked if he could join up. They welcomed him along, no questions asked.

Located on the outer edges of Romney Marsh, the crash site proved challenging — although not an impossibility, like those wrecks taken by the sea or lost high in mountains. The soft, silty loam offered little resistance to a spiralling Spitfire, and made for a deeper impact; the crater quickly filling in on itself, in amongst the reeds and tall grasses and herbaceous flowerings, with the smouldering wreck quickly extinguished. The wetlands — amidst the wiry flows of arteries and tributaries — quickly subsumed two thousand kilograms of machinery, as would a voracious quicksand. The records showed that the pilot had parachuted to safety: with no injuries, bar a stiff neck and slightly sprained ankle from the landing. He came down the other side of Winchelsea, and didn't even see his aircraft barrel nose-first into the marsh.

A true story; but somehow not *this* Spitfire.

In stark contrast to the mechanised slaughter of war, the site itself sat incongruously tranquil and picturesque, offering views of Winchelsea — the settlement originally constructed on a hill at a time when the surrounding landscape lay under water. The village, with its eighteenth-Century coaching inn, mediaeval church and old stone houses topped with thatched roofs, bore no signs of modernity when viewed from the crash site; providing the sense that, rather than hope to find a lost fighter plane, flight itself had not even yet been pioneered, and the date could have been 1857 or even earlier still. In another direction, Henry VIII's Camber Castle stood high over the low marshland despite its unusually shallow and strangely concentric walls: a nucleus of stubby conjoined circles, alone in the landscape. To the south sat the beach, its dunes dotted with grassy sprigs, beyond which, sand the colour of the smudges of the scraped-paint sun of

Turner's *Sunset off Margate Pier*. From their vantage point the team could see between the dunes to the wooden groynes, upright or slightly slanted in regimented lines from shore to waterline, and higher up, ancient sea defences: damp-kneed, mildew-tipped timbers, aligned shoulder-to-shoulder — like a massed battalion, holding its nerve — so that no invading ship might force its way ashore. Further beyond this, distant cliffs, and old, tired boats, moored as if washed up, paint peeling, as they bobbed aimlessly on their tethers. A glorious spring day, clear-skied and fresh-aired, a breeze proved chilly enough to leave dog walkers and the occasional sightseers the only people braving the beach, still dressed in winter clothing.

As well as Michael, that fateful dig included one further new recruit: Geoffrey Freeman, recently retired, and with a vast knowledge of plane crashes.

Michael and Pippa were newly together in 1987, fresh with love, ebullient with hope, and blooming with invincibility. He was 24, she just 19 — with a smart mind and sharply-bobbed black hair that, with its no-nonsense style, made her look smarter still; a hairstyle that suited her so perfectly she never felt the temptation to change it, beyond slight variations in length. For almost two decades — until 2005 — they remained unmarried and childless, living through alternating periods of closeness and distance, but always linked back together in some kind of harmony before growing apart beyond repair. Neither wanted children, and both saw marriage as an archaic institution, but as middle-age approached they yielded to both conventions. Marriage seemed less of an issue, but as she approached forty, Pippa suddenly felt an almost unfillable sense of emptiness, a void that, to her, could only be obviated by motherhood. Such a feeling would have made no sense to her former self; a way she'd never thought she could feel. She was not that kind of woman; not a maternal bone in her body. Her youth had faded, her parents had died, and her career, while still very successful, had grown stagnant in terms of surprises; she faced the eleventh hour of her reproductive powers, and a pointlessness hit home. Children seemed the only solution, and little time remained to buffer the decision; once it was over, *it was over*.

He harboured no sense of paternal urgency, and even at forty-five, and with his wife's belly swelling, felt unready and ill-equipped; all the years spent not having to think about such testing practicalities — other than to feel some smugness when seeing parents struggling with a toddler in mid-tantrum in a supermarket, and muttering *There but for the grace of god shall not go I* under his breath — made it feel like sitting a driving test before taking any lessons, having harboured no interest in owning a car. But, for Pippa, it suddenly became insistent; now or never. To delay further would damn the dream, and in those moments, Michael felt that such a failure would end their marriage too. She never framed it as such — no such ultimatum came his way — but it felt like either he fathered the baby or she would leave to find someone else who would. This sudden alteration in his wife felt dramatic and unsettling, but he also accepted that she had the right to change her mind on motherhood, and crave different things from life. No one goes from cradle to grave with the same hopes and aspirations, set on one single course. Like the characters in his fiction, real people had arcs, and went off at tangents. Some grew and developed; others, not so much.

Back in 1987, deep in the first flushes of love — the chemical rush of limerence — Pippa lived away at university, and at times the pair would go weeks without seeing each other. During breaks on those first digs he would take out his notepad and write her letters that he'd then carefully tear from the spine once complete. In other parts of the book he'd make notes on the excavations, including observations about the other members; albeit nothing too damning, lest they sneak behind his back to take a peak — an act he wouldn't put past the more rambunctious members. And working inwards from the back of the book he'd jot notes for his second novel — in contrast to his first, a complex patchwork of ideas that he didn't yet know how to pull together; knowing only that, at some point, it would all somehow collide. On that first dig he took himself away, down to the dunes, to eat his sandwiches and watch the tide spread itself with tiny flickers and sparkles on the sand, writing down his thoughts when the rain eased to nothing heavier than a fine spray.

1956

Hayes, Middlesex. Back in 1932, when teaching at a modest boys' school, George Orwell — no stranger to hell-holes in those days before his name-change from Eric Arthur Blair — labelled it "one of the most God-forsaken places I have ever struck"; albeit more for its bland conformity and factory-forced monotony than the serious deprivation he'd experienced in the East End and further afield. In the early 1930s the town struggled to cope with the rise in industry and the lack of housing, so new homes were constructed as quickly as possible, spreading out from the railway estate on which Stanley Smith later grew up. It grew into a grey industrial hub on the expanding outskirts of London, reeking of smoke and, on rainy days, strong coffee and chocolate, from the Nestlé factory chimneys. "The population seems to be entirely made up of clerks who frequent tin-roofed chapels on Sundays," and "the rest bolt themselves within doors," Orwell noted. By the mid-1950s, Hayes had started to emerge from post-war austerity, with many of the bombed-out houses repaired or replaced.

In many ways, the town existed as a mere junction; an intersection, on the way to places far more exotic, the Great and the Grand passing by. It led to the Grand Union Canal and the Great Western Railway, and to the Great West Road and the Western Avenue. By 1956, London Airport sprawled towards its doorstep. A nexus, at the heart of various transport spurs, and yet like a heart, best left unseen.

As such, it felt like the kind of place an ambitious young man would want to leave. Stanley Smith aspired to more, but Frank Carter — a lover of the simple life — and his family felt settled in the town they called home. Frank's son James followed in Stanley's footsteps at the cricket club, although their participation never overlapped: the latter's brief tenure a few years earlier curtailed by worsening asthma. Though a relatively new convert to the sport, James — his red hair adding a sense of fire to his rangy run-up — proved a very promising bowler, whose height helped to bamboozle the smaller batsmen prevalent in his age-group.

For all the infrastructural connectivity of Hayes, the River Thames, however, did not pass especially close. And so an industrial town had no softened, watery edges, beyond the banks of barge and flyboat-laden canals; no bucolic riverside vistas of leisurely rowing and punting. If the Thames had instead flowed directly east from the South Bank — as might seem logical, were a river urban-planned and efficiently coursed — it would have cut right through the heart of Hayes, but instead it snaked strangely south at Brentford and Kew, down through Twickenham and Kingston, and only later curved north, to return to its central London latitude; as if the uncouth industrial town had to be given the widest of berths, on the way to Windsor, Eton, Bray — where the views cost serious money, and the monarchy played.

And a certain kind of ordinariness befalls any town with roads named *Keith* and *Trevor* at its core — falling just either side of perhaps its most remarkable feature: The Old Vinyl Factory, and the EMI complex as a whole — monolithic buildings emblazoned with *HIS MASTER'S VOICE* — which contributed to giving the world television, radar, stereo technology, and the switch of record speeds and sizes from 78s to 33s and 45s. It pressed the albums and singles of big-name recording artists of the day; and within a few short years, those of the Beatles too.

Across from the EMI complex, on the other side of the railroad tracks that in 1935 provided the setting for the world's first ever stereo sound film, *Trains At Hayes Station* — a steam locomotive trundling past the Nestlé factory — stood the Fairey Aviation works, which supplied the RAF its legendary Swordfish, and which now developed record-breaking fighters and innovative compound gyroplanes, set to revolutionise the industry.

* * *

After the final whistle of the week sounded, Frank Carter rushed out of the Fairey foyer into the bright July daylight, the sun still high in the late-afternoon sky. He brushed past Stanley Smith, a draughtsman he knew only by sight — and the occasional *Hello* — hurriedly re-entering the building to grab some forgotten paperwork; neither recognised the other, in their haste. Both were finished for the weekend.

Stanley's fiancée sat patiently in the car outside. He had recently graduated to the fully-qualified wages of a man emerging from both his apprenticeship and the following "improver" phase, and with Alice contributing a reasonable wage from a new job, they could afford to set about buying a beautifully-set but semi-dilapidated detached house abutting fields and woodland in nearby Harefield. Until he could officially carry her over the threshold, they wanted to take another chance to view the property destined to be their marital home, to plan the necessary renovations.

They drove through Uxbridge and on into Harefield; past the hospital — a pioneer in developing heart surgeries — with its detached tuberculosis sanatorium, until they came to the last house on a stretch of country lane, beyond which stood fields and woodland, and a fine-running brook. Generally structurally sound, the property had long-since fallen into disrepair: in need of new windows, floorboards, carpets, as well as a kitchen and bathroom; some replacements more urgent than others. The entire decor looked old and tired, and often unclean. The previous owner, a man in his eighties, had failed to maintain or update the property, and even to clean it properly as he neared the end of his life; only escaping dying in the house by a couple of days, when a neighbour helped organise a transfer to the nearby hospital to oversee and manage his final moments. Even for a bargain price, Alice did not like the idea of sleeping in a room in which a man had recently died, so at least that didn't transpire. Still, it left a daunting amount of work. While clearly no skilled artisan or tradesman, Stanley possessed a reasonable handiness — and a clear talent for problem solving — to undertake much of the repair work, while Alice would concentrate on the decor, fixtures and fittings. Even in a state of relative dereliction, both could see the potential, with views — certainly to Stanley, after his railway estate youth — that seemed almost priceless; as well as air much fresher than the smoky town that often triggered his asthma. While a little further from their places of work than ideal — a fifteen-to-twenty-minute commute — nowhere else had come close to matching the value they could get for their money. Once married — the wedding now just a week away — they would take possession of the keys.

1940

Weather-permitting, it became part of Charlotte's routine to wheel Pilot Officer Hallfreðsson out into the verdure of the hospital grounds, her patient propped up in what seemed little more than a cumbersome, over-sized wicker perambulator, the contraption squeaking over the cobbled stone path flanking the quadrangle as she edged it forwards. While other nurses desired to be his chaperone, she asserted herself to become his main promenading partner. In those early walks, as she pushed his muscular mass — albeit a physique gradually losing its tone through inactivity and an inability to eat solids — he could say very little; she had to lean forward, over his shoulder, to push her face beside his, and try to discern the sounds echoing in his gullet. With practice — on both their parts — he could form words in this throat, to expel through clamped-together teeth — to ventriloquise — and she did her best to decipher them. She'd repeat what she thought he had said, and he would shake or nod his head in reply.

She had learnt that his mother hailed from Scotland, and had moved to Iceland in her early twenties after meeting his father, a fisherman from a northern village — albeit its name, Akureyri, she could not meaningfully unscramble from the sounds. His father's expanding fleet of vessels had taken him on a trip to the Isle of Arran, where his mother lived. She — Maud — taught her son English, with a thick Scottish brogue; although he had seen many American movies in the later years of his childhood, at the one local cinema, and found the accents influencing the way he spoke, as his peer group followed suit. At least, that's what Charlotte could decipher, in a strangled tone that made it hard to detect any accent and, at times, any meaning at all.

That was, until now. This proved a red-letter day: the first without the armature, the jaw now fully unwired.

The large communal gardens stood peaceful after the morning's aerial hostilities. By the time the nurses and patients ventured outside all aircraft had gone — as if it were merely a break for lunch at the Oval. Despite the calm, the last of the curving, cross-hatched contrails — slowly spreading and dissipating — still hung in the sky like the fraying wool of an old Aran jumper.

The less-seriously injured, and those more advanced on the road to recovery, lounged on patchwork picnic blankets laid across the grass in the late September sunshine, their crude wooden crutches and walking sticks beside them, while other up-patients sat in wheelchairs — in some cases, used more like portable deckchairs — behind bright red wind-breaks; all casually reading books and newspapers, or playing draughts, as if on a sandy beach, in a time of peace, insouciantly listening to the tides rush ashore. They checked the previous day's dogfight scores in the way they would once have done with the cricket, buoyed by the positive results as, like injured teammates forced to sit this one out, they rooted for their team. Most were dressed in regulation hospital blues — cobalt suits, white shirts and red ties — except for a couple of men in striped pyjamas and tartan dressing gowns, one of whom perused lists of actual cricket scores, from matches the year before, via the distinctively yellow-covered, brick-thick *Wisden Cricketers' Almanack*. Also shielded from the wind were two full-sized beds, transported outside on their wobbly castors, so that their bed-bound occupants may experience the reviving properties of a sky-full of fresh air — once the cordite and avgas fumes dissipated — on such a glorious day. If warm and dry, they rotated 'outside' beds, so that each man, unless in too serious a condition, could have his turn once or twice a month, before the winter set in.

The war had scarred these airmen in all manner of ways, but in such moments, when the sky stood quiet, the conflict appeared a million miles away. Some, Charlotte sensed, felt a nagging impatience at the speed of their recovery, like caged animals eager for freedom, to do what came naturally; men who were damaged, but far from broken. Men both burnt and burning with a desire for revenge, to even the scores. Others, it seemed, hoped to stay indefinitely, the thought of a return to action producing a churning in the gut — even terrors in the sleep; although most would never openly admit such fears, except perhaps to a trusted nurse in private. They wore brave faces, donned like masks — to anyone but their tender attendants, for whom the façade could slip. Others were ambivalent about returning to duty, simply wanting to escape the repetitive hell of countless surgeries, and the confinement in a cramped ward; happy to go wherever sent.

Charlotte wheeled Viktor to an empty bench, set back from a row of newly planted saplings, with a view over the lush hospital grounds, all the way to the adjacent airbase; and in the other direction, a slither of sea sliding out to the horizon. They engaged in general chit-chat, discussing the weather and other such trivialities. His accent, now fully-throated and open-mouthed, had a clear Icelandic tang, with certain words stretched with inflections and odd emphasises — of became *off*, have became *haff* — but his vocabulary seemed generally impressive and his syntax mostly that of a native English speaker, with the occasional aberration thrown in. At times he almost sounded Scottish, before the strange Norse twangs returned, or the jarring, conspicuous pronunciations or slang lifted from American movies. With that unique mix of influences — and the deepness of the timbre — no one, to Charlotte, could ever sound quite the same.

Bombs had fallen on nearby towns, and men — on wards and operating tables — were dying a mere matter of yards away, and yet here they sat, talking of how 'perfectly splendid' it was for the time of year. At first, with so much to ask him — now that he could speak freely — Charlotte could not hone in on any one particular subject, so the weather sufficed. And it *was* such a remarkable day that it bore repeating, as, with his wheelchair parked next to the bench, she held his upper arm and softly exhaled, the last of the tension of work — for now, at least — expelled. She let her body fall perfectly still, to let the world wash over her.

Viktor, by contrast, soon began shifting about in his seat, constantly readjusting himself, redistributing his weight with the points of his elbows. Did he do so to alleviate pain and discomfort, she wondered? — or had he the restlessness of a man for whom, after life in the cockpit, time now expired at a different rate? A man acclimatised to travelling at almost four-hundred miles an hour, for heaven's sake; up in the clouds, no less, when few experienced much beyond forty miles per hour, on terra firma. Earlier that afternoon he referred to his Spitfire as 'his falcon', as, on the ward, she helped lever him into a contraption that he likened, by contrast, to a dodo; but she sensed that *he* felt tethered at the talon; a bird of prey, fettered to a post on the ground.

I sense with such sadness that the sedentary life shall not suit someone so habituated to red alert. The way he looks at the sky — it's like he wants to return there, like he belongs above the clouds. A place I most fear to go.

"What is it like up there, in the midst of the battle?" she asked, craning her neck to the skies as she spoke — at sparrows and seagulls circling and gliding, free and at peace on the gentle breeze, arcing and looping and diving, perhaps simply because *they could,* in the absence of dogfights. He gave what she took as an odd look, as if it were the silliest question imaginable.

"It is a totally different world," he said, eyes widening. "Such beauty, the whole sky is yours, the clouds … then chaos and noise. Planes — British, Jerries — speeding across the sky. Whew! Who is who? Who is delivering the fatal shot? You just pray, in the back of your mind, that it is not your turn to be hit. But you cannot worry, or you will freeze."

Charlotte didn't struggle to imagine him at great altitude, strapped into the cockpit of his Spitfire, busily checking controls and scanning for signs of enemy fighters. Even with nothing more threatening than a finch swooping into the skies he habitually rotated his head clockwise, then anti-clockwise — less falcon and more owl, scanning for prey. The fingers of his right hand twitched beneath their bandages, as if on standby to depress a trigger.

"It is so hard to see the bastards, moving so fast, coming in from the sun. You must have a rubber neck — that's what the pilots call it," Viktor said, exaggerating his own movements.

"Like an owl?" Charlotte said, thinking back to her observation.

He laughed. "*Please!* — more like the white-tailed eagle, from my homeland, if you do not mind. Owls are not so … what is the word?"

"Fearsome?"

"Yes, fearsome. But also *majestic*. Eagles, falcons — whichever. You become one with a machine like a Spitfire — it is you, you are it. Still," he added, his eyes dropping, his head bowing, as he looked over at the hospital roof, "I became the prey. I was shot down out of nowhere. I was the helpless bird."

He described to a captivated Charlotte how he never saw the Messerschmitt ME109, with its sinister yellow nose, until it proved too late — dipping down on him from a cloud, suddenly bobbing at his rear — by which point bullets had riddled his fuselage and pierced his engine, and the victorious German fighter climbed away, job done. Viktor thought he could land the plane, but then the fire spread, and in those moments, as the controls began to fail, he resigned himself to death.

"I cannot believe how very brave you are," Charlotte said, squeezing his upper arm; seeing, with mental clarity, the terrifying drama, as if rewatching a movie.

He let out a slight hiss, like the release of a pneumatic brake. "Brave? Ha! I do not think so. *Stupid*, yes."

Charlotte looked alarmed. Was he joking? It didn't feel like it. "Stupid? Why ever so?"

"Because when up there we are too dumb to be worried. It is a sense of untouchable … *untouchableness*? Is that a word?"

"I believe so. I certainly know what you mean."

"Maybe some men have the terrors. I have seen some ignore the scramble bell ringing. They sit, frozen stiff, although I am not looking back at them for long. But to me, I feel so in control up there, and … well, I never felt like I will be shot down. Not once." He shook his head. "You cannot think about dying, but I think that if we do, we do not fear death itself. God, if he exists, will take us. When it is over it is over. But the *dying* — maybe that is something to fear."

"Yes," said Charlotte, feeling the words at her core. "So, did you ever think of dying and what it would be like?" she asked, resting her hand over his bandaged forearm, just above where the wounds were raw. "When your aircraft was on fire? I think it to be ever such a human thing."

"Yes … and no," he said, staring blankly ahead, unable to look her in the eye whilst uncomfortably putting his mind back into the cockpit; before closing his eyes, to remember, or perhaps to stave off the most vivid of those visions. "I could not handle the fire any more. I would happily have died to feel that no more, that is for sure. But I did not think about what death would be like, or what might follow. There was no time. As a child I once held my hand over the stove for as long as I could manage, and I remembered that instinct to pull it away when it got too hot. You do not even think at that point, you just pull it away, as you know it is too dangerous to keep it there. Your body does it for you. I needed to get out of the fire, but I could not crash into the hospital. I was resigned to death, for sure … but then I was suddenly going to kill people in this building. It is better to die in pain than to kill nurses and doctors and men already badly injured, I do think."

"Thank you," she said, trying to keep track of his darting eyes that were now wide open, and feeling a hint of moisture collecting in her own. "I think it shows that you are indeed *most* brave, and not in the least bit stupid."

"Hmm," he said, in a neutral tone; not disagreeing, but not agreeing, either. Charlotte didn't know how to react, and so said nothing. With her hand resting on his forearm, she gently rubbed her thumb against his inner elbow. "Here is worse, though," he said, sharply, over the gentle chatter of birdsong, the soft rustle of leaves on the slender saplings. "I feel so helpless here. A cheat. A *failure.*"

"Don't be so silly," she said, taken aback at the venom in his voice. "Please. I shall not hear such tommyrot. You are a hero, first class — and let that be the end of it."

1956

Sighing with a sharp flinch of anxiety, Stanley stared down at his brand new shoes; further polished into black mirrors whose toes, amid the delicate curlicues of decorative stitching, reflected the clouds threatening to converge overhead. The beautiful morning of his and Alice's wedding day — the sun rising into clear blue skies, viewed through the open window after he nervously awoke alone at dawn — had been hijacked by an ominous weather front, threatening to dampen the scene outside the thirteenth-Century church.

In keeping with his general fastidiousness, he arrived early for his own wedding, just as he'd arrived early into the day itself; a walk of less than ten minutes from his parents' house taken with thirty minutes to spare. His mother and father would soon follow — they took care of the final adjustments to their clothing — and he planned to meet his best man, Eddie — who lived close by — on the high street before turning down the path to the church, which Stanley kept safely in view; a few early congregators already lingered outside.

It felt like he'd been walking in someone else's shoes, their newness unsettling. A fresh chapter, but should it feel this alien? The new suit and shirt also felt too starchy, hemming him in. It almost felt like fancy dress: playing the role of a smart, grown adult, ready to take on the requisite responsibilities. In no sense did he feel even remotely *princely* — yet he awaited, as he saw it, the young princess. To his mind, Alice was the real thing, and he was just a plain man in a fine new suit.

With so much time to spare he stared across at the familiar church — beyond the skewering stones and monuments — with its tall square bell-tower of flint and Reigate stone, identical inset blue clock faces on each of the four walls. The church stood within a capacious graveyard populated by yews, oaks, beech, ash and horse chestnut, all situated beyond an elaborately roofed lychgate. Amid the industrialised town — with its endlessly spewing chimneys — it felt like he could cross the road and enter into some kind of bucolic Eden. Directly beyond the churchyard lay the sprawling Barra Hall Park, with its banks of red roses in flowerbeds kept by a scrupulous park-keeper, to where they hoped to alight after the wedding for some additional photographs; and adjacent to that, the cricket club, with its lush outfields and air of Sunday leisure, where, briefly — and unsuccessfully — he once tried his hand at the game.

"Hello there," said a voice, and Stanley turned to see someone he recognised but could not place — at first thinking the man, and his family, were distant relatives, eager and early for the nuptials. But no, it was Frank Carter, the lathe engineer from work — unrecognisably smartly dressed, freed of his oily overalls — out for a walk with his wife and his two children: a son and a daughter. Even so, for a moment — his thoughts lost in the potential unfoldings of the day — Stanley still did not recognise the man. Then the roundness of that bespectacled face and the plumpness of the lips struck a chord, and dragged him away from reveries; in his mind briefly flashed the image of Alice's altogether more alluring face, as it might appear later at the altar, and with it a sense of impatience at all this stalling. The man's son stood tall and thin, his red hair short and bright; yet the girl — short, with a slightly tomboyish style despite a skirt and a round face — carried an older countenance. The man's wife looked plain and stout, but warm and sincere.

"She'll be a beauty, won't she?" Frank said.

"P-pardon me?" Stanley asked, thinking about Alice.

"The Rotodyne. What a machine she is. Coming along nicely."

"Oh, yes. Indeed," Stanley said, nodding.

"Not long now," Frank said, smiling.

"No."

"Dunno about you, but I think we'll all be flying about in Rotodynes one day."

For a moment, as he pondered the vision of skies brimming with compound gyroplanes, Stanley worried that he'd made some terrible faux pas in not inviting his colleague and his family to the wedding — before comforting himself with the knowledge that, given how little they knew each other, no such invite made sense. This already proved the longest conversation they'd ever had.

Frank's wife, Gloria, tugged at her husband's arm, gesturing towards Stanley's boutonnière with a nod of her head. "I think the man is busy," she said, aiming for subtlety.

"Beg your pud?" Frank asked with a downward glance at his wife, and then, the penny belatedly dropping, added, "Oh, a big day?"

"Yes, getting hitched. Ss-small affair, though — friends and close family."

"Of course," Frank said, amiably. "Some blokes ain't happy about the old ball and chain — always griping and whatnot — but marrying Gloria is the best thing I ever did. Well, may I be the first to congratulate you," Frank added, offering his hand, which Stanley shook. "Best of luck, dear," Gloria said, as she led her husband and children back on their way.

Guests continued to arrive — some by car, others on foot — but Stanley stayed on the other side of the road, half-detached. The guests were early; the wedding before theirs still underway. Eddie, however, already ran a couple of minutes late for their pre-wedding rendezvous. Stanley didn't even recognise many of the people gathering; Alice's distant relatives, he presumed, and perhaps some of her old schoolmates. Her closest friends travelled with her as bridesmaids, in the car behind hers in the procession, making their way from the family home. As if mirroring their financial status, his family — grouped together, as his parents met with his aunts and uncles — seemed much smaller in number than hers, while his friend-group also seemed thin. Even Eddie, as his best man, could not be deemed an extremely close friend.

His speech impediments, and his allergy to sports, left Stanley as a bit of a social outcast at school; not unpopular due to anything he actually did, he gained the air of someone to avoid for fear of guilt by association: the mentally retarded boy to steer clear of; a boy who, in truth, was much brighter than most of his tormentors who called him stupid. He just struggled to articulate his thoughts. They could share their halfwitted ideas with their limited and often vulgar vocabulary, yet act superior. No one actively disliked Stanley, but they deemed him an oddball.

Unsuited to speaking, and yet too sharp-minded and curious to be a labourer, his ideal career required infrequent vocal communication. He liked to write, until forced to read his work in front of the class. Drawing seemed easiest, as it usually didn't require any accompanying oratory; others may be asked to discuss what they'd drawn, but the teachers soon stopped asking him and just admired his draughtsmanship. Indeed, technical drawings — that also made use of his mathematical mind — required the clearly written listing of details, to prove self-explanatory. After all, he wouldn't be on hand on the factory floor to decode the schematics — they needed to convey the full information. As such, despite narrowly failing his 11-plus that kept him out of grammar school, he later passed a particularly testing technical examination in order to attend Southall Technical College, that offered apprenticeships at various local giants of industry, including EMI, Fairey, and AEC — the company that manufactured the famous red London buses.

Despite his parents intentions, he grew up an only child: subsequent potential siblings miscarried, with one, a sister — even more distressingly — stillborn. As such, he had no brother to fall back upon as a best man. Part of no sports teams — the only attempt a failed stab at cricket — there were thus no teammates, and his work colleagues were mostly older men, with whom he had little in common; and anyway, he avoided smalltalk at the office and on factory floors, as he did in almost every other area of life. The incessant chatter required in pubs and the works' club also kept him away, or if present, at the periphery. He liked dances, as well as the cinema and the theatre, with silence not just preferable but often required — where others did the talking.

Some of the pals he used to knock about with on the estate, or zip around with on pushbikes in town and into the surrounding countryside, had moved away or joined the forces for their national service, as had some fellow students at the technical college, and so it fell to Eddie to do the honours. Never an especially close friend, he inadvertently led to the incipience of the relationship: the pal who, as luck had it, ran into an ex-girlfriend at the funfair the night Stanley met Alice; and as such, Eddie's disappearance helped open up a path of fate to where, left alone — and thus, spared the judging eyes of anyone who knew him — Stanley felt free, at the steps to the Ferris wheel, to make his approach. Indeed, in childhood and adolescence, Eddie could frequently just *be there*, amid a group, without invitation. A year younger, he could be something of a straggler, a hanger-on; but then he'd disappear with his own pals from school, or to play football and cricket with friends, and at organised clubs. They'd sometimes scrump together, jump on the trolleybuses, ride their bikes down the Grand Union towpath, catch tiddlers for jam jars from the brook or try to catch actual fish with makeshift rods in the canal. Stanley recalled Eddie's presence the solemn day the recently-deceased King passed under their feet in plumes of smoke and bellowing steam, carried from Paddington to Windsor in a coffin train carriage, as the boys stood on Bourne's bridge, in the shadow of the giant bright-white EMI factory complex.

In the middle of recollections of childhood scrapes, Stanley saw Eddie strolling towards him: the hint of a five o'clock shadow, even though he'd just shaved. Though younger, he had been using a razor since his early teens. The nose — broken in a sporting clash — complete with the style of suit and the slicked-back hair, the slightly crooked smile and his general swarthiness, gave him a slight Chicago-gangster air, but a totally affable chap all the same, as Stanley often noted to Alice when discussing, and perhaps justifying, his choice. In truth, she didn't really know his friends, and Stanley himself had somewhat drifted away from them. He had spent most of his time with her after they began going steady, and didn't feel inclined to double-date with his slightly plain old pals and the more simple girls they'd likely bring along. He tried his hardest to keep his worlds separate — and largely succeeded — but here, on this day at least, it all collided. He had even managed to gradually implement, to family and friends, the middle-class accent he adopted for Alice at the fairground, suggesting it derived from exercises in a book on locution and stammering.

"Got the ring?" Stanley asked.

"Course. I ain't stupid," Eddie said with a beaming smile that bordered on gormless.

"No," Stanley said, unconvincingly; suddenly anxious about the speech Eddie would later give, as well as his own, for very different reasons. The pair turned to cross the road, and made their way down the path to the church. By now, all of the invited guests had arrived, and milled about outside; some merging into larger groups close to the medieval lychgate, others remaining separate in small clusters at the margins. There were older men in double-breasted suits, younger men in single-breasted jackets, some adding a waistcoat; women in smart outfits, pleated skirts to the shins, hands and lower arms covered by black gloves of leather or silk, with most wearing some kind of headwear. At the fringes, the strangers and stragglers: the balding man with swept-over hair greasily tacked to his scalp; a pair of old, woollen-hatted women with sucked-in mouths and ornate spectacle frames, behind someone carrying an infant dressed in a smart smock. A trilby here, a fedora there; a flat-cap or two. Beside them all, a car emblazoned with *JUST MARRIED* and the various tied-on paraphernalia, for the wedding that preceded theirs.

They now awaited only the bride and her father, in the hired Bentley; as well as the bride's coterie: Alice's mother, the maid of honour, two further bridesmaids, as well as the flower girl and pageboy, who would all follow in the family's own vehicles behind the wedding car. Finally, Reginald — Alice's older brother, entrusted with Stanley's new colour ciné camera, to record the day on its fleeting five-minute reels, and who began by filming at the family home. He would drive the bridesmaids in his father's Austin Westminster, after a family dispute in which Alice refused the offer of an uncle's fancy new Jaguar.

Several of the smaller groups met and greeted Stanley as he and Eddie moved to stand under the lychgate, although others were careful not to crowd in. Yet all eyes were on him, as the groom. He glanced back beyond the canopy of trees and the red phone box on the side street that cut through the sprawling graveyard; out towards the main road, where no new cars appeared. Under the cover of trees a flock of birds chirped, as the sky grew ever more overcast.

His mother approached to survey him — cockeyed, left and right — and then straightened his tie, before flattening an errant flap of hair back into the side of his head. She spat discreetly onto a hanky and wiped a speck of dried shaving foam from his neck. She surveyed him once more, and nodded. The photographer — a habitually busy man who seemed capable of stillness only when about to depress the shutter — interrupted, to take control: lining up the groom and best man outside the broad oak doors with the ring on display; Eddie forced to hold it aloft, goofily, as if to confirm that it had not been mislaid, with Stanley coaxed into looking relieved to see its presence. Amid darkening cloud they stood dazzled by the silver-bowl flash whose searing brightness bounced off the ancient masonry.

The preceding ceremony continued to run over, and in those initial moments Stanley had feared that Alice would turn up before he and the others had entered the church, and that they would catch sight of each other. Perhaps the driver — rehearsed at such eventualities — would hurriedly go around the block, before such a sighting could occur, all bad omens avoided. Yet if she arrived much later, she'd alight into a rainstorm.

A commotion in the church signalled the overdue conclusion to the previous ceremony, and so the Smith/Mortimer party parted like a flock of sheep, as the newlyweds — unknown to Stanley and Alice's family and friends — walked out arm in arm with smiles of elation. As that congregation were ushered off to the lychgate to pose for group photographs, the vicar welcomed the Smith/Mortimer party and began hurrying people inside.

Stanley took a few steps back and stood to one side, seemingly unnoticed by the eager guests who streamed past on their way to take a pew. He couldn't shake the nagging fear of what Alice's lateness might mean; just a matter of minutes, and due to arrive last anyway — but all the same, he felt no little unease. Eddie finally located him, and almost literally dragged the reluctant groom into the church.

One last forlorn glance back out to the road — still no sight of Alice's car — as, finally, the heavens opened.

Fine rain fell fast from dull skies, yet the stained glass panels beyond the altar still sent colour, like thinned-out liquid paint, along the polished tiled floor. Bold flowers lined the pillars of the ancient arches as Stanley made his way inside; past the overly-bright statue of the Virgin Mary, painted playfully years earlier by an irreverent Eric Arthur Blair, who admired the church and its clergy enough to endure its services as a non-believer, and volunteered to help with the upkeep. Faces — familiar and unfamiliar — turned like two rippling tides to see the groom at the top of the aisle, and offered warm smiles. A truly beautiful scene, with just one thing missing.

Time, to Stanley, had never slowed more than those interminable minutes at the altar. Even his thoughts seemed to stammer and stutter as he checked his watch again. Eddie smiled, ruefully. The congregation were too polite to say anything too audible, but there hung a low hum of chatter across the wooden pews; a whispered unease that rose and fell like a rippling wave, with intermittent sharp snaps of *shh*. Since meeting Alice and settling into a relationship full of acceptance, Stanley's stammer had generally calmed — certainly when alone in her presence — but now it unspooled in unspoken words, conjured to accept incoming condolences.

* * *

On the front right-hand seat of a bright red double-decker bus, Charlotte Bradbury — on her way through Hayes to London Airport, with an over-stuffed bag perched upon her lap — thought nothing of the traffic jam, as summer rain sprinkled the scene. Eventually the bus snaked past a broken-down wedding car, with its giveaway cream ribbons tied from silver bonnet ornament to wing mirrors. Two men tried to push the empty car towards the pavement, to the sound of honking horns, with no sign of a bride.

Half a mile away, the mixture of relief and elation gave way to an almost palpable explosion that flew up into the rafters as, in a hurried gaggle, several women and a middle-aged man burst through the door of the church, under the arch of the man's umbrella. The organist quickly struck up Mendelssohn's *Wedding March*, as Alice's father laid aside the umbrella and helped her to compose herself — straightening her veil, as the maid of honour tweaked the dress — before proceeding any further. At the sight, Stanley felt his eyes well up, with a mixture of emotions that had never before quite combined within body and mind.

The photographs, taken shortly after the service, helped memorialise the way Alice appeared to Stanley as he watched her turn onto the aisle, and into full view. Her face, behind the veil, alive with joy; he felt his heart — already beating out of his chest — further inflate, with pride and love and relief and longing. Once closer, she put a hand to her mouth when she saw a tear rolling down his cheek.

Yet the photos never quite captured her expression, as in that exact moment when their eyes met. All the same, the smile — before she covered her mouth — felt seared into his mind, with no need of a reminder. Up close, her makeup appeared slightly smudged by the race to the church, marked by a drip of sweat and a few stray specks of rain. Yet to Stanley she remained immaculate. He hadn't been allowed to see the dress. Just months earlier, the lavish wedding of Grace Kelly and Prince Rainier set the new style for aspiring brides to follow. Alice's dress inexpensively imitated the finest materials money could buy; and yet in its own suburban way, remained far from cheap, with a mixture of silks and lace radiant on — to Stanley — every bit as beautiful a model as the movie star in Monaco.

With the soft back of her hand as they faced one another at the altar, Alice gently wiped the damp line from his cheek, as she held back tears of her own. Then both smiled, and sighed, and shook, and then laughed — together, at once, in synchronicity; the unbearable anxieties of the past half an hour exiting their bodies like an exorcism.

"Dearly beloved, we are gathered here today…"

The vows were rushed — Stanley stammered, stuck on his own name, which meant the vicar spoke even faster to compensate — and in almost no time at all, after the coos at the first kiss, they stood outside in the lightly drizzling rain, as what seemed like dozens of darting women with small cardboard boxes swept in to fling a cloudburst of confetti that fluttered and flittered and fell; flooding the dark sky about them like a colourful snowstorm.

2009

Dave Smith, dappled with a fleeting burst of light through leaves and branches, casually leant against a broad tree, exhaling smoke from behind a coarse hand cupped over his cigarette, as the wind tried to extinguish its gentle smoulder. A burly man, the smoke wisped back into his face, momentarily shrouding his rugged features. He watched nonchalantly as the mechanical digger forced its tracks over brambles, weeds and bracken, and, with an oddly balletic grace — almost *en pointe* — hoisted itself over a pair of fallen boughs whose exposed roots were frozen in mid-air; the machine momentarily tilting ominously, before, with a swing of its arm to redistribute its weight, righting itself. As Dave enjoyed the first of his many cigarette breaks, Michael and most of the others busily worked with shovels and hoes, scraping the target area clear of its nettles and thorny vines, as Alan Johnstone — a man in his sixties, and co-leader of the team — swung the rod of his metal detector back and forth across the ground, divining for shrapnel. With the first piece of evidence, Alan confirmed their suspicions. From the topsoil, he lifted a .303 bullet, still in its casing. Once the digger got to work, Dave dealt with the most strenuous manual labour — lifting the heaviest buckets and shovelling more mud than anyone else, often with a cigarette hanging louchely from the corner of his mouth — so no one argued when, at the outset, as an unwritten rule, he watched on like an indifferent spectator.

As the digger crunched its way towards the cleared rectangle of land, Michael took a quick glance at his phone, and then flipped its lid shut at the sign of inactivity. Pippa must be awake by now — Ethan would have made sure of that; jumping on the bed, screaming "Get up, Mummy! Get up!", with his boundless daybreak energy.

Just a few weeks earlier, as a kind of second rite of passage after the gentle introduction of the nursery, Ethan started school. Michael joined Pippa in taking their son in for his first day, and both held back tears as afterwards they drove home in stony silence. For more than a year Ethan had been going to the nursery, for a couple of hours a day, but this felt seismic. Michael felt unable to share with his wife the grief he felt, at the unexpected sense of loss upon their child reaching this landmark — a good thing, he understood; a developmental milestone. Yet it felt like the first step on the road to separation; a process his own stupidity, in attending the dig, helped to rapidly accelerate. Why had he chosen to get away? Perhaps Pippa felt the same sense of loss, but communication had grown strained ever since the boy's birth. As much as Michael loved his son, he felt sidelined by his arrival, and things never quite recovered. No one quite explained — and for some reason he never quite guessed — that the bond of mother and child could feel so much like a team in which only two may play, where the father becomes an observer from the sidelines; his fragile ego, bruised by the process. Yet, whatever the validity of such conclusions, he felt extraneous. He had not been the one to carry the boy *within*, for nine months; nor, after the unique pain of childbirth, could his body supply natural nutrition. He changed nappies, and cooed, and lifted their baby high in the air, but none of it stopped the tiny infant forever reaching first for his mother. Michael's masculine strength and bravery — not that he had a great deal of either — were not required to defend her from marauding rival tribes, nor did she even need his provision: she worked from home and, even before he lost his regular job and began the fragmented existence of freelancing, earned more than he did. Weighed down by the practicalities of motherhood, and replete with this new unconditional love — for this new *being* — Pippa sometimes failed to even notice her husband in the room. Why should she care if he sometimes went off to do his own thing?

In driving rain that arrowed through interwoven branches at sharp angles, the distinctive yellow-skinned JCB skimmed the topsoil, clawing at mud with its deep bucket: an oversized crustacean, flailing its ungainly pincer. Six men stood and looked on at the trench dug by the seventh, controls in hand, peering over the windscreen; the ditch deepening foot by foot. The first few feet comprised wartime backfill beneath the post-war topsoil. Decades of rain, and the gentle but incessant push of gravity, had failed to compress the earth to quite the same density of the surrounding soil, with its millennia of compaction. It sat looser, full of rocks, dead leaves and decaying branches, as well as the severed networks of fine tendrils — the slenderest of roots — that circuitously wended back to sturdier stems like tributaries traced back to a flowing river. Puddles pooled in the pit — dispersed with every lifting action, only to drip and pool once more; drooling from the sides of the jagged-toothed jaws as they rose and fell. With the initial layer or two scooped out, the arm momentarily at rest, three men stepped into the hole. Thigh-deep, Sanjay — whose grandfather, a WWII sapper, rebuilt bridges and cleared mines with the Bombay Engineer Group in Abyssinia and Italy, before emigrating to England shortly after Partition — lifted the first find: a spur of metal, unhinged from its original housing. "A rib from the tailplane?" he asked, passing it around. They clambered out, raised their thumbs, and passed the piece to Trevor, the group's co-leader, as the digger resumed.

Strata of mud — its familiar, dull earthen brown — and clay — more ochre in hue — were distinguishable within the walls of the trench. But then, deeper down, they hit the distinctively stained blue-grey layer, with its oily, petroleum stench; and at its outer edges, small pockets of corroding aluminium: thin scraps of metal turned to a pale blue dust.

With the hole now several feet deep, and the clay wet and claggy, a number of angular remnants of metal could finally be seen jutting from the cut earth, as the teeth of the bucket scraped away a more revealing layer. Then a sharp clang, as the bucket caught on something more substantial.

"Whoah, whoah," Alan shouted; the digger swiftly switched to idle. All darted quickly into the trench — even the older guys, forgetting their stiff joints and aching backs in the rush; scurrying down like soldiers at the Somme escaping a shelling. Michael and Sanjay scraped at the earth with their bare fingers, although Trevor used a trowel and Dave wielded a shovel. They exhibited none of the extreme care and precision of traditional archaeology, where dirt could almost be tickled — with fine implements, and even delicate brushes — from around a buried artefact until, hours — or even days — later, it finally yielded. Here lay nothing as fragile as a thirteenth century skull, or a prehistoric urn; and they had only a weekend in which to dig, not months or even years. They sifted quickly through debris, easing out strips and slithers; wobbling parts free, like a loosening milk tooth, until the sense of suction abated and it gave itself up with a dull pop. The more recalcitrant finds were shovelled at their edges, until finally levered loose; brute force never far away. Fingernails scratched mud and clay from the finds: in Michael's hands the pristine stainless steel sheen of a piston rod, glistening through the grime; emerging as if *time* had not penetrated the topsoil, and — but for the telling evidence of mud at either end — it had just reached the end of the assembly line at the factory. Next out, a curve of brass piping that, once crudely cleaned, also showed no patina. Other parts materialised rusty and corroded, with some clear evidence of burning: streaks of charring on surfaces, flakes of charcoal amid the ruins.

Fifteen feet down, they finally hit the top of the Rolls Royce Merlin engine — the serious, heavy machinery; *tonnage*, that could not be lifted, bare-handed, by the combined force of all the men present. Shovels hacked at the ground around it, as if quarrying out a moat. Deeper and deeper, they dug down its metal flanks, wider and wider as they sought to gain leverage from the sides; filling buckets they then lifted up to the surface in a pass-the-parcel motion and tipped onto a spoil heap the size of a mediaeval burial mound, its sides crumbling in the downpour, as Liam, the young new recruit, grabbed piles to sift and sieve.

Rocker valves, carburettor, sump pipe, oil pump, fuel line, induction pipe, crankshaft, engine valve: fragments of each were identified while still attached to the buckled metallic lump, all clothed in a skin of earthy hues; some hanging loose, others still firmly intact. To one side of the engine, a gaping aperture, whose cover had been blown clear: the circle of a mouth, its row of inner gear-teeth sinisterly grinning.

Michael heard a ping — a kind of chime — and, after wiping his hands on his jeans, reached into his pocket for his phone. Certain it signalled the arrival of a message, it took a moment to accept — as he stared at the empty screen — that the noise must have been the sound, in the trench, of metal against metal.

The sun slipped low in the sky, the horizon suffused with rich pinks and reds, as the light within the spinney dimmed. The team — the semi-arthritic SWAT crew — had progressed much faster than anticipated, and as such, decided to carry on until the light fully faded. Enough of the earth dislodged, the engine sat ready for removal. They fed coarse leather straps underneath, then around its midriff, and gathered them back into the jib of the digger. Everyone stood back as the line grew taut. The machine's hydraulics heaved a hissing sigh, before the entrenched engine, initially resisting with the power of suction, finally shifted. The hulking mass twirled as it rose, muddy water — running red with rust — funnelling out from its lower extremities. Almost seventy years later, she'd been set free.

Having lost track of time as the task neared completion in the failing light, Michael, with muddy fingers and blackened fingernails, gingerly extracted his phone from his pocket once more, and flipped it open, its screen sharply bright and green in the gloaming. No messages. No missed calls.

Nothing.

He thought again about that unforgettable first dig in Winchelsea, over two decades earlier, and how, looking back, he felt like a totally different person, writing to a totally different woman.

* * *

After lunch, Geoffrey Freeman — grey-haired, bespectacled and bright-eyed beneath bushy eyebrows — quietly introduced himself to Michael, as the latter, leaning against the frame of the sieve, awaited the first finds. No one seemed to know anything about the older man, who had purposefully kept his history out of the equation, to keep things low-key. With two new recruits on the same dig, it made sense to ask the younger new recruit to mind the spoil heap, and so Geoffrey almost became a spare part, unassigned in terms of tasks, but where he said he felt happy to just watch and learn. He also failed to disclose that he hadn't just joined the dig arbitrarily, with a long-held curiosity about this particular crash site.

"You're new, too?" Geoffrey asked.

"Sure am," Michael said, gently agitating the sieve, as if absentmindedly already at work. "You think you'll become a full-time member?" he asked, talking to the older man with his eyes fixed on the ditch.

"Probably not. I live in Scotland, you see. At least, for now. To be honest, now that I've retired I intend to return to Iceland at some point. Did some time there in the war. Would like to see what it's like, see if it maybe holds anything for me."

The younger man turned to look at the elder. "An interesting place, I imagine. But sounds a bit too cold for my liking."

"In the winter, yes. But summers are not so bad. Quite wonderful, in their own way."

"Maybe one day then."

"Yes, maybe."

Geoffrey went to ask Michael of his line of work, but then the first remnants of the aircraft revealed themselves in the subsoil. First out — having been last in — came the strut of the tail wheel.

Although the loam remained easy to dig through, the sides of the trench needed continual reinforcement with wooden boards, and the water continually scooped into buckets, as if baling out an ailing dinghy. Initially, most of the matter passed to Michael comprised clumps of earth with a smattering of mollusc shells, plus a variety of stones found at various depths. One large lump of clay, almost discarded, disguised a threaded bolt with its nut still in place. Whatever it held had snapped off, the bolt remaining flawlessly straight.

Then, something more confusing. At first Michael recognised it as the curve of a ceramic pot, like the earthenware jars he'd read about during school history lessons; although he felt surprised at its lightness. He brushed soil away with his fingers, as if rubbing dirt from the back of his hand; wiping the pot with the lower portion of his grubby shirt, exfoliating the grime. Could it be mediaeval, a relic from the town's historic past, churned up during the crash? And then, once almost wiped entirely clean, its exposed surface revealed the truth: the dull ochre lacquer of the top of a *skull*, its sutures — those snaking veins of bone fissures — clearly discernible. He felt his stomach fall, his knees grow weak. Instinctively, he wanted to throw it down, as if toxic; a reflex, part revulsion, as he stood in silence beyond the trench, as the others, in their ignorance, beavered away. But Michael held his nerve — locked tight his knees and retained his balance — and, with the item in fingers that were starting to tremble, doubled-checked himself: he could not be right. And then, turning to logic, he doubted his ability to make such an identification: he had no anatomical expertise, so how could he be qualified to draw such a conclusion? And as a writer, he had — as others, now including Pippa, often told him — an overactive imagination. He saw things in shapes all the time; faces in clouds, figures in shadows, and the other hallmarks of pareidolia. But in his heart he *knew*. He'd felt so grown up when acquiring, so soon out of university, a literary agent and an advance from a publisher for his debut novel; and in recent times, such as when wooing Pippa, felt so cocksure — controlling his own destiny, in love, and set to make waves as a debut novelist. Suddenly he felt eight years old again, confused by life, and unsure whether or not to notify the grownups. He had once broken his mother's favourite porcelain figurine — knocked the elephant off the mantelpiece with his boisterous horseplay, his imagination having taken him to a castle besieged by marauding hordes who needed repelling, as they so often did, with a scruffy tennis ball — and trapped himself in a state of frozen panic as he wondered what to do with the broken pieces, the trunk lying limply disarticulated in his hand, as his mother prepared dinner in the kitchen.

Why did he feel so guilty at what he had just found? No one died here — the records showed as much. He'd read through the research himself: fact-checking a bundle of photocopies ahead of his very first excavation, and acquainting himself with the history, to confirm it as the last resting place of the Spitfire of Pilot Officer Timothy Sugden. And Pilot Officer Timothy Sugden very much lived on, alive and well in Worcestershire. He'd even spoken to him on the phone just two days earlier, to double-check his memories of being shot down, and to hear, first-hand, what happened to the aircraft. And yet, despite the unsettling nature of the find, Michael also felt a little thrilled. If correct — and it seemed that he could be — then this was *history*: the quintessential essence of hidden lives, buried treasure, untold stories, human mystery.

"Guys," he eventually said, when sufficiently steeled, although they could not hear him over the sound of their labours. "Guys," he said again, louder, and a couple of them turned to look at him. Trevor stared up from his subterranean vantage point to see Michael holding the skull fragment out, and the co-leader instantly recognised its significance. "Shit," he said, scrambling out of the trench. "What the hell?" he added, as he took the fragment in his hand, fingering its surface, feeling its weight, pinching its thickness, all the while shaking his head. "It can't be," he said, under his breath, although he'd seen such skull fragments before; enough to know, for sure, its significance. By the time he turned and shouted "Everyone stop!", the entire team had already paused, aware that something seemed amiss. Alan, already up beside him, focused on the object displayed in Trevor's open palm.

"What do we do?" Michael asked.

"We have to notify the police," Trevor said. "And the coroner."

"It's a pilot, though?" Michael said.

"You'd have to assume so." Trevor said, still shaking his head. "Unless it's from some ancient unknown grave. I don't know … maybe something from the middle ages, disturbed by the crash. But what are the chances of that?"

"Not gonna be some murder, is it?" Alan noted, moving closer. "What's the odds of someone burying a body on the exact spot where a Spitfire crashed?"

"We have to shut this down, right away," Trevor said, looking down into the trench — where other bones might remain; shaking his head faster, as seagulls circled above. "You've all seen the new laws."

"Sod that," Alan said, placing his fingers around the skull fragment, until Trevor felt willing to release it. "I say we continue. We need to find the rest of him. It's the pilot, right? Has to be. I say we carry on down until we've excavated the rest of him — if there's more — and the rest of the aircraft." Alan looked at the others, who had, one by one, hauled themselves out of the pit. The rest of the team listened intently, but found themselves unable to speak. "Then we can go to the authorities with the whole picture," Alan continued, glancing from one person to another, to see if they would automatically be onboard with what he suggested. "Say that we discovered it all in one go. As this clearly *ain't* Sugden, is it? He's very much alive, so this therefore can't be his plane, can it? So we need to find out whose plane it is. And getting entangled in fucking red tape won't help. We'll be shut down and they'll do their own investigation, and take their bloody time, too. And they'll tell us sweet Fanny Adams. You know how it is with them lot."

Trevor looked at Alan and, after a pause, nodded earnestly. "What will it hurt if we dig a bit deeper? As Alan says, we can say we discovered the bones all together, still in the plane, if we find the rest of him."

"But what if it's not the pilot?" Michael asked, unable to draw upon the certainty felt by the others. "We may be disturbing a crime scene."

"I'm with Alan in that I think that highly unlikely," Trevor said, gently bouncing the fragment in his hand repeatedly, as if to discern its precise weight, and as if that weight would tell him something new. "But if we find anything suggestive of foul play, then we reconsider."

"Foul play?" Michael asked. "Like what?"

"I don't know," Trevor said, unable to avert his eyes from the bone fragment. "You're the one suggesting it may be suspicious. Maybe bullets that aren't the usual .303s we'd expect to find. A knife, a gun. Or maybe rope, or other restraints. Any signs of this not being the pilot. But come on, we won't find any of that. Trust me. We've had all this before, years ago — before the new legislation. This is just another undocumented crash, misidentified or just completely unknown. Some cock-up or other. Maybe listed as lost as sea, something like that — it's easy to see how it could have been assumed as such, given the location."

"He's right," Alan said, as Trevor handed him the slither of skull.

Michael felt too new to make any further comment or pass judgement, and, like the others, wanted to know the full story as soon as possible. 'Spuds', a wiry, jug-eared late-thirties man with numerous scratchy, self-inked tattoos — and whose real name

Michael never discovered — bellowed with a big voice from such a thin body, "Let's fucking do this!"; jumping back into the trench before it had been agreed. For all the rousing enthusiasm, no one else followed.

Only then did Geoffrey — the quiet man in his sixties who had kept himself to himself, beyond a spattering of smalltalk and a brief chat with Michael — speak up. He didn't raise his voice, but the tone — and indeed, the surprise of him suddenly holding forth — drew everyone's attention.

"Look, I need to be honest here," he said, moving closer to the others. "I used to do this kind of thing, back in the late forties and early fifties, you see. Official crash recovery stuff, for the RAF. After the war, after I'd stopped flying Hurricanes and the like."

"You kept that quiet," Alan said, simmering with contempt.

"The point is, I have someone in mind for this — if it's not Sugden's Spitfire."

"What do you think we should do?" Trevor asked. "Are you shutting us down?"

Geoffrey laughed. "Heavens, no. I don't have the authority. Not these days. But it's probably advisable that you contact the police. Then I can help you with the details about who this just might be."

* * *

By contrast, the excavation within the spinney at the edge of the farm, some twenty-two years later, proved distinctly unremarkable: a lovely find, but in terms of the dig itself, no sense of uncovered mystery and personal tragedy. Just airplane parts.

The day, however, still bore great significance. Past twilight, Michael wandered to the edge of the site, checked his phone. It lit up in the dark, casting green phosphorescence across his face. Still nothing. He planned to stay in a local bed and breakfast with the other guys, and to clean up the site — and the finds — in the morning. But what if, rather than Pippa simply being mad at him, something serious had happened? The urge blew over him, to rush home. Was Ethan okay? Suddenly, for no real reason, he began to fear the worst.

He told Trevor that something had come up, and hurried to his car, to drive home. It took just over an hour on the dark roads, and he pulled up outside the house, anxious and apprehensive, but also eager to make amends, and desperate to see his boy — who would now be sleeping — in the morning. Everything at the dark house seemed normal until Michael slid the key into the lock. It went in about a third of the way before it jammed. He tried again, to no avail. And then, clear from the streetlights reflecting on its surface as he look closer: the lack of familiar scratches around its disc from a thousand sloppy insertions; the faultless fresh metal, silver rather than bronze, set into the door.

This was, without question, a new lock.

2019

Thin spring snow fell over a sunlit field of yellow rapeseed, the sky half blackened with soft-edged cloud, half bright and blue. The first signs of blossom, tassels of pink and white and pale green, flourished on cherry and apricot and apple branches; beyond them, splashes of emerald on evergreens, and in the fields, bird nests tightly nestled in bare trees.

Four seasons in one sky.

Stanley nervously crossed the road; sometimes he didn't hear the cars speeding up to the corner, and whenever they saw him they rarely slowed down, doing just enough to narrowly avoid him, as if he had no right in crossing; an old man, getting in the way, a mere inconvenience to other people's lives. Every day he made the walk — a little slow, but still without the aid of a cane — to the cemetery, unless it looked too icy to risk leaving the house. He'd brave the rain, and the snow, but ice — which once almost gave him a broken hip — proved an impediment too far.

The wind, and slivers of snow, bustled at his face as he shuffled along. He carried in his hand a clutch of pink gerberas:

Alice's favourite flower, which he had hand-delivered to the house, and for which he paid with cash, drawn from the Post Office. Once a week he refreshed the blooms on her small plot, tidying away the dead stalks and, with increasing difficulty as he bent with unforgiving knees and hips that gnashed and ground, clearing the litter — cellophane floral wraps, cigarette butts, drinks cans — from the area. At night gangs of youths loitered in the adjoining park, straying into the centuries-old cemetery when they dared each other, unless old enough to not care for such superstition. By day its foliage — thick privet hedges, arching yews, ancient gnarled oaks — added warmth and character, and indeed *life* to accompany the dead; but at night they blocked out the dim streetlights and the glare of the moon, and cut sinister shapes in the dark. Occasionally Stanley found beer bottles dumped between graves, and the ragged ends of hand-rolled cigarettes, whose unusual smell — cannabis, he assumed — remained on his fingers after he carried them to the bin.

His routine involved sitting on Alice's bench, which he recently organised as a memorial; a bronze plaque bearing her name, with the words *In Loving Memory, For Eternity*. The tree that it backed onto he claimed as hers too, with the way it spread its branches out high over him, to shade from the sun and to protect from the rain; even though three other sponsored benches surrounded the trunk to form a square, as part of a four-way share. He talked to Alice from the seat — although he talked to her at home, and talked to her on his walks, and in the garden. He needed no special location; he carried her with him, wherever.

The snow fell thicker by the time he reached the cemetery gates, but the morning sunshine continued to burst down in sharply segmented rays beyond the clouds. Only when he approached the driveway did a greater sense of aberrance envelop him: most days only one or two people were present, except for funerals — and it remained too early for that. To make matters worse, as he passed through the gates he could see the spinning cyan of police lights reflecting on the copse up ahead, before spotting the squad cars. The asphalt driveway lay smeared with the crazed curlicues of muddy tyre tracks and black streaks of rubber, whose paths ran wild up onto — and all over — the grass verges, and back again; figures of eight and doughnuts delineated in the parking area, cut with delirious fervour. The turf stood turned over, ripped out, in curving patterns, leading all the way to Alice's memorial. Only then did Stanley see the car — a small electric-blue Ford with a sporty tail fin — embedded into Alice's tree, its bonnet bent and crumpled, the bench obliterated. Around it, a row of gravestones lay clipped or toppled, and a dozen or more people gathered around the scene, helping each other to right the heavy slabs, while a policewoman took photographs and a policeman spoke into his radio, requesting a tow-truck. Stanley saw the gaping yellow-white innards of Alice's tree, where the bark had been sliced clean away. He *felt* the wound. His legs buckled a little, but he managed to right himself and make it to a communal wrought-iron bench before, with all strength lost, he almost fell onto the seat. He harboured the urge — as if still young — to stride over to the tree and, with superhuman strength fuelled by anger, rip the car away, throw it to one side. It remained a mere urge of the mind, with no corresponding inputs sent to the body. In truth he felt barely able to even crawl to it. The bench could be replaced. The tree had not been fatally wounded, and its scars would darken, perhaps even heal. But he didn't know how much more of this he could take.

The walk home always felt much more difficult. His spirit waned, and now, the added uncertainty in legs rendered less stable by shock. Heading back to an empty house did not pull him with an invisible force in the way that the cemetery did. And on a section of country lane he found no pavement, just an unkempt grassy verge that proved hard to navigate.

He stopped at a break in the hedgerow, at a long farmland track that cut through wheat fields; looked down its narrowly tapering perspective, and the familiar telegraph poles, once seen from the back seat of his first car — the old Morris Minor — that shrunk into the distance on a starry night.

1940

Dust accumulated. Insects settled into nooks and crannies, to craftily build their homes within hers. The water ran rusty for the first few moments, the pipes groaning, the taps gasping and coughing; the cistern clogged and pneumonic, occasionally squealing in discomfort, as if a boot pressed firm upon its windpipe. The basic rations Charlotte kept at the cottage turned bad, in need of discarding, and the waste saddened her, at a time when others were going without. She could scrape the mould from the bread and then toast it, but the milk, lumpen and bilious, was beyond consumption; slopping in foul clumps into the sink's drain as, with the water finally running fast and clear, she washed it away. For all the trials and tribulations of getting home, and the problems, and isolation, encountered — and how it starkly drew to mind the sense of loss, of detachment, of decay — it felt essential to her sanity to make these occasional visits.

Cycling home in the blackout rarely appeals, although occasionally, depending on one's mood, it can actually feel extraordinarily liberating — as if the whole of England is fast asleep as I navigate my way under those gloriously twinkling stars.

Most nights she stayed in her humble billet — an attic room in a house located a short walk from the hospital — and went home maybe one or two evenings a week, to check the cottage over, perhaps spend the night in order to reacquaint herself with aspects of her life of old, before the war moved in. She also returned during her meagre two days' leave each month, but it no longer bestowed a great sense of belonging. Too much had changed — within the village, and within the person who returned, a stranger to her own home.

On the rare nights she slept at the cottage she usually managed to escape the conflict, if only for the briefest of intermissions; alone in the quiet darkness, surrounded by farmland, woodland and the lake that teemed and hummed with life, and which glowed at night. Should a bomb whistle down through the clouds on course for the cottage she feared that no one would notice the explosion, out in the middle of nowhere, close — but not adjoined to — the smallest of villages. Air-raid sirens were not as audible in the remoteness, although she could still just about hear their call; but less of a jolt, less of a wailing insistence on finding instantaneous cover — *Run! Now!* — and more like a polite suggestion to move below ground at one's leisure. Her nerves were never quite set on edge in the way they constantly jangled at the billet and the hospital, even if she feared dying alone; or more pertinently, feared conscious awareness during the act of dying alone.

The cellar served as her refuge, with an old desk and chair, and single lightbulb hanging naked from a cord. In addition, she had recently moved her wireless down, to keep her company, and collected together some tinned supplies, just in case the worst should happen and she somehow survived, trapped within. She felt grateful that she didn't have to scamper across a garden in the cold of night, like so many in the cities must, to the safety of a tiny tin shelter, especially given that she would have to do so alone. She had bricks and mortar above her, and that comforted more than corrugated steel and scraps of turf ever could. With the Imperial Good Companion at the billet, she took out her notepad, and jotted down a thought.

For those poor folk, to be in total isolation in such a cramped contrivance must feel like sealing oneself into one's own coffin, when the bombs begin to fall.

On some nights she could hear the German planes pass overhead, maintaining their course to somewhere deemed more worthy of destruction than a single remote cottage, occupied by a lone woman, huddled in a cellar. Each time she heard their sinister sky-bound march she would think of those poor — albeit to her, unknown — souls scrambling for shelter, unaware that tonight *they* had it coming. Then again, a fractional delay in deploying the bombs, or if the sky swept about a strong breeze, it would instead be the turn of their neighbours, as fate intervened.

She would hear the mass of propellers, and feel a knot in her stomach, tied by the knowledge that good people, through no fault of their own, would bite the dust. Goners, who were not yet gone — but going all the same.

***

Dressed in her smartest general garb — excluding a handful of evening gowns and party frocks — Charlotte felt acutely aware of Viktor never having seen her in her civvies. She walked towards his bed in a checked pale blue suit bought shortly before the outbreak of war: short jacket with wide lapels over the delicate peeking frills of a white blouse; pleated skirt, falling just below the knee; navy blue rayon-velvet turban-style hat, complete with tastefully small white gardenia clipped to one side; and a dark blue overcoat draped over her forearm, to be swiftly donned once back outside. His smile upon seeing her approach beamed broad and sincere. She caught the looks and sly smiles of her colleagues as she helped him into his wheelchair — a more modern, sleek affair than the one used around the hospital grounds; almost feeling the nudges the Sisters were eager to jab her way, as she gathered up the prize catch. She shot back a look of defiance, which slid into a wry grin. Fraternising with the patients had initially been frowned upon, but the liaisons were soon seen as good for morale. What harm could it do? They all found themselves a favourite, although it took a while for a couple of the others to get the message, and back away in their pursuit of the tall, handsome, muscular Icelander.

With a blanket hauled over his legs and his field cap angled jauntily on his head as they faced the piercing autumn cold — the sky crisply blue, a stiff breeze blowing in and up from the Channel — Charlotte wheeled Viktor towards the shoreline. The walk to the seafront proved challenging, especially when pushing a man in wheelchair, although it stretched downhill most of the way. The return would not be quite so simple, of course, but she saw little point worrying about that yet.

The daytime dogfights — the swarms of would-be invaders confronted by the spirited Spits and Hurricanes — had diminished since the previous month. The Germans, after suffering such heavy losses, had taken to flying in under the cover of darkness, to drop bombs, but also incendiary devices that spread fire in pockets that shone in the night like rows of ancient beacons. Their arsenal diversified: dropping crude oil trajectiles that exploded to splatter combustable unrefined petroleum across the target, with houses and automobiles — and any unfortunate bystanders — rendered tarred and highly-flammable, with any growing crops covered and choked with the foul yellow-black gloop. People would retch and vomit, plants would die, and everyone had to pray — as they stood helpless, like petrol-doused penny-for-the-Guy dolls beside a bonfire — that incendiary sticks were not to follow. Attacks during daylight were now far more sporadic, and the pair were left in peace during their promenade.

Some days there is a war. Others, with skies faultlessly blue and clear of cloud and condensation trails, it could for all the world be that there is not, when one feels the divine tranquility of peacetime. Indeed, at times it feels even more peaceful — an exaggerated silence, in being left well alone, providing a peace I never felt the luxury to notice before the onset of war.

The pair turned to face a country lane on a hill that ran almost straight down to the soft wash of the sea. Visibly perking up in his seat, Viktor suddenly implored "Let me go!", thrusting his arms out to his sides, like wings.

Charlotte laughed. "Don't be so silly!"

"You are no fun," he said, pretending to sulk, but with a hint of frustration, too. He had to surrender complete control; let alone fly a Spitfire, he could not even move his own wheelchair. His life lay in her hands, his own hands a burnt mess.

She could hear the disappointment in his voice, so, after a frosty silence, she relented and let go; and for a few moments he was *free*, flying again, weightless on wheels. In that moment he felt transformed. "Wahooo!" he cried, the cold wind fast in his face, as she ran behind, to keep pace. "Já!" Even if he'd wanted to, with his bandaged hands he could offer no firm friction to the wheels to slow his momentum, short of jabbing his already damaged fingers into the fast-spinning spokes and perhaps losing them entirely in the process. He gained speed, although as with his aircraft on that fateful day, he had little control, whilst losing altitude. The descent amounted to nothing more than heading down a slope to sea level, and possibly into the water itself, some half a mile or so in the distance. Compared to his erstwhile occupation, the danger seemed minimal, initially at least; hitting the T-junction onto the main road at the base of the incline presented a different kind of threat, the entering of which could be akin to a game of Russian roulette: to do so at a right-angle to a fast-approaching vehicle could easily prove fatal, with no driver likely to even see him careen into their path, and precious little protection provided by the lightweight contraption. Sensing his acceleration, and fearing that he would soon be beyond her reach if he gathered any more speed, Charlotte sprinted as fast as she could to catch him. Grabbing the handles, she felt her frantically-moving feet slip from beneath her; but, just at the point of getting dragged under the contraption, she managed to skip and jump free, and then, when landing, applied sufficient weight with a downward force to slow his roll — from which point she found herself running in time with the wheelchair and, bit by bit, brought it back strolling pace.

"Spoilsport," Viktor said, but with a chuckle.

"Ooh, you are such a rascal," she said, with a breathless smile. "Matron would have my guts for garters if I took you back in several sections. I should be quite disappointed about that too, I must say, for I also prefer you in one piece. But, well, if you don't behave yourself I shall leave you here and then we shall see how you fare."

With that Viktor's mood immediately darkened again; although, from her position behind him she didn't see his face drop and his eyes narrow. She was right: he felt useless without her; useless without *someone*. For now, at least. He checked himself, fighting off the enveloping self pity, in an effort not to take his resentment out on Charlotte. She did her very best to keep him entertained, in addition to her demanding ward duties. "I need a good wingman," he finally said, trying to find some joviality. Leaning in to hear him, she laughed gently in his ear.

Upon reaching Madeira Drive, the low coastal lane that ran below Brighton's main road of Marine Parade, they looked wistfully across to their right at the two eerily silent piers — Palace closest, West almost a mile further along; their long walkways brutally severed as if an errant battleship or destroyer had smashed its way through when plotting an east-west course, patrolling too close to shore. In truth, the breakages were self-sabotage. In the early hours of a summer night, packs of guncotton were affixed to sixty-foot stretches of the iron lattice subframes that held up the wooden planking, and then, from a safe distance, electronically detonated. Scuttling the structures left no way for invading Germans to use them as landing stages, should they wish to dock at the twin pier heads and drive their deadly armoured vehicles ashore. In addition, the southern ends of the piers, housing the main structures — pavilions, concert halls, amusement arcades — were rigged with tons of high explosives, lest Hitler's Operation Sea Lion forces, undeterred by the missing walkways, try to board all the same, perhaps to run pontoons or temporary bridges over the missing sections. Finally, the entrances to both piers were barricaded, and the amusements — including the miniature racing track at the shore-end of the West Pier — stood eerily silent and unused, beyond the unbreachable cordon. Even the beach itself — the deep shingle shoreline — lay fenced-off with barbed wire, and so they could only look on at the sea, with its gently crashing waves and its fast-dissolving bright white spume, from beyond a barrier; the message — *No fun to be had here* — all too clear.

The salty sea air, all saline and ozone, could prove a partial panacea for her patient. Indeed, Charlotte had only that week been handed a new study, showing that burning airmen who ditched in the sea not only had a swift and obvious means of extinguishment, but their wounds healed more quickly. Upon learning this, she had thought about the shoreline, and if dunking the patients — almost as a kind of baptism — would bring them more swiftly back to normal life; reborn as new men, in new skin; believers in the power of nature, after the fires of hell. Yet — here, at least — there existed no practical way to even get them into the shallows, short of dragging them through barbed wire, and exposing them to potential gunfire from the guards on towers where once people gaily played the amusement arcades.

"It looks so frightfully unwelcoming now," Charlotte said, pointing to the West Pier, "but I had so much fun on there. Hard to imagine, now."

"Not that one?" Viktor asked, tilting his head towards the other.

"Well, yes. Sometimes. But I always preferred the West Pier. I won a teddy bear on the shooting gallery. Monty, my lucky charm. Afraid to say that the little blighter hasn't brought the greatest of luck after all, though one cannot really blame a stuffed toy for the outbreak of war. That would be most silly now, wouldn't it?"

Viktor nodded. "The air is so fresh here," he added, drawing a deep, full breath. "Reminds me of home."

"Tell me again the name of the town?"

"Akureyri," he said, plainly. Just as with his mouth wired shut, she heard only a series of syllables. "Beg your pardon?"

"Ak-kyu-ray-ree," he sounded out. "Fishing town."

"Ah, yes," she said, pulling her coat tighter as a breeze nipped at her neck and shoulders. "And your mother was from Arran. I remember that. I know you told me these things, but I'm frightfully sorry to say that I couldn't always fully hear you. You know, before. So tell me again — how did you end up in Sussex?"

"My mother," he said, the *r* drawn out to *rrr*. "She had an elderly relative down here. A very old man. I stayed with him, and that is how I ended up all this way. But he died, not long after I arrived."

"I'm so terribly sorry to hear that," she said, looking into his eyes, but he remained focussed on the offing.

"That is okay," he said with a nod. "He had had a good life. And he was a big help, in a short time. I got out of Akureyri, to rush to Britain, and now I hear the Allies have moved into my home town, to build an airbase. Maybe I should have stayed."

"Oh, but then you would not be here, with me," she said, in a chipper tone.

"No, and I would not be in a *bloody* wheelchair," he barked, his mother's Scottish accent coming out sharp and cutting in the profanity.

Charlotte gasped, then sighed, audible to Viktor with her chest behind his ears. She did not mind the language — she often heard far worse on the wards — but winced at his anger. It cut right through her. "It shan't be too long," she said, with forced breeziness, as her wind-wetted eyes blinked back fuller tears. "If you do the exercises, as prescribed. You know it yourself — you're already able to walk around a bit, with those underarm crutches. When your hands get better you'll be able to grip a cane. Maybe your leg will be fully healed soon too. Really, it shan't be long."

"Months," he said, ruefully. "More operations. Many more."

"But not years."

Viktor said nothing in reply. He tapped his bandaged fingers impatiently on the armrests of the wheelchair, the skin of his cheeks turning blue. Aside from the piers positioned out of the corner of his eye, when looking over the barbed-wire cordon he faced pure open world: the dark grey sea all the way out to the horizon, the bright blue sky rising up from where the two collided. Were he to focus as if in the cockpit — the natural tunnelling of vision, to remove the peripheral when the danger lay directly ahead — then it could be like a form of flight, with just endless swathes of colour, nothing blocking his view. For a moment the realisation returned him to those joyous freedoms — that fearless falcon, in flight — before reality whiplashed him back into his wheelchair, inert and crippled.

"Let us go," he said, finally, with a swift, short backwards flick of the head to signal the direction.

They walked uphill in stony silence, this time heading not on the country lanes but through the main drag. Charlotte, feeling the strain in her calves, pushed Viktor past the Old Steine and Victoria Gardens, up Grand Parade and towards London Road, where, in stages, open spaces gave way to an increasing number of buildings, until reaching the claustrophobic parades of shops on either side; the stepped-back upper stories — above the commercial façades — of ornate regency villas, peeking out over the more utilitarian frontages with signs, awnings and displays, pushing their way forward towards the street. A century earlier, the front-garden plots had given way to single-tiered commercial premises. A billboard at the commencement of the twin parades of shops shouted *GUINNESS IS GOOD FOR YOU*. Viktor had come to like its dark stout taste. Another advert, for his favoured brand of cigarettes, Craven A, boldly implored beneath the headshot of a beautiful woman: *For Your Throat's Sake*. A creamy, iron-filled pint and a soothing cigarette seemed like such a good idea — who wouldn't want those healthful remedies? — but the pubs remained closed until six p.m., by which time the patient had to be back on the ward.

"Look, Victor's Café," Charlotte said, pointing across the road. "It's time for tea. It would almost be rude to not stop in."

"Huh, they cannot even spell my name right," he said, dryly, but with a hint of humour.

Sparse and utilitarian, the café — simple wood-panelled walls one side, whitewashed walls the other, half-occupied hatstand in the corner — housed tall utilitarian metal tea and coffee urns at its counter. Patrons were seated on wooden chairs at cloth-less tables, the cruet they would later be billed for in crude glass cellars. Viktor requested a seat near the window, so that he could see life on the street outside bustle past: a chance to watch normal existences, away from his familiar viewing fare of invalids and carers and men on the brink of death. He particularly liked to see the British cars, with so few vehicles in his homeland. He explained to Charlotte how there were barely even any roads back home — just a few dirt tracks and undulating black rock lava flows that were, in a sense, like uneven, unflattened tarmacadam. The right kind of material, he said — hard-wearing — but due to the bubbling contours, utterly unnavigable. "It is easier to fly from Akureyri to Reykjavík than to drive."

"Really?"

"Really. Easier to go by boat, too. We have so few roads. It is maybe the same distance as here to Birmingham, but maybe five, ten times as far by sea, and if you cannot fly you have to go by sea. We have no trains, either. This is why I yearned to fly, and had to find a way to learn."

After a short wait an elderly man arrived, bringing to their table plates of mashed potato and vegetables, with generous helpings of gravy. They each received a bonus slab of unidentified meat — possibly rabbit caught on the downs — which the man acknowledged with a wink. "For the airman." In a world of civilians, such men were minor stars, and had Charlotte been in uniform, she would likewise also have been thanked for her duty.

Appetites whetted by the walk and the fresh air, it didn't seem to matter that the fare proved no better than that cooked up in the hospital canteen, where meat remained a necessity — a medicine — in helping to rebuild strength. Yet even in this rudimentary restaurant it felt far more exotic — a treat — out in the civilian world. In his better hand Viktor could gingerly grip a fork or a spoon, but found it impossible to hold a utensil in both. As such, Charlotte leant across to gather his plate, putting it next to hers, to dutifully cut up his food as if he were a child; his reaction, unseen, one of gratitude tinged with resentment.

"So," Charlotte asked, after dabbing her lips with the napkin. "Tell me more about Akky — sorry, whatever is it called? I really must write it down."

"Ak-kyu-ray-ree," Viktor said, patiently.

"Yes, Ak-kyu-ray-ree," she said out loud, then once more again, in her head.

"Oh, it is very sleepy — compared to here, anyway. Mostly fishing, but also good agricultural land. It is a fairly big place by comparison to most other places back home, but that is not saying much. A lot of Iceland is dead earth. Volcanic rock, covered in snow and ice. Big mountains, glaciers. We can only live–" pronounced *liff* "–around the edges, closer to the shore, at sea level. But Akureyri has good crops, too. To be honest, I live a fair bit north of Akureyri, somewhere even more quiet, but it's the nearest town of note, and I spent a lot of time there, so that is what I say. And even Akureyri has just a few thousand people, I believe. Brighton is many, many times bigger. London — well, it is like a totally different planet."

"It sounds most lovely," she said, with a warm smile. "Quaint, simple … honest. And peaceful. I do so envy those with a less frantic life. I should like to go there, one day."

"Well, I would like to one day go to London too, to see it properly," he said, chewing on a tough chunk of meat; his jaw, though largely healed, still aching when eating. "All I have seen is passing through, on the train, and on the Underground — and you cannot see much down there. From Scotland I came to England by train, straight after arriving. I ended up down here almost right away. In such a hurry, silly fool that I was."

"Well then, we shall go!" Charlotte said with such gusto that those sat at the nearest tables glanced her way. "When you are fit and able. That shall be our aim. A trip to London!" She raised her coffee cup like a champagne flute, and he smiled, imagining the freedom.

Sitting across from him, Charlotte took the chance to look closely at his face, speared by sharp sunlight refracting through window glass, exposing every ridge and furrow, highlighting the shape of every subcutaneous muscle, and ducts of veins that intermittently pulsed with blood, and all underlying bone; at the bubbles of white scar tissue on his cheekbone and jaw, and, most notable of all, those piercing eyes, brighter than ever as the rays blew deep dimensions into the blueness that encircled the pupils. She'd only had limited time to look at him properly, to really study him close-up, since the armature came off, his teeth unlocked. Prior to its removal the pair had often sat side by side, her on a bench in the hospital grounds, him parked next to it. When they walked anywhere, she stood behind him, pushing. She had faced him when administering medications or changing dressings, but with no time to stop and ponder — no time to look this deeply into his eyes. Even the time she shaved his body in the washroom, eye contact proved difficult, in that early enforced intimacy, with his face shrouded in metal.

In the café his big blue eyes looked deeper than any I have ever seen. It was as if I could see straight into his soul, so far did they seem to recess when this otherworldly light struck them. Nothing cloudy or shady, but pure and open and ever so beautiful. Eyes that went on forever.

"Given what you have described, however did you learn to fly?" she asked, looking into those eyes whilst biting into a slice of wholemeal bread that came with the barest film of butter. "You know, what with all the quietness of … the fishing village."

His face lit up, alive with a rare joy. "Oh my, it was exciting! In an old floatplane — a Fairey Swordfish. Three years ago — God, it feels longer. A family friend, Einar, set up a small airline," — he laughed, heartily — "but we did not even have an aeroplane! A year later, they finally had enough money, so they bought this old Swordfish with floats. When I turned twenty I got a chance to learn. Pfft! was nothing like a Spitfire — biplane, big floats to take off on the water. Top speed of almost nothing — just about enough to get into the sky. Not easy taking off on Iceland's seas, with the winds and the waves. What a way to learn!"

"And that was enough to allow you to fly a Spitfire?"

He laughed. "No! Not a chance. But it helped, of course. The RAF said I had to fly Tiger Moths, which were really easy. Even more basic than a Swordfish." He laughed again, even louder.

"They also made us run around on the ground, too, practising formations! And on bicycles. Very silly. At first, when I arrived, they wouldn't even take me, as it was only British allowed, and even though my mother was Scottish, I was not officially of these lands. But very soon that changed. Suddenly I was in training, and then soon I was in a Spitfire. It is all a bit of a blur, happened so fast."

Viktor appeared more animated than Charlotte had ever seen him, his face flickering with fast-moving expressions, his eyes darting around as memories flitted in his mind, his lips twitching in and out of grins. "The Spitfire — she took off and, *woahhh*, it felt like I was headed to the stars! Could never even *imagine* such power! I had never moved even half as fast. Second sortie I shot down my first Jerry, he didn't even see me coming. He stood not a chance. I felt invincible." Then the glee on his face evaporated, as if a switch was flicked, and suddenly his eyes were downcast. "And then ..."

Charlotte sat patiently, but he never returned to the still-hanging sentence; instead shovelling a morsel into his mouth, and chewing it gingerly on the better side of his jaw.

Viktor's mood seemed unrecoverable after that; not fully sullen or morose, but never able to locate the lighter side. The laughter lay unreachable, beyond some invisible rubicon. They paid up, and Charlotte pushed him back to the hospital, her legs starting to ache, the uphill efforts and the increasing whip of the wind too great to allow for easy conversation. They forked right at St Peter's church, past curving façades and the entrance to Hanover Crescent, heading east, in the direction of ever-increasing greenery, out towards the open spaces of rural landscapes; moving back into countryside as daylight drained from the sky.

"Are you okay?" Charlotte finally asked, leaning forwards to hear his reply. Instead, he simply nodded his head, somewhat unenthusiastically. She went to ask if he felt warm enough, but stopped herself — presumably it had been covered by her previous question. She had the sense that he wouldn't have answered anyway. And what could she do, even if he *was* cold? He would certainly not take her coat — not in a million years. She could spare it, with the exertions warming her to the point where she felt quite hot, but, without doubt, he would have felt condescended to. Did he even feel the cold, she wondered? Iceland must have been freezing — especially in the winter. Plus, flying in incredibly thin metal planes at the altitude of the greatest mountain tops would surely have felt positively Siberian — and it's not like they donned thick fur coats and ushanka hats in the sky. Still, she didn't like the idea of him feeling cold whilst in her care — it had been his job, when up there, to look after the country, but it now fell on her to look after him.

Passing the simple, square-fronted Duke of Wellington pub — still over an hour from opening time — Viktor asked to be parked beside the entrance steps. Did he want a cigarette, she wondered? Charlotte manoeuvred him as requested, and when she turned to face him, found him trying to button up his overcoat like a little boy whose dexterity had yet to fully develop. All fingers and thumbs, she thought, then noted the inappropriateness — quite the opposite: *fewer* fingers and thumbs; just bulky bandages. She watched as he fumbled and fiddled, but dare not intervene.

"Damn the rotten *bastards* who did this," he said with a scowl, giving up with outward hand movements, as if to push away some invisible figure who had been closely guarding the buttons. Had he been able, then he may have removed the coat and thrown it to the ground in frustration, but he felt trapped within it, sat on its tail, and unable to even master the most basic of tasks to fasten it. "Could you do this up for me?" he finally asked, angry at the coat and the Germans, not her. Charlotte leaned in, and with that he grabbed her face in his cotton-webbed hands — in his thick, soft paws — and kissed her with every ounce of passion coursing through his agitated body. She felt her knees buckle, ever so slightly.

After a few seconds, in which, after the initial shock, she kissed him as passionately as he did her, Charlotte guiltily broke away. It suddenly felt wrong; inappropriate, as if breaking a taboo. Nurses at the hospital were steadily pairing off with patients, but this felt like a step too far.

Then, had it really been so wrong?

No sooner had I pulled away than felt suffused with the queerest regret. What a damned fool! A bomb could fall tomorrow, upon which my name or his. What harm, then, such impropriety? Tomorrow never comes, and yet for some, today ends well before midnight.

They completed the remainder of the journey in silence, but just before they reached the hospital she leant in and gave him a peck on the cheek, that she let linger longer than she would for a mere friend. Careful to look into those deep blue eyes, she thanked him for the most lovely time, and told him, with great emphasis and sincerity, that they *really* must do it again soon.

2009

Pippa redecorated the marital home just days after Michael moved out — a bold, strident wallpaper to obscure his pale emulsion — and before long, painted over his existence with another man: Douglas, an absurdly tall and broodingly handsome silver-haired architect originally from New Zealand, who commuted to London from Brighton every weekday. It moved so swiftly that Michael wondered if she knew him from before the split. Had the pair been having an affair? He could easily blame her, and rage at the betrayal; and yet, if so, would he not have simply driven her to it? And had it really been *that* quick, given that her love appeared — in hindsight — to have ended well before the actual relationship finally gave way? Her heart, he presumed, had been cleared of his awkward presence for some time beforehand.

To study only the visible evidence of Michael and Pippa's marriage — in photos and videos, taken in the years before the collapse, and laid bare in a stream of passionate early letters — an observer could be forgiven for thinking it perfect. They didn't take pictures of the unhappy times, the fights, the boredom, the increasing distance. They didn't capture their faults on film, and the letters dried up once they lived together; long before that, even — replaced by phone calls that left no trace, and then text messages that proved ephemeral. The dissatisfaction, and frustration, went largely undocumented. Those love letters sat stashed in shoeboxes on top of the wardrobe, mementos of a thrilling time. Never retained, however, were the harsh words — not written down, nor recorded by video cameras. Words that could never be taken back, no matter how great the desire to do so; etched — indeed, *carved* — into nothing but their memories, right to the core. For a while the good times were mythologised, the bad often overlooked. There were no keepsakes of hellish days — neither picked up a seashell on the day they fought on Brighton beach, in contrast to the way they had collected mementos on an early date there. Their wedding existed on film; their separation, and the road to divorce, documented in solicitor's letters.

Some of the mementos — the signifiers of the good times — now nestled in boxes in Michael's newly-rented flat; extricated in a hurry, at a moment's notice. Pippa and her two brothers were at the family home the morning they allowed Michael to collect the things his wife had set aside as his: mostly clothes, books and records, but with a few surprises thrown in, including gifts he had bought her that were no longer welcome, and yet patently of no use to him. With Ethan at school, there hung an uneasy air of a business transaction over the whole procedure. Michael gave Pippa a hug before leaving, and although she didn't resist, she didn't properly clasp him back. She offered a limp embrace, the safe distance between their bodies — where once there had been not even the slightest aperture — representing a chasm; all intimacy off limits, hips pushed back and away. Where once no light could pass between their conjoined bodies, now a whole beams could shine through. Her older brothers sat tersely in the armchairs, looking on — relaxed and unhelpful, like middle-class mafiosi — as Michael lugged the boxes, suitcases and plastic bags of clothing to the car.

A day later, Michael unpacked the life Pippa had cast aside. He sat in the middle of the lounge in his unfurnished flat, surrounded on all sides by containers crammed with his possessions. Allowed to take no furniture, nor any of their shared household electrical equipment; just everything of no use to his wife and their son, plus things he'd bought for himself. And now here it all stood, stowed in suitcases, boxes, bin-bags and plastic tubs. As he unzipped the two suitcases the sweet smell of what had until now been home — made all the more redolent against the damp pall of the new flat — drifted up into the room. Flashbacks of the items as they had been — in the marital home — zapped into his mind, half imposed onto the new surroundings, semi-vague and partially elusive.

Although technically unfurnished, his new flat — on an upper floor of a 1950s' low-rise tower-block — came with an aged fold-out table complete with a mismatched chair, a basic gas stove in the kitchen, and a rudimentary double-bed with a limp, stained mattress in the master bedroom. In addition, a small collection of inherited and unwanted oddities: a soap-stained plastic duck and loofah in the bathroom; a cheap vase with a glued-up crack from lip to base, empty and pointless — any flowers it once housed long-since deceased — on the living room windowsill; and in the hallway closet, a blue umbrella and a bunched up pair of cotton knickers whose elastic tightly gripped a small cluster of white cat hairs — all of which, bar the vase, Michael threw into a black plastic sack. The living room stood half-painted, two walls in calming magnolia, two in shocking pink; the lighter colour spread across a few square feet of a third wall, before apparently the landlord — or previous tenant — ran out of paint, or willpower; or perhaps, Michael wondered, the will to live. But the third-floor flat accommodated broad windows that allowed the light to flood in, and, if standing on tiptoes, a visible hint of the sea hung on the horizon; redeeming factors, amid the near-squalor. He still had a reasonable amount of his own money in the bank, with Pippa always insisting on financial independence beyond the shared account set aside for the mortgage, food shopping and utility bills, and anything connected to Ethan. Flat-pack furniture, still in cardboard boxes, leant against the wall, alongside some tools and tins of paint, and the packages included an as-yet unconstructed bed for Ethan, for when he came to stay every other weekend, as provisionally agreed.

Michael unpacked his old clothes from one of the suitcases, setting aside some expendable items to change into in order to decorate: jeans whose pockets and knees were frayed, and a faded tour t-shirt of a poodle-haired light-metal band he'd had a now-regrettable soft spot for in the late '80s; a fist-pumping, lighter-swaying concert he attended with Pippa, and enjoyed at the time, but which now seemed so utterly shallow and pointless. He had an urge to get his essentials unpacked, to get himself set — to feel oriented — but it made sense to decorate the flat first, and then, once the paint had dried, assemble the furniture. He opened wide the windows to the main bedroom, and, as the dewy fresh autumnal air seeped in, sprayed a disinfectant aerosol — 'Autumn Breeze' — all over the flaccid mattress, replacing an actual fresh-aired draught with a chemical substitute. Coughing as the particles tickled the back of his throat, he closed the door, to let the product do its damnedest without its overbearing odour spreading throughout the entire flat. Then he located his portable CD player — one of the few electrical items exfiltrated from the marital home — and plugged it in on the landing; the gentle acoustic guitar of *Speed Trials* seeping into the room, before the near-whisper of Elliott Smith spilled out over the music.

Ethan's adjoining bedroom stood small and boxy, with a covering of mould just under the windowsill; the blue-green patch, with a constellation of outlying spores, stark against the pale pink wall. Michael took some sandpaper and rubbed away at the growth, until every last speck of paint and fungus fell as dust onto the carpet. He sanded away some other blemishes, feeling for success with his fingertips, then levered open a tin of deep-blue paint; its colour masculine, less neutral than the colours of his son's bedroom at home. Michael smiled at making his own rules now; at least over such minor details.

Though not in any way artistic — other than with words, when the muse struck — Michael, with the emulsion almost immediately dry, set about overpainting yellow stars and a big crescent moon; the night sky turning a boy's blue into the gender-nonspecific spread of the firmament.

He then dragged the boxed-up bed — dead weighted, like a corpse digging in its heels to furrow the carpet — into his son's room, stripped back the cardboard. Out, like limp gizzards, fell a bloated pack of dowels, screws, wood glue and an Allen key, along with a strip of wood. Before long, struts and braces were spread across the room, along with two-dozen crude plastic brackets to hold together the horizontal support slats. As expected, it didn't quite assemble as directed — the instructions resembling a photocopy of a photocopy of a sketch of a sketch, after being faxed via a faulty machine — but three strikes of a hammer solved one of the issues — a screw refusing to budge any further, until blunt force intervened — and one slat remained unconnected, but stayed in place under the weight of the mattress.

By the time Michael returned to the living room, *Say Yes* having concluded the heartbroken delights of *Either/Or*, dusk had descended. When he pressed the light-switch the naked bulb spread an almost eery light, without the subtle diffusion of a lampshade; nothing on the bare walls — as yet, no pictures, no shelves, no clocks — to absorb its brutal glare.

He sat cross-legged and looked at his life, spread across the floor. The bags and boxes full of precious memories turned rank and disposable by time: like beautiful flowers sealed into a shoebox, and opened years later to reveal dry, rotted stalks and a foul odour; Schrödinger's flowers, alive and vibrant until, with the removal of the lid, revealed as long dead. They never filmed and documented the bad times, and yet now even the good times — enmeshed in the mementos they did keep — had grown toxic; every positive inverted by a change in circumstance, happy flipped to sad. The love letters he wrote to Pippa thirty years earlier, that she so ravenously consumed and replied to with haste: now bundled together with recent junk mail and circulars, returned to sender as a rejection. The seashell from that early date, when they ended up strolling along Brighton beach: now discarded like trash. Or perhaps, the inferred message that it will mean something to him because it now meant absolutely nothing to her? And the crêpe-covered album of their wedding photographs — the one possession Pippa had once said she would rescue from a burning building — shoulder to shoulder with his tatty old books about George Orwell, Eric Ravilious and Fairey aircraft, as if packed for an Oxfam shop. She'd even gone so far as to include the signed copy of his debut novel, from the very day they met.

Time had been a blur since Pippa, with a surgeon's calmness and precision, carved the split with those sharpest of words — *I don't love you anymore* — the morning after Michael had overstepped the mark one last time, causing her, in her anger and frustration, to change the locks. It became apparent that she struggled to even *like* him. He'd slept in the car that night, parked outside the house, his trusted door-key newly impotent; downing half a bottle of whiskey that he'd bought to share with the dig team at the bed and breakfast, before settling down in the foetal position — the only body shape the space would allow — across the back seats. She could always give him a copy of the new key, he had thought, as his anger subsided and sleep drew close. But those killer words the next day left little option but for Michael to move out, rather than stay in what had clearly mouldered into a loveless marriage. He'd been worn down too, and at that stage any sense of the absence or presence of love proved difficult for either to gauge, such were the clouds of numbness and disengagement within their own protective shells. *Something* abided, a remnant of shared times and past passion — a kind of muscle memory — but it didn't feel like love; just a faint echo. They felt like squabbling siblings, freed from the pull of the family — ready to leave home and make their own lives, in vastly different directions.

In the final year of their relationship he began drinking to excess. He continued to disappear for days on end with work, often overseas; still — just about — a fine life, in those final days of writing for a leading aviation magazine, with the perks of global travel, although the monthly circulation only ever fell after the internet truly took hold, and air travel tanked after 9/11, so the trips grew less frequent. Over time, he saw everything scaled back. He'd then spend weekends away on archaeological digs, sometimes under the pretext of work assignments. He missed Ethan greatly during these trips, but felt they revived him mentally for time together upon his return, his nerves un-shredded — wires straightened, fraying edges crimped and taped-up — by a few days away from Pippa, and a hotel or hostel room more conducive to sleep. But then he lost his job, and began picking up loose ends as a freelance writer — getting by, but lacking direction and drive.

One by one, in the strange electric light of his living room, Michael sifted through wallets of photographs, taken years ago on honeymoon and on various holidays before they moved to digital photography; before Ethan came along, from which point all the colour and life moved to hard drives. Michael recognised the different branded envelopes — one from an hour-long facility, another an overnight chemist, a third from a postal service that returned the prints within a week — and made associations with the corresponding occasions before even opening the flaps. But inside the half-filled envelopes were now only photos of himself, as well as the landscape pictures and tourist attractions he personally snapped. The only hint of Pippa lay behind the lens, looking at him; and even then, with the passage of time and the pointed return of these images, it felt as if she now looked away — pointing the camera, but otherwise absent. She hadn't gone so far as to tear him out of the shots of the two of them together; or, at least, she hadn't included them if she had. As a couple, either together or sundered, they'd vanished. These were pictures *of* him, *for* him.

Less than a week after the split, Michael and Pippa met in the neutral setting of the local park on a Saturday morning, Ethan jumping on and off swings and slides, running across the spongy black lava-like play surface, after giving his dad a hug. A couple of days earlier the boy's parents had spoken on the phone, to arrange the weekend handover, but with no real discussion of their situation. Her mind seemed clearly made up, and although he wanted to retain aspects of his old life, including full access to his son, it felt unfixable. And that became all the clearer by her body language: *She is gone, long gone*, he concluded.

This time, when he went to embrace her she offered nothing at all in return — not even the half-baked hug — and so he backed off, awkwardly. He thought to the vase on the windowsill in his new flat, and then a far nicer one they once shared at home: when first dropped, it brought pain — its perfection sundered — but also the instant urge to fix it, as tenderly as possible, even if some of the fissures would still be visible. It could never be perfect again, of course, but the cracks would only be seen close up. But when dropped again, and again, and those same fault-lines gave way while new splits emerged, it took longer to find the desire to fix it. It *could* be fixed, but why bother? It would only break again, only with new fracture lines. So in time it simply lay as shards in a kitchen cupboard, wrapped in newspaper, the glue waiting, but never applied. In the end, in pieces lined with trails of old, dried glue, it went in the bin.

"Have you explained everything to him?" Michael asked, as the pair — rather than maintain eye contact — watched Ethan, who instead of using the steps, hauled himself up the shiny metal chute of the slide, before, having not quite made it to the top, slipping back down it on his front, giggling all the way.

"I have. He was upset, of course, but I'm not sure he fully understands. I didn't want to go into too much detail with him. He's looking forward to having a new bedroom. He's very excited about that."

"It's all decorated and ready," Michael said, awaiting some kind of congratulation that never arrived.

He then looked hard at his wife, and wondered when she would become his *ex*-wife. Was it now? Had it already happened? The familiarity they shared already seemed oddly distant, and he tried to see in her the young women he first met. Barely five-foot one, with a super-sharp bob of black hair and a slightly pointy nose. An unremarkable mouth, too; thin lips, non-distinct teeth. But huge green eyes — sharp and strigine — accentuated over time by additional eyeliner; and a clear femininity in her figure above the waist: almost shapelessly narrow hips — boyish, even — but a surprisingly full bust for her slight frame. The exact same haircut, give or take an inch or two, since they met — only now its blackness dyed, to cover the grey. Unusually for a Saturday morning, she wore full make-up. He tried, and failed, to remember the last time she looked this way in his company. For years he had stopped appreciating her attractiveness, and only saw it afresh too late, as he tried to look through the eyes of Douglas, the man who'd replaced him. She made an effort to look nice, and surely not for her husband — unless just another way to say *Fuck you*.

"Look, I really need to go," Pippa said, abruptly. "I'll nip off now, while he's not looking. Drop him back tomorrow night, will you?"

For years Michael had promised Pippa that he would change — and he meant it, deeply, indubitably, in those moments of panic, before the bad habits consumed his good will. Before Ethan came along the irksome traits were just selfishness, pettiness, stubbornness — along with some drunkenness — and nothing as extreme as the way in which he later self-indulgently unravelled. At times he would go to great efforts to alter those off-putting character flaws — after all, he too hated what she had come to hate — and did so successfully … for a while. But slowly it crept back, bit by bit. Like a chainsmoker giving up too late, the cancer had already formed, the lungs riddled, the damage metastasised. He was, ostensibly, who he had grown into; not a terrible person, but someone too inclined towards life in his own bubble. A few of the improvements stuck — at least, to some degree — but overall he seemed little better. Perhaps over a greater period of time, with repetition of the drills and mantras, and with the motivational levels staying close to desperate — because desperate seemed the only place where it made proper sense, where it broke through his self-deception — he could have made a more substantial difference, and altered what resided at his very core, but like overstretched elastic pulled this way and that, he snapped back, with a sharp rubbery slap, to his old self. Maybe now the reality of a need to change — to hold together his collapsing life — would take greater hold. Too late for his marriage, maybe he'd finally wake up to the blatant wake-up call, and smell the coffee he himself brewed.

It didn't help that he retained some romantic vision of the writer as a free spirit, who could justify the suffering of others — and not just himself — for his art. His first novel raged out of him, finished at the tender age of 24 — the work of a Bright Young Thing, lauded by broadsheet newspapers and literary journals, after signing a three-book deal with a well-respected publisher. It sold reasonably well, without ever allowing him the lifestyle or fame he'd imagined it would bring, and without ever salving the itch of the outsider. There were launch parties, book tours, and a few adoring fans, including Pippa — back then a literature undergraduate he met in a small bookshop after a reading to a dozen attendees. But no life-changing sums of money, no real celebrity. He didn't need the fame and the cash —

at least, that's what he told himself — but harboured ambitions for respect. He could do better, and he knew it.

Yet his second novel proved a far more painful affair, scraped out of his imagination onto notebooks and scraps of paper, and then onto his new Macintosh SE, bought with the proceeds of the first; a horrible experience of wondering if he'd used up his cache of ideas in one go, and fearful of repeating himself. And how could he write about life when he'd yet to truly *live*? The debut novel now felt so shallow. With the bravura of youth he had the arrogance to think he had something to say; a few years on — still in his twenties, although the drafting and redrafting would stretch over well into his thirties — he felt less certain. There also lingered that one stinging review of his debut — in a popular broadsheet — that tumbled about his head whenever he sat down to write, goading him — hearing it in the reviewer's mocking voice, which he imagined as thin and full of snark — about the clichés and stock characters he relied upon. The second novel took six years to complete, and vanished without trace: a heavy tome, that may as well have been placed onto the surface of the sea in the middle of the ocean; vanishing, not a single wave made. By then journalism paid his way; the humiliation of being dropped by both his publisher and his agent offset by the progress he made at *The Aviation Enquirer* — a job he initially took out of necessity when the advance from his debut ran dry, but which rekindled a childhood interest in the world of flight.

Yet there remained a third novel, he sensed, balled up inside. The lack of a publishing contract meant the work could gestate, and percolate, loosely forming within his mind, unspoilt by the firm choices — for better, for worse — of *specific words*; a mix of feelings, sensations and visions, almost dreamlike in their composition, and semi-elusive, without solid language attached. One day, he told himself, he'd get around to dredging it all up, pulling it all out like a fishing line hauled from a cluttered canal with tangled, spinning stories attached.

Without question, he had indeed now lived. Now, as fifty approached, he could look back at genuine messes made, and loves felt, and hearts broken, and careers ruined, and new human life created, and parents lost, and separation from his child, and see that he had experienced life in a way only guessed at twenty-five years earlier. He had succeeded, and he had failed; multiple times on each side of the divide. And yet, did he want to haul all *that* up, and share it with the world? And would the world even want it?

***

Ethan stood nervously in the doorway of Michael's new flat, holding his action figure by its hand, so that it dangled beside him, its feet inches from the floor, like a man desperately clinging to a ledge by his fingernails. Supposedly full of his father's familiarity, this new world — a place to which he had never been — made no sense. Nothing about it resembled 'home'. "It's okay," Michael said, reassuringly, leading his son by the hand into the living room, as the plastic figure continued to swing and flail in the air. On the table sat a new box of Lego: a construction set — digger, cement mixer, and crane, unformed in cellophane bagfuls of mostly yellow, black and grey plastic bricks. In the corner of the room hunkered a small television and a cheap DVD player, with a few of the boy's favourite films, piled on the carpet. Elsewhere, new furniture: two big white beanbags in place of a sofa, their concave shape perfect for slumping into; a second chair for the fold-out table; and a desk and chair adjacent to the window, a space which doubled as a study. Ethan saw the Lego and smiled, but first wanted to see his bedroom. "Show me, Daddy." His face lit up — his eyes big and wide — when he saw the night sky on the walls, and the solar system bedding. He walked right up to the moon, stared intently at the paint from mere millimetres; perhaps expecting to see details, when all it revealed stood fuzzy and undefined. Then he turned and walked back into the lounge, and sat himself at the table, in front of the construction set. "Let's do this, Daddy," he said, placing the action figure on the table, with its back to the wall, so that it faced them, in order to spectate. "Come on!" he said, as if he'd been waiting an hour.

Ethan assigned Michael the role of putting the Lego together, with the boy turning the page on the instruction booklet — sometimes too quickly, sometimes to some random page. The boy also sorted the bricks into piles based on their colour, and then, when shown the illustration, located the necessary pieces. He also assembled the four little workers, who, for some unknown reason, then started to fight; possibly some kind of miniature labour dispute, with their workaday tools — spanners, hammers, wrenches — suddenly firing lasers. Within fifteen minutes Ethan flitted again, looking at the many types of empty cardboard box that lined the far wall. "Come on, Daddy, let's make a castle," he said, abandoning the existing build project — spilling a headless plastic torso onto the table — to imagine a new construction on a completely different scale. When Michael remained staring at the instruction manual, trying to identify the type of brick illustrated — counting the number of little round pegs, up to two rows of twelve — his son took his father's hand and dragged him from the table. "This will be the biggest fun."

These boxes arrived with no corresponding manual. Its architect: four years old, instructing his father as to what went where. At times Ethan stood sizing up the boxes for where they could go, and then suddenly he hid inside one, saying "Can you see me?", or swinging another around. He span in circles with long, narrow boxes on his arms, like propeller blades, until one edge dislodged the vase on the windowsill. When it fell to the floor it shattered with a sharp pop — sundering its old sutures, but also, just as with the old one at the erstwhile marital home, creating new fragments, fresh pieces. With a sharp intake of breath Ethan let go of the box and froze on the spot, his arms rigid by his sides.

"It's okay, Sunshine," Michael said. "It's just rubbish anyway."

1974

Dawn sunlight crested over distant Scottish peaks as winter, crisp and icy at dawn, crawled back into the territory of spring; returning only after allowing, by its absence, the last of the snow on the caps to melt, before — upon its belated return —

refreezing the liquid as shining sheets of verglas. The whistles of lone birds carried on the otherwise noiseless skies of the glen, until Geoffrey Freeman slammed closed the doors to the Morris Minor panel-van that, like audible radar, sent its clanging echo out into the landscape, reverberating on crags and fells and escarpments on its way back to the trio of men in the valley. This sudden sharp sound led to another: a rasping call or cry, from some unseen, unrecognisable creature, that screeched like the last gasp of a strangled bagpipe.

With gloved hands still warm from mugs of coffee decanted from a suitably tartan flask beside the van, the team set out on the long trek from the carpark to the site; shoulders and arms loaded with backpacks, camera equipment, shovels, camping gear, basic medical supplies and the specialised utensils of the aviation archaeologist. The trip to the site and back could be done in a day, but any problems would necessitate the construction of some kind of camp.

"Lovely morning for it," Geoffrey stated, taking in a deep breath as he surveyed the prospect; inhaling what seemed the freshest air possible.

"Beautiful," noted Alvin Griffiths, a Trinidadian history professor, with a cadence that lilted lightly with each of the three syllables. "Though as you know, a bit cold for my liking," he added.

"For once, your complaints are valid," Geoffrey said, with a sincere smile.

"I really can't believe you two talked me into this," the third man, Timothy Hodge — frowning, with a fat jaw and loose jowls, all hanging together to form a countenance of disgust — grumbled in characteristic fashion, as they took the first steps towards their remote target. A retired aviation engineer, Hodge — only ever referred to by his last name — had recently taken early voluntary redundancy. "I gave up work to have some lie-ins, for crying out loud."

"Well, the views are much better here, my good man," Geoffrey said, looking round at his companion, who already — just one hundred yards into the trek — straggled behind. "No factory walls here, you see. No acrid fumes."

The colour palette of the morning, accentuated by the sun's lambent orange glow, sent a mix of muted rustic hues across the vistas: shades of pale grass and lichen rendered cuprous and russet, clustered amid the juts of reddish rock and slate whose true greyness would only gradually reveal itself as dawn turned fully to day and the light burned increasingly blue-white. Panoramas paled toward the horizon, thick layers of atmospheric perspective thinning out the colour on the furthest ridges of highland; the depth clear in how pale each peak appeared, with the mountains themselves rendered two-dimensional shapes. Behind the three men, whitened by a pall of fog hanging over the lowland, lay the carpark, already some distance below, muted and obscured. They hiked in a constant vibrant middle-ground — an aperture of clarity — forever leaving one misty land for another.

The three silently negotiated the shoulders of a cluster of Munros, with their softer curving peaks, shaped like sand dunes covered in moss and shale; their peaks, up above, more regularly mountainous, more jagged and pyramidal. Iron-rich rock, veined with ferrous striations, lined the path of flinty shingle and scree scrunching beneath their steel toe-capped and hobnailed boots; Hodge occasionally grumbling about potential blisters — he could sense them forming — as he continued to lag behind the other two men, who did their best to ignore him. Man-made rock structures and stone piles appeared occasionally as lone — and apparently lost — sentinels, oddly bereft, until eventually the path appeared untrodden, at the point where the impact of human life ceased to leave a trace. All they knew is that at least two people — maybe the first — had hiked a trail in this direction and located some industrial wreckage that, due to the rust and weathering they described, suggested some distant airbound catastrophe. The debris didn't lay at a particularly treacherous height — but miles off the beaten track, even for hikers, and obscured in a small gulley, at a couple of thousand feet, between peaks that rose on either side.

The compass, rather than tracks on the ground, now led the way.

The early spring of 1974, it could instead have been any point in history after the ice age, whose monolithic glaciers slowly carved the topography. The trio's quest: to locate the wreckage recently reported by those highly-skilled mountaineers: possibly that of a small commercial airliner from the 1940s or '50s. Geoffrey, as usual, had a specific aircraft in mind. Now working in Scotland, he hurriedly assembled this team of three, ahead of an impending investigation by air, when the availability of two Sea Kings arose.

Eighteen months before the trio of Geoffrey, Alvin and Hodge set upon this mission, a Fairchild FH-227D bound for Santiago had crashed into the Andes, where, in eventual desperation, the Argentine rugby team it carried took to eating, slither by difficult slither, flesh carved from thigh and buttock; stripped from those who had died. It served as a stark reminder of the reality of a crash, and the aftermath, faced by survivors. Geoffrey had wondered if he'd rather have been one of those who perished immediately; he certainly couldn't envisage himself resorting to cannibalism, even if pushed well beyond the boundaries of decency, in the feral drive for food. He just didn't see how his body would literally stomach it. Indeed, not a big meat-eater in general, he'd concluded that he'd rather be eaten than have to chew and swallow the flesh of someone else. The thought of someone else eating his icy calf or his thigh — or even his buttocks — did not fill him with the slightest horror, as clearly, at that point, he would know nothing about it; although he flinched at the idea of his flesh on display, with some strange sense of modesty that transcended death. It almost felt like donating his body to science, in that others would benefit — as long as they treated his corpse with dignity, when forced to extract its fats and proteins and marrow.

If they located the aircraft, then would the survivors — if there had been any — have resorted to such extremes?

* * *

Despite no prior flying experience, Geoffrey signed up with the RAF in his early twenties. Taking to the training aircraft like a natural, he found himself fast-tracked to pilot Hurricanes. Having commenced an engineering apprenticeship before the outbreak of war — which he ditched in an instant in order to enlist — he later returned to conclude that education after 1945;

thereafter flying only for pleasure, or in an occasional testing capacity.

The Battle of Britain, in its own macabre way, proved amongst the best months of his life: so much adrenaline and gratification, camaraderie and passion, despite — or perhaps heightened by — so much death. He lost so many dear friends, but every day that he survived — just like every German shot down — felt worthy of celebration. It all passed so quickly by — gone in a flash — and yet, looking back, each day provided hundreds of small memories, that, when reviewed, made the summer seem to last forever. A year later, the summer of 1941, close to the Arctic Circle, felt even more magical, until things went awry.

In 1948, newly married to an outwardly shy and timid — but at times, privately assertive — young woman named Dorothy Taylor-Smythe, he joined the MRES: the RAF's Missing Research and Enquiry Service. His role involved the identification and documentation of specific aircraft wrecks and, in some cases, overseeing an exhumation of the entombed crew, in order to provide fit and proper burials. Those unlucky enough to fall beyond the bounds of the British Isles often went unrepatriated. Simply left — although, as at times he saw it in his frustration, *abandoned* — as war graves. It irked him that the Americans went to every length to bring home their fallen heroes, but the MRES' budgetary limits, like that of the United Kingdom as a whole in those austerity years, had gone way beyond a simple tightening of the belt. Never intended as a permanent operation, a mere year after Geoffrey joined the department the MRES headquarters were closed, the operation scaled down to the RAF Graves Service; and again, before long, that too shrunk to just a handful of operatives. At that point he moved to Farnborough, taking on a position as a junior civilian air-crash investigator, juxtaposing his knowledge of flying with some reasonable engineering expertise. As such, he soon visited several manufacturers: their factories and their developmental workshops, their wind tunnels and their test strips. He returned several times to the headquarters of De Havilland in Hatfield, after the catastrophic Comet failures between 1952 and 1954, that were, at the time, the biggest puzzle in aviation; the Comet having seemed like the industry's greatest post-war achievement, only to keep falling from the skies.

By late 1956, Geoffrey's time at Farnborough neared its end. He'd agreed to take a less demanding job adjacent to London Airport, and would soon be moving his wife and young son — not coping well at his first school — across to Hounslow. Immediately following the boy's birth, Dorothy had fallen into a deep depression that often manifested as extreme anxiety. Rather than improve, her neuroticism seemed to worsen with the passing of time. Geoffrey's frequent travelling, including extended trips overseas to examine stricken British aircraft, put too much of a strain on the relationship. Despite a whole host of doubts, moving to London Airport felt like a fresh start, to try and offer more time to his struggling wife and child. Generally eager to make a go of things, at times the prospect aroused an anxiety all of his own.

His final investigation centred on a DC-3 that went missing on a flight from London to Glasgow; an aircraft that literally fell off the radar. He had, he later realised, seen the plane itself taxying to takeoff from the new viewing galleries of the Queen's Building, although he had no recollection of the specific aircraft amongst the many he and Monty looked at that day. Of all the planes they did see, none appeared to have any obvious issues, or else he would have remembered. At the very least, he would have found a way, there and then, to contact the control tower. Even the slightest hitch on the ground could prove disastrous at ten-thousand feet, or when coming in to land. He certainly remembered the snowstorm — they beat a hasty retreat inside when it rolled in, lest he be chided once home for exposing the boy to the freezing precipitation. Did he not know how bad little Monty's colds could get? The blizzard certainly made for poor flying conditions, although no one realised just how severe and far-reaching the storm would prove.

1956

With Gladys temporarily detained, in the anxious hours before the DC-3 hit the mountainside and broke apart, it required the air hostess at the front of the aircraft to rush to the rear with the sick bag, as the black-haired girl in the row in front of Frank and James vomited in the bounce and bluster of turbulence.

The young hostess, so serene and full of bright smiles at the start of the flight, looked perturbed. She smiled at them both, as they looked on with concern, but it seemed a false smile; forced, not through insincerity but, Frank suspected, *fear*.

"It'll be okay," she said.

Frank looked at her name tag, taking a moment to focus.

"Thank you … *Alice*," he said, trying to force his own smile out from underneath the anxiety.

Part Two

1940

The cottage first existed as an old two-up two-down farmhouse; later extended, in keeping with the general style, in two directions. Charlotte's father, Edward, inherited the farm from his parents, years after moving out — and into white-collar work as an accountant. He moved back in with his young family, adding the extensions over time. Without warning — no prior scares — Edward died of a massive heart attack in 1934, and Charlotte's mother passed away after a battle with cancer a year before the declaration of war in September 1939, following months of steady deterioration interrupted by increasingly brief periods of respite. Charlotte's elder sister Kitty lived in Glasgow, studying maths, and although she returned for part of that summer, it had largely been left to Charlotte to care for their mother. The sense of purpose it provided — despite the ultimate, if not unexpected conclusion — helped to change her own thoughts from an initial plan of studying English or journalism; the war merely confirming a need to enlist at nursing college. She would have happily sold the property, given its size and the mixture of memories, but Kitty wanted to keep it, for the next few years at least, in case she had to move back after graduation. They had discussed leasing it out, but no decision had yet been made, and so it sat empty for most of each month, except on the days Charlotte returned to check things over, and escape her cramped billet.

In truth, unless selling it — with the finality of never having to set foot inside again — Charlotte couldn't bring herself to hand the cottage over to strangers, and barely had the spare time to prepare the property, or to find willing occupants. As she pottered around, giving the place a gentle dusting — wiping shelves, shaking a rug outside — she tried to imagine what others might do in the cottage, and how she'd feel about it when she had to clean up after them. This — the dust that had gathered — was *her* mess, even if it accrued in her absence.

As a compromise, she told herself that if she ever heard of any desperate, bombed-out families then she would intervene, but she knew of none. It saddened her that its rooms were not full with the smells and sounds of children; she had no such maternal yearnings herself, but the house and its surrounding land suited young tenants. It seemed perfect for a family — perhaps even an expanded one, with the arrival of evacuees. A house, she concluded as she moved from room to room, should have life pounding cracks in its floorboards and chipping paint from its skirting boards, not lying cold and dark and unloved.

Despite the property sitting empty, the land still served a purpose. Although previous generations of her family sold off nearly all the sprawling arable acreage over the years, to the point where her grandfather retained just half an acre still tended by a neighbouring farmer, there remained plenty of fertile ground beyond the lake, stretching across to where the boundary fence separated what became her family's garden from the fields in the mid-distance. In the spring she had set aside a large plot for use as an allotment, to help the nearest village with its supply of fresh vegetables: her contribution to Dig For Victory. On her days at the cottage, even as the nights drew in and with much of the vegetation withered, she could be found wielding a hoe, greening her fingers and blistering her palms until long after dusk.

She needed to feel a hands-on contribution, away from nursing, when time allowed. She needed to touch earth and muck; to nestle in the ground those delicate seeds that miraculously bloomed into life, oblivious to the presence of war: for they grew, if tended, irrespective of whether or not bombs fell — unless, of course, obliterated by a direct hit. She found it such an unexpected therapy, making something grow so that others might reap the benefits, in the face of unceasing death and destruction. Not all of her patients survived — some arrived beyond hope, while others, sometimes for no obvious reason, slowly deteriorated and slipped away — but the plants mostly thrived with just minimal tending. And any that did not were unworthy of tears and anguish; perhaps they would simply flourish in the next season, or something fresh could grow in its place. Well into October, the last crop of potatoes was due, before the ground froze over and sealed them under rock-hard earth.

Viktor, making his own slow progress, served as her source of motivation: everything about his existence in her life filled her with a greater sense of purpose. Anything that had potential to help the community found those very uses applied to him. Her every thought of the future contained his presence. One day, she imagined, he would help her tend the carrots and the tomatoes and the runner beans.

The simple act of digging potatoes felt the most precious to Charlotte. It seemed to encapsulate the very essence of maintaining a normal existence in an overbearing war. It gave hope — signalled that everyday efforts were not in vain, and that out of the darkness could come light. In their way, potatoes, deep and unseen, were like buried treasure. Once out of the ground they reverted to plain old spuds — misshapen brown lumps that offered reasonable sustenance and nutrition — but at the moment the fork dug into the ground, and agitated the earth — so that the first glimpses of those mottled skins snuck into view — it became a treasure hunt, a voyage into the unknown.

The deeper one digs, the more one may find, in a whole host of delightful and strange shapes and sizes. Always when I think I have discovered them all, one more appears: the very last surprise.

* * *

The raucous sound of a big band, topped by giddy laughter and cries of joy, reverberated around the smoky room, as younger couples jitterbugged and foxtrotted with vim and vigour, and then reluctantly vacated the floor so that older couples — some of the men with limps, and lopsided upper torsos drooping left or right — might waltz and tango; their chance to be Josephine Bradley and Victor Silvester in *Let's Make a Night of It*. Around the perimeter sat men too immobilised or unwilling to dance, but still able to share in the infectious gaiety — feel the beat and the bass and the brass of the band in their chests — and partake in the consumption of alcohol, puff away at cigars, pipes and cigarettes; feeling that bit closer to a return to normality.

With war cast momentarily aside, the Christmas dance appeared a great success. Every nurse had taken the chance to wear her best dress, while doctors and surgeons were suited and booted, with up-patients resplendent in their hospital blues. The ballroom also heaved with locals — many with connections to the airbase or hospital, including those who worked menial jobs, but also some of their friends, and a few strangers eager for a good time. Charlotte wore her favourite black Schiaparelli-style frock, with its playfully large floral buttons, and her last unblemished pair of silk stockings, saved for such an occasion.

Despite dressing to the nines, she could not relax; something — or rather, *someone* — remained absent: only a couple of hundred yards away, laid up in a nearby building and still unable to stand on his own two feet. Despite her best efforts to tease him out, Viktor insisted that he could not stand to witness the fun "as a bloody cripple". She tried to hide her disappointment, but could hear it in her own voice when she told him that she understood. As a compromise, she promised to pop in and check on him, and perhaps wheel him outside for fresh air and a cigarette.

Sensing their chance, other men asked her to dance, but she found excuses to decline.

With the aid of hindsight, perhaps I actually sensed something else — something altogether larger — was wrong, but I fear such superstition to be tommyrot of the worst sort, that one only sees after the event, to make oneself feel in some way superior. Hindsight really is no form of wisdom.

As the evening wore on, Viktor's absence started to feel overwhelming, further sparked by Charlotte's own increasingly conflicted feelings at seeing so much joviality: if *he* could not enjoy it, she suddenly felt unable to do likewise. She couldn't wait any longer. She slipped quietly from the ballroom, quickly crossing the street that separated the hotel from the hospital, covering her hair from the wind-blown flecks of sleet-snow with a magazine grabbed from the foyer; eager for him to see her at her most glamorous. Almost at the heart of the hospital, at the central crossroads of corridors, she heard a whistling sound, which developed into something akin to rustling paper, that in no time at all grew closer and louder. She felt a fierce ripple of air, just before the sky fell in.

Dazed and choking, Charlotte found herself — as her eyes opened — flat on her back, the world around her a dark haze permeated by slithers of light whose glow dimmed in sinister drifts of swirling smoke and dust; the air apparently sucked right out of her lungs and replaced with grit, her throat suddenly a rolled-up cylinder of sandpaper, volcanic ash settling on her tongue. All the while, some kind of bell rang in her ears. To one side lay the barely visible — but sadly, visible enough — body of a night porter, a steel beam crushing his skull to the flatness of a pancake.

She managed to lever herself upright, fumble to a stand. Giddy, she no longer knew where she stood within the vastly altered landscape of the hospital — the existing layout rendered meaningless in a mere matter of seconds by a series of *Sprengbomben Cylindrisch*. Old walls were gone, new walls — constructed from haphazard piles of rubble and collapsed ceilings — erected. Signs that once pointed to various corridors now vainly directed their arrows up at the sky. She needed to find doors that still led to the outside world, or new openings carved out by the explosives. Pockets of fire burned, but small in size, and at reasonable intervals — the bombs, it seemed, only of the explosive variety, and not accompanied by the added menace of incendiaries. Still, it only needed a small spark to find its way to a leaking gas pipe, and further hell would break loose.

Unsteady on her feet, she moved through the particle storms blowing about her in the gloomy hulk of what she recognised as the operating theatre, its distinctive stainless steel apparatus — whose uncovered surfaces glinted with orange reflections in the murk — helping her regain her bearings. She called out for help. "Hello? Anyone there?" She shouted again, louder. The only sound she heard: her own voice, deep inside her head, muffled by the ringing in her ears. Shouting harder led to fits of rasping coughs, but instinct kept her calling out; she cleared her throat and spat out gritty, bloody phlegm, then called again. Replies may have been forthcoming, but she couldn't hear. Below and to her left, unreachable figures lay silent and motionless in smouldering craters, the floor having caved right into the basement morgue.

She stepped into rooms shorn of their uprights, bereft of ceilings — merely collections of rubble and masonry, into which fine drifts of snow blew and melted upon contact with the hot atmosphere; the pureness of the precipitation obliterated in an instant, with an unheard gentle fizz and hiss as flakes dissolved on contact. Light and dark, good and evil, all at work in the swirl about her. Despite atheistic tendencies since childhood — with the premature death of both parents confirming rather than confounding her lack of belief — she found herself mumbling to God, on the off-chance that He existed. Was He listening? What did she have to lose in asking?

I fear I did not make the greatest sense, but He need only look at me to understand the points I made. There came no reply, no sense of anything spiritual, no sense of a guiding hand — just chaos. Where was V? Dear Lord, where was V? Was he okay? Oh how my soul trembled.

Charlotte resolved to make for light, or life — whichever she happened upon first; unaware of her bleeding, mainly from superficial cuts, but also a handful of fairly nasty gashes on her legs and arms; and a deeper one on her side, that would later need several stitches. Her head hurt, and her joints ached — a rag-doll stretched too far in all directions, threads coming loose at the seams — but felt not even the slightest hint of the lacerations. In the near-dark, her sense of smell went into overdrive, with nostrils full of powdered concrete and spilt guts; of vaporised human blood, and flash-fried skin and flesh; of pulverised brick and wood and plaster; of mangled latrines and exposed sewer pipes; and of soot and smoke and ash.

Walking in the dark, across unsteady ground, proved tricky — her balance adversely affected by the ringing in both ears, at a pitch which altered like someone tuning a wireless, before, minutes later, finally dissipating into the wail of sirens raging above distant screams, shouts and murmurs. Did she hear the outside world, or her own damaged eardrums?

Walls continued to collapse, ceilings to cave in. She thought about removing her high-heeled shoes, which had never been the easiest to walk in, even on the flattest surfaces. Yet she traversed a mass of rubbled masonry, twisted metal and jagged shards of glass — even splintered bone — unsafe for the naked sole. She persevered, until reaching the toilet block. The Gents stood half-obliterated, and she could see straight into this previously private chamber. An isolated fire lit the scene, half-obscured by smoke and dust. In the remnants of a confined toilet cubicle, a single foot set at an unnatural angle from the ankle protruded from a mountain of debris: all that remained visible of an airman who, in his short life, braved all altitudes of aerial combat, but who could do nothing, sat on the loo, to escape what rained down upon him like some biblical catastrophe. The lack of a cast proved it wasn't Viktor, provoking a sense of relief, followed by a stab of guilt at her selfishness. She could do nothing for the man, she concluded; unable to even consider lifting any of the concrete and ironwork that formed his tomb. Death had surely landed upon him, in one unsurvivable deluge. If she made it out, she would inform those tasked with search and rescue, and with recovering the corpses.

On she moved, wading through fast-flowing streams of near-freezing water that gushed from broken mains pipes, dousing pockets of flames as it washed over rubble, like waves lapping against a rocky shoreline. Every step taken involved careful consideration, but she sensed a growing momentum; until her shoe pressed down on something soft, like a mattress, beneath the murky waterline.

As a distant torch beam, waved in hope, drifted across the room it became clear, when she looked down, that she stood on the headless torso of a patient, still dressed in partially shredded striped red pyjamas, his neck an indescribable mess, his head nowhere to be seen. Her heel stabbed against his stomach like a bayonet. The tattoo of a rose — with its uniquely personal *JOAN* stencilled on a curving scroll — on one partially severed forearm identified him as airman Hopson: a likeable, if occasionally excessively cheeky and immature young man. Her knees buckled, and she retched without actually vomiting, and somehow managed to regain her composure and continue towards safety. There existed no middle ground between success and failure, she told herself, as parts of the building continued to crumble: *You either make it, or you don't.* Tears welled in her eyes, the byproducts of smoke and tragedy, gummed up on eyelids with layers of dust and mascara. She made for the distant torch beam, that, as she neared, finally pinned her like a follow-spot. "Lady, over here!" came the shout of an RAF fireman, chiming out above the drone in her ears like a declaration of love, as she moved toward the light.

I am certain that I will forever more hear those words, in that beautiful thick Geordie accent, whenever I think back.

A blanket touched her shoulders, and she finally relaxed. Almost immediately she began to shiver. In the next heartbeat her legs gave way, unceremoniously sending her onto her backside. Yet her thoughts went to Viktor. Where was he? Had he suffered a similar fate to poor Hopson, whose headless body lingered within her optics, ghoulishly flickering across her mind's eye whenever she tried to focus on the face of her Icelandic airman. Those patients were sitting ducks. So many of those convalescing proved too helpless to make their own escapes; half-slaughtered lambs, ripe for butchery, in pens that hemmed them in. Even if he had wanted to, Viktor could not run away.

A tearful VAD helped Charlotte to her feet. The girl, trembling, handed over a hot water bottle and led Charlotte around the main buildings towards the largely unblemished canteen, where a temporary emergency room-cum-command centre swiftly sprung into action.

And there he sat! — her foreign airman, safe and well, in a wheelchair, wrapped in blankets, smoking a cigarette, his hair and face grey with dust. A living ghost. Momentarily she lost his features in a fog of exhaled smoke and vapour, and then he saw her.

He smiled like a Cheshire cat when our eyes met, and I felt a flutter inside, the queerest mix of soaring heart and sick stomach, still full of the terror of what might have been — and what had indeed befallen so many others. I scarcely dare believe what I saw. I thought that, yes, perhaps He might exist after all. Then, I thought back to Hopson, and other innocents, and to the entire blasted war, and that brief flicker of faith faded away.

She would later be informed of someone dragging Viktor from the burning building, having discovered him crawling over the debris just within the entrance. Earlier, right before the blasts, he sat in a wheelchair in the porch, sheltering from the snow, lighting up a Craven A, listening to the muted distant hum of the big band and marvelling at the beautiful light snow — whose drifts reminded him of home — when he heard the whistles, before the payload pierced the roof. The overexcited VAD, Stella, told Charlotte that he had toppled himself out of his wheelchair and dragged himself inside to look for survivors. It left Charlotte to wonder, with no little vanity, if he had sought one particular survivor to rescue, or had it just been an impartial act of bravery. Viktor knew she'd be at the dance, but she'd also promised to pop in to the ward, to say hello. Hurrying past in the cold wet air — swiftly ushered along — she witnessed, as she glanced over her shoulder, a man so very calm in appearance, puffing away, as if resuming the very cigarette from which he'd been so rudely interrupted. She could only assume that a burning hospital appeared less daunting to him, even without the ability to walk, than a smouldering and uncontrollable aircraft travelling at great speed. By contrast, to crawl inside a bombed building — with standing rendered impossible, and where those who *could* stand moments earlier were now on hands and knees, or flat on backs, or shorn of legs — must have felt to him like a full sense of control.

He looked so utterly unaffected by it all, so insouciant, so devil-may-care. Did he now value life more, or less? Either way, I knew, in that moment, that I loved him even more. I had lost him, only to find him again.

The unharmed and the walking-wounded arrived from devastated parts of the building, with scraps of equipment rescued from an untouched corner of a ward, or some undamaged store cupboard: bandages, tubes of unguents, medical utensils in need of fresh sterilisation, mobile lighting rigs, towels and blankets. Someone even thought to bring a vase of flowers that had been tipped onto its side, but not shattered; utterly unnecessary, and yet representing so much. Helpers found a kettle and started boiling water. Nurses, doctors and surgeons arrived in droves from the aborted dance, still dressed in their swankiest suits and swishest ballgowns. Scores of people flitted and scuttled and orbited, like clusters of chaotic planetary matter eventually coalescing into one coherent, organised whole.

Sat at a table, nursing a tepid, tasteless mug of coffee whose limited flavour vanished with the dust and phlegm mixing unfavourably with the iron-tang of blood in her mouth and throat, Charlotte stared out at the night sky through a window whose glass, as the only significant damage sustained by the canteen, had been blown in. She stared past men and women dashing about, often in highly inappropriate elegant attire, hurrying to help remove the wounded and the deceased — whole, and in parts. She stared at the munitions dump in the distance, glowing the most beautiful but destructive shade of orange.

She wanted to help. Surely she could do her bit? Alas, her legs still refused to support her weight. They could not even convey her to an upright position. She had not been shaking when trying to make her escape, but as soon as she made it to safety her whole body rattled and shook, in a constant spasming. The paralysis, as she sat and stared at her drink, left her feeling guilty, and utterly inadequate. People needed her, and to her great shame, she could not help.

Midnight: the mess-hall abuzz with the frantic gestures of able-bodied doctors and nurses — some able to find clean gowns and aprons, others still in formalwear — attending to a series of bloodied casualties, administering splints and medication as fast as they could be located. Those laid out on gurneys and makeshift beds included several members of the medical staff. Two healthy VADs as of an hour earlier were pronounced dead. One of the girls to die — Margaret — Charlotte had considered a friend. Not an especially close friend, but a friend all the same, with a certain warmth to the niceties they shared. They had spoken at length about their shared love of the West Pier, and how they looked forward to it reopening after the war. Margaret had her own wartime sweetheart: one of the senior surgeons. A married man, Charlotte made it clear to Margaret that she did not approve, but also added that it was probably none of her business, and, in these testing times, certainly not her right to be judgemental. That both women were so newly enamoured made them kindred spirits, eagerly sharing updates on their beaus. Margaret now lay as one of at least ten fatalities, with many others — dead or alive — still sought in the hellscape of wreckage and rubble.

* * *

In the translucent morning light, with broken outlines of buildings puncturing the mist, the destruction of the hospital looked even more pervasive; the peaks and valleys of what remained edging into focus through the haze as Charlotte hobbled up the hill — across cobbled stones encircled with glassy rings of ice encapsulating specks of powdery snow — from her downhill billet. It elicited an audible gasp: the surprise at the sheer extent of the damage; instantly sobering to see the building — partially covered in the snow that fell in the hour or so after the fires were extinguished — suffering such familiar injuries: burns and breakages. These, however, were well beyond her powers of repair.

Blast it, she said, under her breath, unaware of the pun.

Time had passed so strangely in the ten-or-so hours since she left the ballroom. Barely refreshed, she needed to see and speak to her Iceman. At just after midnight, once the nearly undrinkable coffee went cold, she had found the strength to will her body back into motion. In her partially torn black dress, and still in unhelpful high heels, she insisted on pitching in with the recovery efforts, once her own wounds were stitched and dressed. To nip away to find Viktor meant betraying those in greatest need.

In turn, she patched up cuts, applied tourniquets, issued painkillers — doing her bit in some kind of automatic daze, until total exhaustion cloaked her in the heaviest of invisible cloths, layer by layer. Only at five in the morning did her head find its way onto its blessed pillow, and she sank instantaneously into a sleep that would never be allowed to last as long as required; her body aching for *days* of slumber. Barely had her eyelids met before she stretched to silence the frantic rattle of the spiteful alarm, and scrambled for her uniform, which hung neatly on the back of the door, above the crumpled, cut-up and bloodied black dress lying lifeless on the floor like a butchered mink. *Everything* hurt. A stiffness had set in, and the flesh wounds — to which she had been so oblivious — now smarted. She dressed in a semi-somnambulistic haze, and though feeling no sense of hunger whatsoever, ate cold toast on the short uphill walk to work.

Arriving back at the scene, she had expected to see a fair number of the surviving patients who weren't housed into the canteen squeezed into the one intact wing, whose electrical issues, she assumed, would prove easily solvable in the morning light. Instead, she returned to a hospital containing no patients at all, riven with bomb craters and the damage of water and smoke and fire, and myriad shattered windows. Though still upstanding, the one surviving wing — still without power — stood totally unusable due to flooding from a burst mains pipe, into which coursed raw sewage. The death toll now stood at a dozen confirmed, with a handful of others still unaccounted for.

Those with life-threatening injuries had been ferried to nearby hospitals throughout the night. The rest were either discharged early, if their convalescence neared completion, or, if still in need of ongoing treatment, moved shortly after dawn to other RAF hospitals around the country; ones not situated so dangerously close to an airfield. Viktor clearly fell into the latter category — and so he'd gone: wheeled up a ramp and driven to East Grinstead, some 30 or 40 miles away, where they specialised in pioneering burns treatments.

Whenever shall I see him again? East Grinstead may as well be Outer Mongolia. With the news my desperately faked stiff upper lip collapsed. *I excused myself, and broke down and sobbed most pitifully, for the first time since the unspeakable carnage. Yet even then I could not fully indulge the sadness, so required of me was it to put on a brave face and return to duty. I had to hold it all in, and I could feel its internal stabs, inside my aching skin.*

With all the gusto she could manage — her limbs loosening and their aches lessening as work warmed them up, and as both adrenaline and two tablets of Aspro overrode pain receptors — Charlotte joined in the cleanup operation on the shattered wards; half under cover, half surreally open to the elements, as cold winds blew settled snow crystals and dust particles and flecks of ash across the building. Sombre faces passed word around that the hospital would almost certainly not be rebuilt. What had once made sense — close at hand for the aircrews — now represented jeopardy. On one unrecognisable ward a wooden window frame dangled from its brick aperture like a loose milk tooth hanging onto gum; *By the very skin of its teeth*, Charlotte later noted. Two ward sisters lifted a sodden mattress from the floor, blood and dust and ash soaked deep into its fabric. In the corner, a young Irish nurse knelt in prayer over what she recognised as spattered brain matter. Out in a parking bay, beyond stubs of wall, lay a half-crushed ambulance tipped onto its side like a mere tin toy discarded by a little boy; giant craters plottable in a straight line from the driveway all across the once-lush hospital grounds, out towards the airbase.

Charlotte's stitches, beneath the dressings, now itched like hell. Every time they screamed for her attention she thought to those with *serious* injuries, and more pointedly, those no longer alive, as, in deep silence, she sifted through the detritus. As yet, none of the usual gallows humour that the nurses often shared in darker times — to stay sane — had arisen; this, it seemed, deemed even too grim for that.

After an hour or so the sun broke through parting cloud and dissipating fog, as it might to signify the end of a terrifying storm. Its muted winter glare reflected on the pools of water — many frozen over — and the shards of broken glass, and the 49-year bad-luck cumulation of smashed mirrors strewn across parquet floors, as Charlotte sombrely swept piles of debris towards the wall.

Her thoughts kept switching to the absence of the man who had just been driven from her life: the mixture of relief at his unblemished survival amidst a score of deaths, and indeed, the perk that he awaited more specialised treatment, that could speed his recovery, at a location less open to attack; but also, just how far away he already seemed, and how greatly it reduced her chances of ever seeing him. A dozen hours earlier he belonged to her, to see every day. Leaving the broom leaning against a wall, she made her way to the ward in which Viktor had been housed, using the outside landscape to make sense of its location. His bed — or at least what she took to be his bed, given the disarray — lay as a bent and broken frame, springs distended and contorted into unnatural shapes.

Suddenly I felt ever-so-thankful that we were both still alive. Mere separation can be overcome, I resolved, as I stared at the mangled mess of mattress and frame, which could so easily have been his deathbed. Distance need not prove the end. Death, by contrast, is never surmountable.

2010

Khaki grass, swept back across a black-rock shoreline at the brink of dawn; rugged grey-green sheafs, thriving at intervals from the volcanic shale; wild tunes whistled by Arctic winds swirling off the cliffs, curving around the beach, encircling Michael standing on the shore, as a sweet orange hue spread across the sea from the east. Unable to sleep, he had wandered from his hotel room out into the slowly lightening sky; a lone human, aside from those manning a distant fishing boat. He stared out at Reynisdrangar: the basalt sea stacks upright in the spume, stranded like a broken pier, as still and as dark as nighttime sentries. Cormorants squawked and squalled overhead, squabbling, over food with petrels, fulmar, shag, gannet. There hung a sense of unease in the air, perhaps from the way the birds fought and shrieked.

Homesick, he'd abandoned his plans to stay indefinitely and, having done at least some productive research on Kaldaðarnes and the missing planes — to make the trip worthwhile — booked a flight home, to leave on Friday. He'd see out his trip in Vík, chosen for its remote beauty and relative isolation.

It had seemed such a smart idea, to get away from England. Yet it simply confirmed how much he hated to shut out the thought of his son — to practice the art of compartmentalisation, and almost pretend the boy didn't exist; as, on some subconscious level, the pain continued to burrow jagged holes at his core. Yes, he could suppress his feelings, but even in the background — like an ignored fire raging in an adjacent room — they took their toll, as would rising heat, and smoke silently seeping under a locked door. Then, the times it all broke through, wild and fierce. Though he could do nothing in England but wait, he now wanted to wait *there*.

How had his son — the best thing that had ever happened to him — come to represent such desolation and sorrow? Rather than help, the physical distance — when thoughts and memories and daydreams piled forward from the back of his mind — just exacerbated the feelings. Images of Ethan frequently arose in his mind's eye, uncontrolled and random — almost naughtily so, in the way that little boys disobey their fathers — and so he tried to focus on something else instead. Jóhanna had taught him some basic meditation techniques, focusing on the breath, counting every inhale and exhale, slowing the rampage of images that flitted through his mind; or watching them pass like clouds in the sky. She had extolled the power of nature, and the need to let oneself feel as small as possible; the tiniest grain of black sand on the beach. In that sense, Iceland remained perfect. He took a deep breath, and a sense of peace arose, with moments of pain-free existence, feeling the cold sea breeze on his face and the fresh air pierce his lungs. But then Ethan jumped in, pulling at his attention as if tugging his trouser leg.

The birds began to scatter, skittish and spooked. In the distance — at the horizon — the dark orange sea lay as a sheet of glass, smooth and flat; but closer to shore it repeatedly shattered, as waves swirled up and clattered down. Some kind of storm appeared to be brewing to the west, high in the mountains. Did thunder just clap in distant clouds? Something rumbled, an uneasy shifting as he sought stillness.

Michael turned inland, walking along the rockier shoreline adjacent to the black-sand beach. Dried tubes of long-deceased rhubarb, almost fossilised, spiked from strips of turf. Thick grasses like pelts — the downy strands of yak's fur — draped over rocks beside fine-running rivulets trickling to the sea. Higher up: the church on the hill, popping from the dawn landscape with its white walls, tainted orange by the low sun, below its bright red roof and steeple. Lower down, houses crouched in knuckled clusters beneath rock-faces, protected from the wind in one direction, exposed in others.

The previous day he visited the nearby beach, behind a black sand dune, to see the shell of a wrecked Douglas C-47, the military version of the once ubiquitous DC-3; a hollow funnel of whitened aluminium, pocked with holes, minus its wings, like some silver seal washed ashore and left to rot. But this archaeology post-dated the war; well-known and well-documented — indeed, a surreal tourist attraction, beloved of photographers — it had ditched in 1973, in typically tricky Icelandic weather. Michael sensed something almost metaphorical in its treatment: the *Skytrain* of World War II, dropping hundreds of thousands of paratroopers beyond enemy lines, and given the name *Dakota* during its Commonwealth service; but its time, by the early 1970s, coming to an end. And so, instead of repair and repatriation, the stricken plane found itself stripped of all valuable instrumentation and abandoned on the dark volcanic beach.

A day later, and unexpectedly — given the early hour as he walked the Vík shore — Michael's phone began to ring, teetering on the edge of a signal. He recognised Jóhanna's number, but upon taking the call he could barely hear her over the crackle and cutout of the line, and the rumble in the mountains. Scraps of words drifted out of the earpiece, as she frantically — panting, with the phone tucked under her chin as she drove at high speed — repeated herself, until the line held long enough for him to comprehend.

"What are you doing up?!" she asked, sounding equally shocked that he'd answered.

"Couldn't sleep. Why the hell are you phoning?"

"To leave a message," she said, sounding like *to leaf a message*. "It is blowing!"

"What's blowing?" he said, walking along the beach in the hope of the signal boosting, images of leaves now in his mind.

"The volcano. Oh, *Helvítis fokking fokk!*" she exclaimed in her native tongue, having previously translated the fairly new Icelandic expression to Michael as, roughly, *What the fuckety fucking fuck.*

"Katla?"

"*Not* Katla."

He sighed in relief — not the big one she'd warned him of, as the great slumbering menace, overdue an apocalyptic eruption. If Katla blew, and blew big, Vík, where he stood, would become its Pompeii, its Herculaneum. He'd be one of the human shapes delineated by pumice in two-thousand years' time: *Idiot On Beach, Using Phone.*

"The storm?" he said, as if asking and answering his own question, as he gazed towards the distant mountains.

"No, no storm. Earthquakes, and lightening due to the eruption."

"Shit."

"Yes. Helvítis fokking fokk!"

The peak of the furiously rising plume burst into slow-moving cloud stained orange with sunlight that arced over the horizon; the rays as yet unable to reach down to the ground in Vík, which still lay in darkness. The cumuli, hanging limply, were brutally subsumed by the furore. Soon, great mountains of ash blew east and south, towards the beach that Michael had swiftly vacated, as tremors snaked along the shoreline.

As memories to Michael, these sights, in time, were overwritten with video footage from the soon-to-be circling helicopters and intrepid explorers and daring filmmakers; what he actually saw jumbled with what the mass media later projected, and repeated. But a sense of the *experience* remained; his human smallness, in the face of nature's fury.

Ash began to settle like snow, inches thick, as Jóhanna — Michael alongside her in the passenger seat — raced along the ring road, the yellow, metre-tall roadside markers barely visible, and the steep camber of the surface — the flanks falling into gullies — lost to the view; white lines just about clear enough to follow, the horizon unseeable through a dusty haze. Ash sprayed from tyres of the cars ahead — vague dark masses with muted red taillights — like water from puddles of dust.

"Eyjafjallajökull," she said, in the usual blur of sounds that, as before, left only *jökull* recognisable. "The one that has been rumbling for a while. But no one saw *this* coming. Not this big."

They drew closer to the eruption. Clouds of slate-grey dust spooled and unfurled in a continuous column from the caldera — out of the raw-red opening at five-and-a-half thousand feet — that reached a further five miles high, darkening the sky, turning day to night. Rolling eruptions, specks and flecks of black, launched like potent missiles. The bubbling curves of grey-brown clouds, whilst at the edges, futile mists of steam.

The caldera burst right through the glacier — six-hundred feet of compacted ice; the meltwater cooling the lava to form black-glass particles projected like fizzing fireworks, along with catapulted rocks: obsidian, formed of fire and ice. The world turned greyscale by ash and silica, colour diluted, diffused. Lightning pulsed at the volcano's peak, as red-hot lava spewed and ash bellowed. The smell of sulphur — and something else, like burning hair — streamed into the car's cabin via the heaters.

"*Fokk!*" Jóhanna blurted, her mind racing, the car slowing. "I must stop. I can't see."

They stopped at a lay-by, sloping out of the car as the wind howled and whistled. Black sandstorms blew from the backs of vehicles that sped by, eery headlights approaching out of nothingness. Others, defeated by the conditions, abandoned at the roadside. Footprints were ploughed into the powder, tyre tracks cutting trails.

On the far side of the caldera, the meltwater from hundreds of metres of ice flooded down the mountainside. It could flood this way, too. Jóhanna concluded it clearly unsafe to go any further, and before long the authorities approached in a lit-up SUV, and an impatient police officer told them to turn around and get the hell out of there.

* * *

The fine fur of a rare red fox — dark orange strands flicking delicate and free from the smooth ice under which its body lay trapped — caught the eye of two American hikers on the far side of the Eyjafjallajökull glacier. Late April, the volcano had only recently ceased its chaos-inducing eruptions. The meltwater — *jökulhlaup* — had dispersed in floods, as magma flash-thawed skyscraping columns of impacted ice. Just days earlier, in the malevolence of the active caldera, meltwater regularly sloshed into the volcanic vent, eliciting an even more explosive response; eight-hundred people from the surrounding area swiftly evacuated, European air travel ground to a halt.

Eyjafjallajökull duly becalmed — although still officially off-bounds — and with planes back in the sky, the daredevil hikers climbed up from Stakkholtsgjá canyon to stand on a ridge, staring down at a glassy expanse of ice mottled with ash, smoothed out by the floods. Peering closer, the fox seemed trapped under some kind of metal sheet, from which its fur protruded. Intrigued, the man and his girlfriend hacked at the ice with their mountaineering axes — the surface layer shattering with streaks of lightning-like lines, forming fissures and clouding crystals, blurring their quarry as they burrowed closer. With the ice increasingly unclear as they chipped away at it, it took the tips of their axes chinking against the metal below to confirm when they'd reached the necessary depth. The pair, on their knees, scraped the icy fragments aside, and, with all their might — the woman pulling the man, as the man pulled the metal — pried the corner of the sheet upwards.

Clear beneath smooth ice to a depth of a few inches — protected from their picks by the metal sheet — lay two flattened but unmistakably *human* faces.

The fox — it became clear to the hikers, their stomachs sinking — was not a fox after all; instead the red hair of a young man, with another man's face pressed tight beside his, preserved to perfection under the glassy ice.

The frozen pair, in eternal futility, holding on to one another for dear life.

* * *

Once retired, Geoffrey Freeman entered the world of Icelandic aviation investigation and archaeology as an unofficial advisor, after his relocation — drawn back in the mid-'90s by myriad magnetic forces — to his wartime home of Akureyri. Iceland clearly lacked the technical and technological knowledge — and resources — of the British air industry, and as such, he found himself conferred with something of an exalted status. He could remain an expert, without the pressure of full-time employment.

Before long, the newly-formed Icelandic aviation archeology team invited him to join, and enjoyed the chance to travel around the island and make new friends. Decades on, he remained sprightly and active well into his eighties, and even nearing ninety in 2010, had no debilitating signs of physical or mental decline, beyond an occasional slight unsteadiness on his feet and worsening vision that his spectacles never quite perfectly adjusted.

Geoffrey and Michael Marston had exchanged numbers after the aborted Winchelsea dig in the early summer of 1987 — Michael seizing upon Geoffrey's belated admission to a fascinating career in aviation, to add to his list of contacts in the industry. The older man, after emigrating, later invited the journalist over to participate in digs. In return, Michael had recently written an article about the state of aviation and air crash investigation in Iceland — the litany of lost craft in a snow-bound war — including a brief profile of Geoffrey, looking back at his flying experiences, his post-war missing aircrew research, then his nomadic investigative career, after he escaped north-east Scotland for north-east Iceland; noting that, short of the Arctic Circle, Mr Freeman had no places to which he could flee north-east.

A few weeks ago, Michael had phoned Geoffrey to let him know that he'd pitched up in Iceland on a whim, and that he might make a detour to Akureyri to stop by. Michael's focus remained the deserted Kaldaðarnes airbase, and the Ravilious mystery, but he also planned to kill some time, away from his troubles back home. And yet, just before Eyjafjallajökull blew, he had changed his plans: looking to return home, to sneak surreptitious sightings of his son until the court case; deciding that even if he couldn't be in contact, he could serve as some ghostly guardian angel, doing his bit — an hour here or there — to monitor the boy's progress and, should some kind of emergency arise, be on hand to intervene, and to hell with the consequences. What kind of father would be denied partial custody — and by what kind of court system — if rushing the boy to hospital after some type of accident?

Eyjafjallajökull's impudence reversed his plans. First he found himself stuck in Iceland, with all aircraft grounded; European skies emptied for a week. Some time later came the call from Geoffrey with news of a monumental discovery. Even with the airports open again, Michael now had a reason to extend his stay. *Here* was a story to write about. Fate had intervened, and as such, he felt a duty to uncover the consequences. The older man invited the younger to the scene of the discovery; with Geoffrey himself invited by the protégés onto whom he'd passed his vast knowledge. The team suggested he find a chaperone to help keep him safe, and Michael provided the obvious solution. It would not be an easy site to access, but the pair could be flown up to the ridge by helicopter, where they could find a secure area to observe proceedings.

After dropping-off Geoffrey and Michael in a flurry of disturbed snow and ice, the helicopter stood by, waiting to airlift the two corpses to the hospital, for pathologists to make the necessary examinations, including x-rays. At first, after the hikers reported the horrific scene they uncovered, the assumption suggested recently deceased mountaineers: foolhardy adventurers caught out by the eruption days earlier. The clothing did not seem quite right: thick and bulky, perhaps knitted jumpers; certainly not mountaineering gear. The truth only outed when investigators studied the strange metallic sheet: most of the registration number legible on a fraction of squashed tail fin — cleared of all ice — below the Union Jack of British European Airways.

Geoffrey had spent decades hunting this very aircraft, including false leads on various Highlands mountains. Never once did it occur to him that it could be anywhere north of Scotland, unless it ditched, lost, in the North Atlantic. Yet he knew of countless commercial and military flights that veered hundreds of miles off-course, often beyond the capture of radar. In 1989, Varig Flight 254 headed on a course its navigator plotted for 0270° that actually required 027.0°; crashing 700 miles adrift of its intended destination, despite three further decades of technical advancement. An earlier example: *Star Dust*, the beautifully named British South American Airways Avro Lancastrian airliner, disappeared just after the war, in August 1947, on a flight from Buenos Aires to Santiago; its venture up to the altitude of the hitherto unknown world of the jet stream — attempting to escape the weather — leaving it flying into invisible, unimagined gale-force headwinds, seriously slowing its progress, the pilots blissfuly ignorant. When eventually the plane descended — having flown for enough time to traverse the Andes — it smashed down into a wall of rock and ice on Mount Tupungato, to be subsumed, on its near-obliteration, by a glacier; only emerging more than 50 years later as the glacier shifted its cargo down the slope and, bit by bit, ejected it onto a plateau. There were countless other cases — of getting lost, veering miles off course — in the billion-or-so commercial flights in all that time, without even getting onto various military mishaps. Even in the 21st Century, the problem persisted. The state-of-the-art technology of the new millennium did not fully eradicate the issue.

From descriptions, Geoffrey knew the bodies to be the father and son, Frank and James Carter. They lay crushed together in compacted ice, pried from their metal shell. It proved impossible to airlift to the site the equipment necessary to excavate the frozen tableau as one, and so the team gently poured warm water, heated by small gas stoves, over the ice to defrost the scene and separate the bodies from each other — and from the remainder of the airplane — without damaging the evidence. The corpses themselves would barely be thawed by the process, and thus remain preserved for further examination.

As had occurred in similar crashes, the glacier had consumed the plane — or, at least, parts of it — and Eyjafjallajökull's meltwater had washed bits free, spitting out a scrap here and there. One propeller lay visible, its once-straight blades curved like giant false eyelashes. Yet despite the weeks of extensive scouting that would follow, the rest of the plane could not be located: just the tail section, and its two huddled souls, frozen in time. The remainder could be lost anywhere for miles around, under tonnes of ice that could not be easily penetrated; one day they too might melt or spew back into view.

Michael and Geoffrey silently stared down at the father and son, finally separated from each other after decades of frozen coupling. The two corpses now lay on their backs. Neither of the men who looked down at them felt able to speak; taking the chance for an unofficial mark of respect.

The bodies' flesh had ossified — whitened and hardened to porcelain or alabaster, their hair and faces peeking out through a perished thin material that resembled stocking nylon, the fabric only fully intact in rings gathered at their necks. Every stitch of their clothing could be discerned; every pore of their skin apparent.

Under James' red hair, perfect teeth in an open-mouthed rictus that could be read as the final fixed point of chattering teeth, or some kind of improbable half-smile. Distantly gazing blue eyes, almost dreamily so; a boy, forever on the brink of becoming a man — apparently still alive with a thousand-yard stare in the photographs taken, yet never to move a muscle or take another breath on film or in person. Beside him, Frank's brown eyes were also wide open, but uneven, one looking askance; his fat lips pulled tight and wide in a toothy grimace that exposed blackened gums — an expression that, unlike that of his son, screamed of distress. His unkempt hair lay ragged, in need of combing straight. He appeared slightly shrunken in death — thinner than in the photographs Geoffrey still had on file — perhaps mixed with some weight loss in however long they remained trapped alive.

Geoffrey shook his head, solemnly, and Michael nodded in agreement.

1941

Countless blurs of war: memories merged, condensed, concertinaed. Time distorted in both directions in reminiscence, with mere moments living long in the mind and entire weeks lost to the spark of synapses, as if the wiring to a vacuum-tube computation machine frayed and severed, all inputs lost.

In hindsight, East Grinstead, for Charlotte, seeped into an indistinct cloud of several visits, in the half-year between Viktor's transfer from Brighton and his eventual summer discharge. Icy lawns soon gave way to spring's banks of daffodils, which themselves wilted in the shade of the budding blooms of buttercups and primrose and bluebells, as summer silently snuck in.

In his midst — surrounded by the wonders of nature — were many of the worst burns cases in the country, with airmen at various stages of reconfiguration and restoration and rehabilitation, via pioneering plastic surgery. Like the daffodils, some would quickly die, to be replaced by a more hopeful patient in the assigned plot; a bed, too, in which to flourish or wither.

Charlotte thought she had seen the worst the war could do, but the sights at East Grinstead haunted in a new way. These were patients who, in truth, should not have been alive; a slightly Frankensteinian air of life sparked into deceased flesh, as rapid advances in medicine restored the hitherto too-far-gone.

Men, cursed with crooked smiles and rubbery yellow faces, beset by the droop and list of savage palsies; eyebrows singed away, scabrous scalps where hair had once grown. Men, without eyelids, gazes permanently set to the widest-eyed stare, that left them appearing constantly alarmed, even when smiling. Men, noses as long and pointed as the dishonest Pinocchio, but made of *flesh*, not wood. Men — burnt and blistered, patched and plastered — with the probosces of Bornean monkeys, fat and thick and surreal beneath their eyes. And strangest of all, men, with the trunks of elephants, hanging from the centre of their warped faces, with the tips — the spouts — sewn tight to their forearms.

That first time, as she awaited the arrival of Viktor, she sat just inside the doorway of the famous Ward III, and did her best not to stare; but could not help but take surreptitious glances, to try and make sense of what the room contained. The men, dressed mostly in nightclothes — but some in full RAF uniform — gathered in a structure little more than a long wooden hut, as the low early afternoon winter sun cut shafts of light at near right-angles through the rows of bright broad windows. An old coke stove simmered behind a piano, at whose stool sat a man in striped pyjamas, surrounded by three singers in dressing gowns; beating out a tune — *It's A Long Way To Tipperary* — through bandaged hands as the trio swayed with pints of beer syphoned from a nearby cask. The aromas of ale and pipe smoke and perspiration — so masculine to Charlotte that they may as well have been pure male pheromones — rose above the familiar hospital background notes — most noticeable on the walk through the main building — of kaolin, calamine and bleach, in what could otherwise have been the snug, the saloon, the raucous rugby club bash, the East End singalong; the barrel rolled out, the breezily lifted knees of mother Brown, the lustily repeated calls for any old iron.

The exchange of a steady stream of letters kept strong Charlotte and Viktor's connection. Still unable to easily grip a pen, his oddly formal missives were dictated to a nurse, who transcribed every word in a remarkably neat and decidedly feminine hand. As such, Charlotte sensed a reluctance to speak as freely as he otherwise might, but stilted conversation beat no conversation at all. Even so, what started out as *Dear Viktor* and *Dear Charlotte* became *Dearest Viktor* and *Dearest Charlotte* early in the New Year, and by the time she made her maiden trip to see him, *My dearest Viktor* and *My dearest Charlotte*.

The litany of abnormalities on Ward III seemed never-ending, as the men went about their business as if not carrying a care in the world. Cleft lips, false teeth, clown-faced rictuses. Men, wide-eyed and tight-skinned and uneven-smiled; ears withered, eyebrows askew. A fallen eye, the cheekbone depressed, the socket smashed down, the eyeball appearing loose, as if at any moment it would simply slip out. Tubular snouts with plastic cylinders as nostrils, inserted into the voids, between newly-constructed septa. Fingers lost: clumps of digits, stumps of knuckle. Wigs, toupees, dark glasses and hearing aids, donned without vanity or self-pity. Disguise-kits, to look normal.

Though impatient to see Viktor, the room held so much fascination; the details later filled in via conversations with her Iceman, and the doctors and nurses she managed to take aside for brief chats, as a fellow medical professional. The men without eyelids were waiting to have flesh from their underarms sewn on as replacements — without which, scar tissue would begin to contract, leaving them unable to ever shut their eyes again; from which point each cornea would thicken and blindness quickly follow. However, the various pedicles — transplanted onto the faces of every man who had lost his nose — evoked in her the greatest intrigue. Up-patients at the initial stage of the process casually strolled around the entire hospital with long columns of flesh cut from their stomachs: one end remaining attached to their gut, the other joined to their forearm or shoulder, like freakishly mutated umbilical cords. Once the blood flow within the pedicle grew strong enough the surgeon severed the gut end, to transfer that tip to where their absent noses once resided, hanging with a ludicrous sweep from the centre of the face. Those towards the end of their many operations were less remarkable in appearance — if they didn't have additional dramatic distortions — but were still an unusual sight. With the pedicle finally detached from the arm or shoulder, and with the majority of that excess flesh cut away, it initially left a crude bulbous facial mass. Such men awaited the final surgeries, to hone and sculpt and whittle away flesh with an artist's skill and precision — often by the pioneer, the man they referred to as a deity in these parts, Archibald McIndoe — in order to provide them with the rough approximation of a human nose.

Am told that Spitfires and Hurricanes can be built more quickly than any new pilots trained, so anyone here who is not beyond hope will at some point resume his duties, so long as he retains the stomach for it. Hard to remain humble, midst these fighters.

Burns, and the rapid and devastating disfigurement they cause, had been a regular part of Charlotte's life ever since the first planes were shot down over England; and in a couple of cases, dating even further back, to the crashes from test flights and training exercises. Now at East Grinstead she encountered men who perhaps represented the worst of all fates; worse, she felt, than those who perished in an instantaneous, lights-out demise, with its blessed relief. Only modern medicine kept them alive.

As the pair sat in the hospital canteen on her second visit — or was it the third? — Viktor talked about the various airmen with whom he shared a ward, and the kinship he felt. He detailed the improvements he saw, but — to which she could relate — also told of those who made no progress, or worse still, swiftly regressed and wilted. As he spoke he held a smouldering Craven A between the first two fingers of his better hand, while using the balls of his palms to lift the cup to his lips; the bandages protecting the naturally tender skin of the inner wrist from the heat. In those moments his face disappeared, behind chunky ceramic, cotton mittens, the smoke from the cigarette, the steam from the coffee. She couldn't help but smile: such adult vices, nicotine and caffeine, yet still the childlike air to his struggles, like a little boy in cumbersome mittens.

Some of the men, he explained, were sanguine. They could not alter the past. Others, however, remained full of rage; their anger almost reflected in their glowing redness, that seemed to pulse with their rapid heartbeats. A senior doctor told him that those with a constantly-refuelling rage — as if their hearts pumped avgas, not blood — healed less quickly; the body demanding, in a losing battle, that they let it all go. These men were told as much — advised that all buried feelings are *buried alive* — but they just couldn't do it. They continued to fight their fate, reliving the moments trapped in the mind, the looping literal reactions of fight and flight, that sabotaged their immune systems. A particularly serious case resided in the bed next to Viktor: minor brain damage, broken jaw and cheekbone, lost fingers, missing teeth, and a patchwork of scorched skin; the bones in his legs broken into myriad fragments, and with no hope of them knitting back together, gangrene had set in, and both were duly amputated. With them went some third-degree burns — that unique pain removed with the legs — although plenty of other burns remained on his torso. When awake he seemed full of rancour, and in his sleep he screamed profanities. He'd made no progress in the three weeks Viktor had been there. Yet one case felt even more heartbreaking.

V told of a poor young wretch, described to me as arriving in a frightfully bad way, in both body and mind. My soul wept for the poor mite. War can be cruel in so many different ways.

Placed in the bed directly opposite Viktor's a mere fortnight earlier, airman Urquhart lay freshly abandoned by his fiancée. She had taken one look at his deformed face and his horrifically crippled body — his handless arms mere bandaged stumps, with which he tried to muster the strength to wave — and ran out crying. The next day she left a letter at reception. Within the envelope lay the engagement ring.

Charlotte listened, horrified, and yet unable to avoid pondering how she would feel in those same shoes: the girl a mere 17-years-old, and at the same age she herself had been naïve and immature in both affairs of the heart, and also, like most others under the age of forty, oblivious to the stark realities of mechanised mass-scale warfare; the way it churned people up and spat them out. Like the girl, she too had been born after the end of the Great War, and while not uncommon to encounter amputees, the physical — if not mental — wounds of Ypres and Passchendaele and the Somme were often healed by the time of their childhoods; while the black dogs of depression and the permanent nerve-shredding of shellshock often saw men locked out of sight in mental asylums, or stuck at home, or in pubs with a jar until closing time — whichever way, hidden behind closed doors. Viktor was damaged, but not *deformed*. Nor did he seem defeated. Indeed, he seemed on the mend.

Later, in her diary, she pondered if she could still love Viktor if as hideously disfigured as Urquhart or one of various others, standing little chance of a full recovery. She hoped so, but — disappointed in herself, at her instinctive reaction — she could not be so certain. Urquhart, Viktor had explained, seemed to lose the will to live, and though others had survived similar injuries — a few had even survived something a little more extreme — he died just three days later.

With no life beyond these walls — no relatives sending letters — Viktor's stories revolved around these men, and the medical staff who attended them. The nurses, Charlotte noted, appeared even more attractive than at the places she herself worked. Here, as with air hostesses, looks counted; the women — still fully qualified — purposefully chosen, in these most extreme of circumstances, for their luminescent beauty and cheery countenance, as if these virtues held the true powers for male convalescence. Compared to the nurses who came in and out of the canteen, Charlotte — so used to praise for her looks, and proud of her appearance in a way that stopped short of vanity — suddenly quite felt plain and inferior. One nurse in particular, passed by Charlotte in the main corridor upon her arrival, looked as icily beautiful and unblemished as Ingrid Bergman, her flowing long blonde hair — impractical, but luscious out of fastenings — falling elegantly down the sides of her face. Charlotte wanted to ask Viktor the identity of the woman who helped write his letters, now picturing this potential pin-up; hit by the paradox of the intimacy nurse and patient shared in those moments — did the nurse sit on his bed beside him? — while he had her transcribe his feelings, even if not in the most stirring of language, for *her*.

Though biased, Charlotte believed Viktor, by quite some distance, the most dashing of all the men she had seen in the ward; while several of those who looked like they would once have been handsome now had seriously skewing impairments. Would the nurses, she wondered, home in on Viktor, in a more calculating manner than she herself had last summer? For her, it felt like fate: he had fallen before her, after all. He had, as she liked to tell him, crashed into her life. So, she duly claimed him. No one here had seen him in the moments when he faced death head-on, and as such, what right did they have to his affections?

"Are you okay?" he asked, noticing how she had fallen silent, suddenly seeming distant and distracted.

"Fine," she snapped, picturing that stunning Bergman lookalike. "I'm sorry," she quickly added, squeezing the exposed fingertips of his good hand. "It is such a delight to see you, it really is, my darling — I'm just frightfully tired. I'm not sleeping at all well."

"What has happened?"

She sighed. "The usual. You know, those blasted nightmares. Every night. For the life of me I just can't stop seeing poor Hopson. Feeling my foot on his chest, or seeing his headless body chasing me. Sometimes I see myself running him through with a broadsword. Other nights it's a bayonet. It's … most distressing."

He nodded, attentively. "Try these," he said, reaching for the packet in his breast pocket, as a cigarette fumed in his fingers. "Doctor's orders," he said, with a snorting laugh.

"And they shall help me sleep?"

"Afraid not. But they can help during the day. Go on, try one."

"Thank you, my dear, but if it's okay, for now I'd rather not."

"Suit yourself," he said with a slight shrug. "Not for now, then. But maybe soon I shall write you a prescription," he added, and she laughed with a fraction of the old girlish giggle that, these days, only he seemed able to locate. She watched him inhale clouds of smoke, and the sense of tranquility that washed over his face, flickering gently across sated eyes. He then squeezed the dying butt into a pulp in the ashtray, and reached once more for the packet.

"On second thoughts," Charlotte said, as Viktor struck a match and held it towards the fresh cigarette drooping from the corner of his mouth — and as the smell of sulphur and camphor sparked into the air — "I think I shall like to try one — if you still insist it be most medicinal, my dear Doctor?"

2010

Time slowed whenever Montague worked on clocks and watches. He could both stop and start the hands moving — omnipotent in the world of the windup. Yet he lost all sense of the *actual* minutes passing; taken from temporal reality into the world of flow. His horological expertise, like any eventual mastery, a distant cry from the confused chaos of the beginner. He began as a child — some time after his father's departure — by taking apart one of the many old clocks in the house; unable to resist uncovering the hidden magic that made it all work. The first he yanked and levered apart with a fork and a blunt butter knife, to send springs and coils and gears flying across the kitchen table, as his mother slept in her armchair in the back room. After an hour spent trying to fit it back together, and succeeding with not one single part, he guiltily bundled it into an old shoebox and hid it in the garage. Yet the urge returned, and he occasionally retrieved the box and fiddled and finessed the mechanisms with his father's abandoned tools, until some started to make sense, and a piece or two fitted back in place. Next he found a broken wristwatch that once belonged to his father, of which — in contrast to many of his other unrecovered possessions — his mother had failed to dispose. Again, it never quite fit back together, but in time he came to understand the mechanics.

With super-magnifying spectacles in place of his normal pair, he peered down at the 1920s fob-watch on his desk, received the day before in the post. Strangely, it had been despatched to him by the writer from the aviation magazine he used to read: Michael Marston, the man talking about Concorde on the radio the morning he found his mother's cold clammy body. Marston's accompanying note mentioned that an acquaintance had recommended his first-class watch repair services, and provided a return address in Brighton, along with an enclosed cheque. Beyond that, it seemed just another job.

Montague's own watch hung loosely on his wrist as he worked, its dial facing inwards, the oversized chain strap flapping as, one by one, he manoeuvred a range of tweezers and micro-screwdrivers, tweaking and turning the tips of the tiniest fragments of metal and essential mechanisms: balance wheel and hairspring, chapter ring and escapement, barrel bridge screw and pallet fork jewel.

Decades earlier he'd converted the third bedroom — the spare — to a study, with Dorothy having no use for the upstairs part of the house anymore, and the prospect of guests utterly unthinkable. He focused the glow of daylight bulbs onto the desk, whose light glinted from the stainless steel tools laid out on all sides. His hands were steady, as long as he kept a constant stream of nicotine.

While he could not yet find an actual address, he discovered — via an article by the very same author who sent the watch — that his father now lived in Iceland, which made little sense. Perhaps he could contact Mr Marston to find out more, when returning the watch. No phone number had been included — just the Brighton address — so a letter would have to suffice. The only identifying mark on the watch: the crudely stencilled name *Viktor*.

With a surgeon's stillness Montague teased the Breguet balance spring, carefully adjusting the stud on the balance cock. Switching to miniature rubber bellows, with thumb and forefinger he squeezed a tiny burst of air, to clear away ancient dust, with a gentle *pfff*. He then peered out the window, over the special glasses as they slipped down his nose; imagining what he could see if his eyesight allowed, and Stephanie stood in view.

* * *

Haloed by his hallway light and the security lamp mounted a couple of feet above the doorbell, time slowed, as Montague observed Stephanie close-up — and, for the first time, without the interference of greying net curtains or the grubby stained-glass panel; his natural hyper-vigilance taking in all the details, to the point where his eyes, big behind their lenses, wandered up and down — not from lust, but from an obsessive need to know everything. Even as she spoke in an agitated manner, he remained ultra observant, and slightly detached.

There were so many new details to take in, to add to his established knowledge. Stephanie's oddly thin face — now seen as peppered with small moles and blemishes — sparked a contradiction noted from that first day: suggestive of a slender body, but below the neck she widened to a stouter physique, plumping out in classic pear-shaped form.

Up close, he could now see that she possessed a broad, large-toothed smile only dampened by a discoloured canine and the unusual degree of exposed upper gum, part of which, above the dull tooth, also appeared dark and discoloured; a minor blemish, compared to his own shameful mess of a mouth. Down her shoulders and back fell girlishly long straight dark blonde hair, streaked with grey and in places splayed with split ends; hair that, by now, most women would have cut back to mid-length, if not shorter still, and where others may have reached for the dye. At times, and in certain lights, and especially when viewed at a reasonable distance — which had been most of his experience — its length made her appear youthful and attractive, and yet at others it added to a sense of strangeness and dislocation from the ways of the world. Even so, he saw mostly only feminine elegance in the way it fell down her back and sometimes partly over her shoulders and across her chest. Frequently — such as now — she wore jodhpurs and riding boots, even though she didn't appear to own or ride horses; and from beneath the v-necks of jumpers popped the collars of men's shirts, even though she didn't appear to have a man.

But in this moment she needed a man. Panicked, she required his urgent help. He listened, as she quickly explained her emergency; while simultaneously scrutinising her aspect in what felt like slow-motion.

"Hi, I'm ever so sorry, but one of my pipes has burst," she said, with panic in the rhythm but not the accompanying volume — insistent, yet softly spoken, almost daintily so; with a slight lisp, as if the tongue flicked a boiled sweet.

"Oh, right, yes. Yes. Come in. I'll get something," he blurted, immediately turning his back on her — instantly feeling more at ease as he faced away; heading to the kitchen, as she moved tentatively into the hallway.

"Shoes," he shouted through. "Just let me get my shoes. And, er … a wrench. I have one … somewhere. In the garage, I think."

Stephanie stood in the dark hallway, diminished by the overbearing decor and the excess of *stuff*. She cowered slightly, as if the sheer weight of ornamentation might fall in on her.

"Buckets," he shouted. "I'll get some buckets," he added, frantically, unsure of the location of the buckets, and the wrench, and his shoes.

"Stopcock?" she shouted back, leaning forward to project the word, although her version of shouting sounded more like a forceful whisper.

"Pardon?" he called, facing away, but loud enough so that she could still hear. He moved from his back door into the garage, to sort through the tools that lay in the only available space, just over the threshold.

By the time she replied she had followed him, out towards the rear of the house. "Where's the stopcock?"

"Good point. The back garden," he said, and brushed past her, wrench in hand, heading into his kitchen, putting the distance back between himself and his neighbour; taking control as, with some strange energy, he marched down the hallway and out the front door. He didn't need showing into her house; encircling the hedge that separated the properties at a brisk pace — up his path and then back down hers, with lengthy, purposeful strides — and racing through the door that she'd left ajar. Had he listened, he might have discerned that she only wanted to know the location of the stopcock, and that she could perhaps have taken it from there.

It seemed easier for Montague to keep moving, and the faster the better; to curb the sense of dread that stillness — and any accompanying silence — would provoke. Even if he didn't know what he was doing, he had to *look* like he knew. It felt as if his testosterone levels had spiked; the hormone mainlined, and flowing to every fibre of his being. He didn't come to the rescue with some wishy-washy tub of butter or a mug of sugar, as might be portrayed on a television advert, so that she might avert some cake-baking catastrophe; he came to the rescue with an adjustable wrench and sleeves rolled up. He came to the rescue *as a man.*

Despite the lateness of the hour, he found himself in a light and airy house. A mirrored layout of his own floor-plan, in this version the hallway had been knocked through to form a bigger living room, and, in stark contrast to next door, the added space and the lighter colours suggested warmth and openness. Her dress sense wasn't overly feminine — the mix of the girlish long hair with the more manly clothing — but her home, to him, had a strong female aura. Pale floral wallpaper, intercut with a dainty dado rail and tasteful wooden-framed photos; all lamp-lit and bright and fresh. There lingered the smell of lavender and camomile, which he recognised from his mother's herbal teabags, pleasant and soothing — the sentimental pull of the familiar. Yet, something didn't feel quite right about picturing Dorothy here, as if in some way cheating on her. He paused — suddenly aware that he'd left Stephanie well behind, and should perhaps allow her to catch up before going deeper into her home. And so, for those few seconds, he tried to study her living room — soft, feminine, welcoming — without giving the impression of being nosy. Large format art-books — one on the Pre-Raphaelite painter Dante Gabriel Rossetti, another on the print-works of Eric Ravilious, and a third on the floral symbolism of Georgia O'Keeffe — lay on the coffee table. In the corners of the room were the plants he'd seen her carry in on moving day, that, like children not seen for months, had grown and changed, and presented at new angles; one even going so far as to slouch like a teenager with its back to the wall, a limp leaf hanging like a dank forelock. As Stephanie finally reached the front door he moved on, towards the back of the house, into the unlit kitchen. Several steps behind, she said "through there," as he crossed the threshold.

Though darker, sufficient light spread from the living room to see the problem. Water dripped insistently through a crack in the kitchen ceiling, centred across a bulge of sagging plasterboard: a kind of inverted volcano whose increasing pressure would at some stage have to give, with explosive consequences. Soothing aromas gave way to the heavy fug of wet wood and plaster, with a fog of humidity that caught in the throat. Water beaded up and fell from the slinky polished-metal spurs that housed modern halogen bulbs, where to flick the switch at the wall would send sparks, or force the snap of a circuit breaker in the fuse box. A washing-up bowl sat on the polished wooden flooring under the cascade of drips, whose rhythm rang as a constant tap-tap-tapping, with just enough of an interval between each to separate the sounds of individual droplets hitting the reservoir in the near-overflowing container; any faster and it would blur into one unbroken stream.

He opened the back door and stepped outside; locating and lifting the tiny metal cover of the mains tap that, just like his own, resided a couple of feet onto the concrete patio, and, like a vet about to calve a cow, reached down blindly into its dark void; grasping for the cold brass fingers of the stopcock. Once gripped, he managed to turn it just enough, clockwise, without the need of the wrench. At this point he could sense Stephanie looking over his shoulder, which conferred to him an even greater sense of vigour and stature, despite sprawling awkwardly on the cold ground. He had a vision of his father, oiled forearms and smudged elbows, underneath the old Morris Minor in the garage, shortly before he absconded, and the car found itself entombed. With the image came a sense of just how big his father had seemed, and how — thinking about it for the first time — he never had the chance to watch that height gap diminish. While he did of course grow, to the average height of an adult male — indeed, taller than his father, he suspected — in some strange way he never grew beyond half the size of Geoffrey; and so, even now, in his imagination, his father still towered over him, twice as tall.

His muscles taut and primed, Montague flipped himself upright with a strange athletic power, if not exactly any obvious grace, and made his way into the kitchen as Stephanie moved from the doorway. As if controlled by an adjusted timing valve, the drips slowed to a steady, slower beat; the sagging ceiling gently emptying out its bulge. With the decelerating water, however, went his sense of purpose: a strange mix of achievement and self-sabotage, as if he'd blown up a balloon for a captivated audience and all that remained was to let it go, to deflate itself into obsolescence. "Well, that's that," he said, acknowledging his success, but only underlining the fact that he served no further purpose.

"It was very kind of you," she said, warmly, but with her arms crossed over her chest, so that her hands gripped her opposite shoulders, which she absentmindedly rubbed, as if cold.

"I don't think it will collapse," he said, motioning at the ceiling. "At least, I hope not."

"No, I should hope not too."

"Um, I'm sorry I can't fix the actual pipes — I mean, I could try, but I wouldn't really know what I was doing."

"That's okay, I'll find a plumber tomorrow. When it's light."

Ever since that very first sighting, Montague had exchanged dialogue with Stephanie, immaculately constructed back-and-forths that showcased his intelligence and his humour, formed within the safety of his own mind. He had a stockpile of witty ripostes, entire frameworks of sparkling badinage, several examples of which were now springing to mind; yet as they stood in silence listening to the slowing drips, she failed to produce any of *her* lines, like an actress stuck awaiting her cue. And naturally his prompts would make no sense, as she hadn't even seen his script. Presented with the perfect situation to display that humour and charm, all hope of extemporaneousness, improvisation, ad-libbing wit, vanished in the company of others; the wiring somehow coming loose when time to put it into practice. Preprepared lines, of which there were many, unutterable, as they tumbled and jumbled on the way from his brain to his mouth: opening lines, faked off-the-cuff observations, slick repartee, all closed down in the loss of structure, as sentences liquefied into gibberish. A similar malfunction left him incapable of telling jokes. The middle sections, and the necessary punchlines, never held their form, as he feared a panic setting in, which only exacerbated the situation, as it all dissolved.

Lost for anything further to say, he followed her lead as she silently walked towards the front door. She didn't actually ask him to leave, but he essentially found himself shown the way out. "Thanks again," she said, as he stepped outside, and she moved to lean against the back of the open door. "I'd best start cleaning up."

"Oh, you don't need any help?" he said, which struck him as something obvious to have said back in the kitchen — something simple he could have accomplished.

"No, it's okay, really. I've already taken up too much of your time," she said, and began to half close the door, narrowing the field of view; tapering the situation to near-shutdown. "I'll get onto someone first thing tomorrow." She carefully positioned her politely smiling face beyond the edge, so that he could see her gratitude, all the while slowly closing the gap until she slipped out a soft "bye" as the door clicked shut.

Montague walked up her path and back down his own, into his house, which seemed darker than ever. He closed the door, and allowed himself fall back against its resolute solidity, so that it supported his weight. He took a deep breath and let out a sigh of relief; a sigh of success. How could she not have been impressed?

The next day — clear blue sky, frostbitten pavements — Montague came home from the shops to find a potted plant on his doorstep, with a brief thank-you note. In the coming weeks he kept an eye out to thank Stephanie in return, but their paths never crossed. He wondered: should he have written her a note to thank her for her note? It all seemed a bit cumbersome. Even with his general misapprehension, and misunderstanding of most social mores, it felt an unnatural thing to do.

1941

Every type of face filed past Charlotte as, in near-summer sunshine, she stood on the shallow steps of the Shaftesbury Memorial Fountain at the heart of Piccadilly Circus; standing with a restless fidget in front of the plinth for the famous statue – only with the winged cherub now relocated to Cooper's Hill in Egham for safekeeping, the fountain itself concealed behind crude wooden boards advertising National War Bonds.

Sallow-complected, moustachioed, elfin and petite, olive-skinned, chubby-cheeked and ruddy, fresh-faced and pimpled, gaudily made-up, bespectacled, balding, narrow-nosed, high-browed and wide-jowled: they all passed Charlotte from several directions as, in the middle of the scene, she bobbed her head and alternated her balance on tiptoes, looking to see if *he* stood behind those nearest to her, whom she had already discounted. She sunk back onto her heels and checked her watch. He was late. She consoled herself: after all, he needed to take the overground from Northolt into North Acton, followed by a tube to the West End, and the trains could no longer be relied upon like clockwork.

It had all happened so fast — *too* fast, for her: Viktor's discharge from hospital, his re-admittance to the RAF, his secondment to Northolt and 303 Squadron, to fly with the hotshot Poles and Czechs. The pair's chances to spend time together — planned as two decadent days at the cottage, upon his release — were dashed by the unrelenting speed of war; the lack of time to take a breath, the hasty rearrangements and postponements of chaotic lives. Due to staff shortages — a couple of nurses downed with tuberculosis — she could no longer get as much time off; and before he knew it — and in need of something beyond the sterility of hospital walls — he ended up back in the dispersal hut, awaiting the mad clangour of the bell as the call to scramble. Only now, rather than race his colleagues with his youthful bravado — in the past, always the quickest — he half-jogged, half-limped to his Spitfire; the disability more stark the faster he tried to run. Now always the last into the air, he remained a natural once up there, where legs are an irrelevance. The top brass knew as much; the reason why — so long as he still had the stomach for it — they felt so keen to have him flying again. Occasionally his hands would cramp up or spasm, but a lot of the time he felt no other kind of pain inside his gloves; a strange senselessness to contact and the cold.

Charlotte's heart sank when she first heard the news of his return to action. He had made no secret of his desire to fly again — she knew it was inevitable, as the pair had discussed on her precious visits to East Grinstead: the clear drawback to her role in helping him recover. But could he not have waited just a little longer? It was still only early May. And so, complete with permission slips, they scrabbled to meet for just one single night in London, with no time for him to get to the south coast and back, and no time for her to go to the outskirts of west London and return in time for her next shift.

Sweat beaded up on the nape of her neck, falling colder the further it slid down her back. Appropriately thrifty since the onset of war — and with clothes rationing imminent — she had just that week broken the habit and treated herself to a new outfit, at no small cost, from a Brighton boutique: a grey-blue bolero jacket and matching pleated knee-length skirt, with a black-and-white polkadot blouse, and a pair of elegant black butterfly-bow gabardine shoes with two-inch Cuban heels. It felt too warm for even a thin woollen jacket, but she had been taken aback by her reflection in the shop mirror when first trying on the combination — the high-cut of the jacket, just below the waistband of the skirt, suiting her figure in such an unexpected way that she almost thought she saw a display advertisement; requiring her own movements to break the spell. It didn't need the cooing and clucking of the young and eager female sales assistant to confirm it — nothing had ever felt quite as right before, and wearing it out this first time made her acutely aware of her own attractiveness in a way she'd rarely before experienced. Even her favourite black Schiaparelli-style dress — before its reduction to rags by the hospital bombing — had never quite fit her as she'd hoped; it didn't quite hug her figure in all the right places. A sense of confidence washed through her; further enhanced by the anticipated reaction of Viktor, who found her alluring even in a nurses' uniform that, while not totally unflattering, hardly appeared seductive or the epitome of style. He'd also seen her in her smart civvy garb on their brief outings from the hospital, but all those clothes predated the war, and suddenly they all seemed a little frumpy. This represented high fashion, with the thrilling tinge of first-worn newness; smart, but also decidedly feminine. It all added to the bubbling sense of anticipation.

Every face: was it *him?* Trilbies and bowlers and flat-caps and Homburgs emerged upwards from the Underground stairs, until unfamiliar faces beneath the hats, as the steps were ascended. No, not him. Would he even be wearing a hat?

Then: what *would* he be wearing? It hadn't even occurred to her. His uniform would give him priority on the trains, but this was a special occasion. As far as she knew he had no civilian clothes, but perhaps he had acquired some during the transfer from Sussex to west London, or had time to shop on a quick excursion from the base, in a brief respite from the constant sorties. Unlike most patients, he had no home to go to upon discharge, although she recalled that he briefly stayed with some distant relative in Brighton, before the old man died. Viktor had tried to telephone her, from the hospital administration office upon his release, but ended up leaving a message, and the details of the eventual rendezvous were sorted via urgently posted letters. On the back of the envelope she had written '*S.W.A.L.K.*'. In reply — via the advice of an airman who said he knew what these things stood for — he scrawled, in his spidery, awkward hand, '*B.U.R.M.A.*' An unfamiliar acronym to Charlotte, when she asked a fellow Sister in the mess hall to decipher it, she blushed at the answer, and the reference to being upstairs ready. Another nurse chimed in to say no, it meant *be undressed*. Still, the 'my angel' ending turned Charlotte's blushes into smiles.

In typical fashion she'd arrived early — indeed, over an hour early; catching a much earlier train, just in case of delays. She then spent the spare time window-shopping down Oxford Street, before finding a small bookshop on New Bond Street. She opted for a slim volume: *East Coker* by T.S. Eliot, whose *The Waste Land* she had read when fifteen, and which cemented her love of words, and inspired her to buy *Burnt Norton* before the war. Little more than a plump pamphlet with its simple yellow cover, *East Coker* fit neatly into her slim handbag, along with some simple cosmetics, cigarettes and matchbook, medicines, and a pencil and small notepad, should she get the chance to jot down any observations; hating the drag of cumbersome luggage. Over her shoulder she carried the requisite string-handled cardboard gas-mask-box, which potentially held space to squeeze in any further knickknacks she might pick up during the day, should her handbag not suffice.

She also arrived prematurely at Piccadilly Circus, and having checked that Viktor wasn't also early, sat on the steps — after wiping away some dust — and studied the litany of unlit signs, whose neon strips and coloured lightbulbs would remain switched off during the blackout. Gordon's Gin, Haig Whiskey, Bovril, Schweppes Tonic Water, Jacob's Crackers, Swallow Raincoats, Brylcreem, Sandeman's Port, Ever Ready Blades, Votrix Vermouth. The familiar claim — that Viktor agreed with — that *Guinness Is Good For You*; that it *Gives You Strength*. Wrigley's chewing gum, *For Good Health*. Further down, high up on a Shaftesbury Avenue façade, Craven A's bright red curving sign, for *Extra Quality*, a smouldering cigarette in an ashtray above the entrance to a bank, on the junction with Great Windmill Street. Her brand of cigarettes, too; ever since Viktor offered one in the East Grinstead canteen, and she eventually relented. That very first one, months earlier, did not taste at all pleasant or health-giving, but in the circumstances — in his company — it felt comforting. Before long, it became a habit. As well as shaving the edges off her nerves, they served as a reminder of Viktor's smoky scent, to help keep him close in his absence. He had gifted them to her, in a broader sense. It brought to mind his lips, and that, at any moment, they could be inhaling the same smoky air. Any time she lit up she thought of him, and then wondered if he did the same with her.

Staring at the advertising arrays, she felt a pang of regret that the signs would not come to varicoloured life after dark — she had always wanted to see the famous lights. That said, she felt far keener to deny the Luftwaffe a good bead on them; to light it all up would present an arrow pointing right at the target.

She took out her new book of poetry and read the opening line:

In my beginning is my end.

So much noise to take in: the hoarse thrums of a circle of engines — mainly black cabs and red-and-white double-decker Leyland Titans — all choking out coarse black diesel fumes; some revving, some idling as they awaited movement ahead, as a pony and trap — as if wandering lost from *The Hay Wain* — traipsed slowly down Coventry Street. Horns parped, and people sitting or standing near Charlotte on the island chattered incessantly, gabbling and guffawing. The next line of the stanza, as she stared at the words, failed to register in her mind; her thoughts, drowned out by her environment, drifting to Viktor. So she placed the book back in her bag, to save for the train ride home, and took out her pencil and notepad. She jotted down a couple of things, but she had fallen behind with her journalling; no longer sending redacted versions to the Mass Observation Project, on account of never finding the time to type up her personal diaries, which, in turn, were increasingly sparsely written. Any longer-form writing she reserved for letters to Viktor.

As such, she had taken to making the briefest of notes, sometimes coded. *V, Piccadilly*, might be all she would write afterwards, knowing that the rest would live vividly in her mind. Still, anything truly significant usually merited a few lines, at the very least.

She told herself that one day soon — in a year or so, the war at an end — she could go back and fill in the stories, expand the cryptic notes, maybe write it all up as some kind of memoir.

Until then, she retained things like train tickets, and receipts for items bought on a specific day, to slip into the diary. This ephemera, in their own unique way, would tell part of the story, keep track of the fine details.

Time wore on, and Viktor's lateness stretched past thirty minutes, and she started to feel anxious.

Joyously, out of nowhere … *there he was!* — Viktor, resplendent in his uniform, field cap donned at a jaunty angle, walking steadily with a clear but not extreme limp. Charlotte's heart soared, the butterflies in her stomach flying frantic figures of eight. She wanted to run straight towards him, jump into his arms, but traffic flowed around the roundabout; and even if she were to do so, she didn't know if he could hold her weight, given his bad leg, and if his hands were up to the task. So she waited for him to cross. Once he reached her, he took control, lifting her in his arms, and while locked in a kiss he span her round, pivoting on his good leg; seeming as strong to her as her father, when, as a little girl, he lifted her high — rendering her weightless — as her arms clung around his neck. Lightheaded, and now gossamer in weight, too. Viktor's kisses felt familiar, on this special day; almost like a very first date.

For several months she had carried an almost imperceptibly-increasing anxiety in her body, which first started to percolate after the Christmas bombing: recurring nightmares about Hopson's headless corpse just one of many types that disrupted her sleep. Then, a snowballing of tension ever since Viktor — first taken away from her to another hospital — returned to the far greater dangers of active duty. That deep tension all seeped away as, strong and robust — restored — he held her tight, and though their bodies were in contact in various places, the soft skin of their lips totally dominated their senses. The joy, and the relief, and the ecstasy: she felt fit to burst; with jubilation, but also into tears, in the confusing swell of emotions.

"Oh my," she said, when finally he put her down. "Here, let's sit," she eventually added, lowering herself onto the warm steps after an extended stare into his eyes; suddenly aware again of the public location, in a courtship that had known precious little privacy.

Viktor checked his beloved fob-watch, pulled from his pocket and glanced at for the briefest of seconds, before he slipped it back out of sight. "Sorry I'm late," he said, shrugging. Unlike his limbs and bones and skin, the watch had somehow escaped that fateful crash unscathed, as his weight fell on other parts of his body. Twenty years old — almost as old as him, passed down from his grandfather on his eighteenth birthday — it faultlessly kept the time, as if nothing at all had happened on that most unforgettable of days which, ironically, he himself could barely remember.

Charlotte looked down at his hands: free of bandages for the first time. Instantly she took them in her own, skin touching skin, not cotton; now *his* hands, as they would remain — all operations complete. They appeared in some way shrunken, perhaps due to her familiarity with their usual padding; his fingers, with abiding scar tissue, still drawn slightly in towards the palm, the skin coarse and crocodilian, but still more human than the fabric bandages.

"It is so good to see you, my darling," she said, letting go of one of his hands, to hold just the one closest to her, as they sat side by side on the fountain steps.

"It is a great day, my dear."

Without thinking — and lacking the cue of the bandages — she squeezed his hand tight, and he winced.

"Oh darling, I'm ever so sorry," she said, wide-eyed with horror at her error.

"It is okay!" he said, smiling, giving her a gentle nudge with his elbow. "It didn't hurt. Promise."

"Really?"

"I am mostly rubber now anyway," he joked, before reaching into his tunic pocket for his packet of Craven A. "They can make a tyre out of me when I bite the dust."

She took a cigarette from the offered box, and he lifted his smart silver lighter to her face as she dragged in the benefit of its fire, feeling the first wisps of warmth and smoke through the filter; exhaling a fine cloud through her nose with a sated sigh.

"So, this is London," he said, marvelling at the architecture, the traffic, the bustling life. "Whew!"

"So very vibrant, isn't it?" she said, trying to follow the path his eyes took as they darted from landmark to landmark, vehicle to vehicle, person to person. "Imagine how busy it would be if there wasn't a war."

"But, no, I would not like to live here," he said, with a shake of his head.

"No? Why ever not?"

"It is nice to look at, to experience, but soon it would become too much. I need the sea. Don't you need the sea? The sea, or the sky. For me, at least. *Heima* — back home, Akureyri — I would go for a swim in the sea at first light, no one around, just me and the birds circling overhead, maybe. Those silly creatures — waiting for me to catch them a fish. Such freedom is similar in the sky — no one to bother you."

"Aside from damned Jerry."

Viktor laughed, his run of successes springing to mind. "Well, those bastards usually don't last long!"

Having finally left the small central island the pair grabbed coffee and cake in a low-key café, then wandered the streets window-shopping, stepping around piles of rubble — concrete, glass, slate, metal — swept into the kerb, gathered from in front of stores that bore the brunt of bombings, and which stood in various states of disrepair. Women — with hooded prams and buggies, girls skipping about in pretty floral dresses and impatient boys in shorts — queued at food shops and market stalls, as Charlotte and Viktor unhurriedly sauntered from window to window, skipping those boarded up or still clearing away glass blown to such smithereens that it returned to glittering particles of silica and sand.

Wearying, the pair decamped from the heat and sunlight into the darkness of the London Pavilion; sitting on the back row of the enormous theatre to kiss and cuddle, as the movie *Road Show* — a comedy set inside a lunatic asylum — played in the background. People in the many rows in front seemed lost in laughter, but it all just became a muffled hum to the pair, sat amidst other courting couples, all ignoring the movie. Time seemed to fly by; the film over in no time at all, and soon the projectionist would start it again, after a reel of Pathé News.

Though they had not been watching, it seemed sensible to get up and leave with most of the others as the credits rolled.

Even with the onset of dusk they exited into what suddenly felt like harsh sunlight, until their eyes — so often closed in the dark theatre — adjusted to the orange glare. They roamed the backstreets, passing a couple of pairs of working girls — the so-called Piccadilly Commandos, dressed for night action — before happening upon a quiet drinking den that looked the part. The doorman duly saluted Viktor at the entrance, and led the pair down a narrow dark staircase, into the low-lit cellar. Candles flickered and reflected on the rows of spirit bottles, glinting off pints of beer and the crystal soda decanters lining the bar. Cramped and smoky, faces that turned their way — mostly men in uniform or dressed spivvishly, and a couple of women in the garb of the good-time girl — were under-lit in a slightly eery manner, eye sockets momentarily rendered voids in shadow, until these ghouls moved and the light instead caught their eyes, suddenly bright and alive and twinkling in the recesses, as if flicked on by a switch. A path cleared to the bar, two men on stools edging out of their way, a pretty young NAAFI in uniform moving to the other side.

Viktor and Charlotte took their drinks — Guinness for him, Gordon's for her — and sidled over to the corner, to try and talk in private, but where anyone in the small room could have overheard, had they been inclined to lower the volume of their own conversations. Instead, the din — and later, the wail of the air-raid sirens — concealed their sweet nothings.

The topic eventually turned to his experiences at Northolt, as she eagerly sought stories of derring do, albeit with the edginess of knowing that, at any moment, he could have died; whilst simultaneously holding the joy that he clearly had not. He told of the camaraderie of the Poles and Czechs, but also the friendly but unwavering competitiveness, to score the most kills.

When he spoke of manoeuvres amidst the familiar swarms of yellow-nosed ME109s she felt an overwhelming sense of pride, mixed with a queasiness at how such missions awaited his return, after this night of personal ceasefire. He sounded invincible, and had lived to tell these stories of success — sometimes of kills, other times of high-speed escapes and safe landings with a bulleted fuselage riddled like a cheese grater — as if it were a mere sport, but the margins of error were so slight. Could he keep riding his luck? He had already survived one horrific crash. Did that make him more likely to avoid a second? Did these things work like that — like lightning strikes? She knew that each successful flight improved the odds of surviving another flight — the first few sorties, when least skilled and experienced, were always where the risk proved greatest — but the more flights, the more in harm's way he would put himself.

Every single day since his return she had run scenarios through her mind, assessing and reassessing his ability to stay alive. Could he truly be as talented and fearless as she believed — as an ex-comrade of his had once confirmed to her, recounting Viktor's uncanny abilities and unerring bravery — and if so, were his prospects of survival only increasing with the honing of his skill? Or did that fearlessness take him into ever-more dangerous dogfights, where lesser pilots would sensibly just get the hell away? Out of the highest-risk category, with all his experience and expertise, it still took just one lucky shot, or one piece of shoddy maintenance from an overworked ground-crew technician, and he could bite the dust. And so, when he offered to buy another round — above the muted sound of fresh air-raid sirens — she eagerly let the gin, along with the packet of cigarettes they shared, increasingly loosen the edges of those sharp concerns.

Past midnight, Charlotte and Viktor swayed giddily a yard inside pavement edges painted with a black and white checkerboard pattern, to aid kerbside visibility in the dark; with just enough ambient light in the unlit streets to follow their faint path. Up ahead, the small, extra-dimmed lamps of Piccadilly Circus hove into view; the only other street-level beams the low-slung sidelights of the occasional car, that, in the exaggerated darkness, illuminated with added power, and drew attention to the circular junction. Distant in the sky, clouds lit by arcing beams that flitted across their plumes. Beneath the clouds, the occasional bright glimpse of a silver barrage balloon somewhere over the Thames, swept by searchlights.

They had planned — or rather, had planned to plan — to find and check in to a hotel or bed and breakfast, but the day, sped along by alcohol and distorted by lost time in the dark theatre, had got away from them. Both needed to be on the first trains home. So they decided to make for the tube station, hunker down with the sheltering masses until the system kicked back into life, and the bustle woke them up. But, as they lurched in that direction, Viktor suddenly took her hand and led her through an unlit archway.

They staggered giggling down the alley that led behind another drinking club, stopping to kiss, then heading further into the enclosed space lit only by the glow of the almost-full moon. They tottered into a concrete yard, past an industrial dustbin, and crates of empty beer bottles, towards a corner cut off from the moonlight. Car-beams — from the few passing by on the main road — drifted softly along the wall opposite. They moved with mouths locked together, hands held out like the blind, to feel for unseeable obstacles, until they ran out of room and reached the rear of a building. The path clear, Viktor thrust Charlotte up against the cold brick wall, and in one smooth movement hitched up her skirt, grabbing at knicker elastic to pull it from her waist and hips down to her knees. It took her totally by surprise, and yet, at the same time, it felt totally natural, and utterly thrilling. Despite some initial fumbling he seemed to know what he was doing, his legs more than strong enough, his hands able to move with ease. She closed her eyes in bliss, and dissolved into the flow.

In no way how she'd always imagined it — in all her fantasies she had only ever envisaged a bed, soft sheets, gentle passion, the luxury of privacy, and more recently, Be Upstairs Ready My Angel — but she *wanted* him, regardless. Waiting be damned. To wait any longer represented torture, aching for their uncooperative schedules to align; all the while aware that, even with his skill, the odds of surviving the summer were far from perfect. As if to further dispel any sense of guilt or impropriety, there could at any moment, she knew, arise the sickening wail of closer air-raid sirens, signalling the imminent risk of death and destruction. But by now, even if one were to sound, she knew that she would simply ignore it. Waiting be damned; *bombs* be damned. Their bodies would be found fused together in the rubble, lest they be blown apart.

Though reciprocating eagerly, the occasional intrusive thought jabbed and punctured her bliss: anxious of being discovered — a sudden sense of self-consciousness cutting through the wooziness, even though, as with the threat of an air raid, she didn't want to stop. The thoughts nagged at her, until she gradually lost awareness of all sense of location — of time, of place — and sank into the physical contact; losing herself in the near-pitch blackness, to feel only the sensations of his body interacting so intimately with hers. In the moments when not kissing, her mouth suddenly freed, she wanted to scream; and so gritted her teeth, holding in an unbearable surge of head-pressure — heart-pressure — that felt too great to dare release, lest she totally lose control. She felt physical pain too, and discomfort, and brickwork digging into her back, but it all melded into a mass of confusing sensations, that, in addition to all the alcohol, produced a delirious, light-headed euphoria.

She felt her knees go weak, jittering with a slight tremor, but between the wall and his body her feet floated on tiptoes, her weight mostly held by his; his rough fingers digging into her thighs and buttocks like a pliable version of Bernini's Proserpina, pulling her more closely into him, raising her up. Totally off the ground, she wrapped her legs around his lower back, her fingernails pressing into his jacketed shoulder blades, until she found a way to get them under his tunic and shirt. All sense of time disappeared in the darkness. Rather than an out of body experience, she had never before felt so much *within*.

When almost at an end she felt his legs trembling, and his body grow tense. Moments later he hastily withdrew, and his body shuddered then went slack, and he slumped forwards, momentarily, as if struck a blow to the back of the head by an unseen assailant; his chin resting on her shoulder, his forehead pressed to the wall. In one movement he flipped around, away from the wall, and off Charlotte's trembling body; turning his back against the next patch of wall and sliding down its cold brick surface. Following his lead and suddenly unable to support her own weight, she gingerly stepped over his shadowy body and slipped down beside him. Unable to speak, both breathed heavily, as they corrected their clothing. She nuzzled her head on his shoulder, and he rested a coarse hand on her quivering knee.

Sirens began to sound in the mid-distance, but the two just sat there, side by side, unseen and utterly untouchable.

They sat like that, in total silence, for a length of time neither could measure. Eventually, feeling a slight chill and tiring of the harshness of the wall, they made their way with a slight stagger to the Underground station, and with the platforms and the lower reaches fully occupied, made their bed for the night side-by-side near the top of the stationary up-escalator, to somehow — for a few hours — find themselves sleeping like babies.

"Let's meet here," Charlotte said, waking as the station began to whirr into life. "If we ever get separated, let's meet here, at Piccadilly Circus."
"Why?"
"When this blasted war ends, I mean, and if we're not together. Please, my darling — rush here. As soon as you can. Just like the millions on Armistice Day, heading to all parts of London. Come and find me here, by the fountain, and we can celebrate together."
"But I'll see you before then. I'm not going anywhere."
"Just promise?"
"Okay," he said, with a shrug. "I promise."
"You won't forget?"
"No, I won't forget."

1956

Blue-white moonlight slipped through the smashed windows. The orange glow of a flickering oil lamp caught on the cracks in the shattered panes, and on the jagged edges of the broken glass. On coarse and uneven bathroom floorboards these sources blended in differing balances of cool and warm light, interrupted by dark patches of shadow; light also falling into the void of a missing board, as if lost into a black hole.

In the lukewarm bath, Stanley, with his back to the taps, sat facing Alice. Their new home — still uninhabitable — had no electricity or gas, and therefore, as yet, no running hot water. Duly prepared, they brought along two gas heaters to boil pots to fill the tub; a task that took over an hour. They also had sleeping bags, laid out in the master bedroom. To counter the mustiness of damp and dry-rot, Alice filled bowls of home-made potpourri, although the broken bathroom windows allowed in hints of a fresh late-evening breeze. With cold water from the tap Stanley filled another pan, as Alice reached over to relight one of the stoves, with its glimmering orange-blue flame adding to the different hues of light.

Back from the hazy joyous heat of their honeymoon, Alice had wanted just a taste of their new life together — what the future might hold — long before the house had been readied. One night. Just like camping out, she had said. How hard could it be to spend a night in their new house, which at least provided a roof over their heads, if barely any modern comforts? They had purchased the stoves and sleeping bags for camping trips, taken in the Morris Minor that, when the back seats were folded down — something that never occurred to him that first special night on the lay-by on the country lane — proved just about adequate as a double-bed.

"Let me shave you," Alice said, feeling the stubble on Stanley's chin.

"It'll mess up the water," he said, with a gentle splash from his submerged hands, as if to highlight its current cleanliness. "You'll get covered in hair."

"I'll rinse off after."

"Can you even see clearly?"

"Clearly enough. And I can feel. I want to *feel* you."

He reached for his obsidian-handled foldout cutthroat razor that sat on the porcelain sink, laid out ready ahead of a morning shave before a reluctant return to the office. He loved his job, but his heart now hung slightly heavy with a vague dread at the prospect of the nine-to-five, away from his new wife.

Alice worked as much soap as she could squeeze from the bar she twirled and twirled in her hands, the goop liquified with an intermittent splash of bathwater; a foamy lather the consistency of cream forming around her fingers and the crooks of her thumbs. She felt Stanley's face in the way that a blind woman might inspect the husband she had never seen. In the process the soap smothered his emerging whiskers, from chin and jaw, down across his jutting Adam's apple to the base of his neck.

"This is all mine," she said, with a tender smile. He handed her the blade and, gingerly, she scraped it down the side of his face. It crunched as it cut through bristles of hair, sweeping a clean line of soapy mulch from his cheek. He would have applied more pressure, had he been in charge of the blade; but she exerted enough to do a reasonable job, and he wasn't about to insist she press any harder. He couldn't help but flinch as she moved down onto his neck, even with absolute trust. One slip and she may not even feel it gouge his skin; a deeper cut and they'd return to Casualty, a repeat of the night they met. Instead, she barely left a rash, with her tentative strokes of the sharpened stainless steel. She then tenderly scooped handfuls of water that she softly pressed into his face, to run down his chin and neck, back into the bath.

He turned around, and carefully rested back against her; his weight softened by the cushion of water.

"Our wedding was so magical, wasn't it?" she said, as from behind she wrapped her arms around his chest.

"It was, my dear. Of course, it wasn't the best day for it," he said.

"It was the *perfect* day for it," she added, with a calm tone that took no umbrage to his finding fault with the weather, which lay beyond their control. "For it was the day that it was, was it not? It could have been no other, and now, it cannot be any other."

"You're right. It was — it *is* — our wedding day, isn't it? For all time, it will be our wedding day."

"For all time."

"Although I feared that it almost *wasn't* our wedding day. You know, what with the car breaking down."

"I was *always* going to be there. Wild horses could not have dragged me away." She laughed. "It just so happens that wild horses might have been a quicker way to get there, but there you go."

Stanley chuckled, the movement in his chest sending small waves of water into the sides of the bath. "Next time — not that there s-shall ever be a next time — we shall book a herd of wild horses, white ribbons and all."

"Stanley ... Did you doubt me?" she asked, looking deep into his shadowed eyes as he craned his neck to face her.

"No, not *you*, my dear. But maybe *me*. Maybe I wondered if you deserved better."

"Oh Stanley, why ever do you say that?"

"I just feel s-so blessed. I don't quite feel that I did anything to deserve to be this happy."

"Are most people not this happy?"

"I fear not, my dear. I fear that most people *do* live lives of quiet desperation. Life can be awfully humdrum, and — well, just look at the people we know. Some are happy enough, I suppose. At work, I overhear men moan about their wives. Mates moan about their young women. Few people seem genuinely enthralled by their lot. They don't even seem contented."

"Well, we haven't been tested, I suppose," she said, sounding a little solemn. "I mean, if what happened to your parents ... but no, I can't even think about that."

"My sister, you mean? S-Samantha?"

"Yes. I'm ever so sorry for mentioning her. I know it's difficult."

"It's okay. You know it's okay. We can talk about anything, you know that? I was too young to remember anything about it — what happened — but it did teach me the ... *fragility* of life, once I came to understand it all. An aunt explained it a few years later. But as you know, Mum and Dad won't even mention her name. They went to the trouble of naming her, yet it's too painful for them to even say that name. And I can't even say it properly, half the time."

"They cope, in their own way," Alice said, her hands crossed on Stanley's chest. "And we shall cope, I do think, with whatever life throws at us."

"You really think so?"

"I hope so. I mean, I *trust* so. Not that you can ever tell beyond all doubt, of course, but as long as we talk — like this — then I believe we can overcome *anything*."

2010

Smoke wisping from the taut-knuckled grip of two fingers, Montague leaned against the jamb of his open back door and looked out at the yard; drawing from the hand-rolled cigarette with puckered lips, as if sucking poison from a stinging wound, before exhaling pale white clouds with a soft sigh.

But anxiety soon bit back. He flushed with embarrassment every time he thought how the upstairs windows of Stephanie's house overlooked his garden, and the way that the garden — at least, the modest and orderly green rectangle of his childhood — lay lost under decades of neglect; time folding over itself in layers of organics and dirt, with the occasional man-made item tossed or drawn into the detritus. It never occurred to him to see it as shameful, until his new neighbour arrived.

Once — albeit briefly — his father's pride and joy, the lawn hadn't been mowed for more than fifty years; nothing had been cut back or tended to, hacked or snipped, unless by neighbours into whose territory it encroached. Montague's severe allergies kept him from undertaking any form of gardening. After his father walked out, and his mother took ill, no one remained to tackle it. Within just two summers the whole yard needed scything down: grasses growing tall, with flowering stalks; bushes conjoining and intertwining; vines wandering from trellises to wrap themselves around drainpipes and wind along fences and sidle up the trunk of the lone apple tree; clematis spreading and thickening and blossoming with unlimited ambition, as if nothing should be out of reach; weeds running riot amid the blooms pollinated from beautiful arrays in neighbours' gardens; nettles disobediently nestling in corners, commandeering the perimeters and setting flowers in shade; ivy coiling around thorny bramble limbs, choking an old tree stump, strangling a rose bush. Decades on, it lay almost indefinable: as wild and wilful as untouched woodland deep in the heart of an unpopulated island.

The tall grass wilted each winter, its culms falling face-down in weeds, as if collapsed in stupor. In amongst it all, the perennials dug in, needing little sunshine to thrive: cherry laurel and limelight, bindweed and knotweed, yarrow and broad-leaved dock, sprouting and hanging over — or wrapped up with — thick and bristly mosses. The undergrowth thinned each year as the days shortened, but even in winter it never opened itself up to inspection; enough evergreens to compensate for the flaky deciduous plants that appeared emaciated, perhaps even dead. It all gathered itself in, hunkering into a tighter mass, ready to pop up again when the weather changed.

Left alone, all those years — not so much unkempt as utterly untouched. It subsumed the rusty tin trashcan, the concrete-drummed grass-roller, the wooden bench, a trio of gnomes, the collapsed metal swing, the wooden trellis and various sticks for the plants or vegetables to cling to, and anything else lying out there the day his father walked away.

With good humour, but also a paternal unease at his son's frailness, Geoffrey often encouraged his boy to battle through the welts and hives that peppered his pale skin in the spring and summer months, and to ignore his reddening eyes — which of course his son then rubbed, to make worse — in order to live an *external* life: to help plant potatoes, collect the tomatoes, unstring the runner beans, find the best apples from the tree to cook. Anything to get him outside the house. For a while he tried throwing a ball to his son on the lawn, but even with practice, Monty simply could not catch it; the ball would just hit his chest as he hopelessly clapped his hands together, or sail right by. Geoffrey, himself no expert sportsman but always eager to give something a go, tried kicking a football back and forth, but that proved even worse; the little boy getting so frustrated at his repeated failings that, when finally he did manage to connect, he did so with an aimless, rage-filled toe-punt that sent the ball flying with an unswerving straightness over the fence, smashing the neighbour's window; terrifying Ginger, the family cat taken in as a stray by Dorothy, a year or so before the animal disappeared.

Montague recalled the summer's day his father tried teaching him to climb the apple tree, but his mother, aghast at the sight, screamed at them both from the kitchen with such gusto that the little boy — awkwardly hugging the trunk, yet to even reach the first branch — fell to the ground on his backside with a bump. With that, Dorothy came running, as if he'd fallen head-first from the roof of the house onto the concrete patio. She scooped him up and carried him inside, fret and panic etched onto her face, as she laid him out on the settee, as if a bed in a hospital casualty unit.

Once Geoffrey abandoned them, Montague immediately marked the garden as off bounds. His father's domain — and so it made a certain kind of sense to abandon *it* in return. He no longer had anyone to push him, to try and get him to ignore the severe physical discomfort of the outside world; no one to say don't be 'such a baby', which, without malice but rich in frustration, Geoffrey would sometimes end up imploring.

In the years that followed, Montague gained a perverse thrill that he didn't yet understand from seeing the garden go to ruin. But then, at the age of eight or nine, he started to fear its darkness, its ability to spread and multiply. At night he grew anxious about its presence, lurking down beneath his bedroom: a monstrosity, like some mythical beast, combining the many heads of Hydra with the twisting hair of Medusa and the lithe, searching limbs of the Kraken. Weeds and vines turned evil, wending and winding their way to him. Then, the venomous sting of the terrifying Triffids — whose existence he discovered upon overhearing a dramatisation on his mother's wireless — that he feared could climb the walls to the house with creeping tentacles and enter through his window.

Even if he'd wanted to tidy it all those years ago, Dorothy would strongly object at any foray into the garden. Once an adult, he still reflexively deferred to her judgement about his sensitivities to all manner of allergens. And by the time she passed away the garden appeared beyond all hope. Where to begin, on such a mammoth collection of interwoven organic matter, as knotted as a million unattended kite-lines in a gale? Every now and then he would look at it with purpose and intent, perhaps even donning gloves, only to feel the sense of energy and resolve drain from his body before even lifting a tool.

Imagined through Stephanie's eyes — seen as if from her rear windows — Montague finally decided that the time had come: a hot July lunchtime when, out of nowhere, the need to dismantle the shambles grew to an obsession. It felt impossible to ignore: a taunting reminder of multiple failures: *a man not even able to control his own garden,* he imagined her thinking. What did it say about him? Yes, he'd turned off her stopcock, but that remained the sum total of their meaningful interactions. He now saw everything through the filter of Stephanie's eyes, and it did not look good.

Donny, the middle-aged male neighbour on the other side — surprised to see Montague at his door — agreed to lend him his chainsaw. A few other rusty — but not broken — garden tools were accessed from the fringes of his own overloaded garage: a hoe, a rake and some still-usable secateurs leaning against a battered wheelbarrow in the confined space.

Aware that Stephanie could even end up an observer — the clattering and clanking would certainly alert her, if, as Montague suspected, she sunbathed on the other side of the tall fence — he felt that he had something to prove. Would she head up to her bedroom or bathroom to look out at the commotion? He certainly would, if the roles were reversed; curious, but not voyeuristic. A week earlier he'd even seen her in a bikini, walking to her lounger; eager to stare, he forced himself to look away, as if her state of near-undress meant crossing a line.

Pollens could not dictate to him for the rest of his life. His father's richly-entwined and perpetually undermining legacy — the mess he bequeathed — needed slicing and hacking and tearing to pieces. His mother's cotton wool — he could still almost feel its virtual presence around him, like a smothering cloak — required ripping clean away.

Double-dosing on antihistamines for good measure, Montague stripped to his white string vest, untucked from threadbare cotton shorts held up with a length of curtain cord; an old checked shirt wrapped over his nose and mouth, tinted lens covers clipped to his spectacles. The chainsaw, chugging in his hands with its gasoline splutters — the noise, the smell, the vibrations — took him back to the adjacent London Airport as a boy, in its pre-Heathrow days: the viewing gallery, and the propellers of aircraft on the tarmac, archaically spun into life while others roared into the sky. The chainsaw's rugged thrum rumbled up and down his forearms as he gripped it double-handed. Suffused with vigour, he waded into the overgrowth; his hairless arms so pale that the rivulets of veins — throbbing to the surface as his muscles tensed with the weight of the saw — gleamed bright blue, and beads of sweat sparkled and trickled. Without discrimination he swirled the chainsaw around, lacerating the landscape; nothing spared — birds and insects flying and crawling away as fast as they could flee.

His eyes watered. Rashes ravaged his skin, flies flittered about his face. A fat jet thundered overhead, momentarily severing the spreads of sunlight that pierced the dark lattice. This is what it felt like to be a *man*, he thought, as twigs and leaves and spores fizzed into the air around him to the sound of clanking metal, and the smell of burning diesel and dissected wood. He felt virile, potent; a guerrilla, fighting jungle warfare. He could cut down the fiercest of enemies without blinking; although his shoulders and forearms soon ached, which meant taking a brief break, before manfully resuming.

Vines and shrubs were no match for the spinning blades, and splintered at the merest hint of contact: thistles beheaded, bushes disemboweled. In no time at all a path cut right down the middle of the garden, up to the foot of the apple tree. He reached up and sawed, in mere seconds, straight through an overarching branch: bright flaxen flesh bared beneath the bark, sharing its rings, bleeding sap. He sneezed, wiped his eyes with the uncontaminated underside of his vest, onto which oil and a film of green transferred. He felt the urge to sneeze again, but held it in; smiling at his victory.

And then, an uneasy feeling, at what lay uncovered. Freed from its all-consuming canopy: the skeletal remains of a small animal. A cat, no less: dimly familiar red collar bowed around the neck vertebrae, beneath its weirdly alien-like skull with its small sabre-teeth. Had *this* been where Ginger got to? Grass had grown through the gaps in the splay of bones, and rotting apples lay about their scatter, but the animal's disarticulated form — loosely grouped together — remained recognisable.

Layers — stripped away to reveal his childhood. It had all been here, all along, in the dense and dark foliage. He lifted Ginger tenderly, bone by bone, and placed him carefully onto a mound of leaves in the wheelbarrow. He wasn't sure he'd even loved the cat — the dumb creature only made his allergies worse. And most of the time it avoided him anyway, with a wary sense of distrust of a child that had once tried, in all innocence, to lift him by his tail, as if it were a blatantly obvious handle. But sometimes, on rare but comforting occasions, Ginger would come and sleep on the foot of his bed, and purr with contentment.

And then the sneezes returned; so strong that to try and hold them in would blow the back of his head clean off. He suddenly heard his mother's chiding voice: 'You *stupid* boy! I *told* you. *Stay indoors!*'

Scratching his arms he surveyed the scene. "*No*, Mother", he said to himself, half aloud. "You're wrong. *Look at what I've achieved.*" And then, purely to himself — without a nod to Dorothy — "Look at how I *feel*."

Early twilight, and with heavy and aching arms he downed tools. For all the effort the garden contained no less matter — just redistributed matter: cut into smaller pieces, dismembered, displaced; piled against the back of the house, on the weed-strewn and mildewed patio. The garage, packed to the rafters, offered no route to the front of the house, and the barrow would not fit through the backdoor, let alone down the cluttered hallway. And in all the excitement he hadn't thought to order a skip.

But it would all surely *burn*.

And so he set about carrying the leaves and shrubs and branches, the twigs and the stalks and the grass, back to the edge of the garden, away from the house; piled high to form a loosely defined pyre, in the shade of the thinned-out apple tree. Ginger lay there, too, as a flattened jumble of bones. Rather than be buried he may as well be cremated along with the rest of the garden, and the remnants of his childhood. Several matches were flicked to form the fire, to no avail, until the heat from one finally contracted a dried leaf into a tiny black circle of burning matter, which in turn ignited the surrounding debris into patches of pitch-dark material with a bright yellow-orange flaring at their edges. Moments later, a whoosh of brighter, all-consuming colour.

Waves of heat radiated, singeing the overhanging branches, whose moisture slowly desiccated with wafts of steam. Acrid smoke tickled the back of Montague's throat; its apparent toxicity taking him by surprise, given the organic origins of everything in the pyre, and how humans evolved around such fires. He glanced up; were Stephanie's curtains twitching?

Stripped bare, Montague lowered himself into a bath of cool water, his red-raw body tessellated with blotches of pale flesh in between the rashes and scratches, the sun having burnt all exposed skin, while the remainder — protected by his vest and shorts — retained an almost luminous whiteness. His hands and knees were stained green and black, and smears of smoke feathered his forearms. He felt *majestic*, his muscles throbbing with blood and his veins pumping with endorphins and whatever other primordial chemicals coursed. As he soaped himself with an off-white ovoid slab, he imagined Stephanie picturing him naked and aroused.

Would she want to see this? Would she be thrilled?

Water rippled around his body, flowing between his legs, tickling his genitals, as his hands gripped the side of the bath. Suddenly he tensed, and his eyes flashed. His body slumped, relaxed, in repose against the back of the tub.

All that brutish masculine energy — all that connection to physicality in the landscape, to the primeval power of fire — suddenly seeped away, replaced by a sense of shame. It transported him back to how he felt in that airless hotel — the circular Ariel, on the other side of Heathrow, on the way to Hayes — in his twenties, desperately trying to shed his virginity like an unwanted pox; until, just moments into the act, the blood-flow seceded, and the fleeting sense of virility — all thirty seconds — overridden with sickening unease. How quickly desire turned to nausea. The image of Dorothy had suddenly loomed in the room, shaken and disapproving, aghast at his nakedness, his lust, his procurement of a prostitute; and the further shame at such a premature deflation. With first her hands, and then her mouth, Cindy — as if performing CPR — tried to revive the stricken organ, before, with a shrug, she slumped back onto the pillows and reached for a cigarette, the patient beyond resuscitation. "You still have to pay," she said, lighting up.

1956

The childhood bedroom, transposed as the gateway to perhaps the most significant officiated step of adulthood: the wedding day. With the early morning light spearing in jagged bursts through narrowly opened curtains, Alice, in a state of partial undress, continued her sacred preparations; temporarily alone in the house — everyone else running errands, locating essentials, collecting visitors from the airport, and in her mother's case, popping down the street with the wedding dress to a neighbouring seamstress who could repair some minor — but sufficiently noticeable — damage to the corsage. There remained plenty of time; everyone had seemed to wake early and excitable, and eager to leap into action after a hearty breakfast.

A minor snag: Alice appeared to have mislaid her silk elbow-length gloves, which she swore had been on her dresser when she went to bed the night before. She scanned the low-lit room, suddenly acutely aware of the jarring mix of girlish keepsakes — teddy bears, rosettes for horse riding, Enid Blyton books — and the adult accoutrements on a day of transition. In addition to the silky undergarments she wore, there hung her airline uniforms, and suitcases stuffed with worldly items, including for the honeymoon in Tenerife, and for the big day, bouquets of flowers, and a cache of presents and cards. On those same bookshelves — incongruously alongside Blyton and Beatrix Potter, and no little dog-eared after trips to hotel rooms in Paris, Milan and Vienna: *The End of the Affair* by Graham Greene, *Under the Net* by Iris Murdoch, *East of Eden* by John Steinbeck, and many more volumes. Each proved too modern for the English curriculum at school, where she'd studied the dustier Shakespeare, Hardy, Dickens and Chaucer — and as such, she never encountered such books before meeting Stanley. His efforts to better himself led him to many teenage library visits, and in turn a desire to pass on recommendations, while, by her late teens, for leisure, she'd only graduated to reading Agatha Christie and Dorothy L. Sayers.

Memories of her childhood mingled with visions of Stanley, here in the bedroom, when her parents were away on holiday; and even the few times he'd snuck in through the window in the middle of the night. They refrained from intercourse — but when the house sat empty, or with the dresser moved to block the door, had tried most other things, with increasing skill and mutual understanding. As she moisturised her bare skin she imagined his hands — that would later that day place a ring on to her finger — applying the lotion.

Stanley had joked — or had he half-joked? — just the night before about turning up to see her before the wedding. She liked how he playfully pushed the boundaries, without becoming an irresponsible rebel who got into serious trouble; utterly reliable, but also a little cheeky. He would do unexpected things, and go against the grain, without endangering himself or anyone else.

She had chided him, stating it would be the most terrible bad luck, but then paused, and asked, "But then, why do we need luck?" Even so, she felt it a bad idea, before again, after a pause, correcting herself — she didn't want to base their future on some silly superstition. "Isn't it only bad luck to see you in your dress?" he had asked — to which, after giving it some thought, she agreed that yes, it probably was; and that the dress wouldn't even be around first thing in the morning, as Mrs Hamilton had agreed to fix the damage.

Still, it seemed risky — relatives stayed the night — and would there be time? Didn't Stanley have his own things to take care of?

The floorboards creaked just outside the door, although it could have been a pipe beneath the wood.

Dressed only in her underwear, Alice attended to her ablutions. She lifted the lid on the cream, dabbed a delicate glob on various parts of her body, then began to massage it into skin that hardly looked like it needed any care and attention. She carried on with her preparations, but now with a picture of Stanley in the hallway, sneaking a look.

The smooth, peeking curves — not large, but plumped by a little padding into perfect roundness — of her breasts above the basque cups, led they eye down to the matching ivory knickers beneath a thin band of slightly tanned skin, belly button half obscured; down further still, to the twin curves of silky suspenders, held up by the straps of the basque, with a fine blue garter woven into the one on her right thigh. She thrilled at Stanley peeking through the gap in the door, and how excited he might be, but also, how she had the power to make him wait for their honeymoon hotel room.

Then, the sound again, this time with the clear cadence of weight shifting on the wooden boards. A mixture of irritation and glee swirled within her mind, the ambivalence swaying back and forth. But as Stanley lingered outside, she refused to go to the door and initiate the rendezvous; so that any actions were purely his responsibility. Perhaps he'd change his mind, and leave her in peace, with any issues about bad luck obviated.

"Stanley? Is that you?" Alice finally called out. "I said not to come!" She added, turning towards the door as someone stepped back. Catching him red-handed, she flung it open.

Except there stood Harold, her uncle by marriage, flushed red from excitement, a sickening smile on his face where others would cower in shame. Everything — from her blood, to her skin, to the chambers of her heart — ran cold. He nodded in approval, as she yelled and reached for her nightgown.

"My little Alice," he said with a wink.

Nearly fifty, Harold's dark hair — thinning but not receding or greying — had remained ceaselessly slicked back ever since the war, a spivvish pencil moustache crawling along the edge of his upper lip. Cravat, waistcoat, corduroy shooting jacket — as if dressed for potshots at pheasant. "Can't believe you're marrying that Stanley St-St-Stutterman," he said, saliva spraying purposefully as he mocked her fiancé's stammer. "What a waste. S-silly St-Stanley St-St-Stutterman."

"You *bastard*," she yelled at him, not for the first time, but with a spite more ferocious than at any point in the past. His visits remained blissfully infrequent, but he had first invaded this very room when she was just four years old, to talk of their special friendship. He never went so far as to in any way penetrate, but the abuse — from that childhood day forward, forcing her to touch him — dug deep all the same.

"Little kitty has grown claws," he said, sneering.

Alice stood her ground, both vulnerable and overflowing with defiance. "One day I'll do more than scratch you," she spat.

"You're still a silly little stray, my girl. So, my new Jaguar not good enough for you?" Harold said, full of disdain.

"I'd sooner go to the church in a hearse."

He laughed. "It might suit you more, my dear."

"Is that a threat?" she said, now holding her dressing gown over the front of her body; not wanting to turn her back on this hunter in order to slip the garment on, and unwilling to reveal anymore of herself while facing him. "Everyone will be home soon. I'll tell, I'll finally tell."

"No you won't, you *silly — little — bitch*. You know that as well as I do," he added with a laugh, looking her up and down dismissively, as if eyeing something now disposable. "Anyway, I shall get out of your hair. You're marrying a man who drives a *Minor*, for god's sake. Need I say more? And, well … the blush is now off the rose, I'm afraid to say," he said with an exaggerated shake of the head, before pulling the door gently closed behind him, as if departing after a polite morning tea.

Alice stood shaking, but held at bay the urge to cry. She'd appal her mother and father if she told them the sorry tale — and how would Harold's wife Shirley, her father's sister, feel? However, unlike the childhood tormentings, things were different. Charlotte had Stanley now. *He'd* believe her, even if her family couldn't be trusted to face such a sordid truth. Harold — good old Harry to his pals — saw his every misdemeanour dismissed by the family as harmless; even if none of the misdeeds known to others were ever of such a serious, perverted nature. Stanley, she concluded, didn't need to know either — not yet, and certainly not on this of all days — but if ever Harold tried anything again, she'd get her new husband to defend her honour. Stanley abhorred violence, but he would find a way to make it stop.

Before long, everyone returned to the house, and Alice felt able to put the morning's distresses behind her. If anything, she only felt more certain that Stanley represented the perfect man, having seen such a contrasting sort. When living with her new husband, Harold would certainly never be allowed in their new house. The wedding dress, freshly repaired, fit perfectly, and she felt that any additional attractiveness it bestowed belonged purely to Stanley. Her adrenaline pumped, the excitement palpable, as she focused on her betrothed, and the day ahead, with the worst of it now behind her.

Thankfully, to further signal a day now heading in the right direction, the silk gloves were located, on the foot of her bed — not that she could remember moving them there — and that left nothing more to worry about. Yet as she slipped her left hand into the fine fingers she felt an oozing cold liquid, pooled in the tips, squirm upwards as she pressed her hand down into the garment, with most of the goop copiously gathered in the recess for the ring finger. Confused, she removed her hand to an unmistakable smell and a sticky substance she now associated with Stanley, but which had first been deposited on her childhood nightclothes on a couple of occasions when her uncle and his wife babysat; a substance he had forced her to wash off in the bath, while her aunt sat downstairs, blissfully unaware.

Alice retched, worsened by the nerves of the day, but did not vomit; nor did she cry as, in the bathroom, she soaped and scrubbed and scraped her fingers — and engagement ring — free from her uncle's sickening deposit. *No, that bastard would not ruin her special day.*

1994

In hazy summer sunshine — Icelandic's daylight long, but never as glaring as closer to the equator — it took all of Geoffrey's effort to drag himself away from a transfixion with Akureyri's outdoor swimming pool, teeming with frolicking bathers and swimmers and high-board divers; its modern sleekness a million miles from its ramshackle pre-war origins. A jarring of memories: the past and the present not quite coalescing, like overlapping slides of photographs of a scene, taken in different eras and from slightly different angles, projected at odds onto a vast white wall.

Walking down the hill, the view ahead fell away into the calm water of the fjord, beyond which the rise of its far-flanking mountain. To his right, the sounds of cavorting and splashing in the pool still carried over the tall perimeter fence as he descended the slope; and then — the smaller, almost overlooked pool that seemed to make more sense within the landscape, and stirred the elusive memories he had been trying to grasp at. Had the old pool of the war years — the scene sparked passions — become a mere half-ignored duck pond?

The waters of Eyjafjörður cut through the view ahead: the deepest slit in Iceland's upper spikes and inlets and promontories, where fiery lava once flowed outward to create new land, and frozen glaciers — or the rush of some ice-age melting — sundered and ploughed and brutalised the landscape. Nearly fifty miles long, and many miles across at its widest point, the fjord finally narrowed into the mouth of Akureyri, where from shore to shore it spanned less than a mile, before a fine tail of water carried on south for just a few more miles. Into the bay snuck the occasional humpback whale and white-beaked dolphin, harbour porpoise and menacing orca.

The further he walked, the fainter the splashing and screaming from the pool. Into view, down toward the low-lying coastal headland, hove the clunky, almost Lego-like, stepped-peak steeples of Akureyrarkirkja, the wartime Lutheran church; its apparent height distorted by foreshortening when encountering the spires from above. Those spires grew taller the lower down the hill he descended, but the church never quite fully rose from the illusion of a hunkered position, its foundations on a lower plateau. Completed in 1940 — not long before his arrival in the town with the RAF, after the British took control of the island — its familiar bells denoted the time with similarity to Westminster Chimes; albeit rather lighter and airier than the low and heavy cast-iron London peals.

Akureyrarkirkja bore some hallmarks of the architect who had also created Hallgrímskirkja, the Concorde-like monolith that dominated the Reykjavík skyline. Yet there were striking differences, too. Where Hallgrímskirkja — whose construction in the capital commenced in 1945, with completion a full four decades later — tapered either side in a presaging of a delta-wing design, Akureyrarkirkja, completed just before Geoffrey's deployment, stood inverted: two clunky towers, either side of the peaked roof. There existed another connection to wartime Blighty — its stained glass, housed in the fine narrow windows on the façade, originated back home: the mediaeval glass of Coventry Cathedral, removed for safekeeping in 1939 — with timely foresight, ahead of its bombing into near-oblivion during the blitz of November 1940 — somehow turning up in Iceland two years later, to replace the plain glass panels of Akureyrarkirkja. The sound of the cathedral's peals also brought to mind one of Dorothy's many old clocks, as if from another life entirely.

A sprightly 73 — although he could still pass for 60 — Geoffrey flew to Iceland with an eye to emigrating. Having grown used to isolation in the Scottish highlands after escaping a busier life further south, it didn't seem too radical a step to go back to the place where he spent a cold year briefly heated by intense summer passions. The island represented unfinished business, ghosts in need of fleshing out, before they grew too pale. Could he live here?

And so, for the very first time, he returned to Akureyri, to where he spent a summer at the allied airbase, when the sun never seemed to set. He remembered the geography as if a three-dimensional map had been imprinted onto his brain in a way that later towns and cities never quite achieved; except now, over fifty years years later, the same topography held a far greater density of buildings — by Icelandic standards — compared to the sparseness of 1941. Roads — *proper* roads, where once lay dirt-tracks — proliferated, but the landmarks and the hills and the shoreline retained the same shapes; the air carried the same floral aromas.

Turning right, he walked up a different hill. Across the bay, the glint of thermally-heated water, cascading off a low cliff into the fjord — unchanged in half a century. On either side, tiers of properties: houses slunk back on slopes and inclines, aslant and askew. He could see himself living in one such home, if any were up for sale.

Glancing down below, he looked back towards the low-lying town centre: Icelandic flags fluttering on poles in the harbour, an old boat perched in dry dock. Masts mixed, crossbeams of sails, and silos like giant tanks of oxygen at the port. Though red houses remained popular, he saw less colour in the buildings than in Reykjavik, but far more verdure and variety in the landscape; tree-lined and relatively lush. The winters here were also never as harsh, despite the more northerly location. He glanced at the fjord, and its blurred mirror of icy peaks and low clouds on the still water; staring past purple Nootka lupins and red-berried rowans.

The smell of the sea — or, at least, the sea's roll inland through the fjord — seemed almost magical. His only real experience of the coast — prior to his wartime deployment on these remote northern shores — came on a childhood trip to an overcrowded Brighton beach one bank holiday, where the chaos of day-trippers disturbed all sense of nature. Akureyri, amid the chaos of war, eventually felt like home; but only noticed *after* he'd left, when he felt a sickness for its absence. In time, he settled into various towns and cities across Britain, and Akureyri existed like the parental home a teenager hastily abandons after a quarrel — and then, when too much time has passed, never quite feels easy enough to return to. Now, as a pensioner, he finally felt brave enough to see if — contrary to the saying — you *can* go home after all.

Geoffrey's route took him up to the bright and bounteous botanical gardens, whose varied floral and faunal fragrances mixed with the rising sea air. He first encountered the gardens in their more modest guise as Iceland's first public park — a beautiful space created by the women of the town just before the First World War; one of its creators, Margarethe Schiöth, immortalised in a bronze bust on an obelisk nestled within a hedgerow, close to an octagonal white summerhouse. In 1957 the park officially expanded to become the world's most northern botanical gardens, but its course had been set decades earlier.

The gardens evolved around Eyrarlandsstofa, an old Icelandic house from the 1840s, that greeted Geoffrey once more as he turned right into the entrance, into a world of thousands of species of plants, hundreds native to Iceland and multiple more imported from different climes, to spread their roots as best they could into cold earth. The common and exotic, the native and the imported; yet all thriving — or at least, surviving — in soil not so far south of the Arctic Circle. Sea Pea and mudwort, bristle sedge and burnet rose, harebell and quillwort, snow goosegrass and tufted saxifrage; name-plated species, amid the poppies and tulips and daisies that even a novice could identify.

Geoffrey passed the rear aspect of Eyrarlandsstofa, where further memories sparked in a way that almost took his breath. Further paths curved and snaked left and right; between leaning trees, angling towards each other from either side of the walkways. Further on, taller trees, that tilted and turned and curved; trunks like spines with scoliosis, boughs and branches aloft as arms in distress.

He felt the flood, the flush, of *history*, as vivid memories raced back into existence from seemingly dormant grey matter.

2010

The smartly-dressed pair stepped out onto the swarming late-evening Soho pavement in late summer, as tourists and drinkers and diners passed the emptying theatre and jostled for space. Various languages — spoken to companions or into mobile phones — blended into a strange kind of chirping; the *emotions* automatically translatable, beyond the specifics of words. Usually a teetotaller, Montague's blood stirred with the intermission's alcohol: a double whiskey borne of a paradoxical mix of bravado and the need for a little extra Dutch courage.

Out of nowhere, in a development he saw as fate, things had progressed with Stephanie — to the point where they exited a famous West End show, his companion looking beautifully — if subtly — made-up, her long hair styled into something neater than its usual unkempt free-fall; wearing a light and flowing floral dress so out of keeping with her more typically utilitarian garb. The invitation — offered the day before — that he join her to see *Les Misérables* in London felt like the moment for which he'd waited his whole life: indeed, the overdue invitation to participate in life. It came via a note slipped through his letterbox. Unlike the previous time — the misdelivered bill — this *meant* something.

Sidestepping pedestrians as he waited for Stephanie to button her jacket to a slight late-night chill, the music rang on in his ears; the adrenaline, stoked by such triumphal drama, still coursing through his veins — a rousing story of success for the spirit and the soul, even if wrapped up in an ultimately failed revolution, with many of the protagonists falling along the way. Still, *something* overcame. He felt unsure if he actually enjoyed the music — he preferred wordless classical compositions of the 18th and 19th century, and wasn't too sure about the whole rock-opera vibe — but all the same, he felt giddy on its raw orchestral power and visceral storytelling.

"We must do something like this again sometime," he said, as scores of people brushed by, shoulder-checking and nudging and sidestepping. "Soon! Or dinner, maybe? I'm so thrilled you asked me."

Stephanie met his gaze. "Look, Montague. This wasn't a *date*, you understand? I just had a spare ticket. I thought that was clear?"

The stab, as his stomach sank; or did his heart sink, down into his stomach? Something lurched and fell and ached, deep inside. Suddenly, a dizzying distortion of lights, as his vision began to spin; a colourful clown's grin floating in the crowd of passersby, the sense of a merry-go-round, a whirling waltzer, and then a gaggle of swirling faces contorted by the convex and concave mirrors of the funhouse, all evoked from some childhood memory. He looked up, and in the real world saw the bobbing orange orbital paper lanterns of Soho, and felt an undulation, a sense of seasickness, exaggerated by the varying heights of pedestrians as they drew closer or moved further away.

A motorbike screamed off from the lights with a slide of rubber, then braked hard, and it jolted Montague back to reality.

"Oh, I see. I … well, I thought … what with, um, you looking so … and everything and …"

"I wanted to look good. For *me*. Is that okay?" she said, her tone a little defensive, but not condemnatory.

"Umm, yes. Of course. I just …"

"I did explain that a friend pulled out at the last minute."

"Yes, you did say that," he recalled, hazily.

"Sorry," she said, in a tone that sounded neither apologetic nor guarded; a sorry that seemed to stand for how shitty life can sometimes be, and that, alas, nothing can be done about that.

In silence they walked back to Piccadilly Circus underground station, passing the fountain; Eros perched on tiptoes, his useless bow — or perhaps his wayward shot? — scorned for the inability to bring fortune to Montague's life. What could be expected anyway, from a mythical figure, cast in aluminium and bronze by a Victorian sculptor? The tube ride home also passed in silence, an hour or so feeling like a lifetime.

* * *

Into the cold bath water seeped the oily film of London grime. Arriving back late at night, the last of the hot water used up in eagerness before heading out earlier in the evening, Montague sat in the tub in the dark, feeling the lapping of the gentle tides that the slight movements of his torso sent against the soap-stained flanks of porcelain. The unbearable tension of the tube ride home hung hard in his body, like rampant rigor mortis. He had died, a little, on the inside.

All the dreams — intermittent since his teenage years — that there existed *someone* for him, if only the elements would align.

Women to save him from his mother, and lure him to a new freedom; and then after she died, from his solitary lifestyle.

There were all kinds of on-ramps to a social life that he'd bypassed. The infrequent — but when totalled up, not insignificant — attempts to make something happen; all somehow missed, through bad timing or bad signals or bad jokes, and at times, bad teeth and bad posture and bad personal hygiene. He ran through more clichés, thinking of plenty more fish in the sea: but upon *his* arrival — the fangfish, all teeth and bulging eyes — they scattered. Or perhaps they saw a jellyfish, slow and lacking backbone, and yet somehow deathly toxic. Either way, they swiftly dispersed.

All the little rejections. At some point, he pondered in the dark, he had to question the wisdom — as he leapt eagerly upon another metaphor — of even trying to ride a horse in the first place, if he only ever fell off the bloody thing. The message from the universe? — *Stop trying.*

It all coalesced into a nagging urge to cry, that he couldn't let out; scared to start in case he could not stop. His internal organs felt wrapped in a vice, his ribcage held tight not by a loving embrace but some unseeable constrictor, coiled and concentric, crushing inwards, squeezing pain hard into his core. He stared at the dark ceiling, with its gentle echoes of moonlight reflected up from the bathwater; fearful of clogged breakwaters in calcified tear ducts; terrified that his windpipe would rattle and cough, and offer just clatter and rust; the pain barricaded within.

He had wailed and sobbed when his mother died. Since her funeral, nine years had passed with only the occasional bout of seeping grief; as if pain and loneliness and fear and anger must be tamped, bolted, double-deadlocked down into the darkness. As a child he had the regular release of great howling and weeping, that so embarrassed his father; but which, in the moment, served to rid the boy of his angst — a storm, that cleared the air, and to which his mother responded with care. Now the storm lay stuck, swirling inside his head, a vortex down inside his chest.

After Geoffrey's abandonment, Montague learnt to bottle up his emotions, and to focus on practical matters, so as to not further distress his mother. It served him well until she died — a sense of purpose erased, and some cataclysmic release could not be kept at bay. And yet the loss of control at her demise — the unstoppable flow of hot wailing tears — terrified him, once free of the overbearing and destabilising power. Like a laboratory animal jolted with electric shocks whenever it moved to the opposite side of its cage, he conditioned himself to stay at the edge, safe from sparks.

1941

Early September, and so much had changed since the start of that summer, and Charlotte and Viktor's out-of-time rendezvous in Piccadilly Circus, when, to them at least, the war stopped in its tracks. Down in the depths of that drinking den, and conjoined in a dark alleyway, and then passed out in the Underground, they had obliviously skirted the most lethal and widespread raid of the Blitz: the Luftwaffe's very last hurrah, the final major despatching of bombs, before Hitler switched his sights to the Soviet Union.

The threat of invasion obviated, Viktor now flew defensive missions over southeast England, patrolling quieter skies. Charlotte had finally managed to wangle some extra time off, but with Viktor unable to leave Northolt, she made her way to the heart of London, to take a tube out west to meet up for the evening. He'd be at the local pub, from where he could slip away from his comrades to join her in a nearby tavern.

Time off provided her with another chance to see London and do some shopping, before the lazy journey out to the suburbs, taken with hours to spare. The season had yet to switch to autumn, but the warm days were turning chilly after dark. She felt the drop in temperature the previous night, shivering when smoking outside and then strangely unable to shake it when back in her room. Even with medicinal interventions she struggled to sleep. Although the night air grew ever cooler, the room remained stuffy from the heat of the day. She wedged the window fully open; letting in that sweet cool air, but also a litany of distracting sounds: above the constant, lulling thrum of insects that could have serenaded her to sleep but for the sharper noises of cars backfiring, dogs barking, neighbours stumbling home drunk, cats brawling and mewling in an alleyway. Excitement at seeing Viktor also kept her from falling off the edge into sleep well past one a.m., only to fail to notice when she finally slipped away. Twice she found herself wide awake before six — anxious that she'd spend the remainder of the night staring at the clock, bleary-eyed, until its alarm sounded; only to drift off again without realising. At eight she awoke, disoriented and woozy, but also restless and agitated, all sensations of sleep strangely sated in her brain, but unsatisfyingly so in the body. The barbiturates taken every night to induce slumber — but on this occasion, unable to override the adrenal pulses whenever her mind wandered to their impending rendezvous — often left her foggy-headed the next day; the coffees growing ever stronger to counteract the daze, her central nervous system in constant need of artificial accelerations and brakings. The energy to see out long shifts felt less easily attained without some kind of stimulant, but adrenaline bubbled up unhelpfully in bed, at the anticipation of seeing her man.

 Dressing in the bright morning light, she felt especially dopey, as if she had only just taken the medications. She made it to London via the familiar route to the station and the usual platform, navigated with half-open eyes. The journey unfolded in a blur, and then sleep; she later found herself awoken by a ticket collector at London Victoria, where the train terminated. Again, despite the nap, she could not seem to enter a state more lucid than one of half-waking, unable to shake a shawl of drowsiness as she walked to the Underground.

 Though the night had brought shivers — stumbling out of bed to finally close the window — she now felt, in the Indian summer, exceptionally hot and bothered. The tube felt like an oven, but as planned she exited at Piccadilly Circus, and made for the small café visited on her trip with Viktor. Finding standing room only, she gave up and walked to the colossal and impersonal Lyons Corner House on Coventry Street, spread across four floors, with their famous, anachronistic Nippy girls a byword in swift service. Charlotte gave her order to a young woman in the familiar black and white uniform, with similarly monochromatic checkerboard headband, whose style dated back to the flappers of the 1920s.

The additional items introduced throughout the year to Charlotte's daily routine — medicines and smoking paraphernalia — had necessitated the recent purchase of a larger handbag. Indeed, she had graduated to more of a shoulder bag: a deep, oxblood pebbled-leather model, reduced in price due to a sale. Usually she could feel blindly for what she needed in order to fish it out, but it now seemed easier to just empty the contents onto the table. No sooner had she done so than the Nippy returned with the cup of coffee, and Charlotte had to clear a space, scooping the items to one side with palm and forearm, into a cluster that included the salt and pepper cellars, the sugar bowl and printed menu. Also in the pile were two thin T. S. Eliot volumes, her purse, notepad, pen and pencil, compact with face powder and lipstick, cigarettes and matchbook, and various medications in bottles and boxes. She located the Aspro and swallowed two tablets with a gingerly-taken sip of hot coffee. Her hand lingered over another box, full of Benzedrine Sulphate — the new pep-pills that were her final go-to in search of energy. At times they made her heart beat out of her chest, but a single tablet could see her through the final hours of even the longest shifts. Only lunchtime, yet she couldn't afford to not be on top form with Viktor — time together simply too precious. As she stared at the packaging she felt like she could just put her head on the cleared space next to her drink and sink deep into sleep; her vision flickering at the edges, her eyelids leaden. Still unsure of whether to take the Bennies now or wait until closer to the evening — to have their maximum effect in Viktor's presence — she took an absentminded sip of coffee, and it went down the wrong way. She coughed and spluttered, and that's when everything began to fall in on her.

It wasn't the first time Charlotte coughed up blood. It happened in the early hours after the hospital's blitzing, but its appearance that horrific night on a clean white handkerchief — watery sanguine speckles in the dim lamplight and fire-glow — made sense, her mouth and throat full of grit and detritus. This time she could not put it down to some physical injury. Every subsequent cough felt like a knife to the lungs. She sat staring at the red globules on her napkin, as it slipped in and out of focus. She later thought, when looking back — although also unsure if just her imagination playing tricks — that she had heard the sound of her forehead crashing onto the table, with the crack and clatter of displaced crockery and cutlery; the last thing she remembered, before waking up in a hospital bed, with no concept of what length of time had passed — just the strong sense that it might have been *days*; perhaps even longer.

* * *

Unconscious and febrile, Charlotte — blissfully unaware — had been rushed by medics to St Mary's in Praed Street, then swiftly transferred to Harefield, its sister hospital: a longstanding tuberculosis sanatorium that doubled as an overspill for the Paddington hospital. Beyond the western outskirts of the capital, it stood just a few miles from Northolt aerodrome; the ambulance even drove past the base on its way northwest, out towards the leafy Chalfonts. Harefield's topography — high above sea level — provided the fresh air required of sanatoria, constructed away from London's cloying smog in the aftermath of WWI, and then modernised a decade-and-a-half later. With easy access to the capital, it stood far enough away from what, until recently, had been the target for blitzing in the next global conflict.

A nurse — young, black-haired but very fair-skinned, with puppy-fat cheeks and thin spectacles — stood at the foot of Charlotte's bed, writing something on her charts. Confused, Charlotte scanned the ceiling and then moved her eyes to the woman, aware on one level that the uniform did not belong to an Air Force nurse, but still believing herself to be recuperating in her own hydro.

"The bomb?" she said to the nurse, with the cadence of a question; unable to muster more than a raspy whisper. She remembered leaving the ballroom, and crossing to the hospital as the fine snow fell, hoping to find Viktor in the hospital, and then

… But no, that was *last year*, wasn't it? How did she get *here?* It felt like something had exploded inside her chest. Then she vaguely remembered the coffee, and the blood, and the sound of her head hitting the table.

"No. No bomb here, my dear. Or for you."

"Where's Viktor?"

"Who?" the nurse asked, not leaning in, but turning an ear.

"Viktor," Charlotte said, trying to sit up, in order to get out of bed and sort out this mess.

"Please, lie flat," the nurse said, sharply, placing a firm hand on her shoulder. "Is Victor your husband?"

"Viktor," Charlotte said, correcting the nurse's pronunciation. "We're courting. He's a pilot."

"Well, I've yet to examine them, but I do believe we have all your particulars, gathered from your belongings. Your next of kin will have been notified. I can get someone to contact this Victor as well, if you'd like?"

Meekly, Charlotte asked, "Where am I?"

"Harefield Sanatorium."

"TB?" she said, gingerly; recalling the blood on the napkin.

"Afraid so, my dear."

"Oh my … I think I'm late. What day is it?"

"Wednesday," the nurse said, looking up from the clipboard.

"In that case, I'm *terribly* late," Charlotte said, followed by a helpless sigh.

X-rayed while unconscious, she'd undergone the emergency procedure of an artificial pneumothorax — a collapsing of the shadowy right lung — with the left, fortunately, deemed unaffected by the mycobacterium tuberculosis. The doctor prescribed her rest as *Absolute*, which involved nothing but reclining flat on her back with just a single pillow to support her head; reading prohibited, although she felt too groggy and nauseous to even contemplate it. They even strictly forbade taking deep breaths. She readjusted her posture, realigning her shoulder blades against the firm mattress — the only form of movement that felt possible — but could not get comfortable.

Until the moment in the Corner House, with the blurry red specks on the napkin, Charlotte had no inkling that she could be consumed. But she had sensed *something*. She'd been trying to outrun a vague and amorphous ailment for many months; beginning with the bombing at the end of the previous year, and growing more intense over time. There were chest pains, and at times it felt hard to breathe — but there had been no nasty cough, and no bloody sputum, until that fateful coffee. At times it felt like she was burning up, but she drank lots of fluids and ploughed on. She had lost weight, but the tablets she took, and the cigarettes she smoked, dampened her appetite. Soon, every headache led to an Aspro, every anxious moment a cigarette, every lull in energy a coffee or a Benzedrine Sulphate. And in time, as each lost some of its power as her body naturally adjusted, it became two Aspros, back-to-back cigarettes, stronger coffees, and a large nightcap of gin. Then, when the gin lost its concussive punch, barbiturates soothed her to sleep. She'd just ignored the signs, pushed through, soldiered on.

"A nerve storm, Mrs Bradbury," a doctor in an out-of-town practice had said a few months earlier. Assuming her to be married, he stated with some disdain that he saw too much of it, with housewives like her having little to worry about, but prescribed the barbiturates all the same. She bit her tongue, and took the prescription.

The faster she tried to outrun it all, the more it multiplied its efforts. It could not be shaken. She had nowhere to go, she realised, as she lay supine in confinement, that did not involve taking the bacteria along with her. The external factors — the long, stressful hours, the substances imbibed — played their part, but the cause now lay deep at her core, trapped within. She received confirmation of the potential killer living inside her, clustered in her right lung, doing its time-honoured damage. The war, for her, no longer purely external: a blitz had blown into her very being.

After what felt a mere blink the nurse vanished, yet Charlotte had wanted to follow up on her request to contact Viktor. She continued to fade in and out of consciousness, losing the urgent drive to *damn-well do something about it* without even realising. She awoke angry, but unsure as to what vexed her — or even where she was — before, finally having remembered, drifting off again. The next thing she knew the sun had set, the day falling away.

The following morning she managed to get the nurse to a write a quick message — as curt and staccato as a telegram, but sent by post — that explained to Viktor her location, and why; and then the rest of that day, after a short burst of alertness before lunch, slipped out of her grasp.

She had little chance to take in the beautiful surroundings, the curving modern architecture of the late 1930s, set sympathetically within the countryside, consisting of a seemingly endless row of partitioned, well-lit and airily-ventilated rooms complete with their own balconies, one after another, from one end all the way to the other; repeated in three storeys, to more closely resemble a simple but stylish art deco hotel or holiday camp than a hospital; not too dissimilar to the Ocean Hotel at Saltdean, in which she once stayed, with its famous adjacent lido. The views in Harefield were there; only, to Charlotte, frustratingly out of reach. And yet she could write a dissertation on the patterns and plays of light on the flat ceiling, and the microscopic dimples and divots in its paint.

Though she could only see them when they occasionally landed on her balcony rail, the birdsong from a choir in nearby trees provided its own kind of tonic. Over this would come the sounds of aircraft heading to and from Northolt, flying overhead on defence patrols. *Was it Viktor?* she thought with every audible propeller; unless hearing the more distinctive sound of heavy four-engined RAF bombers heading to, or back from, overseas missions. For the time being — air-raids ceased after that night in May, which a different nurse had confirmed as true upon Charlotte's enquiry — such sounds could not be emanating from Luftwaffe formations, who appeared to have given up the ghost. Even so, could anyone rest assured that Hitler would not try again? The last she knew, Viktor had been engaging the enemy's single-engined fighter-bombers who attacked in sporadic daylight raids, apparently to just provide some kind of irritation rather than any grand plan of destruction and invasion. Now she could do nothing but await his update, in reply to the letter the nurse posted.

Elsewhere on the hospital complex, in a bungalow from the original pre-Great War building, a scientist named Alexander

Fleming diligently worked on perfecting a hitherto little-valued medication.

With so little to see, and no chance to read, sounds provided the stories Charlotte could follow. The muffled movements in the room above, and, less clear, the noises from the room below; the echoing of hacking coughs, whose violence took her back to the Lyons Corner House and her coffee sneaking down the wrong hole; the squeak of trolleys and gurneys wheeled past her room, usually en route to x-rays or surgery, but occasionally to the morgue; and the chatter of up-patients and medical staff in the corridor beyond her room, as she lay and stared upwards, like some poor wretch in a pseudocoma — alert, but utterly paralysed. Unlike those unfortunate souls — she once tended to one at her first hospital — she *could* move; it just wasn't advised. The world around her served as her wireless — in the hours when the actual wireless, piped into rooms via the voluntary radio team, lay quiet — and she had to fill in the blanks to complete the narratives.

2006

Through a pall of intensely thick fog — darkened further by the nearing of dusk — Stanley walked towards the sleek terminal entrance. Outside Heathrow's Terminal 2 and the adjoining Queen's Building stood the signs and symbols of catastrophe: hastily-erected forensic-white tents, peopled like refugee camps, as wasp-like workers in yellow hi-vis vests worn over black uniforms buzzed about, attending to those in need. Everywhere: woollen blankets and the human wraps of thermal foil sheeting; cardboard and yoga mats, laid out as bedding. It just lacked the emergency vehicles, the sirens, the signs of blood and broken bones.

Passing by, Stanley glanced into a tent of the tired and stranded, before the doors of the terminal slid open. The concourse felt more like an old football terrace, overpacked and close to capacity, with the occasional avenue to pass through. Popping out, above the masses: the yellow and black signage, with panels of regal blue. Down low, once-modern stainless steel, now scratched to dullness by a million little touches and collisions. Seemingly endless snaking cordons circumnavigated cubicles and ticket desks and kiosks. Perhaps, unbeknownst to anyone at any point along their circumferences, they lingered in large circles leading nowhere but back around, were anyone actually able to move enough to end up back where they started. In amongst those dressed for the bleak British weather, the optimists, in incongruous Hawaiian shirts and sunglasses, Bermuda shorts and sandals; trapped in the sunless fug of an overpacked terminal.

Stanley glanced up at the large announcement board, its tidings also confirmed on various smaller monitors: over half of all flights — Arrivals, Departures — cancelled. People stared, transfixed, willing their eyes to see an update, or to make the word 'Boarding' miraculously materialise. Christmas only a few days away, the logjam felt like it would take a week to clear; especially if the weather didn't improve soon.

Stanley scanned countenances of dejection. Every posture and position of boredom and despair: heads in hands; chins resting on upturned palms with elbows planted on knees; folded arms; blank, bleary stares, off into the crowded middle distance, or into the coat-backs or rucksacks of those blocking the view. A sea of backpacks and books, hands holding telescopic suitcase handles, half-hearted yoga poses. Those in wheelchairs, suddenly given jealous looks by those left eternally standing. Tantrums not just from children but also adults, angry with airport and airline staff who, despite their wishes, had never been able to control the weather. Stanley thought about the old redbrick control tower, doomed for demolition: did people think it worked miracles, too? Its replacement, the slender, Space Needle-like tower, necessary to see over the ever-sprawling airport, already spiked into the air, ready for operation within a few months. Even it wouldn't offer visibility in fog as dense as this.

It had never been a good day for Stanley, the 21st: the shortest — but also the longest. The sense of unease hanging in the air didn't help, on a rare return. No coincidence: he had been invited back, fifty years to the day — even down to the hour — to when a plane took off and with it vanished the life he thought he had.

* * *

The two men — only having previously spoken by phone — greeted each other with gloved handshakes in the fog-heavy gloaming, the temperature hovering just above freezing on the outside viewing platform of the Queen's Building.

"Stanley?" Michael asked.

"Michael?" Stanley replied.

Neither quite knew the other by sight, even if the younger man had seen photos of a the older — albeit from fifty years earlier; and Stanley having seen a dust-jacket photo of Michael, also of a much younger man. Yet each could discern the other, amid stranded passengers having snuck outside to smoke, some with cardboard cups of coffee; adding further wisps of vapour evaporating into the ever-drifting mist of freezing fog.

"I hate the cold. Always have," Stanley said. "Hate it even more since — well, you know. Christmas, too. Can't be doing with it, even now. Too painful."

The pair fell silent, looking towards Heathrow's vast apron — runways, taxiways and hangars — with everything but the nearest area pale-washed into oblivion. Grassy quadrangles and triangles faded quickly to a watery green, then white. Nearby — close enough — the slow taxiing of pale ghost planes, like sea-going vessels visible only by a mast lantern. A little further, wingtips dipped in and out of vision; reflections on a turning tail-fin; the gleam on a slowly emerging nose-cone; orange runway lights flickering up onto the shiny underbelly of a fuselage.

The viewing gallery barely held true to its word: the fog descended on Heathrow Airport reducing visibility to just 350 feet, a mere tenth of where safety limits start to become a concern. Flights landed by wire, the approaching runway an increasingly rapid series of beeps to the pilots as the electronics took control; but arrivals and departures far more widely interspersed than usual, to keep the blind London skies clear.

Decades ago, this represented the future. Modernist brick and brutal cement, the concrete planters, full of greenery and life; the planters now gone, the shiny pointed cement now dull, and the brickwork heavy with mottles and the unsightly efflorescence of ageing, like liver spots for building materials.

"Fifty years." Stanley said, simple straightforward. "Fifty years," he repeated, the tone identical, the statement unshifting. He could have said it a third time, a fourth time, and nothing would have changed. It needed no hyperbole, no exclamation. It said it all.

"This is going too," Michael said, pointing to where they stood. "The Queen's Building. Terminal 2. It's time has come and gone. This exact view will be gone too. Anyway, thanks for meeting me here. I know it's not easy."

"Well, what else would I be doing? I'm as keen as you to find some answers. How's the book coming along?"

"So much research. It'll take years, I fear. I'm looking into so many different crashes, and disappearances. This is just the start."

"I still sometimes s-s-stammer — *there*," he said, laughing ruefully, "right on cue — when I talk about Alice, and that day here, and what happened after. Generally it got better when with Alice, but the shock, well … Mostly now it's only when I reminisce. Had speech therapy, many years ago now. Cleared up over time. But the cold doesn't help either, obviously," he said, his teeth slightly chattering.

"Strangely enough, I was here that day too," Michael said. "At least, I came to learn that I was, years later. Not too long ago, actually. I have no memory of it, obviously. I was just a baby."

"How strange. What an unusual coincidence."

"Strange indeed, but perhaps not so coincidental. My father was a pilot. BEA, too. So we weren't exactly strangers to the place."

"Oh, so he may have flown with Alice, you think?" Stanley asked, with a tinge of hope in his voice, as if this somehow could bring his wife to life again, via a newfound but distant memory; dead time, decades old, yet bringing new hints of existence.

"I don't think so. Different routes, and she was quite new, wasn't she? But he did die when I was young."

"A crash?"

"No. Or rather, yes, just not in a plane. A motorcycle accident. Hit a patch of ice on a country lane, and slid into oncoming traffic."

"I'm so sorry to hear that."

"Thanks, although it was all such a long time ago. I was only three at the time. I can barely remember him, to be honest. Just this vague sense of his size, his smell, and — this is strange — the coarseness of his face when unshaven. I've seen photos, of course. And at least we got to bury his body."

"I'm still waiting."

"I know, Stanley," Michael said, with a soft pat on the man's back.

"Do you think we'll ever find her? Is anyone even looking?"

"There are always people researching these things, and now I'll be doing more. There's always someone planning some reconnaissance. At this point I'm more interested in the human stories, of those left behind, but I've thought about going up to Scotland and looking. I'll dig deeper into the mystery, do what I can. It's just clear — not that I need to tell you — that it's not in the area everyone expected. It could have veered off course, off into the North Sea one way, or into the North Atlantic in the other — and then, in those waters, it'll never be found, unfortunately. Just a few degrees with a faulty compass or an errant navigational input, and we could be talking the Shetlands, Orkneys, Hebrides — Outer Hebrides. Or maybe it ditched in Loch Lomond — in the terrible weather. It clearly wasn't witnessed, wherever it strayed to, and left no surface evidence."

"I just want to know. To bring her home."

"Of course."

"So, Michael — why this particular missing plane?"

"It's all Geoffrey. He led me to this. To the ideas, to other stories, and for this book on missing planes, all across the world. Then, the fact that it turned out I was here that very day, which just added a little something. In a bit, when we go inside, I'll show you some of the research. Some photos you might find interesting."

"I'd like that. Don't take *too* long on the book. I'd like to live long enough to read it."

Michael laughed. "We've just had a baby — although when I say *we*, Pippa did most of the hard work, as she's keen to point out. So it may have to take a back seat for a while. I fear that I could spend a decade just researching all this stuff. So, did you remarry?"

"No, no. I just couldn't move on. I hear this word 'closure' a lot these days, and that seems to s-sum it up. In that I didn't get any. It was never closed. I always had a silly hope against hope — for the first few years, at least. That she would return, having been stranded in some remote place. Maybe she survived, but had amnesia. People were always talking about amnesia. That's the hope that a lot of people cling on to."

At that moment a figure in a yellow mac and matching sou'wester emerged from the mist; Stanley seeing only the bright waterproofs at first, before a pale face filled itself in amid the fog: a woman he judged as in her late fifties or early sixties, round of figure and cheeks, but even when shrouded in fine wrinkles, a strangely youthful set of features. The woman recognised Michael, and they shook hands tentatively before pulling each other into a respectful, brief hug.

"Lucy, this is Stanley Smith. Stanley, this is Lucy Roberts," Michael said, and so Stanley politely shook the woman's gloved hand, unaware of her significance. Michael hadn't told him about meeting anyone else. The name meant nothing to Stanley, but her eyes lit up in recognition of his.

"Née *Carter*," Michael added, and then, for Stanley, the penny dropped.

"I thought you might pull a stunt like this," Lucy said in reply, but she smiled, pleased with the introduction. She then hugged Stanley, as her significance suffused his body; her tight grip hitting the point home further.

"Are there more," Lucy asked Michael, looking around in the mist.

"No, you two are the only local ones. There are other surviving relatives in Scotland, and some scattered all over the place. Two families moved to Australia in the early and mid-1960s, 'ten-pound Poms' and all that, to escape the pain and the bitter winters, with all the reminders. And others had no traceable relatives — a young couple who had no children, no siblings, and whose parents are now long gone."

"I met you once before," Stanley said to Lucy.

"Really?" she said, with a gentle smile. "I don't remember?"

"My wedding day. You were just a little girl. You were with … well, you were all together. I spoke to your father, for a while. It's not like we knew each other well, your father and I. But you were all passing as I waited near the church."

He could see similarities between Lucy and Frank, whose face he remembered with added accuracy from photographs in the newspapers, that helped cement the image of the man he occasionally saw about the Fairey building: similar roundness of face, fullness of lips, and the wearing of spectacles.

"I don't remember, I'm afraid."

"It probably didn't mean much to you. Of course, I remember almost everything about that beautiful day. And — well, the things that happened six months later, on a far less beautiful day. Our paths almost crossed in Scotland, during the search. I saw you and your mother, from afar. You were heading out somewhere."

"We did our bit, albeit it's all a bit fuzzy now. It feels like it will never be solved. Never be found."

"Sometimes things show up," Michael interjected. "Unless it crashed and burnt to absolute cinders, or it sank to the bottom of the deep ocean, it must still exist out there. *Somewhere*. It won't have rusted and decayed to dust — not yet."

"The waiting was horrible," Lucy said, fiddling with her zip. "We ended up joining in searches around Loch Lomond, but then it just reached that point where — after a couple of weeks — it was time to go home. Mum was tempted to stay in Scotland, move back up there to where she grew up, but we went back to Hayes, and she got a job as a cleaner here at the airport. She'd wax these very floors. She got some compensation — life insurance, I think, that eventually paid off the mortgage, once they were declared legally deceased — and in the end I was able to go to university. Now I work here too."

"Doing what?"

"Engineering, with one of the airlines. Maintenance work, mostly. I thought I'd disrupt the old jobs for the boys malarky."

"Good for you," Stanley said, to which Michael nodded.

"I still can't quite accept that Dad and James are gone. That they won't suddenly reappear. Totally illogical, as I feel it will never be solved, and yet … Anyway, Mum died a few years ago. She got very frail towards the end — but she was never the same after 1956. Yet somehow Dad is still forty-five, James thirteen."

"Sorry to hear that about Gloria. It catches up with us all."

"I just want to know what happened, where they are, before I die. That's all. I know it's unlikely, with each passing year. But you're doing something. Maybe you'll work it out?"

"I can't promise much, I'm afraid," Michael said. "I can help tell the story, at least. Tell it again, maybe in more detail than before. That'll give it some life, as it were. But clearly I don't have an ending. Still, I already have some things that might be of interest. Come, both of you, let's get inside and see if we can get a hot drink if the queues aren't too long, I've got some photos to show you."

* * *

On that bright December day, late 1956, without any way to know what lay ahead, Charlotte broke her usual habit and, suddenly not so frugal, snapped black and white several photographs, in the gloriously low, far-reaching light — shadows stretching passengers into Giacometti statues — before the snow clouds rolled in. Even though she soon heard about the plane that vanished, she never thought to develop the roll of film — never thought her silly little snaps would have any use — and so it ended up stored with countless others for eighteen months, before prints were finally made, and those too were packed into boxes and shelved. Only a decade later would she rediscover them, and realise their significance; eventually posting them to Geoffrey Freeman in Scotland.

With no formal training, Charlotte had learnt via trial and error, and the study of photographs in books and magazines, how to frame an image, capture a moment. She didn't care for zoom lenses, or fancy gadgets, including some fandangled flash; she just needed to adjust the aperture and shutter speed, to capture the natural image without forcing stark fake light into the scene.

From that day, the photograph of the young man she recognised, but whose name she didn't yet know; the young man who stuttered so painfully that she felt twinges of discomfort and empathy whenever he got stuck mid-sentence or mid-word, wanting to gently nudge him as if a groove-stuck jukebox.

Framed by windows, the shot of the handsome BEA pilot, peaked-capped with golden insignia, golden wings on his chest, four golden bands on his blazer cuffs — all rendered silvery in the monotone — bidding a temporary farewell to his wife, who stood stylishly in matching tweed raincoat and slinky hat, with one hand on the pram in which their young son lay oblivious. She looked almost like a fashion model, so smartly turned out; a glamorous couple, totems of the jet-set age. She would occasionally pop for a drink in Forte's, where Charlotte would see her again, before departing with the child as her husband flew somewhere warmer. At the time, Charlotte felt plain and dowdy — and old — when looking at this immaculate young woman, who, in some ways, had stolen her dream of a life with a pilot. Years later, studying the photo once finally developed and printed, she felt the jealous pangs once more, only now she herself had grown older still, while the woman in the print remained mid-twenties and eternally alluring.

A Dutch angle, the camera tilted uneasily, captured a father and his bespectacled little son out on the Queen's Building balcony, staring out at the aircraft; a hint of movement in the boy as he leapt into a slight blur from sheer excitement. She recalled the man — at that point still just another stranger — as having such a kind face.

Then, the photograph of the father and his teenage son at his window of the plane, their expressions unclear in the graininess of the print, the speckled bittiness only magnified with later enlargement — the detail simply not present in the negative. Years later, Geoffrey — the man in the previous photo — would study the image, to look for signs of damage to the plane — something small that might have fallen off, or been askew; or if the radio antenna — which had clearly been transmitting signals earlier in the flight — in some way hung loose. Yet everything looked as it should.

Fifty years on, all sense of space obliterated, the idea that they stood in the very same space seemed almost unthinkable. Signage and shops and stalls and cordons; a jumble of information and advertising and wares-selling. Above it all, high-hung Christmas lights, and the hanging garlands with sparkling LEDs: a festive irony, like party-poppers at a wake.

And everywhere: passengers, frozen in frustration.

At the perimeters of the terminal, as the trio stepped inside, more sleeping bags and thermal blankets: the haggard, unwashed, red-eyed, strewn about like asylum seekers, homeless and in limbo after a tsunami or earthquake; dignified poses soon giving way to a sprawl in which small comfort could be sought. Trolleys as seats, luggage as stools, seats as sofas. The hell of limbo, of delay; neither here nor there. Christmas in the balance.

In each of the photos, passed between Michael, Stanley and Lucy as they stood in a tiny area of free space, various time-trapped people milled about or walked in the black-and-white background, but a clear sense of space in the sprawling, high-ceilinged 1950s terminal which looked big enough to house every airliner out beyond the glass. All those strangers in an airy building, walking towards their futures, captured and forgotten.

Yet they too — the trio, looking at old photographs, while drinking cardboard-clad cups of coffee — would themselves be visible in the background of press photographs and news B-roll, as examples of too much human life crammed into one space, in the tale of an airport reduced to chaos.

1941

A hellish, seemingly eternal week later, Viktor's reply finally arrived. Even as a child receiving a Christmas or birthday present, Charlotte had not been more giddy with excitement — although this one led to an unfortunate fit of coughing. Now allowed to sit up and read, her circadian rhythms had started to settle into a more normal pattern — although afternoon naps remained a feature of her days, as did bouts of staring at the dark ceiling at four in the morning, often wondering about her Iceman. She had only just moved from *Absolute* onto the acronym *BNGU*, or 'bedpans, no getting up', which, with the aid of a second pillow — hard won, like a trophy — at least allowed her to correspond, and to read a book or magazine; her mind too scattered for fiction, she reread snippets of the yellow-covered *East Coker*, over and over. Any hope of Viktor visiting, even if he could get the time off, seemed beyond remote: male visitors were prohibited — indeed, in a notice handed to her, with all-caps accentuated, they deemed it STRICTLY PROHIBITED – whilst there also remained a clear and unbreachable segregation of the sexes, with an entirely separate ward for men, as well as another for stricken children. Healthy husbands, often saddled with rambunctious kids, were not allowed onto the female wards to see their sickly wives, and so a mere paramour stood no chance. However, just to learn that Viktor was alive and well came as an incomparable victory; even if all it actually proved, with a time-lag like light from a distant star, was his safety *three days ago*. In his line of work, three days felt an eternity.

She instantly recognised Viktor's characteristically scribbled handwriting, with a simple pen harder than a joystick to grip and manoeuvre with great accuracy. Still, at least he had managed to start writing his own missives before his discharge from East Grinstead. Perhaps, she wondered — not for the first time — if his handwriting hadn't been especially neat even before his hands were so badly damaged. Far from ignorant, he had a practical, spatial intelligence, and incredible coordination, rather than anything particularly scholarly; she could picture him as too energetic, too fidgety, to do well in class, whatever the schooling system could provide in a small Icelandic town. An outdoorsman, set on that course from childhood. Unlike her, he wasn't one for books. Even in adulthood he had that boyish restlessness. In the fairly short letter, in prosaic English, he explained how he'd waited patiently and solemnly that night in the pub having slipped away from the half-cut squadron, fearful that something serious had beset her. He noted how he soon dismissed such a notion from his mind, in part to stop an absence of information turning, purely via his imagination, into the worst possible news. He told himself it must be something more perfunctory, especially since the cessation to the blitzing, like the unhelpfully late denial — not for the first time — of leave, for which he cursed her superiors as he strolled sullenly back to the airbase after last orders. He never for one moment considered that she'd fallen ill — let alone to such a dreadful disease. Upon receipt of her letter he promised to visit — only to be told it strictly prohibited. He wrote nothing of his life since that night. Signing off with a declaration of love, she suddenly felt, as she read the words, suffused with sufficient energy to get out of bed, to get dressed, and to walk — no, *run!* — to Northolt; but even the subconscious, reflexive adjustment of her torso to a more upright position dug her sharp in the chest like an enemy bayonet that screamed *Halt!*, and she had to let herself slump back into the feathery embrace of the pillows and, close to tears, give in to her damnable invalided state.

* * *

Weeks merged into a blur. In her way, she'd become a prisoner of war, only without the antagonism, and the threat of death from her captors. Though cared for, she felt trapped and institutionalised all the same; lulled by the routine and the dehumanising sameness of perfectly nice rooms that, taken as an identikit whole, started to feel like prison cells within a block. Like a prisoner, she also had zero freedom to leave.

Initially she'd been too drowsy, after days of unconsciousness, to notice the lack of nicotine and alcohol in her system; too drugged up in other ways to need her regimen of uppers and downers. Her body went cold turkey, wrapped in a fever and lost days in sleep and fog and mania. Most of it she could now do without. But weeks later, still she mentally itched for a cigarette, in part to counter the boredom. Her fingers twitched, eager to feel such a fine, lightweight cylinder, packed tight with glorious tobacco and filled with Viktor's aroma, as if he himself rolled them. Yet even in her weakest moments she did not wish — as safe as it might otherwise be — to send smoke into her lungs, given how it could cause her to cough, even if someone were to somehow smuggle a pack into her room. She laughed at the truism: nurses and doctors did not always make the best patients, yet she knew enough not to take tuberculosis lightly.

Refills of clean air were introduced directly into Charlotte's stricken lung twice a week, applied under local anaesthetic. A doctor checked success of the process via a new state-of-the-art x-ray machine — viewed on a flickering cathode-ray screen, with no need for the generation of a plate. Sufficient progress, deemed by the satisfied nods of the doctor, eventually meant a promotion to *Basins*: the freedom to get up and wash at the sink in her room, but it would take a lot longer still to rise to the heady rank of *Out To Wash*.

The only time Charlotte could venture out into the long curving corridor, aside from her pneumatic treatments, came via the weekly visit to the weighing room: her lone chance to mix with what felt like fellow inmates. The aim, if her treatment continued smoothly: to advance through the gradings, from short periods of time out of bed — one hour, then two, alternated with identical periods of time spent flat out — all the way up to undertaking exercise, after several daily rounds of being up and about. If there were no setbacks, light exercising would graduate to more strenuous exertions, and then, finally, the chance to undertake some work: occupational therapy, on the hospital grounds; and yet still somehow, she imagined, reminiscent of prison labour, minus the chain gang. The choices included bookbinding, printing and leather-working; and, most exotically, for those furthest along the path to recovery, the chance to chip in on the adjoining farm, with all that pure fresh air and natural life. However, for Charlotte, the prognosis suggested that all this would have to wait at least until early 1942, if not longer. No two people reacted the same way to the treatments, with each harbouring their own unique levels of damage and colonisation of the lungs — and each patient adhering to the rules to differing degrees — but with no miracle cure, few deemed worthy of confinement in the sanatorium got out in much less than a year; not even for good behaviour.

Her incentive to do better — to assiduously follow the rules, down to the letter — lay in the desire to see Viktor as soon as humanly possible. She'd become accustomed to waiting, but a year seemed interminable. She could feel the impingement of a vague, nagging insanity; a sense of how she might unravel, when thinking of such distant salvation. A year in here would surely drive her crazy; a year *up there* could kill her beau. Unless — and for this she prayed, in a vague, secular manner — the war could be concluded earlier, a year of flying Spitfires seemed tantamount to a daily game of Russian roulette. He could soon be heading overseas, she feared, to follow the action on the continent, and that only complicated matters.

At one weighing session, as all the women stood in dressing gowns and awaited their turn on the scales, another patient — a newlywed at the time of her incarceration — told of how the powers-that-be had threatened her with expulsion after her young husband had snuck into her room. If the sanatorium felt like a prison, such a fate — cast out, to leave the lungs to fight it alone — seemed akin to a death sentence.

This young woman, Edna, became the closest to what Charlotte could call a friend in those early months — their weekly meetings a brief chance to exchange stories. Edna looked more like a child, her weight loss leaving her with a near-prepubescent shapelessness. She had been working at the 11 Group Operations Room at nearby Uxbridge: the vital control centre, deep underground, which oversaw the fighter squadrons of the southeast. She had been present when Churchill, visiting the bunker as the inspiring figurehead in the act of seeing off the Nazi invasion, first said the words "Never in the history of mankind has so much been owed by so many to so few," before he swiftly repeated them, more famously, in parliament.

While she sent the occasional letter, Kitty never visited her stricken sister. She had made her way to the cottage, back from Glasgow, and immediately began a new job. Two colleagues from Haybridge corresponded fitfully, and although Charlotte loved hearing from her limited network of friends and her distant sister, she felt disappointed if the envelope delivered by hand to her bed — by a working patient, nearing release — did not display Viktor's distinctive scrawl and skew-whiff stamp; the misplacement of which became a running joke. In truth, his letters were always a little underwhelming, in that he didn't express himself, she felt, in the same depth that she did to him; even allowing for the fact that English was not his native tongue. Her letters were long, and full of passion; albeit she increasingly found herself with few sufficiently new experiences to document, and so often resorted to recounting their history, and reminiscing about her favourite moment: a reference to the dark Piccadilly alleyway, or their first kiss outside that Brighton pub, or reminding of the need to rendezvous at Eros, should they be apart when the war ended. His letters, scribbled during a busy life, were far more succinct; he had more to tell, she assumed, but less time to spare. At times she wondered if he was losing interest. However, thinking back to the letters sent after he first moved to East Grinstead — and rereading the ones sent to her at the sanatorium, kept on her simple bedside table — there appeared no noticeable decline in his output: he simply never wrote a great deal to start with. And even though she always felt a slight sense of disappointment when the letters abruptly ended, they remained the most thrilling part of her existence.

1941

The war — the chaos and the catastrophe, a year after the Battle of Britain — felt a world away as Flight Sergeant Geoffrey Freeman, in full RAF uniform, took one of his off-duty evening walks, venturing into areas well beyond the harbour alehouses favoured by his colleagues. Akureyri's relatively lush and fertile soil provided fields of wheat and pasture for flocks of sheep, the farmers threshing, the lambs grazing or gaily jumping and prancing. He passed clumped bales, standing odd against the barren, flat topography that flowed backwards for miles until hitting the distant mountains; smiling, as he passed, at a farmer with his free-running flame-haired horses. Further on, two more horses pulling the scantiest of ploughs, as two women hoed and wrestled the crops. Beyond it all, ice in patches on the distant peaks across the bay: like a map of the world, with white continents and islands and archipelagos, against dark slate seas.

A circuitous route took Geoffrey to the outdoor swimming pool — the jarring cold water of Sundlaug Akureyrar — that lay towards the low shoreline, surrounded by a smattering of houses and small huts and bird-less telegraph wires. As chilly as the sea, it proved a safer place to swim; one day he would get hold of some trunks and give it a go himself. A rickety wooden fence unfurled around the pool's perimeter, below the stepped embankments — a terrace of turf-seating five-deep, peopled by a handful of spectators: flat-capped men and head-scarfed women with fidgety children. The pool's buildings, flanking the rear, presented as a flat row with ten doors for different changing rooms, supporting a ladder leading up to a diving board that jutted from the roof. A street ran behind, up towards the mountains, but were he to venture to the top of the diving board, Geoffrey would view a kind of desolation.

He stood just beyond the perimeter, looking at women and girls in body-length bathers and caps, and men and boys in tight trunks; the males heading into the *Karlar* shack to change, the females to *Konur*. The entire area seemed constructed of flat buildings and corrugated façades: all architecture modernist by accident; the simplest, sturdiest shapes all flat and boxy, the strength of the triangle clear in the pitched roofs of houses, while municipal buildings and sheds were plain and flat-topped. Against it all, the human form seemed more organic, with its curves and juts, its soft flesh.

That's when Geoffrey saw him: the boy — a young man, nearly — muscles rippling, skin sparkling with water, trunks tight to his skin, standing proud on the edge of the board. Sixteen or seventeen, Geoffrey assumed, as this perfect figure spired into the water with the arc of a vaulting dolphin.

As he waited at the steps to climb the high-board again the boy shifted his weight from one leg to the other, and then, by miracle, he became Polykleitos's *Doryphoros*, contrapposto in marble; the classical physique delicate with counterpoise, a heel almost absentmindedly off the ground. Pectorals and abdominals; glutes in clinging wet woollen bathing shorts. Not as defined as that Ancient Greek statue of a young man probably no longer quite a teen, yet Geoffrey could envisage the boy in bronze or alabaster.

Fifteen minutes later the boy — his shocking white-blonde hair wet and a little darkened — emerged from the shack marked *Karlar*, a towel wrapped around his shoulders like a scarf, but still in just his trunks. Geoffrey approached. From there, a blur of confusion. The unsayable things. No words; none would be understood, anyway. The *look* the boy gave in return. The international language of eye contact, held far longer than required, until, like a word spelt the same but pronounced in two distinct ways, its meaning radically altered. In truth, Geoffrey didn't even know himself — not for certain — what the look meant, other than a sense of everything changing. Did the boy's eyes narrow? Was that another clue? Before long they wordlessly walked together, down the hill, as the boy led the way. They glanced across at each other, smiling — awkwardly, yet both soon laughed at the strangeness of the situation, and each other's amusement sparked in a back-and-forth. At Akureyrarkirkja they turned up the hill, and at that very moment almost joyful chimes pealed out. The boy reached out to touch the dark blue fabric of Geoffrey's jacket at the forearm, and then the breast pocket, to finger the winged insignia, woven and proud. He then felt the lapel, lifting it up and then patting it down, with an almost childlike fascination. They continued up the hill, to the beautiful floral park.

They stopped at some bushes beyond the back of a hundred-year-old house, in the limited fragments of light — from the strange Icelandic summer gloaming — that managed to penetrate the thickets and copses and shrubs. The boy moved, and Geoffrey followed, into totally shaded obscurity, a delicious pall of night-blooming jasmine hanging in the air. Still wordless, they fervently kissed and fumbled and caressed and groped, grabbing at groin and buttock; the only almost-word a "Shhh" from the older man, to quiet the hungry younger.

* * *

Smartly dressed in full uniform, Geoffrey paced the shoreline, trying to look inconspicuous, whilst simultaneously hoping to draw attention — *from just one specific person*. He stood fifty-or-so yards from the lone house, a dormer in its triangular roof above a trio of identically shaped downstairs windows, set in stark simplicity. He glanced to see signs of life inside, to no avail, and so absentmindedly kicked at shingle and rocks and tufts of grass at the water's edge.

Between the house and the shore, the eery sight, pierced by the low sunlight, of rows of A-frames constructed from unsculpted wood — just branches, bracketed by scraps of fraying rope — packed and strung with the carcasses of wind-dried cod; 'Iceland's bread', to be eaten with butter. Curving darkened heads and tails caught the light as the decaying bodies contracted; revealing sharp spines, and needle-teeth in the rictuses of open-hanging jaws. The sun landed with indifference on desiccated eyes fallen inwards, flat and hollowed out, matt and dulled; Geoffrey's sense of slight queasiness — excitement and nerves — not helped by the smell of saline and piscine rot.

Eventually the backdoor swung open, and Geoffrey's heart skipped at the apparent eagerness of the boy — he'd lost count of the number of their secret rendezvous — and then, the sight of that strong male body striding purposefully towards him. It took Geoffrey a moment to comprehend, having worked his gaze up from the fast-moving feet, the incongruously thick, greying beard, and the glinting fish cleaver in an upraised hand. The words slung his way — gibberish, to Geoffrey — were at least clear in their *venom*, and made it obvious that he had to sprint with all his might, along the water's edge. He surely had the beating of the boy's father in one key way: speed, against the deficits in musculature and weaponry and rage. Perhaps another man may have stood in shock, frightened into inaction, but Geoffrey had trained his body to 'race like hell at the sound of the scramble bell' — even when barely awake — and his adrenals were sharpened by life in the cockpit. He was lean, and fit, and in the prime of life. Still, this felt as dangerous as any moment in aerial combat, and certainly as unexpected.

The whistling wind flew hard in his face as he leapt over a sprigged bush and sprinted along the bank of Eyjafjörður; escape an increasing formality, he felt, until he slipped and fell — but sprang up quickly, pushing his palms, after they broke his fall, into the shale to pop himself upright, like a bucking horse, after a brief moment on all fours. His trousers and shoes heavy with water; spitting grit and brine from where his mouth hit the floor, nothing else could slow his stride.

It must have been two miles before he stopped running, having dared not look round. He did not want to waste time or lose focus in checking. Yet he knew the boy's hulking father, in the brief glimpse he caught, would surely never match him for stamina, just as he wouldn't for speed. At first, in the moments where the two were closest, as he scrambled to his feet, Geoffrey half expected to find the cleaver closing in on him at the velocity of a hawk when flung by his wild-eyed assailant; half-bracing for its thumping dig into his back, clean between his shoulder blades, in the way he once half-braced for German flak. In those first moments, for every yard of advantage he gained the greater the need for his pursuer to resort to that desperate, last-ditch act — and yet it never came.

Hunched over and gasping for breath, and close to vomiting, Geoffrey felt a trembling arise, at the total mess of the situation; at the certain death of the dream of the still-nameless boy — the killed hopes of adding to all those secret assignations — and the fresh threat upon his own life. The uniform left him easy to trace, should the man desire — although the airbase would not be especially welcoming to a cleaver-wielding fisherman who spoke no English. The time had come to angle for a transfer. As luck would have it, before long the RAF were handing over Akureyri to the Americans, and moving on out.

* * *

Decades later, the route down to the shoreline from the botanical gardens remained fresh in Geoffrey's mind from all those adrenaline-fuelled rendezvous, where he would loiter on the beach until the boy emerged at the time tapped out on each other's wristwatches at the end of the previous encounter; the father often out at sea, trawling for fish — or sleeping off a long day's work — and the mother apparently deceased, or otherwise departed. As he had 53 years earlier, Geoffrey stood staring at the isolated house, apparently unchanged but for a fresh lick of paint.

Almost as unexpectedly as in 1941, a grey-bearded man emerged from the same backdoor. In that moment Geoffrey flinched again at seeing the boy's father. Then, acknowledging to himself in the moment and with an air of detachment, how a sense of flashback could easily override what his eyes were actually witnessing. He'd be in his *nineties* now, at least, if still alive. No man of that age would remain so robust, so upright.

"Farðu burt!" the man exclaimed, gesturing with a hand that the trespasser move along.

Geoffrey stood his ground, the words a blur, but the meaning guessed at. This time he faced no gleaming cleaver to hurry him along. He stared at the man, trying to peel away the wrinkles and the whiskers; peel away the *time*.

Unable to quite make sense of what he saw, Geoffrey raised his forearm and tapped on his wristwatch. The man stopped in his tracks, confused. He drew closer, took in the stranger's face. "*You?*" The man eventually said, straightening from a quizzical head-tilt, eyes widening in recognition.

"You speak English now?" Geoffrey said, taken aback; his ageing limbs beset with tremors.

1945

One man. How on earth, Charlotte pondered as she scanned the delirious, overjoyed multitudes that thronged Piccadilly Circus on that manic May day, do you find *one man* — no matter how tall, no matter how distinctive — in a crowd of literally hundreds of thousands stretching as far in every direction as the eye could see?

And how do you find *him* — that one Icelandic airman — when he was possibly — probably? — dead?

* * *

January 1942 — inside a stolen overcoat that barely kept her warm as the temperature hovered just below zero, Charlotte pulled herself up onto the bus bound for Northolt, paying to ride with money loaned to her by Edna, the sole person who knew of her drastic scheme. Charlotte had just snuck out of the sanatorium after an early breakfast, needing its hearty fuel to walk a distance far greater than any attempted in months. Although she often compared it to an actual prison, unlike the real thing there were no guards or high fences to keep her contained. However, leaving without permission — and permission would certainly not have been granted — could have serious consequences. She pilfered the knee-length coat from the nurses' staffroom, to be returned later — necessary both to keep the cold at bay, and also to disguise her nightdress as she walked from the hospital grounds. Even with its bulky woollen embrace, shivers zipped up and down her bones, and she had to clench her teeth to stop them chattering.

The morning: so obscenely beautiful. How *dare* it? Frozen and crisp, snow from two nights earlier unmelted under pristine blue skies. The sun, low over the horizon, dealt a gentle palette of yellows that seemed far too tranquil. Charlotte gazed out the window at the passing icy-white countryside, at tendrils of greenery frilled with frost; her mind urging the chugging vehicle to move faster, as if it would make much difference in the grand scheme of things.

Three days with no news had turned into four, then four to five. By day six, the lack of a letter felt more than a little disconcerting. It wasn't like the mail had a long way to travel, through various postal districts or even to and from different countries — these were virtually neighbouring towns. With each subsequent day she grew more anxious, and began to plan an excursion as meticulous as any jail-break, all the time hoping to abandon the hare-brained scheme when a letter finally arrived, as surely it would. She might lose her right to free treatment, and even be cast out of the sanatorium upon any attempted return; but why even try to recover if Viktor wasn't there upon her release?

The sense of something drastically wrong had grown into a restless paranoia; a circular internal monologue that went from *he's okay...* to *...but what if he's not okay?* and back, never able to resolve itself. Without news he existed as both perfectly alive, and utterly dead. In her mind she mulled the options of preference, yet to put them in order: deceased, injured, captured, or a loss of interest; perhaps worse still, *interest in someone else*. Each felt hard to bear in its own way, but knowing — whatever proved true — seemed most urgent of all. She stepped off the bus into the frigid air, feeling a duller pain in her chest reminiscent of those early months, and clearly weak from all the bedrest. Bitterly cold, even shallow breaths stung her throat, almost tempting a cough.

On the curving West End Road, circumnavigating the base on her way to the main entrance, Charlotte passed two Spitfires standing close to the perimeter fence; recently returned from duty, steam rose in clouds from their torsos like hard-run racehorses: thoroughbreds, back in the winners' enclosure. They *are* winners, she thought: it's that kind of aircraft, and this felt like a place where winners belonged. Viktor had certainly belonged here — and then she caught herself thinking of him in the past tense.

And yet once she finally did know, not knowing suddenly seemed better.

The station warrant officer, a tall, skinny man with a pencil moustache, and whose name she did not catch, met her at the main entrance. He frowned, then led her to an empty side room — an unused classroom with chalked diagrams on a blackboard — where he broke the news rather bluntly. Viktor chased a Focke-Wulf 190 — the man was very specific about that — out of England after catching it attempting a daytime raid over the south coast. Viktor found himself detached from the rest of the patrol squadron, as, now flying solo, he pursued the enemy. His radio had not been working properly, and, a long way out of sight, his RAF colleagues in the air and on the ground never heard a word from him. Tragically, he did not return after engaging in the dogfight. His aircraft went down over the Channel, close to the shoreline, but just far enough out to sea to make a retrieval impossible; no pilot seen parachuting to safety, or found in the water. With nothing, over a week later, to prove anything to the contrary, it proved an all too common story: missing, presumed dead.

A secretary brought through a cup of tea as Charlotte tried to stifle her desire to howl — instead emitting a guttural sob, until she could later let it all out — as the warrant officer, clearly flustered by this display of heartbreak, beat a hasty retreat. Charlotte broke from sobs to sip at the hot drink, letting it burn her lips. She wanted to feel physical pain, to distract from her crumbling insides. She felt like biting right through the china, or smashing the cup against her forehead, to cut her skin open and burn her face. And then it passed, a sense of numbness rising in its place. She coughed, and its sharpness reconnected her to her body.

Some time later — it could have been minutes or hours, given Charlotte's trancelike state — the warrant officer returned with Viktor's possessions, wrapped in brown paper, as if ready to post somewhere: the letters she had written, the last three unopened; some clothing, including a shirt she had purchased for him; and his lucky silver fob-watch, that he must have forgotten to take up with him. Several of Viktor's colleagues confirmed Charlotte as the woman he often talked about — he had shown them a photograph: his one picture of her, which he kept in his jacket breast pocket, close to his heart. As he had not listed any next of kin, she may as well take his belongings.

When it came time to stand she found her legs unwilling and unable to support her. She coughed, and although not bloody, the sting struck sharper than normal. By this time, having felt the pain of his certain death before the numbness set in, her mind had begun calculating the chances that, contrary to the *obvious* conclusion, he had actually parachuted to safety, and that it simply took time to get all the way back to London; or that he lay in hospital somewhere, in the way he had after crashing so dramatically into her own life, and likewise lay unconscious. Like the life-vest he may have frantically deployed, it offered something for her to desperately cling to.

She could return to the sanatorium — if they would take her, if caught when sneaking back in — and do her best to fight back to fitness, until she felt well enough to go down south and find her missing Iceman.

* * *

To even try and find that one familiar face in the surging Piccadilly crowd felt futile. Yet Charlotte also felt obliged, driven by a sense of guilt, but also the fear that, should the one-in-a-million chance come true, and he somehow kept his end of the bargain — despite having been missing in action for over three years, and despite her failed attempts to locate him or his crash site in trips to the south coast — she would never forgive herself had she not made the pilgrimage.

Perhaps, if the unthinkable proved true, he could still come and find her in her daily life — and yet she no longer resided at the cottage that he had once visited, and she had given up nursing, too, after finally gaining freedom from the sanatorium. Still, the staff there could put her in touch, she supposed, should he turn up after all this time. But to be here, *now* — the promise she had made to him, and even though she accepted that he had little chance of upholding his side of the bargain, she had to be true to hers.

Upon her discharge from Harefield — much later than she had anticipated, in early 1943 — she found somewhere to lodge in nearby Hayes, financed by a stipend from Kitty, working in Brighton as a teacher and gradually buying out her sister's stake in the cottage. Once she felt strong enough, Charlotte went down to Winchelsea and the surrounding area for a week, trying to locate the wreck site as described to her by the warrant officer. She checked hospitals, although fifteen months had passed by the time of her discharge with a clean bill of health. At that point she didn't expect to find some injured, amnesiac pilot still on a ward, but she did ask about anyone admitted at the start of 1942. No one matching his description had ever been treated.

Never before had Charlotte seen so many people in one place. She lingered on the pavement, her back pressed firm again the façade of Monico's café, to keep herself moored. She lit a new cigarette from the tip of the old. She had barely touched tobacco since her discharge; her return to the hospital, on that terrible icy day, only possible after convincing the powers-that-be that she had just gone for a walk around the hospital grounds in the borrowed coat, having found herself going stir-crazy. As a trusted nurse herself, who until then had proved no trouble, they saw no reason to doubt her story, but she suffered a stern rebuke all the same. She now only smoked the occasional Craven A whenever anxiety began to chip away at her, although sometimes the memories it inevitably evoked — previously only positive — could strike with an overwhelmingly malevolent force, until she conjured something comforting to compensate.

That morning, by breakfast, she'd already smoked two: suddenly scared of waiting all day and not seeing Viktor; but equally — and strangely — scared of how she'd physically cope if, against all odds, he *did* show up. Her knees started to quiver at the mere thought. Why hadn't she thought this through?

Suddenly she felt that familiar tug on her own sanity, at the foreseen difficulty of trying to believe such a thing true, were she to find him alive and well; or the craziness that would ensue when seeing him, in the flesh, only to then find it a mere illusion: someone who purely looked the part. It had taken her so long — years — to curb the reflexive thoughts that every man she saw, until disproven by her eyesight, *could* be him. In time it improved to the point where any random man now at least required a similar build and complexion — same hair colour and style, too — to cause hope to rise. As such, the false alarms had grown more rare. But Piccadilly Circus — now heaving with all manner of people — was the very place she had told him, all those years earlier, to rendezvous. Would she again start to see him everywhere?

Once at the edges of the famous landmark a great queasiness welled up, elicited by the incomprehensible numbers crammed around the circumference of the roundabout and the fountain at its centre; the new packet of cigarettes, she feared, might not last the whole day. She stood back as people paraded past, the space on the pavement constantly widening and narrowing as the crowd pulsed. A cheery vendor breezed by with a tray of merchandise: conical party horns with frilly streamers that rustled when blown, *VICTORY* hairslides, tin badges imploring *GOD SAVE THE KING*. Revellers filed past in droves, carrying *WELCOME HOME* banners, spinning the clacking rattles familiar to football terraces, and, gaily bouncing along, two women wearing *KISS ME QUICK* caps. A sailor, daffodils protruding like antennae from his service cap, danced by, a woman's hands clasped to his waist. More quickly joined on, and a conga formed, bobbing along the only available slither of pavement, heads bouncing, cancan-kicks flung out to the sides, as, in separate circles, partners do-si-doed. Everywhere the familiar crisscrossing red, white and blue angles of the Union Jack; and with red, white and blue, once again, on star-spangled banners. Such exultation, such abandon, she thought, dragging on her cigarette as the carefree world whizzed and span around her.

Structurally, Piccadilly Circus had not changed much in the four years since she and Viktor had made it their own. Some of the advertising displays on façades were different, but the whole array remained unlit; the war — in Europe, at least — officially over, but the electricity ban on outdoor signage still in place. At the heart of the scene, the octagonal bell-shaped frame of boards, now with eight identical *SAVINGS STAMPS* adverts wrapped around the fountain where Eros once perched, following the eight angles of the steps — the place they sat almost four years earlier. The changes were more superficial: from almost every storey of every building bunting and banners and flags draped and fell and unfurled, some held over from the coronation in 1937, others purchased recently, with forethought and optimism — Germany in retreat, Hitler dead, the champagne on ice. Confetti sprayed in waves from high windows, like spume from breakers hitting the rocks.

The same space that, back in 1941 — she could not recall one better day — held a normal wartime pedestrian population now looked like it had little room left to squeeze in even a dozen more revellers. Yet still they came. A sea of people. And here the sea rolled, with all its pelagic qualities: buses marooned like static liners, around which heads rippled; waves of hats and caps and hairdos falling and cresting; riptides lapping up against the buildings and the log-jammed vehicles. The sun flickered on the rise and fall of the flat ovals of peaked caps and bright-white sailors' headgear. All day long, with its nauseating motion, it never once ceased to resemble a seascape to Charlotte: constantly swelling and undulating, ebbing and flowing. All day, that same queasiness.

Though she tried to keep close to the periphery, at times she couldn't help but inch her way into the throng, to try and gain a better view; only to find herself lifted off her feet — feet which still moved as if treading water — and carried away with the current. What about this place lifted her from the floor, span her head to giddiness? Oh to be back in Viktor's arms, even in some grimy alleyway.

Somehow she never found herself squashed in the crowd to the point of total panic, on account of the fluidity of movement, but it felt highly unnerving all the same, caught in an unstoppable flow that shifted her at will, and where people could perish. No wonder the landmark had served as a metaphor on the actual seas: Piccadilly Circus the codename for the rendezvous point in the English Channel, as flotillas and fleets formed a year earlier, D-Day. Even *that* had to be less chaotic than this, with enough people present to populate an entire invasion force, all crammed into one tiny space.

On the Underground concourse, as they bade a tormenting goodbye, she had said 'by the steps of the fountain' — and repeated it in letters — but the fountain was surrounded, and for every few brave steps she took toward it — this time feeling safe enough to just get a bit closer — she felt herself carried off in another direction. She feared she might lose her shoulder bag, packed with her essential items — including a new bottle of gin — but always managed to keep a firm grip. Each time, as soon as her feet hit the ground, she hurried to place her back against a wall of a building, sucking in deep breaths before fumbling for a cigarette, as the bricks and mortar held her still, as they once had nearby, when Viktor pressed against her.

At some point, she concluded, she would have to find a better vantage point, to try and see into its heart; to see if Viktor stood on the steps, waiting for her.

Four years. Four years since she had stood on those very steps and, on tiptoes, peered over the passersby filing in various directions in the hope of spying a man she knew would arrive. Now she could not even get close to the octagonal plinth; the crowd there at its densest, clustered like spores of bacteria in petri dish spreading around a central source of agar; no one concerned about her private tribulations. Her increasing agoraphobia did not feel so extreme that she couldn't bear to be out in public, but she could not throw herself into a middle of such a congregation. Yet every attempt to tentatively wade in quickly drew Charlotte too deep, and she had to retreat. To move out there — close to the centre — represented, for her, a loss of control, a lack of swift escape routes.

The concept of deep water struck Charlotte on several levels; a subconscious sense that bubbled, at intervals, to the surface. After all, the sea claimed his Spitfire, although the sighting — fairly close to shore — proved of no great help in learning more, and the tides cannot be turned back beyond their normal limit. No recovery efforts were ever made in such cases, as it was both futile and dangerous. He lay just out of reach.

Afternoon turned to early evening, people continued to pour into Piccadilly Circus, as if all six connecting roads were tributaries feeding into the main body of water, those sea-levels constantly rising. Buses queued all the way back down Shaftesbury Avenue. Thousands must have grown tired and made their exits, moving on to other landmarks, like Trafalgar Square or Buckingham Palace; or, exhausted, started heading home. Yet further surges arrived, the numbers swelling, as more and more people flooded in.

A young soldier, wearing the familiar black beret of the tank corps, received a leg-up onto the side of the monument — able to cling to the upper wooden edge of a *SAVINGS STAMPS* board nearly twenty feet above the crowd, and from there, pulled himself the further few feet up to the ridge. Then, like a seasoned mountaineer, he scooted up the yard or so onto the next ledge, and finally up onto the cupola; mimicking, to great approval, the pose — on one leg — of the missing cherubic statue, to the extent of fixing his aim with an imaginary bow. A small group of American GIs quickly followed in ascending to the higher ridge; the first few helping to pull the next cluster — including some young women — up onto their perch. Within minutes, maybe thirty people were up there; some sat dangling their legs over the lowest ledge, but most stood behind them, in tiers. A few brave acrobats — maybe half a dozen — stood proud on its tip, creating the illusion of rows of people on the shoulders of others, like a literal circus act: a human pyramid, one atop the other, swaying with a deceptively sturdy balance; too drunk or giddy with joy and jubilation to consider the dangers of a fall. Further around the Circus, others hung from lampposts and straddled traffic lights; all vehicles inert, whether shown green or red, as the police fought, often in vain, to clear a path for them to carry on to their desired destinations. Revellers rocked any cars caught in the jam, clambered onto the tops of buses; others lounged on, and hung from, the backs of lorries laden with barrels of ale, that scamps tried to lever overboard. Higher up, yet more leaned from, or clung to, balconies and windows and roofs. A man atop a streetlight stripped provocatively down to his underpants, throwing his clothes to the cheering crowd below.

Charlotte looked around, trying to locate a building to whose upper stories she could ascend — where the windows or balconies were not full of reckless daredevils in danger of spilling down onto the street, with the only hope of a soft landing to fall on some poor unsuspecting sods. She turned around and around.

At the highest point of the buildings behind her, the gut-punch of a giant RAF roundel on a billboard for its Benevolent Fund, next to the *GUINNESS IS GOOD FOR YOU* clock. Viktor existed everywhere, except, it seemed, here in person. As well as the Guinness and RAF billboards, he lived in the Brylcreem ad and the Craven A display. A man with a particularly strong and unfamiliar aftershave merrily waltzed past. It led to a thought: would she *smell* Viktor? Is that how she might identify him? The brand of cigarettes, now also her own; his uncommon foreign cologne, that she had never again encountered; his distinct, piquant pheromones that gave his sweat a stolid, manly odour. That night, in the alleyway, behind the unknown drinking club — a venue not too far away, but which she feared she could not locate, even if able to access an unpopulated Shaftesbury Avenue and take her time to pick it out — meant that his smell, in the dark, seared itself, along with the physical sensations, into her consciousness. She could still *taste* him, too — if she focused hard enough — with the bitter tangs of stout and nicotine on his lips and tongue. With sight rendered unnecessary that night in the pitch black, the tastes and aromas clung to her senses. Yet here, she concluded with an air of defeat, any scent would surely be drowned out. In the heaving mass there hung the malodorous fug of stale body odour, mixed with diesel exhaust spewed from colossal idling engines, and all manner of pipe and cigarette tobaccos with their faintly different tones mixing into one generic flavour. There hung every type of liquor on breaths, and even the occasional acrid whiff of vomit. Viktor's unique signature would die in the olfactory overload, too overbearing even for the best-trained basset hounds to discern and track; her nose all too human for such a task. He could be mere feet away and she would never know, his head obscured by the tallest men around her, and the women and children they lifted onto their shoulders; his smell masked in the revelry of the great unwashed, some of whom had been here since the previous afternoon, soused and pungent and unashamedly puking.

As she skirted around the perimeter, scouting a new vantage point, bursts of song rose and fell. *Roll Out the Barrel, Pack Up Your Troubles in Your Old Kit-Bag, Bless 'em All,* and *It's a Long Way to Tipperary* — rousing and triumphal, their words known better than Sunday-school hymns, belted out with brio, if not great melody, and lacking the pleasant harmonies and sharp timing of a practiced choir; more like a drunken chorus around a pub piano just before closing, with verses suddenly dying out — just a few people left singing — before the next full-throated song started up. It took her back to East Grinstead, and Ward III, and the deformed airmen singing many of the same tunes.

Charlotte tried to join in, hoping to feel swept up by the fervour. But the festive spirit eluded her; the lingering sense of attending a funeral while everyone else celebrated a wedding. Out of the blue, as she indolently mouthed the words, a sailor took her waist and kissed her, cheerfully and fully and forcefully on the lips, and with such great ardour that she pushed him away in fury. Strangers everywhere were kissing with abandon, and in other circumstances she would have just given in to the moment. She did not think it so very bad to be kissed; the anger: that the man was not *Viktor*. The stranger, initially taken aback by her reaction, muttered some confused insult, but then joined a conga-line and joyfully bobbed away.

Defeated, she retreated again, to catch her breath, and to survey the scene from a distance; once again desiring a better vantage point, but unsure of how to reach one. Could she just breeze into a building unannounced and uninvited? Perhaps someone in one of the properties had binoculars or opera glasses that she could ask to borrow? If she were to definitely spot Viktor — if her eyes did not deceive her — then, she resolved with great fortitude, she would head back down and wade into the masses — into the deep, dark waters — to make contact.

* * *

Daylight fading, the hands of the Guinness clock approached the perpendicular split of nine p.m.. The crowd seemed as densely packed as ever. People continued to pour into London for the night party — for them, it hadn't even got started yet. Yet as the hours passed, still no sign of Charlotte's missing Icelandic airman.

The crowd eventually thinned at three in the morning, until, as daylight approached, only a few stragglers remained; wandering — sometimes stumbling — in the dark, trampling over the detritus of flags and bottles and confetti and cigarette butts. A few drunks lay passed out on the fountain steps, slumped against the advertising hoardings, with others asleep on the pavements and in shop thresholds. Some, Charlotte realised, already lived on the streets. The bombed-out and destitute and displaced, still sheltered nightly in their thousands in the Underground — now a nightly shelter for the homeless, rather than just a place to escape air-raids.

And so, once again, as the crowds vanished, Piccadilly Circus became the place to which she and Viktor staggered back, heading from Shaftesbury Avenue towards the Underground. She remembered, mere minutes after it ended, carrying the slight sense of shame at their alleyway tryst — wondering if others on the station concourse would notice the dust and dirt and scratches on the back of her dress, or any stains on her legs — but not one ounce of regret.

Four years on, she still did not regret one single bit of it: they had lived in the moment, and taken the opportunity; an opportunity that seldom returned, and which, she now knew, lay almost certainly forever beyond reach. She sat on the steps — the steps where they once sat — and pulled the bottle of gin from her bag, spinning the lid until it flipped off and bounced away.

"To my Viktor," she said out loud, raising the bottle in salute, to chink it heartily — *"Slàinte mhaith"* — against his phantom glass.

Part Three

2018

The Piccadilly Line: an almost timeless pleasure at Uxbridge, the old Art Deco station — with its pre-war contradictions of brutal concrete and delicate stained glass — still a tranquil place for Stanley to embark in the rush-free mid-morning, with just a smattering of other passengers dispersed along the full length of the train; each careful to place themselves at suitable intervals within the carriages. He shuffled into the first compartment he came to — the rear car of the linked convoy — and took a seat adjacent to its back wall, facing the opposite row. Eventually, with a grind and squeal, the train inched into life; trundling past the suburban sprawl, travelling against the grain of London's expansion, out to in. Greenery grew sparse, until all outside light vanished in the descent into the Underground. Rattles and clacks amplified in echo within the dark tunnel, London pulling inwards. It felt too hot for this excursion, but no other day in the calendar would make as much sense. At his age, there might not be a next year to wait for.

With each stop the carriage gradually filled. As the other passengers internalised everything, Stanley found himself edged into isolation. Disarticulated headphones — ear-pods — cut him off from his neighbour; the tinny rumble and bomp and tish extruding from the gaps between earhole and curved white plastic a stark reminder that his tastes — that old sweet music — were terribly antiquated. In the air, every kind of sweat, every hint of fragrance, the tang and drip and exudations of summer's hottest day hanging heavy in the heat-trapped compartment.

The subterranean tube tunnel all but retraced that drive in the old Minor all those decades ago, Knightsbridge Station burrowing below the eponymous road; then Hyde Park Corner — up to Stanley's stop at Green Park — arrowing underneath the A4 where the name changed to Piccadilly. It felt easier being transported — passive, the passenger ushered to the destination — but he could never quite get used to ceding all control in life, to fall fully into the flow of others. Although all those years ago he hadn't really known what he was doing — his first ever date, navigated via unfamiliar roads, after a few more tentative steps into the adult world when booking a restaurant by telephone — the sense of empowerment as he drove Alice into the heart of London felt intoxicating, along with the joys of her presence. He'd become, for the first time in his young life, the master of his own destiny; or, at the very least, wrapped up in that illusion. He sighed, fragments of that day fleetingly clear in his mind before the current world crashed back in.

Decades on, thoughts of Alice now existed on an elliptical orbit; always coming back, but not always at obvious and regular intervals. Spinning out, then spinning in; sometimes more closely than others. But, as age took its toll, and neural connections withered and atrophied, he feared those dim, distant memories that looped away — flying off too fast — continuing on and on, out into the blackness, never to wrap back around. He saw this as one last-ditch attempt to induce collisions in that endless void, and maybe send lost fragments of his wife — a smile, a look, a phrase, a fragrance — hurtling back into the light.

Finally there came a pleasant increase in oxygen as Stanley alighted at Green Park, squeezing past a jostling crowd eager to barge their way on before he could get off. Upon reaching the end of the platform warm gusts whistled at him from the tunnel

— a whoosh, like an airlock slammed shut — and then the pyroclastic surge of heat pushed ahead of the impending arrival.

He emerged into oppressive heat and blinding light opposite the Ritz, able to walk to Old Bond Street and approach the scene in the very same direction as in 1955, only now on foot. In all those decades the density of central London had intensified — taller buildings visible beyond old rooftops, cramped pavements, tightly packed roads, crammed with oversized vehicles. The spaces had contracted; compacted and enclosing, encroaching on his elderly senses — themselves in a constant state of wariness — with unsettling claustrophobia. The sweltering city heat dug deep into concrete and brick and tarmacadam, and like evanescing steam, shimmered back into the air. Every last inch of the capital felt earmarked: built-up, parked upon, signposted, locked down. Brightly-coloured bunting hung across Piccadilly: reproductions of artworks draped in honour of the Royal Academy's 250th anniversary. It added a sense of celebration, with more beauty and vibrance hanging in the air; the warp and weft of London's layout, hatched and crisscrossing, further assaulting the senses.

Without realising, Stanley walked straight past his destination of Old Bond Street, whose opening lay obscured by signage and the blockade of highly-invasive roadworks: green plastic barriers and freestanding steel fences lined as palisades; the entire width of roadway closed off to traffic, to the point where it became hard to even envisage where he parked sixty-three years earlier. He had followed the path of the cordon, which took him along a protected footway on the inside lane of Piccadilly, and only then realised that he had walked too far.

Old Bond Street, as he turned back to face it, looked unrecognisable. Not only the disfiguring roadworks, which blocked a clear perspective on the open road where he parked the Minor. As he sidled down its narrowed pavement, past workmen hacking at the road, what were once quaint façades — jewellers, art galleries, clothes stores and banks — were now almost exclusively high-end fashion stores, whose natural clientele, milling at its entrances, comprised sheikhs and oligarchs and Western bankers. Gone was Gieves, the tailors whose window they stared into, in front of which Alice had complimented him on his own suit. Also gone, the jewellers whose prices made their eyes water. Gone, too, Yardley's, the perfumer, who bottled Alice's adorable aroma. For a split second, that very scent sprayed within his mind, along with a flash of her standing by its windows — but then, as he grasped to hold onto it, it slipped away.

The street seemed fairly upmarket even then, of course, but it now felt obnoxious and charmless. He had only been back to the area once in all the subsequent years: in 1959, a trip which ended with a small purchase at one of the less-significant art dealers, also now gone. That had been another stifling day, although in contrast to this cloudless afternoon it unleashed the most ferocious thunderstorm, that soaked him to his core. He'd avoided London, whenever possible.

Beyond the final barricade, before the entrance to the still-familiar Royal Arcade, clustered a pack of white vans flanked by workmen in hardhats, as pedestrians filtered past.

How would he have imagined 2018, back in 1955? Stanley tried to think ahead, from that moment more than six decades earlier. There were none of the flying cars predicted by the science fiction of his youth, so gleefully devoured; no space-age metal buildings, no geodesic domes and flying saucers nestled amid these particular historical buildings; no jetpacking commuters hovering a dozen feet off the ground — and yet even so, it felt so *changed*. London had sped up, perhaps fivefold, as he slowed down by what felt a similar rate.

But then, looking further down Old Bond Street: a red phone box painted a shade so redolent it flipped progress on its head; and, at the junction of Burlington Gardens, a u-turning taxi: an aged Austin FX4, whose world-famous curves first appeared just three years after he and Alice walked this very stretch of road, and where, with the compression and distortion of time, he had begun to see them in his memories of 1955. Wasn't that, after all, *always* the shape of the London cab?

He turned onto Burlington Gardens, whose pavements were too narrow to contain the throng. Burlington Gardens became Vigo Street as Stanley passed Saville Row, to where Gieves had long-since relocated. Greeting his exit to Regent Street stood another timeless sight: the red double-decker bus, although its shape appeared distinctly more modern; slicker than the old Routemasters and AEC Regents of his youth, but still clearly of the same lineage. On trips to his local town he saw such things — red buses and post boxes and phone kiosks, and the fleets of black cabs — but nowhere near as prevalently as here; and the red telephone boxes — indeed, even the soulless silver ones that frequently replaced them — had all but disappeared from his usual small ambit in the age of the smartphone.

The banners and bunting on Regent Street were even more varicoloured and vibrant than at the entrance to Old Bond Street, strung at intervals across the road just above the roofs of the buses, spanning convex-to-concave elevations, left to right, as the road curved in a quarter-circle. The Café Royal appeared closer than he recalled, all frontage retracted; simplicity and quality, lost behind a far busier street scene. Had it even moved location? Two buses parted at the junction ahead — giant red curtains pulling left and right as if in one stage-managed act — and Piccadilly Circus stood unveiled, a giant bank of blinking video screens dominating the façades where once stood classic animated signs and neon logos. Gone, too, any hint of subtlety in the content of the adverts themselves: a digital panel, clearly bigger than the double-decker that passed below, spinning out the word *Sexy*, followed by a close-up of cleavage hoisted up in a cotton bra, then a tight shot of seductive female eyes, and a jump-cut to a hand moving suggestively across the waistband of a pair of knickers, before concluding with the manufacturer's logo as the loop resumed once again. Beaming from the largest of several subdivided screens — twice the size of the others — this seductive flesh made itself hard to avoid; what would almost be classed as soft-core porn in his youth unashamedly foist into the approaching view, skin and underwear and overtly moist lips popping in full colour over the passing traffic, and dominating the other four adverts, whose messages could never compete as visceral and eye-catching statements. He thought back to Alice in her bridal underwear, and how beautiful she looked; and how this, by contrast, felt cheap and tawdry.

Stanley's eyes then moved toward the top-right screen as it temporarily flashed the familiar rich-red branding of Coca-Cola — the single hint of continuity — and suddenly it all made a little bit more sense; like a lone familiar landmark on a rebuilt city skyline, albeit itself reformed and modernised.

And yet, aside from the sprawling digital fascia over Boots chemist at the junction with Shaftesbury Avenue — where once hung the Guinness and Coca-Cola signs, like vivid works of art — and, further into the distance, on a single rooftop LED display where Coventry Street met Haymarket — the advertising spaces of old were gone. Classic architecture — the London Pavilion's two regal façades, and to the east, on Glasshouse Street, where it tucked in behind Regent Street — all now denuded; relieved of clutter and revealed as if society had grown more tasteful.

Beyond the removal of neon, the entire road stood reworked, the Shaftesbury Memorial Fountain moved to the right as he approached; relocated closer to the Criterion theatre and Lillywhites store, both now enclosed in scaffolding. The *circus* was no more: nothing at all circular about the junction in 2018, with the roundabout itself — the stepped surrounds of the fountain, where he and Alice sat in Anteros' shadow — now engulfed in a wider triangle of pedestrian paving. The exact geographical space where he and Alice kissed — the heart of the scene, the bullseye — now a road surface boxed with yellow hatched lines that faded under the daily rolling mega-tonnage. The exact geographical coordinates of that intimate moment were now trundled over, second after second, by non-stop traffic, ploughing ever onwards. Perhaps the steps were still the very same stone slabs, removed and relaid a dozen yards away. But Anteros and the fountain, and those very steps at his feet, now felt like an afterthought, a sideshow, shunted to the periphery; the main aim to get vehicles through the junction to the handful of off-shooting roads as smoothly as possible. He tried to locate the *exact* step they sat on — facing the Pavilion and the Monico's façades — but the entire terrace brimmed with teenage tourists, French or Italian, seated as if at the theatre.

Everything about Stanley's memory, his experience, felt cast to one side; bulldozed, rolled over and obliterated under the unbearable weight of time. He had returned to reconnect with Alice, but everything seemed wrong. Rather than revive lost memories — such as her aroma, briefly sparked outside the old Yardley store — it mostly felt like existing ones were overprinted by unhelpful new memories, in the way that he'd occasionally mistakenly shoot one ciné film on the reel of another, which then superimposed itself onto — rather than totally wipe away — the existing images; leaving the original half-obscured and ghostly, half-overlain with a different point in time.

In broad daylight the absence of those old neons could not be fully felt; the way the colour that night in 1955 blew the receptors of his retina. At night, rather than an entire panorama of opulent lights it could now only be one charmless wall of moving images.

Adjacent to the young tourists, glimpsed almost by accident, a sight that jolted Stanley as he belatedly focused: an older man and woman — possibly American, he guessed, by their clothes — holding hands as they sat on the steps. Her long grey hair, her smile, and something about her eyes behind smart spectacles. The way she rested her head on his shoulder. It *could* have been Alice, perhaps — a vision of how time might have treated her. The man, though seemingly shorter and with a much sharper nose, could have been Stanley. The couple didn't know it, of course — but they had stolen his life; they had experienced a future, when his lay in the distant past.

A sudden sound from the sky had Stanley craning his neck: an Airbus roaring overhead, surprisingly — if not alarmingly — low; lining up on the Heathrow glide-path within the geometry of rooftops. Tens of thousands of feet higher up, moving with the eery slowness of great speed when seen at great distance, the speck of a shimmering jet, the sun reflecting upon its silver body.

Another time. Another *age*.

Never before had he felt quite such a strong sense of outlasting his welcome — to *still be here*, on this planet, so far away from the life he once had planned.

1957

The brace and lattice rafters of the gargantuan Fairey Aviation factory roof swept high over Geoffrey Freeman's head: a firmament of girders crisscrossed with skylights, whose projected shafts refracted in delicate triangles and diamonds and rhombuses, their shapes intercut by rails and pulleys and brackets, with rows of conical lampshades hanging low on the end of long electrical cords; all casting shadows of a similarly complex weave. Into apparent infinity — beyond the length of any football field — ran evenly-spaced floor-to-ceiling pillars; adding further angles to the manic geometry — a visual chaos, midst an audible cacophony. At various workstations steam hissed and vaporised into wafts of smoke; metallic dust glistened in clouds hit by sunbeams, and from workbenches flew girandoles and Catherine wheels of sparks; to fall onto a floor littered with metal filings and shavings, and delicate spirals of sheared aluminium alloy, and fumbled rivets, all left for the nightshift to sweep up, lest productivity drop in their recovery.

No stranger to vast mechanical complexes, still every single one of Geoffrey's senses felt assaulted: the stench of hot metal, burning oil, molten solder, and familiar sour male perspiration. *Perfection*: the sense of action, of purpose — man and technology, muscle and apparatus — united in the effort of creating flying machines. Male voices rose above the din: phrases and conversations decipherable in mere fractions: "two-thou of a inch, Bob," and "hold it steady, Tom,"; something about Queens Park Rangers and Brentford spoken by men on a tea-break. Further down, smatterings of suitably industrial language whose hard syllables struck like the echoing fast-hammering hardware.

Fine-suited in a world of greasy overalls and rolled-up shirtsleeves, Geoffrey followed a shop steward through to the drafting office annexed well beyond the far side of the building, unable to hear the man's directions — or perhaps just smalltalk — over the tumult. Occasionally the steward would turn his head to direct words behind him, but then turned to face forwards again before completing the sentence.

Geoffrey could feel the thrilling pounding in his chest as he walked. The vibrations rode up his shins into the cartilage of his knees, that damped like shock absorbers. The pair of men passed workers with their shiny tools pressed against rows of blunted, noseless planes, still awaiting their cones; men propped inside the aperture, legs hanging over the edge along with coils of wire. The women of the war — those icons of factory life — were gone; the only feminine figure the elderly tea lady, who, post-menopausal and shorter-haired, also had a slightly masculine countenance, as if hardened by osmosis to resemble a careworn mechanic. The man led Geoffrey past airframes and engines and wing assemblies, dangling from chains like cattle carcasses rattling down the rails of an abattoir.

He took it all in; breathed deep to inhale the unique tang of *manufacturing*. Rarely did he see aircraft under construction, although he frequently saw mechanics at work on wings and fuselages, after years in the RAF, where he witnessed the repair and refitting of the Hurricanes and Mosquitos he flew — and later when stationed overseas, Lysanders and even the occasional Fairey Swordfish; making time, whenever possible, to share a cup of tea with the ground crew, to show his appreciation for their less-heralded efforts, in a manner that some of his pals, either too afraid or too haughty to fraternise, dared not do. With so much change in his life since 1945, he struggled to comprehend, on some level, that it all ended more than a decade ago; in some ways it still felt so fresh. And yet those crazy early-war summers were now closer to two decades ago. His post-war work proved important, and he felt proud of the mysteries solved and solutions he helped posit, but it never seemed as absolutely vital in any given moment. He now experienced a much safer existence, but at times it didn't feel quite real. He still saved lives — just in a less direct manner.

While it lacked the puzzle-solving nourishment of his own work, Geoffrey found a glorious beauty to the masses of men at their machines, wrangling and fettling, wrenching and torquing, in the creation of future potential. In recent years his working life had been a series of industrial post-mortems; this felt more like mechanical midwifery. It didn't help that his latest investigation — the one that brought him to Hayes — had stalled: more than six weeks in, they had yet to even locate the crash site.

As he walked past spars, struts and bulkheads, laid out on the floor or spreadeagled in jigs in need of final nuts and bolts and rivets, Geoffrey witnessed the reverse process of his own work. He worked with aircraft in tatters, cast far and wide, bent into unnatural shapes and sometimes torn beyond all recognition;

often smoke-damaged, and sometimes, after great efforts, dragged from the bottom of a shallow ocean. Even so, he helped reconstruct those once-scattered aircraft remnants in giant hangars, albeit in loose formations spaced across the ground, where seams would have faultlessly met other seams, had they not been so violently sundered. Rather than fully rejoin, they placed debris side by side, like jigsaw pieces arranged in homage to connection, never welded back together; a loose collection of calamity. Those small, intentional gaps — sometimes the proof of where, as seen with the Comets, metal fatigued and violently sundered with an explosion of cabin pressure — were often adjacent to huge empty spaces, where sections could not be salvaged, or were perhaps simply obliterated. Though the hangars were almost always grand, sometimes the recovered wreckage looked almost apologetically minimal.

Pinned to the wall in a short, narrow corridor: a photo of the original headquarters in Piccadilly. The two men then passed a capstan lathe, its arrays of levers, its hand-wheels and its two main headstocks — live-centre and dead-centre — all inert, as the company sought out a new machinist, following the likely death of its erstwhile operator, Frank Carter.

The drawing office proved far more peaceful, if not entirely soundproofed. Rows of draughtsmen, in smart shirts and ties, several bespectacled, some bald or balding, were hunched over drawing boards, books of charts and graphs and calculations piled high on desks beside them, set-squares and compasses and protractors to hand, anglepoise lamps lighting the fine details. Plans, blueprints, templates — all pencilled-in and inked-up, by skilled and steady hands. Some looked up as the two men entered, but others were deep in concentration. In their free hands some held lit cigarettes, while one or two kept theirs on the go in pursed lips, expertly avoiding the ash staining their work. In their midst sat two draughtswomen, diligently scribing, heads down. At a towering drawing board towards the back of the room stood a senior-looking, moustachioed man in his late fifties, pipe dangling from the corner of his mouth, his triangular set-square riding up and down on the movable horizontal T-square as lines were drawn.

The draughtsman Geoffrey had come to see — the man named on the docket — stood beside the apparent master, who, after introductions were made, said solemnly, "Go take your lunch break now, Stanley. No need to hurry back".

* * *

"So, tell me about Alice. What was she like?"

Geoffrey and Stanley sat facing each other in a greasy spoon cafeteria situated halfway between the Fairey factory and the train station. The two men sat at a table next to the wall, under the black menu board, with its white pop-in plastic letters and numbers, itself pinned to cheap wood-panelling. Bright-windowed on a mid-February lunchtime, the glass hung heavy with condensation, blurring the world beyond. Every other table sat occupied, with a group of four navvies adjacent to a conductor and a locomotive driver from the railways, and in the opposite corner, a man wearing the apron of the shopkeeper; all bar one eating hearty fry-ups. Also dotted around the tightly-packed room were bespectacled old ladies with hats and headscarves and hairnets, often eating far simpler fare, with pasteurised orange juice and pots of tea. Stanley, his sandwiches still stored in his work locker and therefore still fine for later, ordered a pot of tea with a round of toast and a slice of Battenberg, while Geoffrey requested coffee and a Bakewell slice. Though it would just be more bread, Stanley no longer needed to cook himself anything for dinner, a task that seemed far more onerous now that Alice's absence stretched eternally beyond a night or two.

"Sh-she was the most kindhearted p-person you could ever meet. Really. Sh-sh- … Sh-sh-ssh—"

"Relax, Stanley," Geoffrey said with a warm smile. "You're not in any trouble."

Stanley, frustrated with words, looked at Geoffrey: the older man's face pinched, the features drawn in close to the nose. Such a prominent gap in the upper front teeth might have rendered someone else slightly imbecilic, but even if Stanley had not known the man's background and achievements, he could discern a sharp mind from the darting speed of his eyes — behind thick horn-rimmed glasses — that appeared to constantly process information; not in a furtive manner, but as if in constant recalibration. Older, he guessed, by perhaps a good fifteen years, Geoffrey possessed an avuncular air, but also a quiet authoritative confidence — a gentle sternness, as possessed by the best teachers at school, who, if necessary, could make their point with a whisper, where others would bully and shout and, when talking to him, humiliate. In truth, Stanley warmed to this kind of man, who reminded him of Mr Dunbar, his long-time English teacher: a real gentleman, as he remembered him — but no pushover. He found it tended to be the blue-collar workers who mocked his speech impediment — to his face, at least, as he passed through the factory. He sensed that the white-collar types did so behind his back — they certainly weren't averse to thinking him simple. Although apparently not from some elite school, a man like Geoffrey projected an air of class, without appearing supercilious. However, even though Geoffrey did his best to put him at ease, he still felt under interrogation.

"Sh-she was s-so understated," Stanley said, wet butter from the toast glistening on his upper lip, until he wiped it away with a paper serviette. "Very clever. Knew a lot about a lot of different things, but never cared to be an expert in any one thing — could have done all kinds of great things in life, but only wanted to do what interested her, while it interested her, like flying and s-seeing the world. Travel — that was her thing. Was only s—posed to be for few years, just to see new p-places and experience different cultures, maybe learn a language or two along the way. Sh—sh— ... Sh-sh– ... Had a quiet wisdom, did Alice — beyond her years. Why do you ask? What does it have to do with what happened?"

"Oh, mostly curiosity on my part," Geoffrey said with a smile. "And, you know, checking every angle. From our point of view, it helps to know just who was onboard, just to be sure. Making sure everyone was proper and above board, mentally sound and whatnot. Skyjackings are extremely rare, you see — mostly seen overseas: Eastern Europe, South America and what have you — but these days we have to rule out air piracy as a matter of course, especially when there's nothing else to go on. A Douglas DC-4 was skyjacked just a few months earlier, in Bolivia. We don't want people getting ideas."

Stanley's eyes narrowed. "Heavens, no. I hope you don't sss-suspect that Alice could p-p-p—"

"Certainly not, Stanley," Geoffrey said, almost choking on his coffee at the younger man's alarm, before laughing. "Good lord, not at all! You must forgive my clumsiness in mixing my lines of questioning. No no no — I merely wondered if there were any previous incidents she might have mentioned to you? Any regular passengers who seemed in any way unhinged or who had made threats against the airline? That kind of thing. Anyone at all threatening, and what have you?" he added, before levering a forkful of cake into his mouth.

"No, nothing like that. But nervous fliers who wanted to get off at ten thousand feet — sssh-she had a few of those. Always joked about them. Used to s-say that sh-eed hand them a p-parachute and tell them 'well, there's the emergency exit, dear — off you pop'."

Geoffrey smiled, Bakewell crumbs clustered in his teeth.

"And," Stanley continued, "that to get to wherever they were going it was 's-straight down all the way'. But just a joke, you understand," he quickly added. "Never actually told them any of that, as far as I know. Usually found them s-something to give them to calm them down. S-some people would get into a terrible state."

"As I can only too sadly attest to, aircraft *do* crash. If you were only to focus on the ones that crashed, then it would seem complete madness for anyone at all to ever fly."

"I guess an airplane landing safely does not make headlines."

"Indeed. People see the tragedies and, well, it's understandable, isn't it? Not everyone can get the sense of the probabilities."

Stanley shook his head, a rueful tilt to the side of his mouth. "I wish we'd at least get some answers with Alice. Where the airplane went down."

"I know, Stanley. One day, hopefully. We're doing our best."

Stanley looked alarmed. "Oh, I didn't mean to imply otherwise"

"No, it's okay. I understand," Geoffrey said. "I have to say, it was a surprise to find that you even existed. In terms of Alice, I mean. The airline didn't even know she had married. We spoke to her parents, you see, and they told us about you."

"Had to be kept a s-s-secret. It's not allowed, marriage — although lord knows why."

"So, you took her to the airport that day?"

"Yes. As normal, whenever I wasn't working. I'd finished early that week — took off the last day of work before Christmas — so I drove her to the terminal. Does that matter? To the investigation, I mean."

Geoffrey took out a small notepad and a pen, but placed them on the table, the pad closed and the pen sealed with its lid. "Again, it just helps me to know more about who was onboard — if anything was out of the ordinary, that type of thing. You may have seen something when you dropped her at work."

"Nothing unusual," he said, "although I wasn't really paying any great attention. I mean, I wasn't looking out for anything. I went to the Forte's café to get a cup of tea and some sandwiches, and after eating those, drove home."

"Sometimes something will stick in your memory. Did you know Frank Carter? He worked at Fairey, too."

"I heard he was on the aircraft — the others at work told me after he didn't return after the Christmas holidays. Actually, now that you mention it, I think I s-saw him at the airport that day — but I wasn't expecting to see him, s—so couldn't be certain. He wasn't close enough to talk to — p-passed by in the distance. With his son, I think."

"That's right — James Carter."

"Frank s-ss-seemed a nice chap. Never really talked to him p-properly too often, though, beyond saying hello. Though I did bump into him and his family on our wedding day, funnily enough." Stanley, concern suddenly etched on his face, leaned in, to whisper. "Is it s-s-suspicious that I saw Frank?"

"No, Stanley, not at all. We know for a fact that he was on the plane, flying to meet his wife and daughter in Glasgow. So obviously he *had* to be at the airport. Just a bit of a coincidence that you worked with him. That's all."

"Well, as I admitted, I didn't know him well," Stanley said, suddenly feeling a little foolish.

"No. Quite. Anyway, we're not exactly expecting any hijackers or whatnot. It's all highly unlikely. It will, almost without doubt, have been some kind of mechanical failure or pilot error in the abominable conditions. But as I said earlier, I have to ask — just to make sure nothing was off about the day. Even down to making sure there wasn't too much luggage onboard, that kind of thing."

"Well, if it helps, Alice only had her handbag, as the return flight was due back at night."

"Look, to be perfectly honest, without any firm evidence — without even having found the aircraft — I'm just spinning my wheels a bit. We know it went off course, but until we find it we can't say precisely why. The conditions doubtless played a key role, but there may have been other factors."

"Oh, I see. So do you know *anything* about what happened?" Stanley asked, absentmindedly prodding at his cake with a fork. "Other than what the newspapers have s-said?"

"Very little, I'm afraid, beyond speculation. No issues reported with the aircraft beforehand. Logbooks at the maintenance hangars all in order, all work up to date, no lingering mechanical issues. Pilots highly respected, clean bills of health. One thing we know for certain is that radio transmissions ceased, and that she disappeared from radar. As I said, nothing found at her last known coordinates, or even within a substantial radius — so she may have flown on for a bit longer, keeping down low, maybe on purpose or maybe not, and thus below detection. May have been disoriented, trying to get sight of land, get a fix on the ground. Up in the squall it's just hopeless. I flew often enough in heavy snow, during the war — Lysanders, mostly, for a whole winter in Iceland. Awkward bloody things they were, at the best of times. And occasionally even flew one of your lot — the Swordfish. Lots of accidents in Iceland — good location strategically, up in the North Atlantic, but a bugger of a place to fly during the winter. Scotland at the same time of year can be much the same. Maybe not quite as bad, but you get my drift."

"I've never even been to Scc-Sc … north of the border."

"Beautiful part of the world, the Highlands. Quite fancy living there one day, to be honest, when it's time to slow down. But not the best place to be stranded in the winter. If it's any consolation, anyone who survived would probably have died quickly from hypothermia — just fallen asleep in the cold and never awoke, I should imagine."

Stanley blanched, closing his eyes as if to blot out a vision, even though the imagery in his mind's eye could not be banished. "I try not to p-picture it too much, to be honest. Too p-p-painful to even think about it, although s—ometimes I can't help it. But if that's what you really think — about how it can be just like falling asleep — then I guess I shall have to cling to that."

"Sometimes we find people and that's exactly how they look — fast asleep, maybe still even strapped into their seats. Can happen due to a lack of oxygen at altitude, or when freezing, or the smoke from a fire if the fire itself doesn't consume them. Some get knocked unconscious — a bump to the head that doesn't even break the skin — and never wake up. To all the world they could as well be asleep. Obviously we see some far more unpleasant things, which you needn't think about, but plenty of times they just look like they are sleeping. I hope that helps."

"It does."

"Look, I'm going up again soon. One last time, before I finally switch to my new job at London Airport, which I've had to delay taking up. You are more than welcome to join me on the search."

"I'd like that," Stanley said, smiling. "Would at least feel like I was doing s-s-something."

Geoffrey and Stanley walked back to the factory in the fine, chilly drizzle of a fleeting shower that sparked, in the distance above the whitewashed leviathan of the EMI complex, a pale rainbow. With a little more time to kill, Geoffrey had asked for a quick glimpse at this new Rotodyne he'd been reading about in the newspapers for a couple of years now, ever since declassification of its development. "She sounds like a winner," he'd acknowledged, about to bid Stanley farewell outside the station, before the two, upon that thought, decided to turn back to hangars, for a quick guided tour.

"This is the p-prototype," Stanley said, as they moved into the giant shed, the hulk of a gleaming fuselage flanked by men busily crafting and whittling at workstations. Stanley led Geoffrey to the large, rectangular aircraft hull, minus tail, cockpit and rotors: just the body and the short upper-mounted wings. "Well, the core of it," he added.

"Have to say," Geoffrey said, looking perplexed, "she looks entirely like a plane, in this form. Albeit a very strange plane. Not at all the right form to be a helicopter."

"It's very much in a rough shape. It'll make s-sense when you ss-see it finished. Engines and rotors are being assembled in another hangar. Tail assembly being worked on in S-s—tockport. Then the whole thing will be joined together at White Waltham, and all test flights will take place there."

"Ah yes, White Waltham. Of course, your previous testing strip has come quite a long way," Geoffrey noted, circling the workbenches and moving closer to the aircraft.

"London Airport, you mean? We never got a p-penny, from what I understand."

"I still remember it as the Great West Aerodrome from the war," Geoffrey said, inspecting the wall of the fuselage, feeling the thickness of the slender metal skin like a tailor discerning the fineness of a silk. "Incredible to think that that same scrap of land is now that sprawling airport. Then there's Northolt, too — I flew there briefly as well. You probably know all this from Alice, I expect, but until a couple of years ago BEA had the busiest hub in Europe at Northolt."

"S-she only joined up last year," Stanley said, his voice catching when he added, "BEA had moved to London Airport by then."

"Yes, '54, wasn't it? It's all changed so much in such a short space of time. Things move at quite some pace these days, don't they?"

"Here, let me shhh-sh-ow you s-something," Stanley said, turning towards an anteroom off to the right of the workshop. "You can't really get a feel for the Rotodyne from that sh-shell." He led Geoffrey to a small, unlit room, the staff absent, away on their lunch breaks. He flicked a switch until a long fluorescent tube overhead clicked and strobed into life. On the wall were pinned various grand schematics, and on the central workbench, perched like a proud statue on a plinth, sat the perfect scaled-down wooden model of the Rotodyne, honed like a sculpture. On several occasions it hand been draped on thin wires in the wind-tunnel, to discern its aerodynamism.

"Wonderful, isn't she?" Stanley asked, like a proud father.

"Ah, now I see what you mean," Geoffrey said, as if it now made more sense, without making *total* sense. "It's … *interesting*. To say the least."

As he inspected the model — circling it as if pondering a creature splayed on a veterinary table — it gave him the sense of a mutant near-abomination: beautifully crazy, crazily beautiful … or neither, and just some bizarre white elephant? Based on all that he had read, they'd aimed to create the near-perfect all-round aircraft, to take aviation up towards the 21st Century. Yet it looked illogical and unnatural, whilst — he had to admit — retaining *something*. He saw so much to admire, in its ambition and its Swiss Army knife-like variety and utility, but also so much to confuse.

"Impressed?" Stanley asked.

"Hmmm," Geoffrey replied; a sound caught between assent and disapproval. The wisdom of fellow aviators — aircrew spoke frequently of the aphorism during the war, especially with the Spitfire — insisted that if a plane looked right, she *was* right. She will have pleasing aesthetic curves and aerodynamic logic; birds soar gracefully when they fly, and by stark contrast, house bricks do not. But the Rotodyne, in trying to enable the direct vertical ascent of the helicopter with the fast forward motion and strength of the airplane — allied to the broad, passenger-carrying capacity of a bus — managed to look like a glorious monstrosity: an ugly duckling; or, more apposite, as he continued to through his mind a whole host of creatures, an *emu* — that, logically, could never fly.

And yet, if it did — and Stanley had assured him that the finished prototype would — then Geoffrey knew it could change everything. As with the record-breaking Delta 2 born of this very factory, it would surely help make Fairey the biggest and most important aviation company on the planet.

"The future," Stanley said, with a smile. "S-safer too, I hope, than ... well, you know."

* * *

It all hit Stanley suddenly, as Geoffrey, after a firm handshake, made his way back to the train station. Stanley crossed the factory floor to the lavatory block to locate an empty cubicle and, locking the door behind him in the far stall, sat on the closed toilet lid and silently sobbed; eager that no man hear. The emotions — from all the talk of Alice –arrived like a delayed tsunami following a sea-bound earthquake: layering higher and higher, moving nearer and nearer, as the conversation with Geoffrey unfolded; held at bay for as long as necessary — until he could find a private moment, in the pungent stall — before finally it felt too much to bear and he suffered wipeout. At times, when discussed, she seemed so viscerally alive — in brief flashes — and yet in the same breath, as the likeable investigator spoke, Stanley found himself having to confront his wife's mortality; picturing her perishing, somewhere cold and remote. The man who, via his work, had helped these images return to Stanley, now confirming — not that it needed saying — that those would now be all he would ever have.

The honeymoon in Tenerife: just seven months earlier — although the past six weeks had themselves felt like a year. The memories, already, were gradually atrophying to a series of fleeting images and movie clips, similar to the disjointed, five-minute ciné films, mute and often fuzzy, that he so diligently recorded in the Canaries, and yet now seemed too painful to set up and view. A jumble of recollections, centred around that magical week in the sun.

They flew in on another airline, to keep their marriage secret from her employers. He recalled Alice's sadness that no one from work could be invited to the wedding, with no notices posted in the local papers, lest it let the cat out of the bag; so much silliness, she felt, but also, the desire to keep her dream job. The ring, placed on her finger in the church, hidden for work; tucked beneath her blue uniform blouse on a chain around her neck. As clear as day: the way she kissed him goodbye on the morning of her return to work, and claimed it apt to have the ring hanging so close to her heart. As clear as day, until it started fuzzing at the edges.

Alice, prior to joining BEA, had flown with her family to Italy the previous summer, before months, in her new career, spent crisscrossing Europe. Yet Stanley had never flown before. His sudden nervousness, as if he'd never even considered the fear of flying until clicking his lap-belt. The way she held his hand on takeoff, and, feeling the increasing sweat, held it firm until the Viscount broke through the cloud.

Such heat, the like of which he had never before experienced, from the moment they descended the steps onto the sweltering airport tarmac; the freshest air blown in on warm, piquant sea breezes so at odds to the heavy seaweed stench of colder British shores. The curious verdancy in sun-drenched vistas: white stucco walls, guarded by rich green cacti and spiky palms and hunkering dragon trees. The volcanic loom of Mount Teide — the island that surrounded it having seeped, over geologic time, from its caldera; never part of the great tectonic mass of Pangaea, it instead bubbled up from the ancient seas. Gargantuan cruise ships leaving ports, setting the fishing boats bobbing in their wake. The procession through the streets, of Catholic crosses and festival floats; followed at night by fulminating fireworks splitting into vibrant fissures of colour. Geckos and cockroaches and antlions on ceilings and walls and windows, blue chaffinches chirping in almond trees. Red wine and fresh fish delicacies, a sausage called chorizo, a ring of squid, green and black olives in al fresco restaurants after dark. Alice, self-conscious in a tasteful bikini at the beach, claiming she didn't have the bust for such a garment; Stanley telling her she looked perfect and to not be so silly. Making love at dusk in the humid apartment, the windows wide open to the scent of laurel trees and flowering jasmine.

1959

Semi-opaque sheets, cascading smooth and sleek: summer rain, falling hard and fast against the coffeehouse threshold; only splitting into individual droplets upon hitting the concrete, sending flecks and specks, like fiery sparks, into the entrance with its door wide open in the oppressive heat.

The deluge arrived out of nowhere — the hottest, most thunderous storm Charlotte could remember; calling to mind the dreaded crack and boom of the bombs that terrorised her early twenties. For her, the war ended *here*, of all places: Piccadilly Circus, and the nearby points of congregation and celebration, fourteen years earlier, in a colourful hail of bunting and streamers and fluttering confetti. From her seat a decade and a half later she could superimpose the people dancing and singing, conga lines curling like giant caterpillars cutting through a swaying mass of bodies. She could still feel her anxiety on that day; her sense of hopelessness. And she could see back further still, to a few years before V.E. Day, to incipient love and memories filled with hope, Viktor discharged from East Grinstead, and a darkened alleyway.

She had come to favour this café, along the aorta of Shaftesbury Avenue, for its views of the famous roundabout. As at London Airport, she could turn and look inside — at the strangers, and their lives, which somehow helped to fill her own. Even with the door open the air hung muggy and warm, full of bellowing steam and the fug of damp patrons escaping the downpour; their woollen garments heavy with the whiff of wet animals. From her corner table by the window, with her back to the wall — a tactic to survey all other tables, as well as the outside world — Charlotte watched people hurry in diagonals across the road, or crossing via the roundabout; darting to the nearest shelter, including the foyer of the London Pavilion and the overhangs of shop façades. Some sprinted straight for the coffeehouse door — although with every single table occupied, and a gaggle lingering by the bar, many decided instead to hang around just outside, under the awning, before moving on to try somewhere else.

    Charlotte had selected her seat an hour earlier, before the storm, when the café sat half-empty; placing her holdall on the table to reserve her spot. Upon making her order at the bar she stood in the shadow of the sleek gleaming Gaggia espresso machine that separated her from the staff, as it groaned and hissed and spat. Despite seeing it so frequently over the past few months, the machine still seemed so futuristic: a hulk of ribbed and curving chrome, perched atop the counter like a miniature spaceship. Levers reached high above the servers' heads, pulled down like lofty train signals to the release of vapours and sibilances of steam, all for the extrusion of a thimble's-worth of rich brown liquid. She needed the caffeine hit, but her unease felt greater than a lack of energy; she had awoken with a sense of crippling doubt, one of those indistinct ennuis that plagued so many mornings, and which returned, with menaces, after sunset. There lingered the sense — the smudges — of some unpleasant dream, but its detail had long since absconded by the time she awoke, leaving only an amorphous anxiety lacking content or explanation, but that clawed and clung tight all the same. Age vastly expanded the reservoir her subconscious could draw upon, when dredging up failures and regrets and disappointments, both big and small; victories, for some strange reason, less commonly summoned.

    Her mood darkened further when she caught sight of herself in the espresso machine. It presented her with a distorted reflection, her unavoidable ageing — the callous punches and pinches and pulls of time — accentuated like the mocking of a cruel fairground mirror: nearing forty, the first signs of crows feet, dragged wider and longer; warping the faint wrinkles around eyes and cheeks, artificially bulging the nose like a fisheye lens. All those newly-forming laughter lines, full and deep, despite having rarely seen the funny side of anything in almost two decades; striations flowing from the mouth and, thus moulded, unlikely to do anything other than further deepen, like glacial tributaries gouged at the thaw of an ice age. Deeper still, frown lines, like a vertical gash between the eyes. She saw the dark blue headscarf that hid hair in need of trimming and styling — a garment which none of the younger women were wearing, and which suddenly, she felt, aged her like those older women who still wore hats and hairnets leftover from bygone eras. A strong coffee, and some of these fears would recede, and the day could resume its routine; but unrest lay like a fast-cutting undertow.

An hour later, with her mood somewhat stabilised — if not especially elevated — the coffeehouse surged with vibrance and youthful vigour in the humid, tobacco-amplified pall. Older patrons could always be spotted: one or two men could almost always be found sitting alone, usually suited, with pipe and bowtie, newspaper strewn across lap or table, and occasionally an old woman, who looked more cut out for the genteel traditions of tea and china. The clientele, while mixed, still skewed young: teenagers, and men and women in their early twenties, many with eyes obscured beyond thick black sunglasses or newly fashionable shades with purple-blue lenses. There were berets and beards; Brylcreemed quiffs and neat bouffants on budding poets, actresses and models; wannabe bohemians, puffing on cigars and Gauloises and hand-rolled skinny cigarettes; two handsome, besuited West Indian men in pork pie hats, utterly at home — in this part of London, at least, where anything seemed to go — in their new country. She lit herself a cigarette, her habit back up to a packet a day. If any mycobacterium tuberculosis remained then she would smoke the blighters out.

A few sips from finishing her second coffee, Charlotte found herself contemplating the strangeness of the clear glass crockery, which, even after countless visits to the establishment, remained so odd. Why didn't it shatter from the heat? Hers sat rimmed with froth that clustered like a nebulous circular galaxy, whose depth, when she held the cup up to the light, could be discerned through gaps borne of bubbles. The whole establishment felt so modern: fixings and fittings of chrome, linoleum and Formica, in addition to the see-through cups and saucers, the clear bowls of cubed brown sugar, and the shiny metal ashtrays; although not as space-age and Sputnik as parts of London Airport, which she still visited a couple of times a week. Kitty continued to pay her a stipend, and the various physical and mental illnesses of Charlotte's post-nursing years resulted in the handy top-up of social security benefits. She had tried returning to work, but nothing seemed to last. Perhaps one day she might do something with all the notes she took, and the fragments of stories she jotted down, but would anyone be interested in her story?

Windows — and the views they could provide — proved a necessity; a seat nearby, or, better still, directly looking out through one — to a busy world kept at bay behind broad and toughened glass. She felt increasingly uneasy in the centre of rooms, and in spaces that had no natural light — basements, in particular, especially those with low ceilings — or rooms which, via silly little windows or obtrusive decor, mostly obscured the outside world. On the days when she didn't go to London Airport, one of the alternatives — one of the magnetic pulls — remained Piccadilly Circus, with its personal significance, dating back two decades. As with the airport, she felt most alive here, where reality permeated the fog of a kind of shellshock that had metastasised since late 1940. Crowds continued to fascinate her, as long as she lingered at the periphery; a clear path to a door always a priority. Just the thought of dark basements had her reaching for another Craven A, slipping out a cigarette from its rich red packet.

Absentmindedly, with a reverie that temporarily overlaid images upon what she actually saw, Charlotte looked out at the streets, until focusing fully on their dimpled puddles: spits of rain, twinkling like fairy lights as they reflected distant sunlight, exploding against the liquid surface, before seamlessly joining the pools as the downpour pattered on. Taxi tyres squirted low arcs onto the pavement, while those buses moving fast enough slammed full puddles against the window — violent spurts, at intervals, like a sideways geyser; each causing a reflexive start, as if the glass right beside her were not there, or might break if the force proved sufficient. Perturbed as one struck, she watched the water sliding harmlessly down the glass in a streaky blur before the view, at least until the next fast-moving bus, lay clear and panoramic.

Beyond this, the jarring sight of the figure of a man, smartly suited, seated alone on the steps of the fountain, as the torrent soaked fine fabrics and flattened his hair into a dark wet mop. He looked lost — lost on some deeper level, she concluded, given that no one here, at the heart of London, could be unsure of their location. What was he doing? He carried no luggage, no camera, no umbrella, no briefcase; and so didn't seem to fit the mould of tourist, day-tripper, or the new younger breed of dapper city gent. Her eyes remained firmly fixed on him as, eventually, he slowly stood, stiff-backed and sighing, and ambled towards Coventry Street, only to turn and stare at the spot on the roundabout he had just vacated, as if he'd left something behind. A trio of buses moved slowly to block her view, awaiting, in line, the right of way onto the busy roundabout. As the queue backed up she returned to her coffee and her notebook. Twenty seconds — maybe more — passed before she sensed, out of the corner of her eye, that the large red mass had moved, and so looked up again. And there the man stood, now just a few feet outside her window, eyes fixed back at Eros and the overflowing fountain. He turned his head and stared momentarily at the café — his eyes glazed, as if looking at nothing in particular. At this close distance, and allowing for how his hair slicked down across his forehead — and perhaps thinning a little into a widow's peak — she realised that she recognised him, but couldn't quite place him. A patron of the coffeehouse? If a regular, then of course he would appear familiar.

Then, a strange delusion struck her: a kind of cognitive trick, which she knew a mere trick but which, temporarily at least, she felt eager to indulge. Though roughly as tall, give or take an inch, the man did not look especially like Viktor; but for a moment the rush of recognition, of some type of familiarity — distorted by the unfocussing sheen of rain on the window, and by the way the man's sodden hair slid onto his face, and the blankness of his expression — flipped something in her mind, conjoining concepts, and her heart rushed, for just a second or two ... until she realised — indeed, as she had known on some level all along — that *of course* it wasn't him. To be so young it would have to be 1941 again, not 1959. These hands lacked Viktor's scaly skin, and the man did not limp.

Then, as soon as the spell broke, the truth burst through, hard and fast and with vivid clarity: she had seen him at the airport. The man with the stammer. Indeed, she had seen him there on quite a few occasions, albeit not for a long time — maybe years. Though she still went each week, his absence had never once occurred to her, until this reminder. They had never spoken, but sometimes smiled to each other, out of vague recognition and habit; the kind of person who, upon seeing, she momentarily felt obliged to talk to, which caused her to pause and think of what to say — what had they chatted about the previous time? — until she remembered that no such conversations had ever actually taken place, and there existed no social contract to enforce now. So they left it at a passing *Hello,* nothing more. Still, he always seemed friendly — a kind face. He now looked discernibly older, even though he must have still only been in his early twenties. He carried himself in a different way, the lope and slouch of a man with a weight on his shoulders; age added, exaggerated, by the drenched and dazed and bedraggled countenance, and the moist muss of his hair. Suddenly it made sense to have a proper conversation, discover this man's story; a mix of familiarity and curiosity overriding her usual desire to keep herself to herself. And he looked so pathetic, wet-through.

She tapped on the window, and when he didn't react, tapped again, with a tautened knuckle. This time he looked around. She motioned to him to come in and join her, with a wave as if fanning her face from the warmth. He stared back, a twitch of a smile betraying politeness — an instinctive reaction — when his eyes, in truth, suggested no hint of recognition. She motioned again, mouthing "come here", and slowly he made his way to the door, as the rain beat brutally at his back, flicking at the nape of his neck. Only when he got to within a few feet of Charlotte did there arise an expression of understanding. He may even have nodded his head, but she couldn't be sure; his posture already slouched, his forehead already half facing the floor.

"The airport," Charlotte said, pushing the chair on the other side of her table out with her foot, like stepping hard on a brake. "I used to see you there. Remember?"

"S-sso you did," Stanley said, standing beside the chair. "Knew I'd seen you s-somewhere."

"Sit yourself down. You're soaked. I'm Charlotte, by the way."

"S–Stanley."

He sank solemnly into the seat, water dripping from his sleeves, and from his collar, and running down his face from an unintentional kiss-curl that slid slug-like onto an eyebrow. He sighed, and tiny droplets sprayed from thin lips into the warm air, as his shoulders slumped further, almost to where his elbows had been.

"Can't be all that bad," Charlotte said, distracted by the droplets lingering on his face, as two gathered together on the tip of his nose, almost — but not quite — ready to fall. "Worse things happen at sea, and all that," she added, with an ironic laugh. "At least, that's what I would have said. Once ... *before*. Long time ago. But not anymore. Not since ... well, since I stopped saying 'worse things happen at sea' and silly rot like that, because, well, it turns out, it doesn't need the sea, after all. Plenty of other ways for life to take you out at the knees. Anyway, talking of the sea, you look like a drowned rat who's just washed ashore."

"In that case I wish I hadn't washed ashore," Stanley said, with a hefty sigh that somehow slid from his body, despite a posture not conducive to taking the breath necessary for such a hearty exhalation. "S-sorry. Forget that," he said, pulling himself upright in the chair, wiping the water from his brow, straightening his collar that had stuck, skew-whiff, to his neck. "I'm being very rude." He shook his head, as if to shake himself free of some torpor, and more droplets sprayed into the air. "I really don't mean to be. I just ... well, I sh-sh ... ought not to have come here."

"Why ever not?"

"Long s-story, I'm afraid. Too long."

"You look like you need a nice warm coffee. As it just so happens, I know just the kind of place to get you one," she said, with the slightest of winks.

"Oh, I don't drink coffee," he said, in a detached manner. "Never have."

"Not once?"

"Nope. Never. Tea — I'm a tea man. Was always tea in my house growing up. Tea breaks at work. S-same when living at home with ..." he trailed off, unwilling to finish the sentence.

"Well, this *is* a coffeehouse. Try it. Lifts the spirits."

"I don't know."

"Trust me," she said, with a smile. "I'm an old hand. As someone once said, I measure out my life with coffee spoons."

"Oh, go on then, if you insist," he said, looking round at the chalkboard listing the prices. "Um … I think I'll try one of those expressos, whatever they are. At least they sound quick."

Within minutes a waitress delivered Charlotte's fresh cappuccino, and set down the dinkiest clear-glass espresso demitasse in front of Stanley, and even then it sat half empty.

"Nine-pence for *this?*" he said to Charlotte, when the waitress returned to the bar.

"Ah, but you see, it packs a punch worthy of ten bob."

"Express, indeed," he said, looking at a mere mouthful of liquid in the oversized glass thimble.

"Don't knock it back all at once or your eyes may pop out. Perhaps your teeth, too. So, what are you doing here?" she asked, leaning in. "Really, I don't mind a long story. I'm not going anywhere."

"Memories, I s-su-pose. I thought … Well, I don't know what I thought. I wanted to reconnect with the past."

"And have you?" she asked, wiping the faintest whiff of a white moustache from her upper lip; watching as Stanley tried to ration his drink with little more than the barest sip.

"Yes, and no. I'm not s—sure it was a good idea, to be honest. But here I am."

The downpour abated, but still rain dripped down: from the awnings, and rooftops, off porticos and archways, down lampposts and traffic signs; still beaded-up on the roofs of the cabs and the buses, trickling down windows and windscreens. It evoked in Charlotte a sense of *Singin' in the Rain,* but clearly no one felt like dancing.

No sooner had the waitress cleared their table — ahead of returning with new drinks — than Charlotte emptied out her holdall onto its formica surface: *East Coker* minus its yellow paperback cover; two boxes of Aspro; a silver fob-watch wrapped in a tattered handkerchief; her camera in its case, along with three tin canisters of undeveloped film; cigarettes and the all-important matches; a squat bottle of Gordon's gin; a half-eaten Mars bar; several silver and bronze coins of varying denominations — but mostly pennies; and a small box of feminine napkins. Stanley looked on, bemused, as, one by one, she placed all the items back into the bag — carefully, in contrast to the way she had dumped them all out — leaving just the box of Craven A and the matches.

"Do you mind?" she asked, in a clipped manner with a cigarette already teetering between two lips, a match poised. While smoke could aggravate his asthma, he'd learnt to put up with it.

"No, don't mind me," he said, feeling unable to object.

"So, do you work at the airport?" she asked, after Stanley — now sitting bolt upright — took their drinks from the waitress. He'd opted for a cappuccino too, on account of the value for money that seemed inherent in a full cup, with the added goodness of milk; distinctly unkeen on the bitterness of the shot of espresso, which he had dutifully finished like a medicinal syrup. "You never seemed to be flying anywhere," she said. "From what I can recall. Never any luggage, I mean. Nor that look of a weary traveller. I still see a lot of those. Can spot them a mile off. Not that I travelled either — still don't, even though I still go to the airport."

"No, my wife worked there. I only ever dropped her off. S-sometimes I went for a cup of tea or s—something to eat, s-save cooking myself dinner."

"She doesn't work there anymore?"

"No, sh-sh—"

Charlotte left a pause, to allow his stutter to straighten itself out over the word she guessed as *She*, but watched as he gave up on the sentence and fell silent, slumping back to his earlier downcast posture.

"What does she do now? Sorry," Charlotte added, before sucking in her lips. "I don't mean to pry."

"Ssh-she … Well, that plane that went missing in the blizzard — you remember? The one three years ago, I mean — not the one from earlier this year."

"Yes?"

"Well, Alice was on it. Trainee air-hostess."

Charlotte paused. Thoughts came to her quickly, but still needed rearranging. "Oh my gosh … I was there that day. Christmas, '56."

"Crashed somewhere in the storm."

"Oh Stanley, I'm ever so sorry to hear that. That's frightfully sad."

"Thank you. I'm still trying to come to terms with it. As you can s-s-see."

"My my, that's so eery," she said, shaking her head. "We do have rather a lot in common, it seems. London Airport, Piccadilly Circus, and — well, the senseless loss of a loved one in a somewhat similar manner."

"Your husband died?"

Charlotte exhaled smoke to one side. "We were never married. Long time ago now." She sighed, with eyes briefly closed, and added, "Time flies, they say," with a caustic laugh. "Except when it crashes. But yes, we would have been, one day, I hope. Or *hoped*, whatever the correct tense should be. After all, it's not like I still hope we will, seeing as it was nearly twenty years ago. But I do hope that we *would have*. Eventually. Anyway. He went missing in action. A pilot, in the RAF. Icelandic. Viktor, my Viktor. I called him my Iceman. A Spitfire, somewhere over the Channel. Never found."

"My word, that is rather s—similar."

"Happened a lot more in the war, of course. Occupational hazard. Before your time, obviously, as I'm sure you realise. So many aircraft vanished. Then again, the whole bloody aim was to make the other lot vanish — shoot 'em down, often over the sea. It's what separated the two sides, after all." She shook her head. "You know, I've never really thought about it like this, as he wasn't in the navy, but of course, Viktor was lost at sea — or at least, close to the shoreline. So maybe worse things *do* happen at sea. Anyway, I'm sorry for putting you on the spot. I didn't mean to open old wounds."

"No, really. It's nice to talk to s-someone who understands. And it's nice to talk about Alice. I came here today to think about her anyway." He laughed; a strange and sad laugh, somewhere between a sigh and a snort. "It's funny, but I can't talk about her to the people who knew her. And yet here I am, telling a complete s—stranger all about her."

"I know the feeling," she said, tapping her cigarette against the ashtray.

"It's just too p-painful, to talk to family, or to our friends. They'll say something about Alice that I'm not ready to hear — a memory, an anecdote that'll catch me off guard. Lovely memories — don't get me wrong. But it's as if — and this will s-s-sound funny — when talking about her, Alice will form in the s-ss-s-sss—"

"Take your time, Stanley. There's no rush," Charlotte said, giving his forearm a gentle pat that reminded him of Alice's forbearance.

"—S-space between us," he said, so loud, in a vocal spasm, that caused people to turn and look, before resuming their own conversations. "With bits of my memories and bits of their memories" — he drew a deep breath — "to make this s-s-tereo-s-scopic image, like with those funny coloured glasses at the movies. It makes her whole, and I end up missing her even more. S-sometimes a forgotten memory, not one of the many I run through my mind. It feels new, *real*, and the wounds feel fresh. But it's nice, too, in that I get to remember little details I'd forgotten. I just don't like s-surprises."

Charlotte half smiled, closed-lipped and rueful. "No one I know knew Viktor."

"S-so you don't get to be reminded of him?"

"No, not by other people, at least. I mean, some friends and acquaintances — colleagues, too — knew him, back at the time. Other nurses. But we didn't stay in touch."

"You were a nurse?"

"During the war, yes."

"What do you do now?"

"I'm a fugitive — on the run."

Stanley looked back at the deadpanning woman, as she kept a straight face — her lips unable to betray a smile while taking an overly long drag on her cigarette.

She finally laughed, smoke flushing out. "No, just kidding. My sister pays me some money for the property we inherited. During the war I was … taken ill, and — well, I'm probably not fit for proper work anyway. It's complicated. And for that reason I lead a simple life. If I ever run too low on money I'm sure I can find some temporary unskilled work."

"Not a return to nursing?"

"God, no," she said, sharp with rancour, that took Stanley off-guard. "*Never* again. There was just too much …" Now it came her time to trail off.

"I understand," he said, inferring what he could. "You never met anyone else?"

"I did. Eventually. A couple of times. But they seemed to bounce right off me, in an emotional sense. Didn't leave an impression. Like the heart is all sewn up. Or made of cement. You?"

"Heavens no. Can't even imagine it."

"No, me neither, at first," she said, absentmindedly tilting her cup slightly, back and forth.

"But you felt like trying?"

"Eventually. But, well, they were never Viktor. Not that they ever could be, of course … I don't know. It didn't feel fair on them."

"I know the feeling," Stanley said, now wide-eyed, his hands fiddling with the spoon, tapping it against the saucer, skiffle-style, as his knee bounced repeatedly under the table.

"So, did they ever find the airplane?" she asked.

"No, they didn't. They haven't. S-still haven't."

"I'm sorry," Charlotte said, her eyes peering from over the rim of her cup as she took a sip. "I thought I read that they found it?"

"That was another aircraft. This was heading for Glasgow. Got lost somewhere up there."

"Yes, so many terrible crashes and disappearances."

"It's a big s—sky," he said.

"The biggest, I hear. You must have felt so helpless. So far away."

"I went up to S-Scotland, eventually, not that I was much use. Went up with a crash investigator, a man called Geoffrey Freeman, who—"

Charlotte interrupted, startled; carelessly placing her cup into its saucer with a sound somewhere between a sharp glassy clink and a duller ceramic clank. "Oh my word, Geoffrey Freeman! Now there's a blast from the past."

"You know him?"

"Indeed I do. Or did. Well, sort of. Knew *of* him. My mother's maiden name was Freeman, so his name always stuck with me. I once wrote to him, some years back, but he never replied. Or maybe he did, but I move around a lot — you know how it is, things get forwarded for a while but then they just lose track of you. I found his name in a newspaper article about missing airmen from the war. Thought he might be able to help find out what happened to Viktor. I spoke to some other man, an ex-colleague of Freeman's, but he was no use in finding any information. I'd see Geoffrey's name appear in the papers now and again — saw him mentioned on the Comet stuff, a few years ago. Farnborough too, '54 or '55, whenever it was."

"Well, Geoffrey is a kind man — a very clever man. He did all he could for me."

"In that case," Charlotte said, leaning in, "maybe you could help me get in touch with him?"

"I'd be more than happy to. I can't tell you what he will say, or if he'll be able to help, but I'll gladly pass on any message."

Charlotte thanked him, and then returned to a more neutral posture. The downpour had resumed; her eye caught by the puddles on the pavement as raindrops splattered and dimpled.

"I often wonder about Viktor's parents, back in Iceland," she said, turning back to face Stanley. "Are they still alive? He told me about how he grew up, but never mentioned them after that. And he never listed any next of kin with the RAF. So I had no easy way to trace his family, if he had any left, to share our stories. I tried to send letters to his parents, addressed to his surname — sent them to the town he spoke of, with no actual address — but heard nothing back. I wanted to fly to Iceland, I really did. Always meant to. Almost did, a couple of times. Got ready to board and everything. One day I still might, but as yet I can't… well, y'know. Airplanes and all that."

"I'm the same."

"What about children?" she asked. "You didn't have any, I mean? I can imagine it being, well … so very bittersweet if you did."

"No, that wasn't allowed — at the airline. Even being married wasn't allowed — we had to keep it ssss-ecret from the company. By rights sh-sh-she sh—" he took a deep breath and steadied himself, his body edgy, jittery "–should have given up her job, but wanted to do a couple more years, s-see more of the world.

Would have been forced to retire at thirty anyway — her age was not a thing we could have kept hidden, as they knew her date of birth from when she applied. Sss-she had to be at least twenty to sign up, and after ten years they'd know anyway. Certainly couldn't have hidden a pregnancy. There was no rush to have kids — not for us, at least. Never s-seemed my p-place to force her to give up her p-passion." He sighed. "If I had, maybe there'd be Alice at home, with a little 'un or two by now. Maybe another on the way."

"And you wouldn't be here, now."

"No," he said, crestfallen, as if feeling the loss of all those unborn, unconceived children. "Quite."

* * *

Drying off on the warm walk back to Green Park tube station — still hopped-up on caffeine — Stanley stopped in at Frost & Reed, the art gallery on Old Bond Street he'd glanced into when walking with Alice on their first date.

Hanging just inside the doorway, a tender, almost ghostlike work of watercolour, crayon and pastel, both vague and yet not too abstract — perhaps not quite finished — of the bleak, flat Kaldaðarnes landscape hemmed in, in the distance, by peaks; a strip to one side, the rolling water of the Ölfusá. Hints of colour crept into a frost-bound early morning scene, a Lockheed Hudson readied for flight.

Stanley appreciated the clever perspective: the way the lines of the runway and the distant peaks converged, to draw the viewer's eye to the plane in the foreground, all rendered with a muted palette. The unsigned artwork had no name; no statement of the location it portrayed — he guessed the north of England, or maybe Scotland. He knew little about Eric Ravilious, and had no idea that he was viewing the artist's last work of art; a fact that would take decades to establish. It struck him as simply a nice picture that Alice would have liked, with her love of aviation, irrespective of how it could serve as a reminder of her fate. To block out all acknowledgement of what happened to her — of what he knew, at least — would do her a disservice. It had been her passion.

Stanley, perhaps driven by the demons that arose in the past three years, had also taken a liking to the work of Francis Bacon, but he knew such sinister paintings — or the homages and pastiches that he could afford — would not have been welcome in their shared home as she had envisaged it. No, those were definitely not to Alice's taste. This, he concluded, embodied her style; consulting with her in his mind, and affirming her opinion.

He acquired the nameless, story-less painting for a modest sum, and later, when home, hung it in the hallway, just inside the front door.

1956

They half-awoke before dawn, slipping silently into the shortest day of the year, their bodies sensing the usual time to stir well before any light streamed through the windows. Stanley spooned into Alice, wrapping an arm around her waist, as she murmured and sighed at the comfort of his warm breath on the nape of her neck. She went to say something, but focused instead on other senses — touch, smell; and then, with eyes closed again, another hour passed without either realising.

The next thing they knew the room gathered in the orange glow of sunrise, as this time they blinked their way fully out of slumber. For once the alarm didn't even need setting: signed off work for the festive period, and her flight not due until late afternoon.

Stanley began to caress Alice's lower back, around onto her hip. "Later," she whispered, feeling him start to press firmly into her. "After work."

"Won't you be back too late tonight?"

"Ten-ish. I'll come back, and we can have a bath together."

"Oh," he said, sounding unconvinced. "Okay then."

"I really don't feel like work today," Alice said, her words elongated by the onset of a yawn. "You're already done for Christmas. It's not fair."

"I'll be working on the house."

"I'd rather be working on the house with you," she said, stretching her arms at the release of another yawn, before turning her body to face his.

"You love your job," he said, inching himself into a more upright position on the pillow.

"I suppose so," she said, and then smiled.

He sighed. "Flying is so much more exciting than painting window frames."

The house now stood watertight, plumbed and fully electric-cabled, but it felt like they had sutured its wounds without healing its fractures. Within, dry-rotted floorboards still ran across rooms, wallpaper hung blistered or half-fallen, and for decades damp had risen and spread. But new glass panes — protecting and insulating when required — could now be opened within sash windows, to air the house, as the central heating clunked some warmth within its walls.

Once dressed, Alice made the pair breakfast, with a tea for Stanley and a coffee for herself, as they sat at the table with a newspaper each. A knock on the door revealed the postman with a small package: something else for the renovations, no doubt, out of the many things still expected. "S-s-sorry for all this," Stanley said, apologetically.

Stanley and Alice worked together for a couple of hours, removing old wallpaper. After lunch they took a walk in the woods behind the house, past the gently flurrying brook, as the sun — in a cloudless sky — struggled to gain elevation, sending pale low light through the thicket. A white sheen of frost cracked under their boots with the crepitation of snapping twigs and the gentle shattering of leaves. On an open patch of ground a furtively-bobbing robin wrangled a half-frozen worm from the icy ground. Further ahead, they caught sight of an emaciated fox retreating at the sounds of their footsteps. The couple found themselves startled by its sudden scamper, having not even noticed the animal until it moved. Their sense of unease passed as it shot out of sight; the undergrowth slowly settling back to stillness.

"Tell me about our children," Alice asked, her face illuminated by a shaft of light, his deep in shade.

Stanley stopped in his tracks. "What children?"

"The children we shall have."

"Oh my. *Not yet*, dear," he said, now walking again.

"No, of course not yet. You *know* that. I haven't changed my mind about waiting."

"Oh, I see," he said, as the robin flew past, up into bare branches, worm twirling from its beak. "It was before the wedding that we last discussed it. I thought you might be hankering."

"I just want a hypothetical. A story."

"In that case," he said, discomfort almost etched on his face as he struggled to elicit mental images, "… A son. And a daughter, of course."

"*Of course*," she said, sounding pleased. "One of each. *At least*. What are their names?"

"Names? Wouldn't you help to decide?"

"I want you to tell me what I helped us to decide."

After a pause he said, "Geraldine and Eric."

"Oh. Why those?"

"They just came to me."

Walking with Stanley in line with the brook, Alice found herself startled again, turning to see the same fox — its fur dark and matted, its ribcage showing, some kind of gash on its ear — staring from between a clutch of trees. Their eyes locked for several seconds, a stare across species. Alice had the sense of a wounded vixen, perhaps guarding some starving pups in a nearby den. Again the creature turned and retreated, this time sloping off less anxiously, with one glance back, just to make sure it wasn't being followed.

"How old are they?" Alice asked, returning to the conversation.

"Seven and five. At least, at the point I'm now imagining them."

"Yes, two years apart seems sensible. What do they look like?" she asked, wrapping her arm around the crook of Stanley's elbow.

"Eric looks more like me, and Geraldine — well, she looks like you," he said, but then grimaced, suddenly a little disappointed in himself. "But Geraldine has red hair," he quickly added, to mix things up, to show some imagination. "And Eric's hair is a bit darker than mine."

"What do they enjoy doing?"

"Eric plays cricket. He doesn't have asthma, and so he's good at sport. Definitely cricket, maybe some football in the winter. Not rugby — not yet, anyway. Maybe when he's older. Geraldine likes … horses."

In truth, he didn't know an awful lot about little girls — he almost added 'and dolls', until thinking it sounded clichéd — but one day hoped to learn, first hand, about the whims and fancies of a young daughter. He already sensed that he'd care little about either child's interests — in terms of how they correlated to his expectations — as long as they acted respectfully, loved their parents, and found some happiness in their endeavours.

"They shall love their dog, too," he added. "A puppy. A spaniel. Called … Billy. No, *Victor*. You know, for victory."

"Sounds perfect. One day then, my dear Stanley."

"One day, my dear Alice."

"Golly," Alice suddenly said, startled after a glance down at her watch. "Look at the time. I need to go and get changed into my uniform."

"Oh, my — indeed you do. I'll drive you. I want to stop in at the office to collect some papers. There's talk of snow later. But nothing too heavy, thankfully."

1959

On her favoured front right-hand seat of the upper deck, Charlotte sat positioned like a high-riding driver with her own broad windscreen — but no steering wheel; the actual driver seated directly beneath her, below her floorboards. The bus emerged from the artificially-lighted tunnel into bright natural sunshine, on a direct course — were the road not to later bend to the left, towards the Europa Terminal — with the imposing beacon of the red-brick control tower, in all its unblemished newness. The bus filtered left at one of the two roundabouts, and she alighted at the stop between the tower and one of several uncovered car parks that had yet to burgeon upwards — as they would within just a few short years — into vast multistoreys.

She crossed towards the modernistic terminal through banks of automobiles painted in drab hues: black, mid-blue, dark blue, light grey, mid-grey, dark grey, beige, dull turquoise, russet, brown, cream, and a pale olive green; to mix with the black, dark blue, grey and olive green suits of the men who made the same journey to and from the terminal hub. Not a single shade of yellow, orange or a brighter hue of red, as if the warm half of the spectrum did not exist. And yet airside, as she had seen on so many occasions, there flitted and flurried bright yellow trucks, lorries and buses — highly visible due to their purpose, along with the lurid red of the standby fire engines.

The London Transport Routemaster from which she disembarked — itself a rare example of bright red on 'landside' — turned to start its return journey as she reached the terminal, where the buses owned and operated by the airlines were mostly drab, too; dominated by the grey and white of British European Airways. The destinations on the front of these monochromatic buses listed the names of foreign cities, as if boarding would transport the lucky passenger straight to Paris or Stockholm or Munich without delay or diversion. These special buses pulled up outside one of ten numbered parking bays, each with its own entrance to a corresponding passenger channel, from whence conveyance — like parts-processing at a factory — to the specific aircraft began.

Those without tickets could enter via the main foyer, beneath the line of two dozen evenly-spaced flags atop the Europa façade — not of countries but airlines: BEA, Aer Lingus, Swissair, Air France and others — and ride up to the first floor, where ticket sales staff and customer enquiry teams were gathered inside boxed, chest-high cubicles.

Instead, she walked next door, to rendezvous with the man she'd waited years to meet.

The airside restaurant of the Queen's Building: its curves at odds with the straight lines of the panorama that took in the adjoining Europa Terminal, the adjacent control tower complex and the rows of parking spaces. Those approaching by air — such as Geoffrey just an hour earlier — could see the semicircular aspect to Queen's Building that faced airside, from which ran linear walkways and glass corridors, and the Y-shaped slope where each corridor split into two boarding gates meeting the parked-up aircraft.

Somewhat incongruously, Charlotte felt the restaurant possessed the air of an ocean liner: rows of rounded columns arranged in a curving line equidistant to the broad semicircular façade, situated yards apart inside the wall-to-wall windows overlooking the apron, like rows of funnels running up into the ceiling. The seating consisted of oddly simple wooden chairs, almost as if from a schoolroom; while similarly plain tables were laid out with rudimentary checkered tablecloths and festooned with basic cutlery and crockery, and the crudest pots of cruet.

Yet everything else felt as thrillingly modern — even *futuristic* — as possible, short of an adjacency to some space development programme at the new National Aeronautics and Space Administration in Washington, or the Korolev design bureau in the USSR, that she'd read so much about in magazines. As the pair took their seats, the thrilling roar of four turbojet engines sent a reconfigured Comet into the air — sounding as if another Sputnik launched into space — while elsewhere on the sprawling grounds, the Tupolev Tu-104 of Aeroflot and a Pan American Boeing 707 confirmed the jet-age, this time, here to stay. The bottom halves of the restaurant windows — through which she stared — jutted out at a shallow degree towards the apron, then, just above halfway, cut back sharply to the perpendicular, with thinly sliced louvres: sharp, space-age angles, precisely mirroring the clear-eyed control tower's eyrie, from which men with binoculars diligently surveyed the airport.

Charlotte would not fly — still *no way* she would fly — but as Geoffrey's guest she took the chance to sit in the restaurant a floor below the viewing gallery she so regularly visited: even closer to the planes than on the days she walked the upper deck. They had met at the foyer, and were led to a table at the far end of the seating plan; a slatted wall, like an empty cross-hatched bookshelf — up which ran plants and vines — cunningly dividing the restaurant from the open areas beyond.

The servers, disconcertingly, drew to mind the Nippies of the Lyon's Corner Houses: black uniforms with white collars and a white pinafore; with it, for Charlotte, the sickening sense of sitting in *that* café, the blood on the napkin, the failing consciousness, the year and more lost to the sanatorium. She took a moment to compose herself. As she did so, Geoffrey placed a box on the table, then changed his mind and slipped it down by the side of his chair.

"What's that?" Charlotte asked.

He reached down, and flashed the lid in her direction, without lifting it back up to the table. "I bought it for my son. I'm not entirely sure why."

Charlotte looked at the box, at the painting of a strange hybrid airplane mixed with familiar design features of the helicopters that ran shuttle services from the apron below into central London. A *ROTODYNE*, according to the bold lettering.

"Oh, so you have a son?" she asked, sounding surprised, with no logical reason.

"Well, not one that I ever see."

"Oh. Why ever not?"

"It's a long story."

"Long stories are becoming my speciality."

"That's as maybe, but I am not so good at telling them, you see."

"You won't improve without practice, as they say. Sorry, I don't mean to be blunt."

Geoffrey laughed. "Well, you *are* quite direct."

"I know," she said, smiling proudly. "Seems that I've lost my patience for vagueness and chitchat and general tommyrot. Don't you miss him?"

"It's easier to not have to see the … *frailness*. I still send him presents and cards on his birthday and Christmas, not that I ever hear back — although I don't include a return address. I don't want to confuse the boy. Oh, I don't know. I doubt that anything I do now is of any help."

"What's his name?"

"Montague. Or Monty, really. To me, at least."

An immaculate Nippy in the trademark monochrome maid-like uniform interrupted, to diligently take their lunch order.

"So, did you leave?" Charlotte asked, as the waitress walked to the kitchen.

"Yes," he said, lowering his head, "I'm ashamed to say."

"I'm sure you had your reasons. You don't seem the kind to just … well, I don't really know you, obviously. It's just an impression I get."

"It was all one big mistake," he sighed. "Every last bit of it."

"I couldn't imagine having a child. Does that make me strange?"

"No stranger than a man who leaves his child, I suppose. I just don't want to give the impression that it was in any way easy."

"Of course."

"To be perfectly honest, he never seemed to like me very much. His mother coddled and fussed him such that he took anything I did or said as a punishment. Even as a baby he cried whenever I held him. I tried — well, as much as one can. We just never … hit it off. And then I'd be away for ages on business, on some investigation, and any time I came back he seemed even more like his mother's son, you see."

"You don't think that in time it would have improved?"

"If anything it was getting worse. In truth, it didn't feel like he was mine."

Charlotte's eyebrows narrowed. "What, not *actually* yours?"

"Heavens no. He was Dorothy's, I mean. Not mine. But maybe the fault is with me. Maybe there is something lacking in me. Clearly there is *something* wrong with me. I'm not … well, I'm just not the paternal kind. Let's just leave it at that."

"Will you go back and see him?"

"I don't think that I can. Too much has changed, you see. It's been more than two years. I'll post this," he said, pointing at the box, "when I get the chance. For Christmas. But his mother … it's just not that simple. There are other issues. It's very complicated. Getting a glimpse of the house from the air just now as we came in to land — well, it felt most strange. I've moved to Scotland, you see, and prefer to keep that kind of distance where possible. Work still brings me to London Airport, as you can tell, but otherwise I stay away."

"Yes, your work. Of course. I don't want to take up too much of your time."

"No, it's fine. There's no rush. No rush at all."

"Well, if you're sure," she said, and reached for a cigarette.

"I'm always happy to help, where I can. You never give up this kind of work, even if you switch jobs. Anyway, the airman you contacted me about" he said, reaching into his attaché case. "I was able to find some old records. Viktor Hallfreðsson. Nothing much, I'm afraid, but a few reports." He laid them out on the table, either side of his cutlery. "You may well know more than me, to be honest. There really was no confirmation of his demise, and no reports of seeing his Spitfire go down. Nothing has surfaced since. He could have sped quite far across the Channel, if he was in hot pursuit, or being pursued. We found one lost pilot's Hurricane all the way over in Normandy, when he was seen last in Dover. Your Icelandic chap's radio was shot out, by the sounds of it. There were also a number of sightings of Spitfires being shot down on the south coast — Dymchurch, Folkestone, Winchelsea — that could potentially be his. But they couldn't be recovered, and are lost to the elements. Lots of them, you see. Unrecoverable at the time, and well — it's getting on close to twenty years, isn't it? Often it only gets trickier. They get forgotten. No one is looking anymore."

Charlotte stared at the papers — brief, cold-typed memos, with just a few human scribbles, that added nothing new to her understanding of the events, but provided some kind of connection. "Can I keep these?"

"Of course. They're photostatic copies. Were you and he — this Viktor …?"

"An item?" she asked, looking up from a simple three-line document. "Yes. Not betrothed or anything, but I hoped we would be. One day. After the war, perhaps."

"You never married later, to someone new?"

"No, not me," she said, after an extended drag whose smoke flared from her nostrils. "Never came close, to be honest. Could never quite accept that Viktor was dead. We had a vague agreement to rendezvous at Piccadilly Circus as soon as the war ended. Silly idea, really. He never turned up. Obviously still hasn't. Yet I'm still waiting, in some strange way."

"I saw it a lot, after the war. Some could give up and move on. Others just seemed stuck."

"That's me. Stuck."

"Some men *did* return, you know?" he said, with an encouraging smile.

"Really?"

"Amnesiacs. Prisoners of war. Men hospitalised overseas. Not millions, I'll grant you — but enough. Eventually they made it home."

"But not Viktor."

"No, it would seem not. I have to say, from what I discovered, I have some loose connections to him."

Charlotte's eyes widened. "You *knew* Viktor?"

"Not directly, no. But his name rang a bell. Seems our paths almost crossed. Or rather, we were in the same places at different times. I know Iceland quite well, you see. And Akureyri."

"*Really?*" she said, suddenly sitting bolt upright at the sound of the town whose name she took ages to learn, asking Viktor to repeat it many times. "How so?"

"During the war. Stationed there, for a summer, '41. It was … eventful, shall we say."

"Viktor got out in '40," she said. "Made it to England. Before the Battle of Britain."

"Yes, I gathered. I would love to go back there. One day."

"What's it like?" she asked, hauling her bloated oxblood bag onto her lap, to squeeze in the new manila files.

"I should imagine it has changed greatly. It was developing so fast. We arrived just after they'd built the cathedral — monolithic, grand thing, it was. Fairly ugly, to tell you the truth, but to each his own. Roads were being built. The whole infrastructure, really. Yanks were there too, taking over. It's not an especially beautiful place in terms of the architecture, it has to be said — but it has its own charm. Big mountains, the flowing fjord, wide open spaces. Perhaps not as wide open now. I also flew from Northolt, for a short while, you see. Again, a different time to your chap, but same place."

"How strange."

"Life is full of coincidences, don't you find?"

"I suppose so," she said, scrunching the last of the butt into the ashtray. "It's all about what you look for, don't you think? Maybe they are everywhere, if you pay attention. I mean, everything is at least *loosely* connected, isn't it? I like to sit in the terminal and do just that — pay attention. Maybe there are coincidences all over the airport. Sometimes I think I see things. Perhaps it's like the stars at night — at first glance you see a few, but the more you stare the more that gradually appear, in vast interconnected patterns, as your eyes adjust. I used to float on my back in the lake by the old cottage on cloudless summer nights, looking up at them, as more and more emerged. Especially during the blackout. A different world."

"The same world — up there in the heavens, I mean," he said. "But yes, down here — a different world. Things change, at this earthly speed. Still, the service at this place remains fairly glacial," he added, failing to spot any imminent movement on their lunch.

"You will have been much closer to the stars than I will ever manage. All that flying."

"You haven't flown? Will you go to Iceland."

"No, never. Never — to both questions." She visibly shuddered. "I just can't face it. Not before I saw those crashes and the dead and the dying, and definitely not after. I've tried, believe me, but the fear just takes over."

"It's getting safer."

"That's as maybe. But not yet safe enough. I mean, Munich, just last year — the deaths of all those young men. Just lads, weren't they? So heartbreaking."

"Now, that was a particularly tough one to take. I'm glad I didn't have to go over to deal with that one. I'm not much of a follower of football, to be honest, but I felt like I knew those poor boys, in a strange way."

"So much potential. Such a waste."

"So, what are you afraid of?"

"Not *dying*, that's for certain." She let out a long exhale, steeling herself. "Excuse me if this seems a little too personal," she said, leaning in conspiratorially, lowering her voice, "but I get these moods, that feel like they're smothering me. Nerve-storms, the doctors say. I feel so bad at times that I'd rather be a goner. So

... death itself is not what worries me. Perhaps I fear *surviving* an airplane crash. Being disfigured, disabled, a wretch. All the things I saw at close quarters, all the things that still haunt my dreams. Life's hard enough as it is. Or to be stranded in some godforsaken place, beyond rescue. Or maybe the moment when the plane is going down, and everyone knows death is imminent and unavoidable. I fear all that. Death itself is not the problem. It's the *prelude* I fear. And so no, I will never, ever fly. Never never never."

1962

A ticket clutched unnecessarily tightly in her quivering hand, Charlotte stood at the boarding gate, ready to hand its crumpled form over to the Icelandair stewardess. Charlotte had been here before, only to back out. Now, with the sun setting in every possible way — the doctors held out no hope — that option seemed pointless; her task akin to that of a butterfly that must take flight, lay its final egg, and accept the swift ensuing all-time darkness. She had just enough time for a trip to Iceland's eternal midsummer June sunlight, and a search for the thing she had never been able to rediscover.

In the end, the decision to fly felt simple. The return of TB proved an incorrect self-diagnosis. She had felt mostly fine; a cough, and a little tired, but nothing too serious. Yet days earlier it had come, the hammer-blow news: cancer, and terminal, too; aggressive, and at any moment could take full control, as it massed and merged and metastasised. Treatments — some newfangled toxic chemical concoction, or brutal radiation that sounded like getting intimate with an atomic bomb — were eschewed. Death did not merely wait; instead, it moved in, as, at the same time, she sped toward it. With the swift halving of closing speeds, the two would collide, head-on. Time was tight — as tight as time can get.

She walked to the apron, towards the giant Hunting hangar in the distance, and to the portable stairs pushed up against the Vickers Viscount. She still had time to back out, run away; she had done so before. But it had reached the stage where running seemed pointless; like the stricken Spitfire she witnessed twenty-two years ago — that began *all this*: the love of Viktor, the deep fear of flying — it had a force of its own, on a path that could not be avoided. There could be no turning back. Her legs shook as she ascended the steps to the plane.

Did she expect him to still be alive? Realistically, no. But still the flickers of hope, with his body and his aircraft never discovered: that men at war got lost and escaped to far-flung places, sometimes no longer in possession of their memories; that he had dreamed of returning to the relative peace of his homeland; that after possible capture and torture during the remainder of the war, he felt too ashamed or broken to return to her. Every day she ran through various scenarios, finding ways to bring him back to life.

In recent years it had occurred to her how little he ever said about his homeland, his family, his friends, his childhood; they existed mostly in the extreme present-moment of war. But he must have family and friends and neighbours, who would have photographs and stories and knickknacks, to bring him back to life — bring him back to her — one last time.

She frequently reread all his letters, and yet there were so few clues about his Icelandic past. She made long-distance telephone calls answered by people who spoke no English, as well as the letters marked 'Hallfreðssons in Akureyri' that never went answered. For a while she stopped Icelandair passengers at the terminal as they queued for a flight, to ask if they hailed from Akureyri, until the airline staff asked her to stop pestering its customers. Now they welcomed her aboard their Viscount.

Anxious in her seat, the belt strapped across her lap, she craned her neck left and right, up and down, to survey the cabin, as if in a cockpit like Viktor, scanning the skies for incoming danger. Yet the foe lingered internally; the restlessness, the anxiety, the phobic panic. She had two strong tranquillisers in her bag, but she feared what sedation might do to her; perhaps if the plane started to spiral out of control she could bite into both as if cyanide capsules, and hope they took effect as soon as possible. She couldn't afford to emerge bleary and infirm at the other end, unable to further the journey for however many hours it took to regain both her full faculties and her balance. She feared the temptation of sleep, and how she had no way of realising, ahead of time, which would prove her last.

A digging internal pain took three aspirin to dull. Everyone else looked relaxed, some even ebullient. The air stewardesses smiled incessantly, as if merely a works' jolly to Eastbourne. *Hadn't they ever seen one of these things crash?* Where were all the gritted teeth, the fingers dug into armrests?

The Viscount suddenly bolted into motion, pulling Charlotte firm into the backrest, as it went from stationary to barrelling down the runway in a half-skipped heartbeat. Before long she felt a weightlessness to her legs, but gravity bore her backwards at the shoulders like the pin-down of a twenty-stone assailant, and pain speared within her chest, as she glanced out at the twilit runway buildings speeding past.

Once fully airborne and settled at a cruising altitude, she hauled down the old bulky oxblood bag from the overhead storage rack, recently lightened of load. The camera and rolls of film removed; no time to develop and print any photographs taken, no future from which to look back on a past. Just a single book: *A Grief Observed* by the mysterious N.W. Clerk; and some medications. And then, the bare essentials. Passport, blue and stiff-backed. A tiny notepad, a stubby pencil. One box of Craven A, a small box of matches. A couple of lightweight changes of clothes. Finally, a greater quantity of her old friends, the uppers, than the downers — and the further rattle of a tub of painkillers.

The pills could be popped, to boost and pep and palliate. As her body applied its natural braking systems she could override each organic impulse with the kind of energy that could only be borrowed from the future; a future she no longer needed to cherish and protect.

She had seen how quickly patients could plummet. She'd witnessed bursts of sparkle before the sudden burnout — the surge before death. And she had also seen interminable lingering, as if stuck in the jamb of death's door; no life force — alive by mere technicality. She didn't want that. Of course, doctors advised her not to travel. It might be mere weeks, if she looked after herself. How much of that time could she take on the never-never?

She posted her journals and a batch of specific photos and letters, along with Viktor's old fob watch — which, ominously, had stopped working — and an explanatory letter to Geoffrey Freeman in Scotland, to ask if he could supply any answers she failed to uncover, in the brief time she had left, and though of no use to her at that point, beyond her passing. To keep the search going in her absence would possibly also keep her alive a little longer, too, like an author whose books are posthumously read. The *story* must live on; she clearly would not. Should she find any trace of Viktor, or the life he had up until 1940, there might be time to post another letter to Geoffrey, for one final update.

The descent into Iceland — the sudden altitude falls — were felt as roiling swirls in her stomach, and she gripped the armrests with whitening knuckles. Lights appeared below, growing quickly larger. The touchdown tumult: bumpy and, for a moment, the sense of rising again, before the wheels settled smoothly on the ground.

* * *

Charlotte assumed that the plane would land close to the capital, but Keflavik airport, to her surprise, stood a distance of over 30 miles from Reykjavík. The fairly humble amount of krona she'd exchanged from sterling at the airport had to last an unknown length of time. The already limited number of internal Flugfélag Íslands flights to Akureyri the next day were booked up or cancelled, and, late evening, all coach journeys and public buses were done for the day. Even though she survived the flight from Heathrow, she didn't want to wait a couple of days for another.

The sun still shone low and bright at midnight as she exited the terminal, and so, with her bag hauled over her shoulder, she began to walk the roadsides in the direction of the signposts pointing to Reykjavík. The irony of endless days, at her life's eleventh hour. At some point she knew she'd have to stop and rest, but just getting *somewhere* felt essential, having come this far. She'd walked 30 miles in a single night before, fired by wanderlust and manic energy, during the blackout of the war, in the crazed state of needing to see Viktor; but she was young, and not terminally ill. She felt that same desire again, the inability to stay still; perhaps more so now, as time had never been tighter.

Yet she could feel parts of her body grinding, internal organs distressed by movement. Perhaps she could thumb a lift, but few vehicles passed. She felt confident that a coach or bus would surely pick her up in the morning, whenever one happened by, and as long as she headed north-east, she'd remain on the right track; inching ever closer.

On stretched the barren, featureless roads and the flanking lichen-covered lava fields, mountains always in the distance, giving no sense of ground covered; the only indication of true movement a rainstorm edging in from above the sparsely-iced peaks. Time also seemed to stand still, the twilight never-ending. Grassy and plainly floral aromas barely rose above the tang of sun-warmed lava, mixed with scatterings of sulphurous thermal ventings, and some more distant ongoing volcanic activity that never escalated into eruptions. She'd passed a single unlit farmhouse, and little else, in the first two or three miles of her pilgrimage, before — 100 yards off the road, towards a hill — she reached a tiny abandoned turf house, its grass roof overgrown, its wooden A-framed façade bleached of all brownness, its front door hanging half off its hinges, its threshold spruced by beautiful wild flowers. She felt the first cold drops of rain and, in dire need of rest, turned towards shelter.

Charlotte, in a hut lacking furniture, wasted no time in preparing somewhere to lay: scattering a clutch of flowers and grasses and mosses plucked from the entrance on the hard floor of ragged paved stones. In the permanent dusk that would — without anything but the imperceptible change in the direction of the sun — become dawn, she lay with a herringbone jumper covering her eyes; trying to stay awake, but letting her body recover as much as possible. This could not be where her journey would end — that felt utterly clear. She just had to slow her breathing, rest her eyes, and then, after a couple of hours, take a dose of uppers, to enable the next push when, she assumed, it had to start becoming lighter and the waking world would reappear.

She listened in the scratchy woollen darkness as the turf-house door, half-ajar, creaked in both directions, the sound ascending or descending depending where the rusty lower hinges, that held the door vaguely in place, were pushed from by the wind, and the effect it had on the birch. Her sweater grew damp from the gentle drips of rain, running down the dangling stalactite roots of grasses that grew in the roof, and from the feverish sweat of her brow. Fighting off deep sleep, she slipped uneasily along its edges, and fell into waking dreams: alternating between the shock of being buried in the rubble of the RAF hospital, and the heaviness of her head on the table at the coffee house, and then the near-blank scenes of staring straight up from the sanatorium bed, as the light danced upon the ceiling. Each felt like an ongoing struggle.

She occasionally awoke fully, seeing the light edging a little more brightly — a little further into the room — through gaps in the wood and the half-open door as she shifted the garment from her eyes, but still absent all sense of time. The sound of rain soon stopped, the dripping inside the hovel slowing to the tiniest trickle. The next time her eyes fully opened, the damp sweater removed, it felt like full daylight, until her eyes gradually adjusted. Still, it clearly felt like dawn now, rather than eternal dusk.

She ached all over as she forced her body upright, and felt pain that jolted like an electrocution — in all areas of her abdomen, up into her chest — but, with grit and gumption, she drily downed several chalky tablets that slowed in her oesophagus. She sucked on nothingness, generating and swishing saliva around her mouth to swallow and help lubricate their passage, aided by slapping the back of her neck to dislodge one that felt snagged. She hadn't come this far to choke to death on *medicine*. She dragged her body up to stand and dozily lurched outside, to see the sun high enough on the horizon to constitute a new day.

* * *

Blue light refracted through the tinted bubbled roof windows that curved from side panels up and around merging, into skylights. Everything inside the coach shimmered in blue hues, coloured to match the coach's livery. Windows as widescreen: Charlotte watching the winding world drift past on roads bumpy and meandering.

Life arrived and passed at intervals, in between long swathes of rugged landscape. Mossy, treeless landscapes, and lava whose bulging ancient flows could almost be seen slowing to a halt, before petrifying into a rocky overlay. Other vehicles on the scratty roads were a mix of European and American: a tiny Fiat, a curvy little Beetle; a tank-like Buick; a front-heavy Chevy pickup cabin, trailing a low flatbed.

The coach rolled in and out of small towns; passed villages by the sea; snuck through mountain passes, and over rickety bridges. All the disparate and distant towns in Iceland, finally connected by roads that, for all the nation's efforts, remained fairly rudimentary. Still, these led, circuitously, to Akureyri, and on the way, through the window, came the chance to marvel at a dolphin or whale venturing closer to shore, and inland, the ragged-maned horses running free on roadside pasture, in lands that felt unkempt.

Eventually, more signs of human life: fields of sheep, corralled by a lone farmer; two stout ponies, guided by a man pulling a plough; a bigger farm further along, its owner almost cheating as he drove a giant ground-churning tractor. Then, at some port, the chaos of the clustered fishing vessels, barrels loaded and unloaded as they bobbed on chains, the cargo winched on hoists and a slippery cascade of the day's catch flowing like oily slicks into giant containers. Bare-forearmed men and women in leather aprons grabbed, flipped and beheaded the fish, tossing them into salty vats with a rhythmic grace. Beyond them, blonde boys on boats, gaining sailing experience during the four-month summer holidays. Further on, blonde girls in parks, hoeing and trowelling, as the youth gained a hearty work ethic.

The Eskimos, Charlotte had once read, had fifty words for snow; here they needed fifty words for *blonde*, with strawberry, dirty, mousy, snowy, flaxen and sandy clearly not sufficient. Of course, there were the dark-haired, too — deeper auburn, rich chestnut, a few redheads, through to pure black. But, so far from the equator, pale skin and pale hair dominated. She thought of Viktor's hair, a darker blonde rendered bronze by Brylcreem.

Again, *What if he was alive?*

What would he look like now? He seemed forever trapped at twenty-one, twenty-two; but now he would be in his forties, double-aged. Would that hair have thinned, to the point where he slicked it back or combed it across a pale bald pate? Or would it still be beautifully thick and lustrous, yet possibly greying? Would he now wear glasses? Would his swimmer's build, that he had started to regain in the lead-up to flying again as he pressed-up and pulled-up, be replaced by a sagging middle-aged spread? She'd love him regardless, she told herself; yet she didn't know *this* Viktor, that sparked in her mind.

And yet, officially, he remained frozen at twenty-two, his body buried somewhere, likely trapped inside his aircraft. Had he gone down in flames, like the first time?

Did he get out, for a second time?

Then, her own decline, as seen through his middle-aged eyes. She knew she'd never had film-star good-looks, but what the Americans called that 'girl next door' charm; clearly attractive, until standing alongside the near-models at East Grinstead. She'd lost weight — but for all the slimming, her face looked more ravaged by time. And maybe she'd lost too much weight at this point; wasting away. She'd diligently dyed her greying hair this one last time, *just in case*; but the lines cut deeper. Would her appearance be a shock to him, were they to meet again? Yet that couldn't occur without the reality of how each now looked.

And what would she say to him? Without exaggeration, she had idly and dreamily and loosely rehearsed a thousand one-sided conversations in the intervening two decades; sometimes talking to a spirit, lost to this world, and at others to the living man who — in her outlandish fantasies — swam a thousand miles to safety, or landed in his plane in the ocean and improvised a way to use struts from its broken wings to paddle to shore.

Then, the notion of amnesia. If a full amnesiac, perhaps he returned home — maybe he took identifying letters from family up on that final flight, that helped him find his way back — and lived anew as Viktor Hallfreðsson without any prior knowledge of who that man had been; just some version of him that died in 1942, with the new version of himself, bereft of all backstory, having met and married a woman, perhaps now raising children? Charlotte accepted that he would have likely rebuilt his life, if he somehow got home.

The question she didn't want to face: what if he'd *chosen* to not get in touch; to have moved on without her, knowing full well what he had left behind in England, and having no desire to reconcile — not even write a letter. Then again, what did it matter now, to find out so late in day? At this stage, blissful ignorance could be shattered, as a trade-off, in the deep need to know.

Ultimately — at this, the last minute within the eleventh hour — simply to find evidence of his existence — photographs, stories, faces that shared familial traits — would suffice. Anything to fill in some blanks. Suddenly the God she didn't believe in, and the afterlife she'd previously dismissed out of hand, could provide an eternal euphoric epilogue, if — given the unlikeliness of it occurring in this life — he awaited in the next.

Back to the window, the people outside. Check and flannel, wool and cotton; and the overalls of the farmer, the waders of the fisherman. In the busier towns — still small compared to back home — she saw men in suits, in limited, unimaginative, uniformly dark shades, standing by the side of the road or walking with purpose.

Charlotte watched as a perfectly-complected Icelandic woman, with blue eyes and blonde hair, maybe twenty-two years old — an unidentifiable hint of something that suggested age beyond her teens — boarded the bus and, with a steadied grace, walked the aisle in her direction as the vehicle lurched and jerked, to take the seat beside her.

"Excuse me," Charlotte said, moving her oxblood bag from the chair onto her lap.

"You are English?" the woman asked.

"Yes, my dear."

"Ah, so we're allowed to talk now," she said with a smile and a gentle, lilting laugh. "It's so good the news that we're not at war anymore."

"War?" Charlotte asked, as her mind, increasingly beset by temporal discontinuity and jarring jump-cuts, flashed back to 1945, and Piccadilly Circus: the war over, the wait ongoing. Then ... why was she *here*, when she should have been there? A sense of panic sparked: Viktor, at this very moment, could be waiting by Eros! And then ... no, she'd waited there, hadn't she?

"Yes, the war over the cod fishing," the young woman said with a smile, nestling her own bag on her lap. "The fish!"

"Oh, yes. I see," Charlotte said, dragged back to 1962, but uneasily so. "Your English is very good," she said, as she sought time to make sense of what year this *really* was, to contemplate the evidence of the intervening years. She retrieved a handkerchief from her thin jacket pocket and dabbed her tingling forehead.

"I learnt young," the young woman said, cheerily. "The Yankee radio stations — from the US airbases — growing up, and all those Hollywood films. It all filters through. And the BBC World Service, too, although that was more my mother and father."

"Ah, I see."

"Then, I got to work for Icelandair. I fly to Scotland and England quite a lot. Sometimes to America, so I get lots of practice. I'm Margrét, by the way."

"Charlotte."

"You look hot," Margrét said as she looked closer at her new travelling companion, "if you do not mind me saying. Are you okay?"

"I'm fine, dear. Never been better," Charlotte said, laughing quietly to herself.

"Do you travel alone?"

"Yes. A fish out of water, as it were. Here, I mean. And, well, in general. I always travel alone. I live alone. I never married. I wanted to. An Icelandic man, no less."

"Well, we have some good ones. Mostly. Maybe not the drunken fisherman who spends his life at sea."

"I'm here to find him. The man I wanted to marry."

"Where is he?" Margrét asked, theirs the only voices on the noisy coach not ringing out in the native tongue.

"Akureyri. At least, he *might* be. Near to Akureyri, anyway. It's a long story. He went missing. In the war — the proper war, as it were. Not wars about fish. Do you know Akureyri? Are you going there too?"

"No. Well, I know Akureyri, of course. I have been there, but I am not going that far. I have to be back in Keflavík in two days — flying to New York. I'm going about halfway, to Sauðárkrókur, to my family. Halfway to Akureyri, that is — not New York. Have you been there?"

"Akureyri?"

Margrét laughed. "No, this time I meant New York — as so many people dream about going there. So they tell me."

"Well, I've been to neither. Both always seemed like a million miles away to me. May as well have been on Mars."

"However do you mean?"

"Flying. I just never could. Nor could I get on a ship. So, you wouldn't know anyone in Akureyri, then?"

"Not really — very distant cousins, but I do not know them. I think we have cousins everywhere. So did you fly this time? It is a very long way by sea."

"I did. Finally I flew."

"You survived!" Margrét said, with a warm smile.

"I did," Charlotte said, her eyes heavy, her forehead beading up again.

"You see, it is not so unsafe. I fly several times a week. I'm still here."

"I know. It's only the aeroplanes that crash that I worry about."

Margrét's chuckle seemed more wry this time. "I suppose so, as rare as they are. They don't tell you in advance, though. That would help. Not today, ladies and gentlemen, as this one is going to lose all engine power."

Charlotte laughed, but it caught in her chest and spread to a sharp and spiteful cough. She put the handkerchief to her mouth, pressed liquid from her tongue onto the soft cotton, but did not dare check for blood; concealing the item under the cuff of her thin sweater. Margrét lay a comforting hand on her shoulder, out of concern, with the practiced ease of someone natural to the service industry. "You don't sound so good," she said. "You look unwell, but with these windows, everyone on the bus looks a funny blue anyway."

Charlotte felt the touch, heard the words, but the hacking in her lungs had rattled her entire body, with stinging stabs zipping up her spine and firing fizzes into her brain stem, and in a woozy instant felt her eyes shift into double vision dotted with stars, then slowly glaze over.

As agreed, Viktor stood waiting to meet Charlotte at the coach stop in Akureyri, looking as youthful as ever, dressed spiffingly in full, freshly-pressed RAF uniform, a blanketed newborn baby tucked peacefully asleep under each arm. *Twins.*

Ah yes, they'd had twins — how could she have forgotten? She chided herself for forgetting so many things these days. His hands were bandaged again, and when he greeted her he spoke only in Icelandic. "Halló, hvernig hefurðu það?" he said. He'd said it to her before, one time they met for a date, when pretending that he didn't speak English after all. She recognised the sounds, but apart from *halló*, could not decipher any meaning. He began to speak faster, all weird singsong syllables, and she felt a panic, at how he didn't seem to understand that his words were mere gibberish to her. Then, with a sullen expression, he handed her the babies, giving her stern instructions in Icelandic, then turned and walked away. She gave chase, calling out to him for an explanation. The faster she ran, the further away he moved.

With a sharp unease, Charlotte found herself awaking, unaware that she'd even been asleep; a sense of deep disturbance. Was she on the bus home, after seeing Viktor? Where were the babies?

Who were the babies? The twins. *Her* twins. She didn't even know their names.

"You're back," Margrét, bathed in blue light, said with a smile, as Charlotte looked at the stranger with complete confusion. Who was she?

It slowly came back, reality spreading over the ultra-vivid dream; less of a jump-cut and more like a slow transition shot in a film, where one scene gradually fades out while the next fades in. "Are you sure you're okay?"

"Yes. Well … no. But — it's too much to explain. You don't need to know. No one needs to know."

"You can tell me?"

"Please, I'd rather not."

"As you wish," Margrét said with a gentle smile; the smile of a compassionate nurse with impeccable bedside manners. Charlotte pictured herself sat beside wounded airmen, talking to them when they wanted to talk; knowing when to shut up.

"So, what do you do?" Margrét asked.

"I'm a nurse," Charlotte said, picturing herself on the quadrangle as Viktor's flaming Spitfire careened; and then in the washroom, shaving his inner thigh. "I'm here to see my husband," she added, looking at her companion but not quite focussing. "We have two children. No, three children. Or is it two? I forget."

Margrét — until then, leaning in — recoiled slightly in her seat, pulling back towards the aisle. "You're married? To the man in Akureyri?"

"Yes, to Viktor. We've just had twins. Two boys. Or maybe two girls. I'm never quite sure."

"Look," Margrét said, looking with concern at the woman whose own eyes drifted past hers, and whose forehead glistened with sweat. "We are near to Sauðárkrókur. I really must get off at the next stop, it is just up ahead. Are you sure you are okay? If you come with me I can take you to see a doctor."

"Oh no, I'm as right as rain," Charlotte said, with a wonky smile, and eyes whose focus floated. "I'll see my Viktor soon."

* * *

Once fallen, the sun hovered on the horizon, for hours at its edge, as if slowly surfing across the distant sea, skimming the offing. With every bend the coach took the sun would hove into view, then fly away when a mountain range flipped across that flank. The moon and sun shared the same sky, but on differing paths. She had slept once more, but this time awoke with a clearer mind, as the coach stopped in Akureyri.

As she alighted from the vehicle by the harbour, she could recall that Viktor talked of walking down from the hills through a specially cultivated public park — the pride of the town — built around a house that dated back to early Victorian times. He lived to the north of the town, way up in the mountains, miles off the beaten path, with a view down at the town and the airfield and the harbour. She decided she would walk uphill, for as long as she could muster, to see what she could find. Unsure of the time, it seemed late; the eternal dusk. Tomorrow, she decided, she could go and look for an official building, where records were kept, and hope to find an assistant who spoke English.

After a brief rest on a public bench, she walked past the hotel Hamborg, up towards the twin spires of the clunky cathedral, the streets totally deserted; passing the open-air pool, silent and still, the glassy water golden from the glow of the low sun. Out at sea, from near to far, bobbed tiny boats and chunkier trawlers, but on land, the continuing strange lack of human life. The same applied at the public park — now officially a botanical garden, expanded since the days of Viktor's youth and WWII, after a 1957 makeover. Eyrarlandsstofa, the early Victorian house it all evolved around, sat unchanged, as the park expanded in terms of size and variety. Paths wended, and she found herself wandering within near-maze-like verdancy, the land brought to life with careful, expert cultivation.

She entered a circular section of the gardens, in which a ring of flowers of every conceivable colour seemed to spring from the soil, often tall and wild and rangy: the white of mountain avens; the purple of Arctic thyme; the yellow of plain-old dandelions; the blue-frilled long-necks of lupine; and oranges of surging Spanish poppies.

She put down her oxblood bag, and turned around to survey the full panorama. Yet in turning around she suddenly felt dizzy. Bright pricks of light sparkled on her retina. As she looked up at the light night sky — trying to ward off the sense of vertigo — the flashes in her eyes could almost have been the unseen stars, twinkling without the dark sky to showcase their presence; the visual field flickering phantoms of light from within, not without. Next, a sense of falling backwards — so she looked down, yet now the ground began to spin, the colours of the flowerbeds whirling around as, giddily, she stumbled and lurched, left and right, in the hopes of staying upright. Instead, she just gained momentum, until falling face-first into a flowerbed. Spores and pollen and plant dust spilled into the air, a leaf or two spinning free. Prone in the cushion of earth, floral scents flooded her olfactory receptors, with the bitter tang of soil and fertiliser; the rank taste on her lips, on her lolling tongue tip; the prickles of plant matter and tiny stones on her skin. On went the swirling sensations — the waltzer, the whirligig, the feeling that her body still span upright, in open space, round and round and round — as she lay flat and, increasingly, deathly still.

Then, the sense of sinking slowly into the earth. Feeling the vining flowers crawl and entwine and weave, grabbing and pulling her down. Her skin slipping, her face falling, her sinews dissolving, her bones liquefying; the manic, febrile, unseen slide in and out of consciousness, before, unnoticed by anyone, the final closing curtain of the coma.

2008

The liminal light of the perpetual magic hour of a deep Icelandic winter: stretched to the full four hours from dawn to dusk, so that sunrise blurred into sunset; car headlights adding yellow-white to the orange hues against the white aftermath of a blizzard. Snowbanks, ploughed at noon to ten-feet icebergs, encircled Akureyri's town square, like the walls of an igloo. The square itself remained a misnomer: a *circle* of spindly trees, snaking bench seating, lampposts, flagpoles and flower planters, like some modest modern Stonehenge, rendered just a little more epic by the shunted snowbanks on the ringed pedestrianised road. The only sense of extraordinariness arrived in the scale and heft of its Christmas tree, whose lights twinkled twenty-five feet into the air.

Then, Geoffrey Freeman walked into an unfolding drama. An old man — maybe even older than he himself — sat on the ground beside a jarring pool of blood; its redness so rich it almost sparkled on the fresh snow. By the time Geoffrey drew closer, the flashing blue lights of an ambulance were rebounding like visual echoes, as the long, drawn-out wail of its siren pinged in a circle of reverb.

A small crowd gathered around the old man, blood streaming down his forehead from a half-inch gash that somehow bled like a severed carotid. Geoffrey felt the pain of a fellow elderly traveller, awkward on the floor in the snow; a fate he'd suffered a couple of times as his balance and reflexes waned, his now-brittle bones lucky to survive intact. Still relatively fit for his age, he — perhaps like the old man on the floor — refused to accept that walking in the aftermath of a snowstorm had moved onto the increasing list of things closed off to him as his nineties grew nearer, never to move back onto the list of the possible. There were things his body simply could not do anymore — that not even medical interventions could reverse — but this remained a grey area: he could still walk, and had reasonable balance, but the likelihood and consequences of a fall felt all the greater, as such a reminder showed. Yet he hadn't moved to Iceland a couple of decades earlier just to lock himself away from the world, so that, forever indoors, he might as well be in some grim British care home, propped up and doped-up in some foul-smelling armchair in front of a dumbly blinking television set.

He drew closer to the injured man, as the ambulance driver tried to get the vehicle close enough to park. Having already helped the victim to sit upright, a strapping young man — broad and bearded — removed his trendy puffy jacket and then his long-sleeved white cotton top, to wrap the latter around the old man's head. As he worked the makeshift bandage, a kneeling woman held the old man's hand, and asked him his name, where he lived. Though conscious, he seemed confused, possibly concussed.

Now close enough to see clearly, Geoffrey took stock of the tall, slender men, whose face, dribbled with blood and turbaned with fast-reddening cotton, wore almost every possible mark of ageing: the furrows on what could be seen of the forehead, cut with radiating striations, like the faint metal lines of a dartboard; some clearly throbbing with veins, some hollowed out, cut across with the ridges of a wrinkled brow. His nose had clearly previously been broken, and he had a soft burn scar on his cheek. Geoffrey looked down at the man's hand, in the grip of the young woman's, and saw further scars — *serious* scars, the skin like a gnarled glove of hard-baked rubber. Higher, sneaking out below pulled-up cuffs: ancient forearm tattoos like smudged bruises, inked blues and browns and greens; the possible hilt of a dagger, perhaps the tail of a serpent.

"He doesn't know his own surname," the woman said in her native Icelandic, looking up at the latest onlookers. "I've asked a few times. He doesn't know where he lives."

Geoffrey felt his own eyes widening, his attention further ramped up. He had once heard a story, but never believed it true. Told to him a few years after he arrived back in Iceland, it detailed the local man who, during the war, somehow escaped his downed aircraft in France and found his way first to Norway and then back to Iceland via various ships and a small fishing vessel. The pilot returned to the wife and young child he had hitherto abandoned in 1940 in the race to join the war effort. They lived on the outskirts of Akureyri, to the north in the mountains, in remote seclusion; apparently the man couldn't stand crowds. The story of the nameless man had clearly passed through several iterations, shared by people increasingly distant to the original source. Geoffrey recalled an obvious candidate, although not all of the details — sketchy though some were — seemed to fully match the first-hand stories he knew regarding the potential suspect; a man clearly believed long dead, but whose body had never been found, including attempts he himself had made to locate it on the Winchelsea shoreline, and the woman who kept asking that he look into it. He thought the tale — of escaping the war, to retreat into obscurity — just a myth; a tall story, told by loose lips in bars, with reckless exaggeration.

And yet, while not an entirely uncommon name in these parts, this man, the woman holding his hand had declared, was called *Viktor*. It all seemed to click into place, as two ambulance-men shuffled him onto a stretcher.

"Are you Viktor *Hallfreðsson*?" Geoffrey asked, hurriedly, as they lifted the stretcher onto a gurney.

"No," the man said, with a shake of his head, although his eyes quickly widened, and then fiercely narrowed in focus.

"You are. You *are* Viktor Hallfreðsson."

"No," the old man said with a further shake of the head; closing his eyes, as if to shut Geoffrey out, before the ambulance men pushed the gurney into the vehicle and closed the rear doors.

2010

Fat jets thundered low over the freshly cultivated garden, casting dramatic fast-moving shadows over the stubby scraps of organic matter that, if somehow still rooted amid the shreds of cut twigs and vines, looked to green and grow again, as the severed paled and dried and withered. Buoyed by the success of this summer's horticultural mastery, Montague felt it finally time to clear the garage. He would order a skip for out front, to cast out decades of junk and tat.

He had not seen Stephanie since their trip to the West End. She must be avoiding him. And yet he had to admit that he hadn't exactly been hoping to run into her. Or rather, the biting ambivalence: he still yearned to see her, but feared the rejection of the encounter going badly, such as her blurted excuse to hurry along, or worse still, a failure to even acknowledge him; pretending, with a blank, that she didn't see him, and therefore, that he did not exist. He recalled the sense of control bestowed by scything the overgrown garden; how he could find strength in the moment of hacking away at his past, as a way to move forward.

The front entrance to the garage — two dark green wooden barn-like doors that opened outwards towards the street — had been bolted shut from the inside decades earlier, with access to the bolt, due to the buildup of stored and discarded items, rendered impossible, as, at the same time, rust gradually seized it up. To take all the junk out through those front doors and into the belly of the skip would first require removing it all via the backdoor, into the rear garden. Only then could the bolt be accessed and uncocked, with the influence of some WD-40.

Not everything required disposal. He hadn't yet decided what to do about the Morris Minor, whose engine had surely fused into immobility, thirty or forty years ago. Would it be worth a reasonable price now, as a vintage, low-mileage car? Even so, he still couldn't see himself getting rid of the vehicle. He'd reluctantly accepted the need to ditch a lot of the clutter, the bric-a-brac, the detritus — even eventually clear out some things from his mother's room — but the car, and some of her clothes, remained too personal. Maybe there were lost fragments from his childhood, buried deep in the vast accumulation.

Disturbed dust, displaced by any kind of movement, scattered and fluffed up into gentle clouds that caught in dull sunbeams permeating the grimy glass of the garage doors. Fresh spirals of spider webs glistened, while heavy, yellowed cobwebs draped like dead, thickened vines. His fear of small creatures and crawling insects remained extreme — the sphincter-tightening recoil of their touch upon his skin, where even just the mere thought made him internally flinch. So he wore long sleeves, gloves and an old flat cap for the task. Family archaeology, stored in chronological order, and unpacked in reverse.

Starting at the edges — the only place possible — he began to haul cardboard boxes and sacks outside into the sunlight. These first retrievals comprised his own junk, from recent years: old clothes placed into black bags; broken glass boxed up so as to not endanger the dustmen and then just forgotten about; broken tools that he intended, one day, to fix; his mother's commode; and old VHS tapes, full of arcane recordings of BBC2 in the 1980s, including one, in a case marked with *Open University Lecture*, that instead contained a disturbing German pornographic film involving wanton micturition on black plastic sheeting. At first it appeared a standard sex tape — the first he'd ever bought — that he found utterly alluring, until, alarmingly, the urine started to splash. He recalled the shameful return from Soho upon its purchase, walking through Piccadilly Circus with the cassette in a brown paper bag, his selection — made hurriedly, to get out of the store as quickly as possible — based on the beautiful woman on the cover, with no idea of the distinctly unhygienic tableau it contained. He slipped the colourful cardboard case into a bin adjacent to Eros as he passed

— what would his mother say if she saw such a thing? — and kept the cassette in the plain paper bag. Once home he snuck into the garage, to hide the contraband. Later, as Dorothy slept, he crept out to retrieve it, scraping off the lewd label and placing the cassette into the disguised case.

Is *that* what women wanted — to be pissed on? Is that what other men wanted to do, too? It made no sense.

Further in he found toys that his mother decided were too inclined towards rough-and-tumble — a cowboy belt complete with plastic pistol, and the football, now deflated, Geoffrey had tried to get the boy to kick — that she had packed into boxes and stuffed into the garage, including onto a row of three shelves set high on the wall, which must have required a stepladder. Back then, just a single layer of bags and boxes on the floor surrounded the Minor, squeezed into spaces, including the foot-or-so between the front bumper — the car had been backed into the garage all those decades ago — and the bolted double doors. Once Geoffrey absconded the second layer soon piled upon the first: the things of his — or connected to him — that Dorothy could not bring herself to throw away, but which required casting aside. Much of it she felt too shaken to examine, and so just piled it high; out of sight, out of mind.

The next layer swiftly followed, when Montague, as a little boy, added his own: the toys bought for him by his father, often on the many trips away with work. Geoffrey may as well have taken them all with him that final day. Why leave them behind, as cruel mementos of abandonment? The man — the distant, shadowy figure — never even sought to contact his own son again; never so much as a card in the post. Not that his little Monty would have appreciated the idea at the time, but he would have liked the chance to decide whether or not he should reject such a gesture. Instead, he never got the chance; nothing ever sent.

Some of that distant shadowiness started to coalesce into something a little more coherent, as Montague's neurons whipcracked sparks: his mind, much like the garage itself, storing evidence deep in layers of darkness and obfuscation; memories that could be lit up, in some form, via a clue from the present moment. He realised that Geoffrey *existed there,* in his mind;

more than he'd cared to believe. Yet also, in many ways, as elusive as the itch on the tiny patch of skin at the centre of the back that cannot be reached from any angle by a fingernail.

Visions stirred upon finding the 400-piece *Good Companion* jigsaw — *Comet Over New York* — with its evocative illustration of the shiny new jet-plane banking over blue skies above the Hudson River. He had completely forgotten the image, and yet, now seen again, he had a sense of recognising a familiar friend from childhood; the time spent putting the hundreds of pieces together, with the patient help of his father.

Other memories twitched into life. In another box, surrounded by desiccated conkers and various sizes of marble, sat the blue plastic Airfix Spitfire Mk I, that the two had assembled — albeit Geoffrey affixed the wings to the fuselage whilst his son glued his own fingers together; another argument with Dorothy, about irresponsibility, swiftly ensuing. Again, the sense of the size of his father's hands, and how big they still felt in his mind as they peeled away the adhesive. Montague smiled at how poorly the construction worked out — perhaps it wasn't so bad for a first try, and it might have looked better had they ever got around to painting it. He placed it outside, in the 'keep' pile.

A bigger, heavier box — under scraps of balled-up newspaper — contained a plush photo album: his parents' wedding. The first photograph — revealed after flipping back a wafer-thin semi-opaque layer of crêpe paper that protected the print — depicted a portrait of his mother before the wedding: much slimmer than he ever remembered, looking proud but perhaps anxious too — something in her eyes. Who was *this* woman? He only remembered the wreck she became. Who had she been before things fell apart? No one else had ever been on hand to tell him, and, to her dying days, she refused to speak of any time prior to 1957 — like some veteran of the Somme who would not hear a word of reminder of that sodden hell on Earth. What had she been like as a girl — full of hopes and ambitions, with a youthful zest?

Montague struggled to even remember his own father's face, or how he spoke; so much time had passed, and with it, the dimming of grey matter that furred up in his mind. The details were so vague. He could sense those hands, but more the size of them, than anything recognisable. All photos had been removed from the house decades earlier, and he'd never felt it the right time to try and find some evidence. And yet here Montague stood, about to meet the man again on the day of his parent's wedding; less than ten years younger than when last he saw him. With a creeping trepidation he turned the page. The next photo: a group shot, outside the church, of bride and groom flanked by elderly-looking parents and aunts and uncles — Geoffrey's only, as hers did not attend — in awkward poses stiffened by starchy clothes that looked like leftovers from the war. Dorothy's expression remained the same — a slightly eery distance to her gaze; Geoffrey's expression, however, *totally obliterated* by the manic scratchings of a black biro. Whether or not the groom appeared happy, or anxious, or excited, there could now be no knowing, as every subsequent overturned leaf of fine crêpe paper exposed a man scratched and scrawled and scribbled into oblivion — a cloud of chaos and destruction above the shirt collar. Disappointed, and saddened by the vitriol, Montague set the album to one side, packed neatly back within the box. He'd keep it too, but sensed that he'd never want to revisit the brutal damage to his father's features, and the rabid anger in those pen marks, that scuffed and tore the paper; photographs of a monumental day transformed into documents of bitterness and betrayal.

Delving into the garage's next layer, he dislodged an old book, and instantly tins and boxes and tubs slipped and fell, as a rotted shelf — relieved of some of its burden on one side — finally snapped in two. Some of his father's old possessions cascaded down, ricocheting before hitting the ground: the dull yet liquid thump of a tin containing thick oil, and a sharp crack, that sounded like glass popping.

Then ... the sudden overpowering smell, a masculine musk: bergamot and lemon vervain, oakmoss and vetiver — unknown ingredients whose fragrance only meant something to Montague in that distinct, hitherto long-forgotten combination. For a brief moment, he could with all clarity see his father's face for the first time. Not some flat, dull image, but almost a hologram, full of vivid depth and shade and life. Not only could he see Geoffrey's image, clear and precise — flickering with detail — but the image somehow transcended his mind's eye, transposed, with mass, into the three-dimensional space in the half-lit garage. There his father stood, just a few feet away, in his blue overalls; perhaps mixed with a visual flash from childhood, aided by the added sense-memory, of Geoffrey wearing that very distinctive shave lotion. He sensed he could not possibly see his father's then middle-aged face any clearer were he to actually be present, the year 1957, such was its clarity; until the image began to recede. Montague grasped at it, within his mind; forcing it to stay, trying harder to retrieve it — like a polaroid that, with more effort in flapping the print, could be shaken into lucid colour — but instead it just grew ever-more elusive.

Other memories stirred. However, the clarity continued to drift between haziness and mere microseconds of something more definite. Hitherto so dismissive of the man, so unwilling to forgive, he found he wanted to hold the image of his father a little bit longer. Could the two make peace? Was it too late?

Born 89 years earlier, the chances were that he had died by now — although the lack of any official notification, which he presumed would still be forthcoming from the authorities overseas, suggested otherwise. Perhaps he could write to some people in Iceland, make some detailed enquiries. And he had the fob-watch, to return to the journalist who once knew something of his father. Why had he stalled on returning it, having fixed it months ago?

Montague picked up the smashed jar of shave lotion from behind an old broken television set. Yardley, with its black, red and yellow *Y* bold on the jar; the glass held together by a label that had almost fused onto the bottle like a tattoo. He located an empty Tupperware container, and placed the jar inside, to seal it with air-tightness; its aroma a fragment of his father that he wanted to retain, given the ongoing lack of photographic evidence.

The three piles outside the garage — keep, discard and undecided — grew surprisingly tall and wide and deep, as if the items expanded in the light, once removed from the dimly-lit space. With tongs from the kitchen he disposed of the desiccated carcass of some kind of rodent, and with a broom swept away droppings and dustballs and dead insects. He jumped back as a moth flapped from the dark, towards the waxen light of the filthy garage door windows.

The path around the Morris Minor now lay clear. The car wore a film of greenish-grey grime, spread all over its turquoise paint scheme; the windows, like those of the garage, dimly opaque. Montague possessed a vague memory of the keys stored in the exhaust pipe, and after fishing through dust and grit and grot with a tentative finger he located the keyring, tucked a few inches in. The driver-side door opened after a weighty tug, and he slid behind the wheel, into a dusty capsule that almost contained fusty 1950s' air. It reeked of something unpleasant — must and decay, rust and petroleum, perhaps even animal decomposition — with the undertones of old seat leather, his father's fragrance now locked out. While his mother retained the Morris after his father absconded, she never drove it again. A journey with his father sprang to mind, and a terrifying trip to the fairground. With that, he quickly got out of the car.

Montague unlocked the boot, flipped up the hood. A stronger smell of petrol seeped into the air. He pulled away some old sheets, to reveal a fairly sizeable cardboard box, that just about fit within the confines of the space. Resting on its side, Montague pulled forward the flaps, and inside lay a series of unopened cards — addressed to Master M Freeman — and several gifts, of various sizes, in wrapping paper. He lifted a small box covered in the green and red colours of Christmas, and tore away the sheet to the sound of rattling within. The lid displayed a painting of a blue-and-white-liveried Fairey Rotodyne, utterly resplendent over Tower Bridge, the Thames with its barges — obsolescence personified in the shadow of the very future of transport — as mere inconsequential shapes far below.

2010

The setting sun slumped wan and muted behind slow-moving snow clouds, the sea eerily still and calm — and icily dark-blue — beyond Reykjavík's curving coastal road, as Michael nonchalantly steered the bend. A memory of Ethan, out of nowhere, smashed like a wave: the little boy laughing — almost yelping — on the wintery Brighton beach as the tide rushed at his scampering feet. "Run! Run!" Ethan screeched, in between giggles — the kind usually aroused by merciless tickles that had to cease when it sounded like he might cry — as they all retreated, only for the boy to run back at the sea moments later, shouting "Shoo! Shoo!" as the water receded. Then, "Run away, run away!" again.

Michael smiled, pleased at such an unexpected visitation, but it proved naturally bittersweet: the lack in his life of such joys, beyond memories, a grim contrast. And then, recalling the moment seconds later, when Ethan fell over as the cold tide bit back, and the ferocity of the boy's tears, his trousers sodden, his face red, his nostrils inflating bubbles of snot that expanded and contracted with his frantic breaths before bursting; nothing bittersweet there, just pain, sharp and cruel and jabbed right to the heart.

Still, soon he would return home. Maybe he could catch some surreptitious glances at his son, before the summer's court case.

Michael collected Stanley from the latter's Reykjavík hotel, a day before both were due to head back to England. A few streets away, they picked up Geoffrey from the foyer of his hotel, for one last special gathering; unlikely there would ever be more, they presumed, given the ages and distances involved.

"You haven't changed a bit," Geoffrey had said to Stanley, when the two met a few days earlier in that same foyer, after the latter's pilgrimage to the glacier, where the Carters and the tail fin were recovered; to where Alice still lay, somewhere close but not close enough. The cold — burrowed deep into his marrow —

and the shock of the end to five-and-a-half decades of waiting, saw Stanley stutter in reply, about how he could never forget that day at the factory, and the subsequent trip to the Cairngorms, in a period of his life that, in contrast to the couple of years before the crash, stayed seared into his memory for all the wrong reasons. Only later did things become a blur, as the wait for news stretched into one amorphous mass of time, where, on a daily basis, another minuscule modicum of hope vanished. No news never *felt* like good news.

And the belated bad news, that the plane had been located, came as a relief, with the chance to stand on the very spot where at least part of the DC-3 remained.

Days later, and still Stanley felt the cold in his bones; his shins, his spine, the ridges of ribs, all cryogenically frozen. Age had seen his stutter generally slip away; until the cold, or stress — and in the past few days, both — sparked a few slips. "That day — the factory," Geoffrey said to him, as the pair sat in the car, Michael driving them in the direction of the edge of a glacier. "The Rotodyne. What the hell happened to it? I mean, I read about it — but even so."

"What a waste," Stanley sighed. "As you know, at least there were no crashes there. It worked beautifully. But we just couldn't get the noise down by the final few decibels to make it acceptable for city flights. Too loud, they kept saying. Project ran over, and over, but it was getting there. We were getting closer. Lots of publicity, lots of excitement, prototype was a dream. Then the government just s–shut the whole thing down. Soon after, Fairey was merged with Westland. And that was that."

"It was so ahead of its time," Geoffrey said.

"Maybe *too* ahead of its time," Stanley noted with a sigh.

"I had planned to write a book about it," Michael said, switching eye contact between the two elders, Geoffrey at his side, Stanley via the rear-view mirror. "Just like the Rotodyne itself, another project that never got finished."

Michael allowed the car to slow a little as they approached the Sun Voyager statue, an abstracted skeletal ship of entangled curves — prow, stern, flanks and oars, all interwoven in stainless steel — which peered out to sea from its ornamental dry dock.

Further on, the roadside soon offered rows of boxy modernist apartments with balconies, and half-built complexes, inert cranes towering over abandoned projects in the wake of the recent financial crash. Bright, beautiful futures, almost ready for advertising as dream homes, reduced to breezed-block and studded-wall half-ruins, bereft of glazing and roofs and life.

"So much unfinished building work," Michael said, eyes darting across the fast-moving landscape.

"They overstretched themselves," Geoffrey said. "*We* overstretched ourselves. I've been here long enough now to say that. We were a very simple country, with simple lives. A land of fishermen." He let out a loud sigh, which almost hissed like steam from a valve. "Then it became about banking, and money we did not own. People got stupid, and greedy. At least, some people did. Most people here are good people — salt of the earth, really — but it's always the hard-driven ones who drive the rest over a cliff."

"Like the Rotodyne, I guess," Michael noted. "So many great unfinished ideas, where people run out of time or money, or both. Things just fade away."

The dual carriageway — flanked by successions of half-built condominiums — funnelled into a road that looked like a motorway — the flatness and shade of tarmacadam, the barrier running the length of the central reservation, the ample areas, resembling hard shoulders, on either side — but comprising only one lane in each direction. Heading out of Reykjavík, everything filtered down to single-file; the human world narrowing, the natural world ahead ever-widening.

"That is most of Iceland's population behind us now," Geoffrey said, as they passed a tall cliff-face with a trickling waterfall, droplets transformed into falling diamonds by the sun. "Ahead, most of our land."

The sky and its thin clouds raced towards them at great speed, flipping across the silver bonnet, skipping onto the roof and into the rearview mirror.

Stanley went to say something, but a sudden sense of vulnerability overwhelmed him, as if to speak the words would lay too much on the line; to unpick the stitches of an unhealed wound. So he fell silent, and stared out as the strange country sped past: rowan bushes and heather, and small, thin trees rising along the pavement-free roads, where only the hardiest flowers emerged from the ancient dead rock of lava flows. Turf houses flashed by, their wooden windows and doors set within overgrown grass and moss walls. Beyond rickety fences, stout wild horses stood or cantered, with straggly blonde beards and windswept manes, side-parted forelocks, buck-toothed as they brayed and bared their gums at passing cars — Vikings, Michael thought, recast as four-legged animals. Every mile or so a white church with a pointed red roof slipped past, or a solitary farmstead, sometimes with a smoking chimney, but — just as frequently — homes that lay totally abandoned, as if all life just walked away. The landscape back- and- front-projected as all three watched in air-conditioned comfort.

The sun set in bands of yellow-to-red behind them, everywhere else a swathe of cool blue hues with a hint of violet where the outer reaches of the sunset melded with the darkest shades of the firmament. Every time Michael stepped from the climate-controlled car during his stay he sustained fresh shock at the contrast; the cold — for which he still braced — biting even harder than expected.

As such, Michael concluded, Iceland was about embracing then escaping the cold. The snow and ice, the frigid winds, were all — like a dip in an ice bath — invigorating in short bursts. They stoked the heart, got it pumping harder; bringing tingles to the fingertips and other extremities — unless exposed for too long, in which case it numbed. But the true pleasure came in the escape, the moment when that cold could be left behind: an opened and then blissfully closed door. For this night, that meant the limited protection of a zipped tent.

"Thank you, gentlemen," Stanley eventually said. "I'll probably never get back here. Not at my age. I just want to spend one more night with Alice."

Once parked they wandered along an ice-carved valley lit by the moon, the glacier up ahead, unseen around the corner, creaking and groaning as it forced itself inland in retreat; as described to him by Jóhanna, the thumb on an ice-hand the size of a city, gradually drawing its fingers inwards, up into a clenched fist.

Underfoot the ground felt like gravel, with the occasional puddle and ridge of ice. Either side, in the near-dark, stood the scree of moraines scattered by the bullying force of ice-age nature bulldozing its way past. Every now and then they'd see a giant boulder, once lifted up a steep incline with no apparent effort, and left there to half-dangle, as if Sisyphus awaited the energy for the next push.

Taking out his phone to check the time, to track how long the trek would take, Michael noticed the voicemail icon, and two missed calls from an overseas number. He instantly listened to the message, and heard Pippa's voice, but digitally distorted, cutting in and out. "Everything's okay" sounded perfectly clear, and bright in tone, but then words dissolved into blips and squeaks, before a possible sign-off about calling again. The signal would only deteriorate the further they walked, so he placed the phone back in his pocket.

"Everything okay?" Stanley asked.

"Seems to be," Michael said, becalmed at how, in amongst the distortion, he could hear only calmness.

Hardly the easiest terrain for two elderly men and one in middle-age, the distance from the parking space to the edge of the glacier remained just about manageable, and then, they would only venture onto the first shelf — the very edge of the vast Mýrdalsjökull, two-hundred square miles of deep, dense ice that simply subsumed the missing airplane. The trio shared constant stabilising grips, on forearms and upper-arms, when the terrain felt uneven or slippy. Geoffrey, the eldest, proved most accustomed to the cold; hardened to Iceland at its most raw. Each carried his own small tent in a backpack, while Michael — probably the least fit of the three, in terms of looking after his body and how quickly he struggled for breath — also transported a small gas stove and supplies. Younger and stronger, with a better sense of balance and less brittle bones, he felt a sense of shame at how unfit he seemed compared to the old men alongside him.

After a dark passage the landscape soon lit up, as, with a bend in the valley carefully traversed, the glacier heaved into view, ahead of a small lake of frozen meltwater trailing in its wake; the moon offering a soft spotlight, to gently illuminate. In the glassy water lay orphaned icebergs, withered away — bit by bit — by day, like decomposing white whales, as temperatures rose slightly above zero, and then set fast as solid ice again at night.

The three men stepped onto one such orphan, recently cast from the colossal mass up ahead, and then stepped carefully across onto the full body of the glacier, skidding slightly on their spike-less soles. Michael looked down, beyond his boring brown shoes, at the blue-black veined ice — bringing to mind deep-frozen flesh in a morgue; subcutaneously lined with basalt and olivine arteries — spewed by Iceland's ancient volcanoes, and covered with a fine powder of snow.

They found a plateau of ice and downed their luggage. For a moment they looked around in silent awe, breathing heavily after the trek, their breath wisping about their features.

"It's not the exact spot where the plane was found, obviously. But at least it's the same glacier," Geoffrey noted.

They pitched their tents in the dark, with the aid of a little artificial light; scrambling inside, once erected, to lay down sleeping bags and a few essentials. Seen from outside, the glows of torches within shone like the illuminated hearts of diaphanous sea creatures. While the elder men took their time, Michael moved on to building a small fire from scraps of kindling brought for a short, ceremonial burn, and some temporary warmth.

Eventually the three men sat around the campfire on small air cushions Geoffrey had packed for the occasion; his bony backside too brittle to withstand the firm, cold ground, with Stanley's similarly tender; their lungs just about able to find sufficient puff to inflate them. Their faces shone in the fire's licking yellow light, the flames flicking tiny combustible sparks into the dark, through a swirling fog of smoke and vapour.

"I brought this along, for the occasion," Geoffrey said, pulling a small bottle of whiskey from his pocket.

"I'm supposed to be giving that up," Michael said.

"One last snifter?" Stanley said, handing out the plastic beakers.

"We have lots to drink to," Geoffrey added. "Some wonderful people to remember. I'd also like to toast that strange and elusive woman — Charlotte Bradbury — who I think, indirectly, brought us all here."

"Really?" Stanley asked, poking at the fire with a small stick. "She was an interesting lady."

"Think about it. I met Michael at the dig in 1987, looking for the Spitfire I thought her Icelandic chap may have been lost in. She sent me her diaries, many years earlier. That dig is when I met Michael."

"It wasn't him though, was it?" Michael pointed out. "In the Spitfire."

"No, but I thought it might have been. It took me there. All because of Charlotte."

"Thinking back," Michael said to Geoffrey, "even though I didn't know it at the time, you also had the photos of *that* day — the day Alice's plane took off — that she had taken. I had no idea I was at London Airport that day, until you sent me copies of those photos. How strange that we were all there that day, at the same time."

"But we were all there often enough," Geoffrey said. "I was about to start work there, even if it didn't last. Your father was a pilot. And you were there most days, weren't you Stanley?"

"I took Alice quite a lot, yes. And Michael showed me those photos, a few years ago."

"I was there with Monty," Geoffrey said. "Tried to show him where we were moving to. It was hard seeing the photo of us together. Must have been four or five years later when Charlotte sent me all the stuff, out of the blue. I hadn't seen Monty since. Still haven't."

"It was hard seeing the photo of my mother and father, with me in the pram," Michael said after a sip from his plastic beaker. "I hardly even remember my father, he died when I was still so young. I want Ethan to remember me, yet I think of how those first three or four years disappear into nothing. You can maybe keep the bond that you build up, as some invisible link — at least I hope you can — but the memories, for the child, just vanish. It's so strange how the mind cannot seem to hold onto anything from those first few years."

"Monty was old enough to remember me," Geoffrey said, solemnly, "although I'm not sure he cares to recall too much."

"Well, I guess I started all this, then, if I've got those right?" Stanley said. "Charlotte cornered me in a café, back in '59. I gave her your details, didn't I, Geoffrey? She asked me for them, after I mentioned your name. That's how we all got connected."

"Ah, that's right. She'd written to me a couple of times, I think, but I never got around to replying. Odd lady," Geoffrey said, smiling. "But quite fascinating, in a wonderfully weird way. Stuck in a loop, she was. But talk about sheer bloodymindedness and never giving up. Would have made a good detective, with that obsessive nature. So yes, we met up in '59 too. At London Airport, just before Christmas, her carrying around this big old bag."

Stanley laughed at the memory of the bag. "I think she had her whole house in there. Maybe a small village."

Geoffrey, swirling the whisky around in his beaker, continued. "Wanted me to chase this ghost — the missing Icelandic Spitfire pilot, as you know. Viktor. Gave me lots of details about him, a few scraps of paper. Anyway, two or three years later, she just sends me a whole heap of stuff — letters, diaries, this fob watch he owned. Terrified to fly, she was, so until then she had never actually come here to see for herself."

"Ah, the fob watch," Michael interjected.

Geoffrey ploughed on. "Anyway, she didn't have long to live — cancer, she said — and just planned to finally get on a plane out here, after sending everything to me. Finally came to hunt him down, to see if he was alive, even though she'd been told his plane went down. I always thought she was a bit nutty, to be frank, but in an endearing way, so it made a certain sense, you see, that she'd finally do something so drastic. She made it to Akureyri, but died upon arrival. She had my name and address on her, so I was contacted by the authorities here."

"She had no family?" Stanley asked.

"A sister, that was it. Anyway, I was fairly certain that this Viktor chap had been shot down over the English Channel, as per the official reports, even if there were no witnesses to his actual demise. Pretty standard stuff. That's why I'd gone on that dig, and of course, met Michael."

Michael interrupted, albeit to confirm what he already knew; perhaps seeking clarification for Stanley. "That was your job, once — finding lost airmen after the war?"

"Indeed it was. I'd had his name on file, and it always stuck in my mind, given that he was Icelandic — I'd already been stationed out here during the war, and it was obviously rare to find such names in RAF documents. But until we met at the airport, it wasn't a special case on my part. So anyway, once I moved back over here, to Akureyri, I started hearing these stories about this pilot who'd gone to fly with the RAF and then, having been shot down a second time, lost his nerve and escaped to Norway via a trawler, and instead of going back to England, gave it all up and returned to Iceland, to live as a recluse with the wife and child he'd previously abandoned. Sounded more like legend than truth, to be honest."

"Wife and child?" Stanley asked. "She never mentioned that."

"She never knew anything about them, clearly — although reading her journals, there's a real sense of haziness about his past. He's a shadowy figure. Anyway, I asked around but back then no one seemed to know anything about who the man actually was — just some phantom, some myth. A great story — the man who everyone thought was dead but scrambled back to Scandinavia and made it back to Iceland."

"I remember it so clearly, her telling me about him," Stanley said. "When we had that coffee together at Piccadilly. How we'd both lost our loved ones. How they vanished, presumed lost at sea. How she and Viktor were going to be married. It surely wasn't the man you're talking about. His plane crashed."

"Well, that's the thing," Geoffrey said with a sense of drama. "A couple of years ago, I'm out after a snowstorm in Akureyri, and I see this old man who's slipped on the ice. Blood everywhere, you see — looked like he'd been hit on the head with a machete. May have had concussion, too. So, as they're about to take him in the ambulance I saw his scarred hands, and part of a tattoo, both possibly matching what Charlotte told me, and what she'd written about. The man's name is also Viktor, but he refuses to answer when I put it to him that he was indeed Hallfreðsson. But when I tried to find out more about him — no luck. Nothing."

"So was it him?" Stanley asked.

"Who knows?" Geoffrey said with a shrug. "It all seems to fit. But no hard proof."

"This is perfect for the book," Michael said.

"Maybe one day you'll finally finish it?" Stanley suggested.

"Yeah, one fine day," Michael said, sounding unconvinced.

"So, tell us more about Ólafur," Michael asked Geoffrey, as the fire withered to smouldering embers. "How did you meet? It can't have been easy, back then, what with attitudes not what they are now."

"It's rather crazy — people might not understand — the utterly thrilling chaos of war, even in a place like Iceland. Heightens the emotions. We didn't even speak, you see — not that first time, and hardly at all. Just sounds. It was animalistic, but also spiritual. It was almost a dream, until it was clear that his father, who also didn't speak English, was going to kill me. I don't think he knew for sure what was happening, but he must have felt I was trying to corrupt his boy. At least he didn't kick Ólafur out of the house, or worse, as he was still there all those decades later."

"That's something to be grateful for," Stanley said.

"My heart first felt love out here, with Ólafur. It was so … *intense*. I hadn't quite trusted my sexuality and my … urges, I suppose, but that confirmed it for me, you see. Even now, it's strange to talk about it. It was something to bottle up. It ended so messily — the first time — that I never dared try again when back home. I suppressed a lot, locked myself fully in the closet, as it were. Not for one moment did I expect to find and reunite with Ólafur again, when I moved back here. It was more out of hope than expectation. I was coming back to Akureyri, not him."

"How did it feel, getting married to your wife after the war?" Stanley asked.

"Well, Dorothy had no idea about my past, you see, and, you know, that kind of thing. I feel terrible for how I treated her, how I lived a double life. But, well … that was what one did back then — got married, lived a lie." He sighed. "I also just found her increasingly unbearable. She became such hard work. She wasn't a bad person or anything, just not someone I could get along with, especially when I felt like a fraud. Maybe she picked up on that too — my distance."

"But you also left your son. I can't imagine doing that," Michael said, then realised how critical he sounded. "I don't mean to judge."

"I know. It's hard to explain. I felt so much guilt. Still do. But equally, I wasn't going to be good for him. Me staying with Dorothy and getting more and more depressed wasn't going to be good for him. You try and do what's best, you see, even if nothing can be best for everyone. At that point, I felt it would be best if I left, let them get on with it. Just send them money. She was smothering him, but it wasn't helping him to have me confusing things by trying to make him stronger, more self sufficient. At least that's what I told myself."

"So you just left?" Michael asked.

"It was never quite that clinical. I did try to make contact, various times, with cards and presents, but she kept everything from him, it seems. So anyway, in time I figured it was easier to just disappear, stay gone. You know how it is — you want to contact someone, and time passes, and then it reaches a point where it feels like too much time has passed. And all that happens is that more time passes, and it only gets worse. You can't just casually check back in again. Every day means an extra day to add to the betrayal. And I had no idea if he wanted to see me, how he would be. Dorothy would have poisoned him against me, even if I understand why she would hate me. She had every right to."

"And she died, of course," Michael noted.

"Yes, a decade or so ago. I got some notification, via my solicitor."

"Not from Monty?" Michael asked

"No."

Stanley chimed in. "You didn't go to the funeral?"

"I was living here. I didn't even send anything. It didn't feel … appropriate."

"Well, funnily enough, I know where Monty lives," Michael said. "I didn't quite put two and two together initially. But he has the fob watch you sent me. He fixes clocks and watches — found him in an old Yellow Pages I had. Still lives in the house you left, it seems — right near Heathrow. I didn't want to say anything to you, once I figured it out, but I sent him Viktor's watch to fix. It seemed fitting."

"Really?" Geoffrey said, shifting like a man half his age to a more upright posture. "How is he?"

"I don't really know. We only corresponded via letter. I don't think he even has the internet. I didn't say much, just asked for a quotation for the work and he sent one. I sent him the watch. Didn't mention that I knew you. Wasn't my place to do that."

"I wouldn't even know him if I saw him," Geoffrey said, his eyes blinking hard in the cold.

"Go and see him, Geoffrey," Stanley said, softly.

"It's too late."

"While you're s-still alive, it's never too late," Stanley said.

Michael added, "There are still seats on the flight back tomorrow, I checked earlier. Come back with us two. You have some luggage packed already, and you told me yesterday that your passport lives in your suitcase. You know where he is, and the house clearly hasn't moved from the airport."

Geoffrey wiped a small icy tear from one eye. "Maybe," he said.

The trio sat in silence, gazing at the majestic scenery. Michael pondered the constant *memento mori* of life in Iceland: in the shadows of mountains packed to the rafters with nature's greatest tinderbox: many megatons of thermal energy, thousands of times the size of atomic bombs; the ground liable at some moment to violently split in outpourings of molten rock, to leave the sky darkened and the land polluted for days, weeks, months, even years. Eyjafjallajökull had quietened down, and beyond aviation disruption, had not had the global effects of Laki, which darkened the entire world in 1783. Yet Katla, another major Icelandic volcano, remained overdue. He recognised the long-bred tradition here of finding sustenance in the wilderness, in a landscape that yields very little to consume, with few crops, few trees. And then, the rich history of men and fishing, out in the island's turbulent waters, with storms and swells and terrifying squalls all braved just to *continue* life, and provide for the families back home, whilst at the exact same time seriously risking it. It felt like a kind of insanity, and yet based on something Jóhanna said on their first meeting, life on a knife-edge — life *felt* — can be like meditating at the cliff edge to sharpen the mind. Life in

Iceland could only ever be at the edge, not stuck in the centre. No one can live in the middle; life can only survive at the low-level perimeter, jutted up against the wild seas, threatened from behind by volcanos and avalanches, from below by the heave and shift of tectonic plates, from above by snow and sleet and gale-force winds. It left nowhere totally safe to turn, so you had to make the best of whatever happened, while you still could.

Then, a sudden, overwhelming feeling of futility, contradicting the brief moment of enlightenment; a sense that his life was totally and utterly wrong. He took a deep breath. "What the fuck am I doing?" he said, breaking the silence. "My boy. My life. I'm running. But I'm running *from* something … and *towards* nothing. What's the … point in that?"

"How so?" Stanley asked, slightly taken aback at the sudden outburst.

"I've lost my sense of home," Michael said, shaking his head. "I don't even know where home is anymore. I'm here, in Iceland, and with you guys, because I have no home. No proper home, at least. But … it's not just about being out of the place that *was* my home — the family house we all shared. It's … it's that Ethan is my home, Pippa was my sense of home." He let out an ironic laugh. "She got on my nerves, and I didn't recognise what we were sharing at the end as 'love'", he said, moving his fingers by mere fractions to shape the air quotes, "but, I don't know — she was still my sense of home. Every day I looked at her, more than I ever looked at myself, and yet the image of her made more sense as a reflection. My own reflection no longer looks right … I'm sorry, I'm babbling."

"Things end," Geoffrey said. "They run their course. You need to find a new way of living. I'm not one to offer advice on fatherhood, clearly, but I've had relationships end in different ways. Life moves on. Is nothing happening with that girl you saw — Jóhanna?"

"No, she's sweet, and kind. And half my age."

"At least you didn't start driving a Ferrari," Stanley noted drily.

"As if I could afford one," Michael said, and all three men laughed. "On Pippa, this new guy can have her. Really. But the pain of not seeing Ethan is just too much to even contemplate, so I just bury it. I wanted to get away from the pain of not seeing him, but I'm just further away, and the pain is just as bad, maybe even worse," he paused, looking up at the heavens. "I have moments where I forget, because I'm not in my old routine — the place where he'd fit into my daily life, y'know? So far away, his absence cannot be measured against those reminders. I'm not having to look at his untouched toys gathering dust, at his drawings stuck on the fridge, the little plastic table and chair I bought for him, where he'd do those drawings and make his Lego — all those kinds of things. But instead I ended up here, wandering around, lost."

"Well, we're heading back tomorrow. What's stopping you from winning back some access?" Stanley asked. "Give me a reason?"

Michael sighed, deep and jagged and defeated, shaking his head. "I don't really know. Maybe it's Pippa's boyfriend's fault. Douglas. Some architect. I could see Ethan until he moved in to our old house."

"Was he the only issue?"

"Well … as you guys know, I did — still *do* — drink too much at times, but when Ethan was with me it was only after he'd gone to bed. And never to excess. Just to help me sleep. I don't think I was too irresponsible. I bought five smoke alarms, one for each room and the landing, to make sure I woke up if there was a fire."

Geoffrey laughed. "*Five?* Sorry. It's not funny."

"No, it *is*," Michael said. "In its stupid way, it *is*. It started years earlier — the drinking, I mean. Of an evening I had to drink to take the edge off, and then drink more to get to sleep."

"Been there, as they say," Stanley nodded.

"Indeed," Geoffrey added.

"But you guys knew when to stop. Anyway, I don't know if he — this Douglas bloke — put her up to it. I just don't think it's that simple. She's not that easily manipulated. She's not stupid, or weak. And she's not even spiteful — at least, she wasn't. But maybe he just backed her up on it, egged her on."

"You think he has that much influence?" Stanley asked.

"If he insisted that Ethan should see his father, maybe all this would be different. I don't know. Or maybe it's the solicitors. They stir shit up, don't they?" Michael nodded, then answered his own question. "I know they do. I don't think I was excessively negligent, but it's easy to twist and exaggerate these things. Maybe in the stories she tells I drink way more than I really do, that I'm a falling-down drunk, that kind of thing. You know how it is, if someone is listing just your bad qualities it paints a certain kind of picture. It's easy to make someone look bad if people just give edited lowlights, a litany of only the things they got wrong. Anyone can look bad, a two-dimensional villain. Then, people — friends, new lovers, family, whoever — just back people up on those gripes, as if they're doing the proper thing. You can end up sounding like a totally terrible person, but it's all an illusion. I just like a few drinks, that's all."

"Have you ever managed to stop drinking?" Stanley asked. "Not that we've helped by forcing you to have another."

"This is just a small one, and there's no way out here to get more — unless I take to drinking the lighter fuel. I have times when I'm doing okay, cutting back, but then something really shitty happens and I can't resist. I need it to dampen the pain, shut off my mind. Flood it with alcohol. The cliché is that you 'drown your sorrows', isn't it? — but I guess it's more like dampening the sound, like putting it all underwater — you can't hear the nagging voices in your head clearly anymore, the thoughts, the memories. It muffles them. It muffles those voices. You can't drown them for good, of course — they pop back up. But you can hold them underwater to suffocate them for a while, to make them speak in bubbles, to mute the message."

"Sounds like you have all the motivation you need to stop," Geoffrey said. "I messed up my relationship with Monty. I'm old now. Even if I come back to see him tomorrow with you guys, as you suggest, I'm a very old man now. You have time. Ethan is still so young."

"I just can't believe she's being such a bitch," Michael said, anger spiking at the thought — suddenly fresh and alive — of being kept from Ethan.

"Now now," Stanley said, tutting. "No need for that language. That won't get you anywhere."

"I'm not saying she *is* a bitch. Just that she's acting like one. She'll have said far worse about me, believe me."

"Look, she is in pain," Geoffrey said.

"She *is* a pain," Michael said. "She's *causing* pain."

"Because she is *in* pain," Geoffrey emphasised. Stanley nodded his ascent.

"Why can't you both just say she's being a bitch?" Michael asked, shaking his head.

"Because we don't know her," Geoffrey stated. "And as I said, it sounds like she is in pain. She's acting out."

Out of nowhere, as if months of pent-up frustration had come surging up into the space behind his eyes, Michael began to cry. Tears stung, running cold, colder, down his face, where they froze on his cheeks and contracted against his skin; his body convulsing with shivers, his teeth chattering between sobs, as the raw emotions and the weather speared throughout his insides.

"Sorry," he spluttered, regathering some composure; as if there existed a time limit on men's tears, especially in the company of other men, and he'd already exceeded it.

"You loved her, once," Stanley said. "She cannot have changed that much. It is just where we are at in our lives that changes, mostly. But the pain she is feeling now must be new, it is not what she felt years ago. Maybe she had no pain back then. Maybe together you kept each other's pain away."

"She's moved on. She's with Douglas. I don't think she's in pain. Not from me, anyway. But this isn't just hurting me. It must be hurting Ethan."

"She will come around," Geoffrey said, his hand placed gently on Michael's forearm. "She will see more clearly when she is feeling less pain."

"I don't know. How can you say that?"

"If you want me to be truly honest," Geoffrey said, angling his head a little, "I can't. I can't say for sure what she will do, as I don't know her. It is just my reading of the situation. If she acted like this throughout your marriage she may just be a troubled soul, constantly in pain, always lashing out, unstable — that kind of thing, you see. But I think she is probably not such a bad person, from what you have said. To have been married so long. She'll wake up to it, sooner or later."

Michael sighed. "She has Douglas, though. She seems happy."

"But he is new," Geoffrey said. "He is a sticking plaster. A bandage. A way to avoid what is going on. It may last, of course. But it's early."

"But how can she be in pain when *she* chose to end things," Michael said, glancing up at the moon, at the reflected light it shared.

"But that does not mean she will not feel pain," Stanley interjected.

"I guess not," Michael acknowledged. He took a deep breath, which he exhaled as one long sigh that blew flecks of snow from about his mouth as the vapour spooled out. "She left a voicemail earlier. Maybe it sounded conciliatory. It was hard to tell, as the message kept breaking up."

"So there you go," Stanley said, with Geoffrey nodding in agreement. "She may be planning to resolve things."

"I just don't know if I trust her anymore. Anyway, I feel like I should be paying you two," Michael said, laughing on an outbreath. "This could be a new form of treatment — glacial therapy."

"Well, we are quite slow," Geoffrey said with a smile.

Stanley stood up. "Look, here's what we'll do," as he topped up his plastic beaker, and filled Michael's empty beaker halfway. "Take one sip, and think about Ethan. Think about how much he means to you, how you need to see him."

Michael, standing up alongside Stanley, followed the instructions.

"Right," Stanley said, pointing. "Now throw the cup into the abyss. Down there."

Michael looked askance at Stanley, but then the penny dropped. Geoffrey struggled to a stand to join the pair — Michael offered a helping hand — looking down at a chasm of ice that trailed off into the darkness. Michael took a swig then drew back his arm and flung the little beaker towards the icy sprawl, a fine spray of fast-freezing whiskey flickering as it fell.

"Now," Stanley said, a gloved hand on Michael's shoulder, "when you think about giving up, you can envision this moment. Remember how far away you feel, how lost you said you feel. Being far from home, miles from your s-son. But remember too, that the beauty of life that doesn't need alcohol. Indeed, alcohol just dulls the senses, and numbs the pain, and forces us to avoid the paths that lead to pleasure — or to contentment, and acceptance. At times I drank to forget Alice, believe me, and what a bloody dumb thing to do that was. Why would I want to forget her? I don't think there's a life of pleasure out there for anyone, but you can find inner peace."

"I found it, out here," Geoffrey added. "With Ólafur, and then after he passed away, on my own. Anyway, time for bed, methinks. I have a big day tomorrow, if I'm going to be getting on a plane with you two."

* * *

Wind whistling and snow lightly falling from the sky to mix with flakes whipped up off the icy floor, Michael clambered bleary-eyed from his tent, only to be greeted by the other two men. He looked at his watch.

"Secret four a.m. meeting?" he asked.

"Bladders and prostates," Stanley said.

"Indeed. I guess I have some catching up to do."

"Takes me an age to get going," Geoffrey said. "Then even longer to stop."

"The danger here," Michael noted, "is freezing in place, I guess. Ideally you want to get it done as soon as possible. In and out. Or rather, out and in."

"Not the best place on the body to get frostbite," Stanley noted. "Not that I have experience."

"Well, its best days are behind it," Geoffrey said, sadly. "I could be rid of the useless thing — just have a hole connected to a catheter or something. It's all it's good for, at my age."

"But for now, be careful," Stanley said to Michael, as the younger man, back turned, wandered a distance deemed sufficiently private. "You also don't want to be stuck to the ice from a yellow s-stalagmite," Stanley added, his teeth chattering.

"It's more orange these days. A brownish orange. Maybe it's just pure whisky."

"But not for much longer," Stanley said. "You can do this, Michael."

"Take a pee?"

"No, get off the booze. Stay off it. We can help. If you ever need support, we'll be on the other end of the phone. I've been there. We've both been there. I've helped other people before."

"All this talking isn't exactly helping me right now," Michael said. "Never been one for urinal conversations. Even a urinal as uniquely beautiful as this one."

"Well, best head back to the tents, then," Stanley said. "To sleep, until nature calls again. So, back here at 4:30am, then?"

"If I can last that long," Geoffrey added. Then he laughed. "It might be easier just to be fully incontinent. Then you just let it go."

"Not sure it would be so pleasant in these temperatures."

"No, you wouldn't want that freezing around your middle."

"Are you two going back to bed or not?" Michael called, still trying to get started.

"Oh, wait. Look!" Stanley said, pointing upwards.

Up ahead, the night sky began to flicker. At first a gentle wash of pale green, gradually building to a sky-bound swirl of oceanic colour.

"The aurora!" Geoffrey exclaimed, excited to show his guests something he himself had seen hundreds of times before.

"Oh, wow," Michael said, lulled by their movement, postponing his attempts and zipping his fly.

"Have you seen them before?" Geoffrey asked the two men.

"Only in Reykjavík," Michael said, "but there was a fair amount of light pollution. They looked very pale, almost white."

"No, never," Stanley added.

"Well, they are nice and strong tonight. Stronger than usual."

At times the colours felt close enough to almost touch, just beyond the summit of the glacier and the edges of the valley, until their true distance — enmeshed in mesosphere, thermosphere, exosphere — lay starkly revealed, as earthly clouds floated past, small and humble by contrast, moving quickly against the colossal backdrop of *the very edge of space*, where particles from the solar winds exploded by their billions against the planet's magnetic field.

Michael stared upwards, at first following the activity with just his eyes, before moving his head to take it all in, as it all rose and fell — what he'd later compare with colossal silk scarves, dyed with the fine-ground dust of precious and semiprecious gemstones, swept and swished, swirled and swayed, in flows across the sky: emerald, jade, peridot, turquoise, alexandrite and aquamarine, mostly — the gamut of the blue-green spectrum — but with the occasional warmer hints of amethyst, carnelian and even the fleeting full-red flush of ruby. All washed together in drifts and turns, spins and cyclones — delicately feathered light, flickering and sparkling just for them.

"They say the norðurljós — the northern lights — dance," Geoffrey said, gently moving his hand back and forth as if conducting a waltz. And that's precisely what they saw: celestial choreography, as two ghostly giants trailed those distinctive silk scarves across the firmament.

Then the trio fell quiet, standing in silence, awed beneath the display; a comfortable peace, with no need to hurry in and break it. To do so would mirror taking a knife to a Rembrandt or a Titian, to slice up its uncanny beauty. Where words were so often forced into spaces, they granted each other tacit permission for silence.

Stanley stared at clouds of colour reflected on the icy meltwater lake, and in more muted form, on the glacial surface. "Bury me here," he said, emphatically.

"What … *now?*" Michael quipped.

"No, at least wait until I've died. But seriously — I really mean this. S-someone, bring me back, then. S-scatter me here. I want to be here, if Alice isn't found before I die. It's so beautiful and peaceful. I'll be dust, somewhere close to her."

* * *

The next morning, back at the car, Michael's phone lit up with missed texts and voicemails. Given their content, the flight home could not come quickly enough; the plane painfully slow, as if he needed Concorde to return from retirement, to speed him supersonically to Heathrow.

* * *

The sparkling airport terminal, with its walls of floor-to-ceiling glass, bristled with irregular motion — paths crisscrossing, haphazard trolley-wheels wobbling and squeaking, sharp-heeled shoes clacking on the richly polished marble. Silver columns held a high roof and half-cut mezzanines; rows of hundreds of circular light wells, with bulbs, rather than sunlight, filling each cylinder. Banks of yellow signage, hanging just above head height. A shiny silver balustrade to allow the travellers, including Stanley, Michael and Geoffrey, to funnel past, like red-carpet guests against the backdrop of bus-sized typography: *International Arrivals*. The old Europa Building, which became Terminal Two, had only recently been demolished, with the new Queen's Terminal under construction, so they exited via a different set of elevated walkways.

And there, across the concourse, stood Ethan.

Michael's heart felt strangely heavy, as if swelling with all the blood in his body. The boy — recognisably his son — looked taller, a bit more angular and recently rid of the last vestiges of baby weight, even in just a few weeks — though it felt like months — since he spied on his son outside the school. It looked like he'd graduated from toddler to proportional child. Pippa saw her ex-husband across the divide, and the pair exchanged knowing nods and half-smiles; but Michael kept his distance, not wanting to rush at his son, despite wanting *desperately* to rush at his son. Ethan just stood there, between the two, awkward and confused; unsure of what to do at the sight of his father, whom he hadn't seen since the previous autumn. Michael dropped to his knees, to the boy's level, but Ethan turned around, to look at his mother, who hung back.

"Go on," Pippa said, and her son — their son — walked forward with some trepidation. Perhaps Ethan understood the significance in the moment he gave himself up to Michael's open arms, but *he* wasn't the one crying. Michael clung to his child with tears streaming down his face, that, as he tried to hold it all in, contorted into a joyous silent inner howl; Pippa, too, crying softly from a safe distance, as Stanley and Geoffrey stood to one side, the latter holding back tears of his own. Ethan could feel his father's body shake; his own happiness of seeing his father again mixed with confusion at the sadness all around him, at his father's tremors.

He pulled away from his father's embrace, in order to look closely at his face, confused by its sadness. The little boy then pressed his thumbs softly into his father's cheeks.

"Wipe your eyes, Daddy," he said with a benign smile. "There's no need to cry."

Epilogue

2020

Stanley couldn't remember the exact last time he'd unpacked the projector and unfurled its accompanying off-white screen; only that when he had — some decades ago — it had not gone at all well. He recalled that footage: Alice, weirdly over-tall — like the *Attack of the 50-Foot Woman* — towering ludicrously over the houses of Bekonscot model village, before — out of nowhere — the screen glowed at the centre with a growing, pulsing yellow-orange orb, from which tiny hot-bubbled black circles quickly grew and separated — like cells dividing — to fill the space, until one giant black circle engulfed the reel; at which point he noticed the smell of acrid smoke and burning celluloid, as he turned to see the first hints of flames licking from the jammed reel. His life — at least, part of it — going up in smoke.

As much as he yearned to view them, the rest of the films lay untouched in their original yellow Ciné-Kodak Kodachrome boxes, safe within a shoebox; memories he wanted to let breathe again — to re-enter his mind, to let dance past the dust — but whose exposure to the light — in this case, the burning-hot projector lamp — could instantly turn delicate moving images into nothing more than a clump of black camphor and nitrocellulose, all life removed from its memory, all recorded past destroyed. Once gone — gone forever.

But *now* … his life had all but burnt away anyway. Now he ran mostly on fumes, trying to glimpse his past at the edges of the blurring frame as the sprawling mass of darkness expanded.

The antiquated Kodak Brownie projector, when tucked up within its protective shell, could easily be mistaken for a small suitcase with rounded corners; it even had what resembled a luggage handle. On the table in the darkened front room, Stanley unclipped the metal frontage and, with tender care, lifted it away, revealing the inner workings. These innards looked deceptively simple, too, until the reels were clipped in place, at which point it took on its recognisable form; almost squid-like in its flow. He eased the empty receiving spool onto its small housing nub, then turned to the shoebox containing the films. He lifted the small, faded yellow box marked *Wedding Day, 1956* — Alice's beautiful script a bittersweet detail — and carefully removed the lid. In unsteady hands he took the reel, and clipped it onto the other nub on the machine. Threading it through the central gripping device and then into the narrow aperture in front of the lamp and behind the lens had been a finicky process at the best of times, but his dumb fingers and gnarled thumbs, complete with deadened nerve tips, numbly grappled with the fine film; no dexterity, no real sense of touch in coarse fingertips. After all the years of abstinence — awaiting some point in time where he knew he'd take the risk — he didn't want to damage the film with clumsiness, nor to buckle or crack the delicate celluloid. He felt stabs of stress, twitching at his muscles and tendons, until a sense of calming patience washed over him — the sense of how little time, in the grand scheme of things, this fiddling would take, and how he would gladly use up whatever time he had left in the process anyway. And so he persevered, gently, stoically, until the movie sat correctly loaded. His hand hovered over the *On* switch, but something didn't feel right. He had something to do first.

With hips grinding, and a cough rattling, he pulled himself up the stairs, and into the bedroom. He opened the stiff doors of the dark-oak wardrobe, and ran his hand over the hunched shoulders of hangers, feeling one suit-jacket after another. He stopped at the single-breasted silver-grey suit, a one-point pocket-square handkerchief still displaying its half-diamond of silk from the breast opening. He lifted out the hanger, laid the suit tenderly on the bed, as if lowering down a fragile, long-lost friend. The buttonhole sat empty, the boutonnière of a simple yellow carnation taken and dried out by Alice in a book after their honeymoon; a book somewhere in the loft, out of reach.

The thought of that carnation — of its particular yellow hue — took him back to the honeymoon — to that hot, airless bedroom — in a recollection of how quickly he got undressed; Alice confidently removing his braces as they kissed, whilst he fumbled — even though his fingers back then were nimble and dextrous: nerves and excitement the problem — for the zip on the back of her wedding gown. All these years later, and eager to be inside that suit once more — as if he could inhabit a different space once within, a different *time*. It took an age to strip down to his Y-fronts. In the dimness of the light fanning from the hallway he looked down at his legs: his kneecaps harsh and protruding through fine, sagging skin whose whiteness, and strange hairlessness — and whose spread of liver spots and varicose veins — he had rarely taken the time to study. It all just crept up on him; crept *over* him. He recalled standing in just his underpants in Tenerife, and how he glanced down at the youthful vigour of his slender yet well-defined quads. How can these even be the same legs? Those sinewy calves and thighs of his youth — which enabled him to lift her, in her delicate silk bra and knickers, with white stockings and a blue garter, onto the bed with a sudden surge of confidence and authority — now stood emaciated and shapeless, barely able to keep his own ailing body off the ground.

He took from the wardrobe a white shirt, slipped his thin arms into its loose sleeves, pulled its starched collar around his wiry neck — eliciting more coughs, more deep discomfort — and fumbled with the top button. The shirt still fit, but he no longer filled its contours on the upper half, his mass seeping lower; the sagging of his belly pulling the lowest buttons tight against his skin, and away from scrawny shoulders. He uncoiled the thin blue silk tie from the hanger's crook and wrapped it around the back of his neck, tucking it under the raised collar; one side longer than the other as it draped down his shirt front, before starting to tie a Windsor knot. In more recent times it had been the black suit, the black tie, the respectful garb of eulogies and last goodbyes. One by one the world had deserted him; Alice the first to depart.

From the foot of the wardrobe he fished out his boxed-up pair of black Oxfords, only ever worn that single day; the soles marked with the smallest scuffs and scratches from the few places walked. He slumped onto the edge of the bed and slipped the shoes over his socks; the leather still coarse and ungiving, his bony feet uneasy in such confinement, the bunion on his left big toe awkward against its instep. He recalled how they dug in that special day, too, with their stiff newness.

He walked to the bathroom — shoes digging and chafing — and pulled the light cord. Under the harsh glare he looked into the mirror. A vision of himself fifty years earlier, looking into another mirror, flashed across the glass — in these very same clothes; so vivid that he had to blink. Not a sought-after memory, with frustrating vagueness, but an aftershock, momentarily sharp and crisp and real — illusorily rich on the retina — before, without realising, he saw only his face *now*, lined with time, creased and cursed, badgered and battered, scuffed and mocked. How did that image — a subconscious surge — come so quickly, and leave just as fast?

What else lay stored deep within the recesses of his mind? Did it *all* still reside there, just tantalisingly inaccessible, bar the occasional glimpse? Did it just need the correct prod to reanimate it? Did it exist in grey matter whose connections seemed to lay permanently uncoupled?

He took hold of the loose Windsor knot dangling against his chest and eased it up towards his Adam's apple, whilst pulling down on the thin end of the tie, until it sat as faultlessly positioned and perfectly weighted as in 1956. Then, the collar straightened, its corners caressed. Next he took a comb and ran it through his hair; this time remembering — a selected recollection, which lacked stark definition — running Brylcreem through his forelocks and, with the widely-spaced end of the comb, getting a quiff to stand proudly upright; before pushing down ever so lightly on its peak, and at its sides, to bond it together, like compressing a sandcastle. Now, he simply combed thin hair back across the sides of his head, and with his hand smoothed the fine wisps that covered the back half of his pate.

One more tweak of the tie knot — not really adjusting it, more a nervous tic that twisted it one way, and then back to how it already sat — and he felt ready.

Amid an off-focus fuzz, Alice — dearest Alice — emerged, as recognisable in a blur as in the sharpest of delineations. But *of course* he would know her at a distance, in a fog, out of focus: the times spent face to face, too near to see clearly; the times spent far away, too great to discern details, where they still knew each other by shape, by movement. He knew her smell, with eyes closed; her skin, by touch alone.

He felt breathless, cut to the core. Actual pain, sparking a violent cough, that caught and rasped. He loosened his tie, but the discomfort lingered. Photographs of the day, of her half-veiled face, were framed on the mantlepiece, the images part of his everyday life for decades; but as she moved to make eye-contact with the camera — with *him*, now, as the focus adjusted to its sharpest, to capture every last twinkle on her cornea — it felt like a punch to the solar plexus. Overwhelmed, he had to look away. At first glance he felt his heart swell with euphoria, and then — inflated, as if to nothing but a bloated bowl of nerve-endings — felt its searing ache, as if doubling in size only to be pierced full of bigger holes, to pour out greater pain.

Yet, of course, he swiftly looked back at the screen. He needed to see it, see his wife, in the process of becoming his wife. He trembled more nervously than at any point that day; feverish, as he sought to bid her a last farewell. He took a deep breath, coughed, and steadied himself. Light flickered in time with the projector's whirrs, as the frame panned across his in-laws' living room. Alice's older brother Reginald — a mere novice — worked Stanley's ciné camera, tasked with filming the day; catching sight of Virginia and William fussing either side of their daughter, as more distant relatives — some whose names he could no longer recollect, as well as Harold, her uncle — sat stiffly on the sofa and chairs, sipping tea. While Harold often came across as abrasive, Stanley could never understand why Alice didn't like the man. Indeed, he had very kindly offered the use of his wonderful new Jaguar for the ceremony, and she refused without explanation.

Such a tragedy, Stanley recalled, that just two years later Harold ended up as a spoon-fed quadriplegic, after flipping the vehicle into a ditch after speeding down a country lane.

Stanley sighed at the muted hues of the film — the vividness of reality at one remove, lost in translation from life to screen. Bleached colours, robbed of their lustre, but *colours all the same*, travelling to him from an era of predominantly black-and-white photography. Those photos had robbed his memory of some of the truth — of his own increasingly vague first-person recollections — even if they captured likenesses, and moods, and smiles; the films gave a fuller, fresher picture, of things he never got to see on the day itself.

Clearly not a particularly skilled or steady cinematographer, Reginald did an adequate job. Stanley knew he couldn't film his own wedding, and Alice's older brother seemed the obvious person to ask. Now, so many decades later, Stanley wondered if he should have made a different selection, opting for someone with more sensitivity to the equipment, a greater feel for the art of encapsulating a world that moved. Would the occasion have been better preserved? What had Reggie missed? It could still only be the same day, of course — the day was the day, was the day — but a different pair of eyes behind the lens could have captured other aspects of its ceremonies: an alternate perspective, a different reality; one that perhaps better chimed with Stanley's own memories. Instead, there were bursts of film where nothing happened: Alice's grandparents standing still, upright and rigid as the camera drew closer, as if posing for a still photograph, and Harold pulling a silly face; eating away a great chunk of precious frames, that moved fast through the camera as they stood inert, as if awaiting a flash. Then, brutal jump-cuts to something else, the few priceless — ever more priceless — minutes of film, eked out with a fraction here and a fraction there, over several hours. With just two five-minute reels, Reggie lacked the option to film everything and then edit it all later; in essence, edited in advance — by guessing the moments worth recording, before the action even took place. Reggie had to depress the trigger and hope that *things happened*: people reacted, joy unfolded. Instead, sometimes nothing; sometimes guests rendered as waxwork dummies.

All sound remained lost, too; never even captured, due to the limitations of the technology; allowed to wisp away into the ether, evanescing into nothing. Not that he wanted to hear himself, a jumble of nerves, stammer through his speech; although Alice looked at him with such pride and love when he got to the end.

Even in silence, muted by the lack of a microphone on the camera and a speaker on the projector, he could see himself stutter, as Reggie panned onto his face, his mouth, and taut lips, fighting to conjure the shapes of speech. He longed with all his being to hear her young voice — the delight in her words, the timbre of her laughter. There were photos, and these ciné films; but her voice had gone, even from his memory. He recalled things she had said, but with an uncertain sense of their sound. Oh to hear her say *I love you,* as applause rang round.

Instead, he watched a soundless wedding, marvelling at his beautiful bride, in the sumptuous dress with its fine lacework above a sweetheart neckline, a delicate lattice that ran across her upper chest and down her shoulders, passing over the white straps of the silk bodice. He'd called her his princess, and she looked it — every inch — in that gown.

In a brief scene at the reception he could even recall their conversation, prompted by his actions on screen — asking, with gestures, what happened to the silk white gloves she'd been so keen to wear; and how she'd said that she'd changed her mind, and held out her hand with its wedding and engagement rings, in her desire to have them on full display.

The happy couple — and boy, were they happy — beaming at the camera.

Her silent smile divided him in two — sliced right through his core; again a mix of utter pleasure and total despair, for which 'bittersweet' felt too feeble a term. The joy of her smiling *at him,* and the beauty of that smile; and the grief of the loss of that time, her smile, their youth.

And of *her,* and their future.

Alice, lost in time; lost with time that no longer existed. Time that blew far and wide and away on the wind, like the confetti outside the church door scattering on the summer breeze.

* * *

The way old men fight the urge to cry. The deep breath. The discreet wipe of the eye, the disguised rub of the nose. The blinking — faster and faster. Stanley held it together like a blocked steel kettle approaching boiling point, rattling but unbreached. The quivering chin; the trembling cheeks; the rapid thrum of loose neck skin flickering over the awkward jut of the bobbing Adam's apple. The more it built up the greater the release. Blowing out cheeks. Biting lip. Squeezing eyelids tight. In the week since viewing the ciné films he could feel the internal collapse, like prolapsing organs. He cried when viewing the films, and now cried again; but hoarse and dehydrated, with tears barely able to flow.

April 2020, and the end felt close. Further weight loss; bone increasingly prevalent through skin. For a year or two, the bile in the bowels, the toxic sludge. Prostate pulses, searing pain centred between his aching hips, worse when he crouched on the toilet. Post-urinal drip, a cold yellow tear wept down a thin inner thigh; at other times, piss like treacle, orange and thick, after an age to get going. Now, the clear red ripple of blood in his pee.

He was not in a good way, and he knew it — made worse by the new cutting cough; an increasing temperature sending him giddy with feverish dreams; the sudden loss of smell, as if his senses were shutting down, one by one. The asthma, controlled for so long, further blocking the supply of air. Alone at home, he could call for medical attention, but what good would that do? Why prolong the inevitable?

He felt a dart of dampness down his cheek, belatedly fallen — saltily, with a tang into the corner of his mouth — as the sun streamed through the window, harsh into his watery eyes.

He lay down wearily on the sofa, felt his eyelids snap shut; closing them as if for the last time.

Moments later he found himself walking in a daze to answer the front door, and — not at all taken aback, not even a pause of surprise — he opened it to Alice, beaming at him, resplendent in her lace-topped wedding dress. She stepped into the hallway — his sense of smell returning, to register the long-locked memory of bottled Bond Street — and she led him by the hand — her soft, soft hand — down the hallway, past the Ravilious painting and into the living room, safely back to the sofa. Her warm fine fingers, like a muscle memory, interlocked as five soft dovetail joints designed for a perfect fit.

He lay back down, and she sat on the floor beside him. They shared a smile — and a deep, loving stare — and then, as if just for a short nap, he closed his eyes. With the faintest moist warmth he felt the pressure of two soft lips, pressing gently against his forehead, until, without even noticing, all of his senses slipped silently away.

Acknowledgements and Thanks

Mairead Mooney, Jules Jackson, Jill Adamiecki, Kristján Már, Ólafur Haukur Tómasson, Hinrik Jóhannesson, Leifur Geir Hafsteinsson, Arngrímur Baldursson, Guðmundur Þór Magnússon, Adrian Mervyn, Ian Fox, Ruth Clarke and Roxanne Baines. Thank you to everyone who helped along the way.